ADRIAN'S REVENGE

Keith A. Davies

Addiction — Conspiracy — Murder — Redemption

Sierra Nevada Destination Services—Grass Valley, CA
ISBN: 978-0-578-40661-9
Library of Congress Control Number: 2018913750
Cover Design: Keith Davies and Joy Porter
Printed in the United States

Published in the United States by New Book Authors Publishing—Madison, WI.

Survival is my only hope, success my only revenge.
Patricia Cornwell — *Post Mortem*

Living well is the best revenge.
Frank Sinatra

Dedication

To my mother and father, Rose and Craig Davies.
Also, my brother Don. I miss them all very much.
To my son, Michael—May the sun always shine on your face
and the wind always be at your back.

PROLOGUE

A relentless barrage of crackling lighting and pounding thunder accompanied Adrian Davis as he scurried from his law office to the nearby Quartz County Courthouse. It was April 8 on the calendar, but sometimes winter stays late on the western slope of California's Sierra Nevada mountains.

The bleak weather cast an ominous pall over Adrian's early-morning dash, but it was an important day for his client. Besides, he knew better than to be late when curt and exacting Superior Court Judge David Rupertini was presiding.

He entered the courthouse lobby, carefully shook his wet umbrella to the side, removed his slicker, placed his pocket items in a plastic tub, walked through the metal detector, greeted the lobby guard by name, recovered his items from the tub, then moved toward the lone elevator.

It was 8:50 A.M. when Davis walked into Courtroom Three and took his place at the defense table. Benedict "Benny" Nicholson, his client, was already there, fidgeting with his long, wavy hair. They shook hands, but it was not an especially cordial greeting.

At 9:00 A.M. sharp, Judge Rupertini entered, took his place on the bench and the jury was brought in and seated.

Another routine day in court? Not at all.

Davis, a tall, slender lawyer just north of seventy, had no way of knowing what awaited him that blustery, dreary morning. He didn't know he would never again empty his pockets into a plastic tub and walk through the courthouse metal detector, nor ever again enter the lobby elevator on his way to the third-floor courtroom.

Benny Nicholson would be Adrian's last client.

PART ONE
Losing Control

Chapter One

Quartz County Superior Court Judge Rupertini looked to his left, toward the jury foreman, the judge's dark hair streaked with natural grey and a serious face reflecting decades in the practice of law and countless cases from the bench.

"Have you reached a verdict, Mr. Foreman?" he asked.

"Yes, we have, Your Honor," the foreman answered.

The court clerk walked over to the jury box, received the written verdict from the foreman and handed it to Judge Rupertini. When the judge finished reading, he looked directly at the defense table and said, "Please rise and face the jury."

Benny Nicholson and Adrian Davis rose as requested and stood expressionless, with no outward sign of nervousness or anxiety. They feared the worst, but they weren't going to let anyone see from their stoic faces what they were feeling inside.

Judge Rupertini then turned to the solemn jury and directed his questioning to the foreman, a heavyset man in his early sixties with thinning gray hair. His wide-lapel suit and thin tie looked as though both had been hanging in his closet for a decade or more. He seemed like the kind of man who would be far more comfortable in blue jeans and a Levi flannel shirt; not a blue suit with a tie older than his eldest daughter.

"In the matter of the People of California versus Benedict 'Benny' Nicholson on the single charge of conspiracy, distribution, and sales of cocaine, how do you find?"

"We the jury find the defendant guilty, Your Honor," the foreman calmly announced.

Nicholson slumped, aware that the verdict would bring serious prison time. Davis remained calm but felt a heavy dose of disappointment rush over him. This had been a case he dearly wanted to win—for his client as well as for himself.

"Thank you, Mr. Foreman, and thank you, members of the jury," the judge said as he released the twelve jurors and two alternates. Without looking back at Benny or Adrian, the jury quietly filed out of the courtroom.

Turning his attention back to the defense table, Judge Rupertini said, "Mr. Davis, you and the defendant will appear back in this courtroom in three weeks for sentencing. During these next three weeks, the district attorney and Quartz County Probation Department will consider and submit sentencing recommendations. Please see the court clerk for a date and time."

"And my client, Your Honor? What...?"

"The defendant will remain free on bail with the restrictions and conditions already outlined in the bail agreement," he told Davis, "including the covenant that he is not to leave the county under any circumstances. Is that understood?"

"Yes, Your Honor," Davis replied, his still-handsome face and a full head of hair belying his age. From the neck up, he resembled Ben Matlock as he interrogated witnesses and appealed to the jury for leniency. But the expensive Italian-tailored navy-blue suit, silk shirt, and Countess Mara signature tie were anything but Podunk.

As the judge left the bench and walked toward his chambers, Davis turned to his client. "Did you hear him, Benny? You can't leave the county, and you must adhere to the bail terms—all of them. Do you understand?"

"Yes," Benny sarcastically replied.

"Good, then let's meet in my office tomorrow morning at ten. We can discuss the options and what you might be facing going forward."

"OK, I'll see you then, but I'm not happy, Davis—not one fuckin' bit happy."

Benny Nicholson was the spitting image of his father, Gary. A handsome face with age lines far exceeding his forty plus years, and teeth that needed serious dental work. The suit, shirt and tie Adrian had purchased for him to wear during the trial helped enhance his courtroom appearance, but it didn't affect the verdict.

Davis knew that guilty is guilty, no matter what clothes a man might be wearing.

He and Nicholson got up from the defense table and prepared to leave the courtroom as the morning sun was beginning to shine through the bank of windows behind the jury box.

The floor-to-ceiling windows allowed a view of downtown Gold City—a historic mining town established in eighteen-fifty during the California Gold Rush. Millions of dollars in gold had been extracted from the creeks and hills in and around Gold City, and its inventory of nineteenth-century brick commercial buildings and stately Victorian-era homes brought thousands of tourists to town each summer.

Devastating fires in eighteen sixty-one and eighteen seventy-six had leveled the town and left it in ruin, but Gold City pioneers were a rugged bunch—determined to rebuild as soon as the ashes had cooled. The mythical phoenix had nothing on Gold City.

During the glory years of "gold fever," some fortunes were made. But failure often came to those who thought all they had to do was pluck gold nuggets off the ground then return to their homes in the East with a bountiful harvest of the precious metal. Gold, however, wasn't as plentiful as most Argonauts thought it would be, and many returned home poorer than the day they arrived in the goldfields.

***

Adrian Davis was a respected defense attorney, a fourth-generation native son, born and raised in the town where he now practiced law. And his son, Michael, now twenty-three and attending law school back East, was the fifth generation of Davis stock to call Gold City home.

After Davis shook Benny's hand and reminded him of the next day's meeting, he exited the Art Deco-style courthouse and was greeted by a light spring breeze—a lingering remnant of the morning storm. Walking to his office on Hill Street, however, he recalled that it hadn't always been a pleasant spring day in Gold City. There had been dark days; some darker than others.

Yes, there was much to be happy and proud about, and many things to celebrate about his seventy-plus years on Earth, but undeniable reflections of regret looked back at him from shop windows as he walked from the courthouse to his office. Regret not just about the guilty verdict and being unable to help Benny, son of one of his best friends, Gary Nicholson, but also Adrian's role in not being able to prevent Gary's death many years earlier.

If only the jury had found Benny innocent, it would have helped ameliorate the guilt Davis had been carrying for so many years; baggage that sometimes weighed heavy on his mind.

But now? What of now? He realized Benny faced hard time—Folsom State Prison, at a minimum, not the Quartz County Jail. And he would have to tell him what to expect in prison when they met the next day.

If only he could have done more.

Chapter Two

Adrian sat at an antique oak desk in his early 1900s appointed office on the third floor of an old Victorian house built in 1866. The elegant former home of a nineteenth-century mine owner had been restored and turned into law offices in the nineteen-sixties. And because of its close proximity to the courthouse, it was a very desirable location for Davis to hang his shingle.

His interoffice phone rang. "Yes, Mandy?"

"Benny's here for your ten o'clock. Should I send him in?"

"Please do and tell him to come right on in—no need to knock."

Adrian got up from his desk and walked toward the door to greet his client. He was still considering how best to break the news to Benny that hard time was inevitable, but he knew there was really no best way—just tell the truth and deal with his client's emotions.

"Please come in, Benny," Davis said, motioning toward a sofa under the window a few feet from his cluttered desk. "Can I get you something to drink? Coffee? Soda? Water?"

"No thanks, I'm fine," Benny answered, thinking to himself that the only way he'd be interested in coffee would be if Adrian flavored it with a shot of Jack Daniel's.

Davis sat in a comfortable leather chair opposite the sofa, facing Benny.

"I'll cut to the chase," he told Benny. "It doesn't look good, my friend."

"So, if it's not good, then it must be bad, eh?"

"Well, keep in mind that this is your second drug-related felony. And it doesn't help that you were still on probation from the first offense."

"Can we cut the bullshit, counselor? Just tell me what you think is going to happen at sentencing."

"Honestly, Benny, I think the DA's going to recommend ten years in state prison."

"Ten years? Ten friggin' years at Quentin or Folsom or some other shit-hole prison?"

"But remember, ten years means that after five or so, you'll be eligible for parole."

"Is that supposed to make me feel better?"

"I promise you, Benny, I'll fight like hell for five years, and then we can hope for even earlier parole. But with that prior on your record, I'm not very optimistic."

"Remember, Davis; it's your fault I'm in this fuckin' mess," Benny angrily shouted.

"Wait, wait," Adrian told him. "If you would have taken the three-to-five plea deal they offered, as I recommended you do, then you would already have half the sentence behind you by now. You were there, Benny, you knew the evidence they had against you and the witnesses they would present. You knew the risk. That's why I suggested you take the deal and not go to trial. But you insisted on a jury trial, and here we are."

"Yeah, but this goes way back to my dad, and you know it. You fucked things up in his life, and now, by not winning this case, you've fucked up my life too. I didn't take the plea because when I took it last time, as you suggested, all it did was ensure that I'd get a longer sentence this time around. Some fuckin' attorney you are, Davis."

"Come on, Benny, we both agreed you were probably going to be convicted the first time, so probation was a hell of a deal. The truth is, I was surprised the DA even offered it. This time, you committed another crime while still on probation. It was out of my hands; it was your doing. And being on probation from your last conviction means a stiffer sentence this time."

Adrian was trying to reason with Benny, but the prospect of hard time at San Quentin or Folsom was making a normal conversation very difficult.

"Remember, Davis; I was there when Dad died. I was only seventeen, and maybe he wasn't the best father a boy ever had, but he was my dad; he was all I had. Now look at how fucked up I am, eh? My life without a dad has been a mess, and you haven't helped things. In fact, you owe me. You owe me big time."

Benny began shaking as perspiration formed on his brow.

Davis stood, pointed a finger at Benny and said, "Now, wait a minute, Nicholson. After your dad died, I tried to find you. I wanted to help, but you went into hiding with those other crazy-ass friends of yours."

"Well, at least they were friends, which is more than I can say about you."

"Give me a break, OK? You didn't finish school, and you haven't listened to anybody's advice these past twenty or so years. You've gone your own way and, unfortunately, it hasn't turned out very well. But it was me who tried to get you to stop selling and dealing that fuckin' nose candy after the last arrest. I suggested you leave town and start fresh somewhere. Anywhere but here in Gold City. Remember? But you didn't listen, so you should have known they'd be waiting for you to screw up again."

Nicholson sat on the couch, pissed, but trying not to show his anger.

"The best I could do for you was take the cases pro bono. And because of my friendship with your dad, I was happy to do it. Believe me, I did my best for you, Benny, considering."

Benny jumped up, pulling a gun from his jacket and pointed the .45 caliber Colt Double Eagle at Davis and shouted, "Considering *what*? That you tried to help my dad, so you say? Well, I know different, and I know what you really did."

"What the hell are you talking about, Benny?"

"I'm talking about how you came out of the mess just fine, but Dad's dead and buried and my life's fucked; has been for years. Maybe it's time for your life to be fucked as well, asshole."

Benny was spitting his words, wildly waving the semi-automatic handgun, but his eyes were laser-focused on his attorney.

"Benny, wait, you got it all wrong; it wasn't me," Davis pleaded.

"Fuck you, old man," Benny sneered as he reached out his pistoled hand and shot Davis point-blank in the chest three times, then watched as the startled attorney fell back over his chair, landing in front of his desk.

Death came quickly.

Benny calmly put the gun back in his jacket and left the office, swiftly walking past Mandy, the receptionist, as Sandi Stassi, Adrian's law partner, and wife, came running down the hall from her office.

Oblivious to the screams of horror coming from the two women, Benny Nicholson calmly walked down the stairs and exited on to Hill Street.

"What a beautiful spring day in Gold City," he said as he passed a tourist taking photos of the building where the body of Adrian Davis was bleeding out.

***

A few days after the funeral—and an inspiring memorial service attended by nearly every attorney and judge in Quartz County, as well as business leaders, politicians, and lifelong friends—Sandi Stassi Davis was at Adrian's desk with her twenty-three-year-old son sitting across from her. Her natural black hair was perfectly coiffed and cut straight in a sixties-like style, flaring toward her face. Sandi was five-five and just over a hundred pounds. She was dressed in a navy-blue pants suit, white blouse, high heels, and Amber jewelry that Adrian had bought her in Prague on one of their vacations. She was sullen but looked professional in every respect.

Michael, on the other hand, wore shorts, tennis shoes, and an untucked dress shirt. He was handsome and athletic—a notch over six-foot, one-hundred ninety compact pounds with brown-blond hair and a million-dollar smile. He was a student at George Washington University Law School in Washington, D. C., but, because of his father's murder, had been granted a short leave of absence.

For twenty-five years, Sandi's life had revolved around Adrian, Michael and the law practice. And now her husband was gone, killed by a maddened client. Sandi, just sixty, was eleven years younger than Adrian, but the burdens associated with his sudden death made her feel much older. Her youthful spirit was deflating before her son's eyes. Where would she take her life from here? What would she do about the law firm? Would she be able to guide and counsel her son as her husband had done so well?

Sandi had lots of questions and not many answers, but today she needed to talk to Michael and do her best to explain to him why someone would kill his dad. He deserved to know why someone could be so angry at Adrian that he would shoot him in cold blood. Three times. Then calmly walk away and let him bleed to death on his office floor.

"Michael," Sandi said, looking up from the desk, "your father had some demons in his past. He made some mistakes, some big mistakes, but he was a good man."

Michael nodded as if already knowing some of the family history.

"Through the years, as you asked questions, we both tried to tell you about his and our history as truthfully as possible. We didn't want you to be caught by surprise, or hear something on the street that wasn't correct, or a truth taken out of context." Michael nodded again.

"As to why Benny Nicholson killed your father, I can't really say. I know we both did our best to keep him out of jail. And isn't it ironic? We defended both of his drug arrests *pro-bono*. Your dad felt we owed it to him; felt sorry for him, because of past history with his dad and Gold City. I guess it proves the old adage, 'no good deed goes unpunished.'"

Sandi paused, not sure what to say next.

"Benny told authorities he did it for his dad and said your father deserved to die. Benny said he just didn't care anymore and just wanted the pain to go away and your father was part of that pain."

"*Pain*? What pain?" Michael asked.

"Your father began writing a book based on all that took place in his adult life up to the mid-nineties. He started writing in two thousand-seven and finished it in two thousand-twelve. Were you aware of that?"

"Yeah, he told me about it but said he never wanted to see it published. More of a cathartic process for him, I guess."

"That's right," his mother said. "It was a soul-cleansing exercise. It was something he felt compelled to write if he was ever going to purge the demons that haunted him."

"Have you read it, Mom?"

"Yes, and some of it was painful," she said, handing the manuscript to her son. "I know that what your father wrote is the truth and that it all took place as he described it because I was very much a part of his murder trial."

"That's when it all began for you two, right Mom?" Michael asked.

"It sure did," she told him, smiling at the memory of their courtship. "Your father and I fell in love during that time, started the law practice, brought you into this world, and tried to right some wrongs. Sometimes we succeeded, other times maybe we didn't, and I know the truth is in these pages. But I want you to read your father's words and judge for yourself."

"Do you think he would *want* me to read it?"

"Yes, I know he would. And he would want you to keep it."

Michael held the unbound manuscript in both hands, staring at it for a few seconds. He had no idea what his father had written, but he knew it would be candid; maybe harsh.

"Will what I read here affect or change how I look at or remember Dad?"

Sandi took a deep breath and thought about her son's question. It deserved an honest answer.

"I don't think it will change or alter your love and respect for him if that's what you're asking, but it might give you pause as to who you think and knew him to be, as opposed to who he was at one time in his life. Your dad told me that no man ever becomes rich enough to buy back his past, but your dad sure tried in every way he could to right his past and square the wrongs."

"Meaning...?"

"Meaning, he was a complicated man, tortured over some issues. But he was a brilliant, caring and loving person about so many other things, including his love for you and me. He once told me: The purpose of life is to matter, to count, to have it make a difference that we even lived at all."

"Well Mom, he did make a difference, especially with you and me," Michael said as he cupped the manuscript with his right hand while kissing his mother on the forehead. Then he left the office, stopped at the reception desk to give Mandy a firm hug and said goodbye.

The drive to Sacramento International Airport would take just over an hour, and he had to turn in his rental car, so he decided to keep the manuscript tucked away in his carry-on bag—better to start on it once his flight was headed East.

Chapter Three

Michael Davis was welcomed aboard the Boeing 757 by a flight attendant in a light-green uniform with matching scarf. He was happy to learn that the flight would be departing on schedule and especially happy that his mother had treated him to a first-class ticket.

"Nice to have you with us today...err, Mr. Davis," the statuesque blonde said, looking at the ticket. "Please relax and enjoy the flight. I'll be happy to get you something to drink in a couple of minutes, and lunch will be served shortly after we're at cruising altitude."

Davis placed his drink order with the flight attendant and pushed the soft, first-class seat back two notches.

Shortly after Davis had settled in and the plane began its slow taxi to the main runway, the attractive blonde brought him a glass of 2013 Cakebread Cellars Cabernet Sauvignon—the sort of vintage not available for those traveling back in coach class.

Michael took a deep breath and a sip of the top shelf Cab, then flipped on the overhead reading light and opened his father's manuscript. It began as a family Bible:

***

Davis family roots in the Sierra Nevada foothills date back to the 1860s when my paternal great-grandfather, followed by my grandfather and dad, all worked in the gold mines. It was a rugged life, but they were rugged men—all of them.

My paternal great-grandfather, a miner from Rumney, Wales—not far from Cardiff—came to California for the purpose of hard-rock mining. And he settled here in the foothills, east of

Sacramento and west of Lake Tahoe. He arrived in this part of the world after the copper and tin markets of Wales and Cornwall collapsed in the mid-nineteenth century.

As more and more mines closed there, men searched for jobs to support their families. They scattered across the globe—thousands to South Africa, thousands to Australia, and thousands to the United States.

Great-grandfather Thomas Davis chose America. And thank God for that.

Once here, Tom earned a dollar a day mucking rock and filling ore carts deep down in the bowels of the Rosebud Mine, a couple of miles from Gold City. Fortunately, both Grandfather Frank Davis and my dad did a little better than that because gold eventually increased in value and wages improved.

Dad, for instance, earned as much as three dollars an hour and worked six days a week, but there was no overtime pay in those pre-union days. Straight time for fifty-to-sixty hours a week kept the bills paid, sure, but while our family lived with the bare essentials, mine owners and company shareholders vacationed in Cuba and lived in big houses.

And during World War Two, when FDR declared mining a non-essential industry, Quartz County mines were closed "for the duration." Fortunately, when Dad returned from WWII, he found work in the lumber mills, got his degree in engineering with the GI Bill, and never again had to go underground to earn a paycheck.

On my mother's side, Grandfather Victor Santelli was, as family oral history recounts it, running from the Italian Mafia. It had something to do with a loan he knew he would never be able to repay, so he booked passage to California. Somewhere in the South Atlantic, he came to believe that a couple of Mafia henchmen were on board, so he jumped ship in Argentina. And that proved to be a good decision because he soon met my maternal grandmother.

After they married, Grandfather Victor brought his bride, beautiful Aurelia Sanchezzi, to San Francisco, eventually settling here in the Gold Country. They had nine children, of which seven survived—the youngest being my dear mother, Rose.

Both of my maternal grandparents died at an early age, whereas the Davis side typically lived well into their late seventies. Sometimes longer.

Grandpa Frank Davis was very much involved in politics in Gold City during the 1930s and forties, and he served on the town council, as did my dad and an uncle in the fifties and sixties.

Grandpa Frank owned and operated a stage and motor coach line in the twenties and thirties, delivering mail and passengers throughout the Sierra foothills. He was also a hotelier, landlord, and saloonkeeper with my Grandmother Alice. They opened Frank's Place on Commerce Street in nineteen thirty-eight, and it quickly became the kind of Gold City bar that attracted hardworking miner's and logger's intent on getting loud and drunk—especially on payday.

Frank's Place was not a bar where customers ordered margaritas and frozen daiquiris. Hell, they didn't even own a blender. Shots, beers, and highballs—that was about it. And some Dago Red for the Santelli side of the family. The place was a saloon, not a bar, and certainly not what was known in those days as a cocktail lounge. If an out-of-towner wandered in by mistake and wanted something fancy, they would be sent to the Miners Inn Hotel bar, a block away. At least the hotel had a blender.

My grandparents had only two rules for customers: "If you want to fight, take it out on the street, and curb the foul language." And from what I've heard, they bounced more than a few burly men looking to settle a dispute with fists.

While Frank and Alice took care of the bar, my dad and uncle managed the family ranch until it was sold in the nineteen-nineties, a few years before their respective retirements.

That pretty well sums up our family history in California from the gold rush to 1980. I've always been proud of the family legacy; hard workers who earned every nickel they were ever paid.

It was sometime in nineteen-eighty that my father called me in New York and suggested I return home to take over the saloon. Frank and Alice were getting too old to run the business, Dad said, and no one else in the Davis family had any interest in taking it over, except my brother Don, but he didn't have the ready cash.

Dad told me that if I didn't come home and run the place, my grandparents were going to sell it. He said that wasn't an idle threat to get my attention, it was the truth, and I needed to understand how serious Frank and Alice had become.

For more than a decade I had been hop-scotching from San Francisco to Los Angeles, and New York, living out of a suitcase, touring with some of the biggest rock 'n' roll acts in the country. Our company controlled the T-shirt concession at major concerts, and it was a very profitable business—for me and for my partners.

The idea of rock bands setting tour dates at major venues, where crowds of 50,000 or more could fit in a football stadium, was in its infancy and we controlled a large part of the business— and its huge profits—without much interference from competitors, except for bootleg products sold outside the venues by scab vendors.

When Buddy Holly and other rock 'n' roll stars toured in the 1950s, they played small auditoriums and high school gyms, hoping to make a few bucks and sell some records. What we were doing in the nineteen-seventies was a whole new ball game—a new way to hustle merchandise and fill our pockets. Life was good.

But then came a sea change in the music business.

As band managers watched T-shirts and other merchandise fly off our concession tables at concert venues, they soon recognized the potential for their own income. And that led to demands for large up-front payments for the touring concession rights.

With less profit in concession sales and considering my unending go-go-go existence, I was attracted to the idea of a slower-paced life. So, I told my dad I would move back to Gold City and take over Frank's Place.

Little did I know that the world I was entering was anything but slow-paced. In my mind, I visualized taking over a small, friendly bar where I might realize a decent income and relax. *Relax?* That was a luxury that evaded me for the next several years.

My grandparents were the best, but never invested much in upkeep or modernization of the bar, so any idea I had of keeping things as they were went out the window the first time I inspected the building. I knew immediately that it would need considerable upgrading and décor changes before I could consider it mine. Fortunately, I had the cash to do it.

Naturally, I had some misgivings about such a big lifestyle change, but I had fond memories of growing up in Gold City. We had two elementary schools and one high school, and our high school class size was barely three hundred when I graduated. We grew up knowing everyone, and that part was both good and bad.

In the winter of 1980, acquiescing to my dad's suggestion, (that seemed at first to be more like a demand), I came home and began an extensive remodel—the kind of work necessary to transform the bar from the 1930s to the 1980s. There were half a dozen bars in town at that time, and their décor pretty much looked the same: Dark and depressing. No life, no energy. I wanted my place to be different.

In the 1970s, Gold City had experienced a major influx of hippies from San Francisco and the Santa Cruz Mountains. They drank a lot—and that was good for the bar business. But many of the city fathers and business leaders were not happy about the demographic shift.

It brought an element to town that, in addition to a preference for good booze, imported beer, and fine wine, they enjoyed smoking and growing marijuana—something a lot of old-timers frowned upon. And when the hippies discovered the foothill climate was perfect for cultivating their leafy crop of choice, many more rolled into town with their VW campers. The floodgates opened, and there was no way to close the spigot.

Heavier drugs, like cocaine, were soon introduced into the community and it was having its effect on the established old guard. Newcomers had their bars and businesses of choice, and the rednecks had theirs. They simply didn't get along, and I could understand why.

When I decided to get off the road and come home, Quartz County, and Gold City, in particular, represented the past, not the future. Our history was amazing, and I had great pride in being a native-born son of men and women who had contributed to the glory days of mining and California's early growth. But the town in which I was raised was in many respects no different than the Deep South.

We had our share of rednecks, and many were descendants of the Welsh and Cornish miners who came here for a better life. They were hard workers, but happy to live in the past and reject the present, including some of the guys I attended school with and considered my friends. And they preferred to live in a town without blacks, Orientals or Latinos—as they were politely referred to back then.

Long hair on men was frowned on, as were tie-dyed T-shirts, natural fiber clothes, and women openly breastfeeding their babies in public.

The value of gold had been frozen at thirty-five dollars an ounce since nineteen thirty-four when FDR signed the Gold

Reserve Act, and anyone lucky enough to find some gold had to sell it directly to the government, not to the highest bidder on the open market. That led to what is called high-grading—a polite term for stealing.

Before the last of the mines closed in the early nineteen-fifties, workers were routinely searched when they emerged from a shift underground. But there were several ways to smuggle gold—especially if the crew had a good plan and no one squealed. One of the classic stories of high-grading occurred when, during a shift change, a crew surfaced with a dead mule sprawled on the elevator floor.

Mules often spent their entire life below the surface hauling ore carts along rails, so mine supervisors weren't surprised when another dead mule emerged with the crew. What did surprise them, however, was a request from the crew chief to allow his men to give the beloved mule a fitting burial.

The request seemed odd, but harmless enough, so the mule was carried to a wagon and driven away as the men followed behind. Once out of view from the mine, the men cut the dead mule open and retrieved several pounds of gold-laced quartz and large nuggets that had been stuffed down the poor animal's throat. Some nuggets were the size of hen eggs and others the size of a ping-pong ball, and the haul was worth several thousand dollars.

The men divided the high-graded booty and laughed all the way out of town.

Grandfather Frank told me that story when I was a kid, and I have no reason not to believe him.

***

Combined with a decline in logging and lumbering in the Sierra foothills, there was a lot of unemployment in Quartz County in the nineteen-seventies. Good jobs were scarce. Bank interest rates were over twenty percent. A lot of families I knew were struggling to keep the mortgage paid, the lights on, and food in the fridge, so when they watched unemployed hippies strolling through town without a care in the world, there was friction—sometimes fist-fights.

For some, it was not a pleasant time to live in Gold City. For others, life couldn't have been better.

I knew all that recent history when I agreed to take over the bar, but I was optimistic that the tide would shift, the economy would improve, and opposing factions would come to live in relative harmony. And they did. Eventually.

When I started remodeling Frank's Place, I worked with the wife of my best friend. She had interior design credentials, and I planned to emphasize the Art Deco era of the twenties and thirties. I had decided to call the place Bogart's—in honor of Humphrey Bogart, of course—so I needed an interior look to match the name.

These days it's called branding; in those days it was simply a matter of trying to get as many warm butts as possible on as many cold barstools as possible.

We had Frank and Alice's antique oak back bar to work with, and we knocked out a wall to expand into the old dining room they had been using for years as storage. We turned the former dining room into a dance room with a large bandstand and dance floor. Also, we installed a state-of-the-art lighting and sound system, hung pictures of stars from Hollywood's Golden Age, and placed highboy tables with barstools and sofas around the dance floor. Accent lighting was everywhere, and the room's look was exactly what I had in mind when the remodeling began.

In the original saloon space, knowing that the antique oak back bar would be the centerpiece, we installed a colorful stained-glass piece with Bogey's image in a white tuxedo coat and black bow tie with the word "Casablanca" arched over his image, and "Rick's Americana" across the bottom. Effective back-lighting accented the glass.

We also hung stained-glass chandeliers from the ceiling to create a faux antique fan system, along with a fireplace area and a large, refinished oak-block bar with a marble top. And as we had done with the dance room, we installed lots of accent and mood lighting.

We brightened up the bar area by cutting into the front walls and installing large plate glass windows that looked out on to Commerce Street. Then we cut an opening in the side wall that led to an existing driveway and used that space to create an outdoor patio for warm summer nights. We even built a small cabana with a service bar.

For the Grand Opening, I organized a private party and invited city and county officials, along with families and friends from the old days. I also invited some new friends I had met during the bar's renovation.

It took several months to finish the remodeling, but Bogart's was, as far as the public was concerned, an overnight success. And the cash registers began ringing up some big numbers.

With success in the bar business, however, you sometimes make strange bedfellows. And it didn't take long to realize that remodeling the bar was not the only change happening in town.

Almost overnight, hippies morphed into real ladies and gentlemen. Well, at least some of them. Women shaved their underarms and put on dresses for the evening, while the guys shaved, washed or bought new clothes. And I couldn't help but notice that their language had improved for the better—at least a little bit.

One of the first observations I made as a rookie bar owner was the open and frequent use of cocaine by all walks of life in our beautiful town. Everyone—from attorneys in public office and private practice, to city council members, law enforcement officials, business leaders, real estate and healthcare managers and, of course, the many hippies who now frequented Bogart's—seemed to be snorting nose candy. And often it was happening in our restrooms. It gave a whole new meaning to the phrase—"going to the ladies' room to powder my nose."

I knew what was happening, and I knew it was illegal, but considering who the regular users were, I felt Bogart's was a safe-haven—for them and me.

In all the years, I was involved with the rock 'n' roll business, touring with the likes of The Eagles, Rolling Stones, Led Zeppelin, Queen, Beach Boys and more, I had never used any illegal drugs. Never. I saw lots of it, naturally, including bowls of coke in dressing rooms with spoons for easy dispensing. I watched musicians shooting up with heroin or speedballs. I saw overdoses backstage and knew entertainers who missed performances because of drug and alcohol abuse. But I didn't succumb to the temptation; I was focused on making money.

About eighteen months after opening Bogart's, however, a cute little darling from Southern California changed all that.

Chapter Four

"Good evening, Wally," I said, as I greeted my burly Bogart's doorman on a busy Friday night. "Any problems?"

"None, boss, just the usual fun night in La La Land."

"Well, let's hope it stays that way. We need all the Lincoln lithos you can collect so we can pay for that damn band tomorrow," I reminded him, pointing at the metal cashbox where Wally deposited five-dollar cover charges from customers entering the bar. That kind of entrance fee on a busy Friday would pay for the band when its gig ended the following night. At least I hoped it would because that's why bars have cover charges.

It had been well over a year, almost two, since Bogart's opened—and the place was jumping. So was most of downtown Gold City. Since Bogart's opening, there were now eight bars and saloons in town. On Friday and Saturday nights, there was live music in five of the eight clubs and the town's nightlife was so popular that on the weekend hundreds of clubbers ascended from outside the community.

They came to enjoy a night of revelry and, if they played their cards right, an after-hours flesh-to-flesh encounter with a stranger looking for the same exciting companionship.

Downtown crowds at some of the clubs spilled out onto the street during warm summer nights. In fact, police sometimes closed Commerce Street to accommodate people wanting to dance to the music coming from the open doors and windows of two popular clubs, including my place.

Opposite Bogart's was the Crazy Lady Saloon. At times during balmy summer nights, lines of pedestrian traffic between clubs reminded me of lines I had seen at rock concerts.

With the birth of Bogart's, the town had clearly become a destination for good times and good music, and both new and old downtown businesses were enjoying a financial boon. Storefronts with "For Rent" signs on the window when I returned to town were now busy shops—many catering to tourists rather than locals.

***

Seated at the far end of the bar, near the new door that opened onto the patio area, a couple of regulars were enjoying the evening with cocktails and conversation. A common mindset for many of us in those carefree days was, "We can do no wrong, life is good, and may this endless summer never end."

But everything in life changes. And every person changes, eventually. Nothing stays the same. And some of those changes would soon take me to places I could never have imagined. Dark places. Deadly places. Places no sane man would want to visit.

"Boys, what's happening?" I asked as I took a stool next to Gary Nicholson and George Allen.

"So, help me, God, that's the truth," Gary said to George as he tossed down some Bombay Gin and tonic, his favorite drink.

George was one of those rare people who could walk into a gloomy room and light the place up. He had an electric personality with three first names, George Thomas Allen. He was twenty-eight, dirty-blond hair, deep green eyes, the biggest smile you've ever seen, perfect teeth, and all of it on a six-foot frame of rippling muscle developed from years of hanging drywall.

He was a popular guy and a real charmer. His good looks, hunky body, and outgoing personality ensured he would not go home alone at closing time unless he wanted to go home alone.

George was a nail-banger by day, an honorable trade, but his avocation was dealing cocaine by the quarter, half, or full grams. A street dealer. Occasionally, he would sell what was referred to as an eight-ball—an eighth of an ounce, 3.5 grams. Clean coke was worth a bunch of money, especially when it was being sold at an inflated price to bar patrons already buzzed from the booze. It was supply-and-demand economics at its best. George had the supply and Gold City customers had the demand.

If a tipsy, anxious customer was willing to pay George a hundred bucks for thirty bucks worth of coke, he was happy to oblige. But as I sat next to my two friends, the conversation had nothing to do with drugs. It was a bit more esoteric.

"Whenever a man believes he has the exact truth from God, he develops the arrogance of theological certainty and becomes a slave to ignorant assumptions," Gary said as he took another sip of his drink.

"What the hell are you two talking about?" I asked.

"Beats me," George laughed. "I never know what the fuck this guy's talking about."

"Well, of course not, you Neanderthal," Gary countered. "I was quoting Robert Ingersoll, America's greatest agnostic, on the damage that religion can cause—at least according to him."

Gary glanced at me then at George with that cocky look of superior intellect that he confidently carried with him. He had migrated from Los Angeles to Gold City in the nineteen-seventies after being raised by a well-to-do, upper-middle-class family. His father had been an aerospace engineer at Lockheed prior to its merger with Martin Marietta.

Nicholson had thick black hair with a ponytail, looking very much like a young Jack Nicholson in *The Witches of Eastwick*, which wouldn't open till nineteen eighty-seven; but Gary was always ahead of the arts and the culture curve. And since they shared the same last name, the connection fed into his persona and ego.

As to his intellect, Gary was educated in private schools and graduated from the University of Southern California with a Political Science/Pre-Law undergraduate degree. His present vocation was importing. That is to say, Gary was the main local importer of cocaine from Mexico and Southern California.

"This guy Ingersoll, you're saying he doesn't believe in God?" George asked.

"It isn't a question of what he believes or disbelieves, at least not anymore, 'cause he's been dead since eighteen ninety-eight."

"You should have figured that out for yourself, George," I chuckled. "Hell, man, everybody Gary likes or has any respect for has been dead for decades. Why do you think he loves Bogart's so much?"

"Yeah?" George asked sarcastically with that big smile of his. "So, tell me, Gary, what's so great about this guy Ingersoll? He ever do any real work, like hang drywall all day or build something?"

"Afraid not, buddy, you got me there," Nicholson answered. "But a writer and poet by the name of Walt Whitman once said: 'Resist much, obey little,' and that fits you perfectly, George. Never have I known anyone with such tunnel vision."

"Damn right!" George said triumphantly, not realizing Gary had just slightly insulted him. "But why are you so taken with an agnostic?"

"The fact he knew that religion makes enemies instead of friends," Gary replied. "In the name of universal benevolence, Christians have long despised their fellow man, inventing and brandishing the most destructive weapons in an effort to defend their pious beliefs."

George turned to me and said, "Like I was saying a couple of minutes ago, Davis, I never know what the hell Gary's talking about."

"So why listen?" I asked.

"Hell, I don't know. I guess because usually whatever he says sounds like the truth. And around here these days, the truth is refreshing."

George finished his drink as my brother Don, the bartender, walked over to where the three of us were seated. I ordered another round for my friends and a Myers's rum and OJ for myself.

"By the way," I told Gary, "Ingersoll died in eighteen ninety-nine, not eighteen ninety-eight. Remember that the next time you quote him."

"How the hell would you know when he died?" Gary asked, sure that I was bluffing.

"Noticed his grave last time I was at Arlington," I answered. "Went there to pay my respects to a college buddy killed in Nam in sixty-nine and couldn't help but notice the memorial to Ingersoll when I passed by it. I saw he'd died the same month and year as Tom Davis—my great-grandfather. I wouldn't forget a thing like that, would I?"

Nicholson grew silent, quietly acknowledging that I wouldn't forget something like that, then turned his attention to a young woman seated to his left. Don had just delivered a fresh drink to Gary and one for his lady friend.

When Don delivered the round I had ordered, he laid fresh napkins for each of the fresh drinks. Our white napkins had "Bogart's" printed in large, bold red letters in Algerian script across the middle of the napkin. Over Bogart's in black, it read: "Here's Lookin' at You, Kid." And under Bogart's, it read: "To the Beginning of a Beautiful Friendship." It was our custom for the bartender or the purchaser of the round to say, "Here's Lookin' at You, Kid," when a round was bought and delivered. So, upholding tradition, I made the toast in my best Bogey voice to smiles and cheers.

Don had been working for me since Bogart's opened. He was

considered our main-draw bartender—someone with personality, good looks and a knack for mixing drinks. Adding to his value was the fact that he had been born and raised in Gold City. He knew most of the locals and could intelligently talk to tourists about the town's history.

And he loved sports—all kinds of sports—and could talk about the gentle sport of golf as expertly as he could talk about the violence of NFL football. When locals walked in Bogart's and saw two bartenders walking the plank during a busy shift, they gravitated to the portion of the bar Don was working.

After I made the traditional toast for the round of drinks, I paid for them with cash. I knew a lot of bar owners who ordered comp drinks for anyone who would laugh at their dumb jokes and tell them what a great bar they had, but I learned from my Uncle Babe, who once owned a popular bar in town, that bar owners who comp too many drinks, come to regret it.

By actually paying out of my pocket, it helped me control the urge to act like a big shot around friends and other customers. And it ensured that cash went in the register to pay bills and salaries. It was something Frank and Alice had told me the day they handed me the keys to Frank's Place. Just as the debate about Ingersoll's contributions to society concluded, a young patron slipped in between George and me. He seemed anxious, but spoke in a soft voice, not wanting others to hear what he had to say.

"Good to see you, George. Can I talk to you outside for a minute?" he motioned with a nod of his head.

Scotty Peterson was a regular Bogart's patron, especially on Friday nights. And as he waited for George to respond, I noticed a light gloss of sweat beginning to appear on the brow of Peterson's twenty-something face.

"Not a chance, asshole," George said in a muffled voice, not wanting the conversation to be heard by others. "You owe me a lot of dough, Scotty. Way too much to give you more credit."

"I know, I know."

"So, when are you going to give me some cash, man?"

"Hey, I know the tab's getting up there, but I've got some serious money due me next week from a job I'm finishing. You know how it is in the construction business, George; it's up, and it's down," he shrugged. "Next week, for sure, I'll be fat again."

George Allen sat staring at his drink, ignoring Scotty.

"Help me out for tonight, OK? I'll square things with you next week. That's a promise."

Allen looked up from his drink and stared at Peterson for a few seconds.

"First thing next week, no later. And you know what comes next if you fuck up and ignore me, right? Understand?"

"Yeah, I know, and I don't want to be on your bad side, man, I really don't. I've heard what that means."

"OK, then let's take a walk," George said as he and Scotty headed outside Bogart's bar area on to the patio.

"What about you, Davis?" Nicholson asked. "You want to party tonight as well?"

"You know I don't play with that fool's gold crap; too expensive, for one thing."

"You got that right, my friend," Gary laughed.

"Glad you understand," I said while patting him on the arm. "By the way, are you coming to the pond party Sunday at the ranch?"

"Of course, wouldn't miss it. And I'm bringing a guest if that's OK."

"The more, the merrier, right? I said with a smile.

"I knew her in Southern Cal. Only twenty-three, but a wild little shit with a great body."

"Can't wait, Gary. Always like to meet new young ladies." Nicholson laughed knowing I wasn't joking.

"What's your friend's name?" I asked.

"Shelly," he answered. "Shelly Summers."

Chapter Five

Michael kept reading, occasionally wandering from the manuscript's text to imagining conversations his father no doubt had during the flush days when Bogart's was a cash cow, and his dad was on the verge of falling in with some bad company.

He wasn't sure what he would discover next about his dad's early life, but he wanted to know the truth—the truth his mother promised he would find in the manuscript. He received lunch and a fresh glass of Cab from the flight attendant and continued reading his father's words.

***

It was a beautiful, bright sunny day in the summer of 1982; temperature in the mid-eighties and everyone in the mood to have a party out at the Davis Ranch, located above town off Lake Valley Road.

My grandfather acquired a hundred acres right after World War Two. The ranch had run cattle and horses, but no longer. By the nineteen-eighties, all the livestock was gone, but located smack in the middle of the ranch was a pond Grandfather Frank created by digging a large hole in the ground and redirecting the overflow of a very productive year-round spring that ran through the property.

With a steady stream of fresh spring water, the pond was as pure as most backyard swimming pools. Even purer than some I had dipped in.

As kids, we spent countless summer days at the pond swimming with friends, as well as rafting and fishing for catfish my grandfather had planted in the pond. Frogging was also a fun summer-night activity, and I recall several keg parties were held at the pond to celebrate family achievements and special events.

As footloose teenagers and young adults, we took advantage of the pond's setting for parties and bonfires with the girls. Truth be told, it was at one of those beer-infused parties that I lost my virginity. Can't remember the girl's last name—Linda something —but I sure remember that first time, and I was determined to repeat it.

One of our more creative friends concocted something called a Spoolie-Ollie Cocktail. Not sure how it got its goofy name, but it was definitely not something we ever served at Bogart's. And after I describe it, you'll understand why.

Granddad had an old bathtub next to the pond with a small flume connecting a spring in order to ensure fresh water for his livestock. Being kids without much regard for the tub's intended purpose, we would empty it, wipe it clean as best we could with towels, then fill it with blocks of ice, a couple of bottles of Hawaiian punch concentrate, with multiple large bottles of 7-Up and the cheapest rose' wine we could find. Finally, we'd dump in the key ingredient: vodka. Cheap vodka, but vodka, nevertheless.

Naturally, you couldn't taste the vodka, and that was the whole point. The brilliance behind the idea was to keep the girls drinking, then, sooner or later—and the sooner, the better—a guy would go into the nearby woods with an unsuspecting party girl for a late-night roll in the hay. Literally. I still blush with a wide grin remembering those early Spoolie-Ollie parties where I had those carnal indoctrinations with young girls as curious as I about our sexuality.

Naturally, the ranch and pond became the site of the annual Bogart's Summer Appreciation Party. We would gather our staff and some of our most faithful regular customers and host a party at the pond—usually on the evening of July Fourth.

Gold City celebrated July Fourth each year with a parade down Argonaut Street. For many of the locals, Parade Day was more like Get Laid Day—or Night, for that matter. The hearty citizens of Gold City loved to party on parade days and then seemed to morph into a night of sexual freedom.

We would close Bogart's at 5:00 P.M. because by then most of Gold City was over at the county fairgrounds enjoying family festivities and waiting for the big fireworks show. We had our own sort of fireworks at the ranch, but not exactly what folks would call family oriented.

Sometimes, more than two hundred people would attend—our way of saying "Thank You" to our staff and customers. In addition to supplying beer and booze, we also catered the party with BBQ burgers, dogs, tri-tips, salads, and beans.

The pond was surrounded by a dozen heritage oak trees and several rose bushes. The area adjacent to the pond began as a small patch of flowers and ground cover that Alice tended to, but through the years Grandpa Frank had cleared enough space for a large lawn.

Later, dad built a gazebo that included a built-in kitchen, bar, and BBQ. And to handle the call of nature for our guests, restrooms were built, as well as an outdoor dance floor and bandstand. It was a ranch to the older generation, but a resort to us.

At the 1982 party, bundles of helium balloons floated in the air above the pond, and round tables were placed on the lawn with eight white wicker chairs at each. I wanted everything to be first-class, so we ordered pastel-colored linen and placed bright centerpieces of tulips and roses on each table. Guys didn't give a damn about the extra touch, but the gals did. To top it off, we had a local five-piece band belting out rock 'n' roll tunes from the sixties and seventies.

The setting was perfect, weather ideal, and soon the area

around the pond was filled with our staff and regulars. Lots of happy faces. Lots of booze. Lots of food. And a very special dessert. It promised to be a great evening, and that seemed to be where it was headed.

I spotted Gary Nicholson holding court over at a table of eight that now sat ten, so I walked toward them to join in the laughs.

"Everyone enjoying themselves?" I asked.

"Actually, we're having way too much fun," someone at the table responded. "Time for you to join us?" she asked.

On the table was a dinner plate with a sizable pile of cocaine and a tiny scoop spoon for easy access to the nostrils of pleasure. I didn't care about the open indulgence of coke at my party; the area was secure from law enforcement or outside influence, so I was not judgmental in that regard. Live and let live was my credo; just try not to hurt anyone along the way.

Sitting next to Nicholson was a young blonde with the greenest eyes and whitest teeth I had ever seen. She was beautiful. The most beautiful woman at the party—and there were plenty of beautiful women that day. She wore pink shorts and a red tube top that left no doubt as to the size and firmness of her breasts. Her body was pornographic, in fact.

I was taken aback when I saw her but thought she might be too young for me—perhaps even too young to buy a drink at Bogart's.

"So, who's your guest, Gary?" I asked without taking my eyes off the blonde.

"Adrian Davis, meet my friend from Santa Barbara, Shelly Summers. She's visiting up here for the summer and might stay, provided she can find work."

"What does she do? For work, that is," I said with a smile.

"I can answer that question myself," Shelly said as she stood and extended her hand. "I can wait tables, cocktail or bartend. You name it; I can do it."

"Can you tap a keg?" I asked.

"Of course, I can, and I can do it without getting sprayed with beer."

"Very impressive."

"So, do you need any help at your place?"

"Maybe, but you can't work at Bogart's unless you're twenty-one."

"Twenty-one?" she laughed. "Thanks for the compliment, Mr. Davis, but I turned twenty-four last week."

"That's great, but I'll need to see your driver's license because you barely look old enough to vote much less drink."

"I assure you, Mr. Davis, I'm old enough to vote, I'm old enough to drink, and I'm old enough to do anything else I damn well please."

"Call me Adrian, please. All my friends call me Adrian."

As we continued with our teasing conversation, Shelly looked at me with a smile that said, "I think I like you."

I blushed, then turned to Gary and asked, "You vouchin' for her?"

"Absolutely," he answered. "I've known this little girl most of her life; grew up with her brother and sister. Believe me, Shelly's a great bartender, and guys love her. So, yeah, I highly recommend her," Gary said as he planted a hand on Shelly's ass.

I noticed Shelly reacting to Gary's ass grab with body language suggesting they were definitely not an item. That was encouraging, but I had other guests to schmooze and food to serve. I could only hope Shelly would still have that same starry gleam in her eyes later in the evening.

"The barbecue's ready, you guys, so go get something to eat, all of you, before you have too much of that stuff and won't be hungry," I announced, pointing down at the platter of white powder.

While walking from the table toward the spread at the gazebo, I took Gary's arm and said, "Nice gal you have there, buddy. How long's she been up here?"

"Arrived in Gold City last week and staying with me until she gets a job and finds the right roommate."

"Pretty ballsy gal, huh?"

"Yeah, ballsy's a good way to describe Shelly. She's an independent, sassy young lady, that's for sure."

"Anything going on with you two?"

"Not even close," Gary laughed. "I gave it my best shot, but nothing. The truth is, my friend, I'm not sure even you could handle her—provided, of course, she gave you a chance."

"Maybe, maybe not, but I gotta try," I said, flashing a mischievous Cheshire Cat smile.

For the next few hours, partygoers came and went. Kegs were drained, food was devoured, and the coke piles eventually vanished. Some people had designated drivers, but many left the ranch with a stern warning to drive carefully going back to town. It was only a couple miles, but a lot of bad things can happen in a couple of miles.

About ten that night, as the party was winding down, Gary walked over and shook my hand.

"Thanks for another great party, buddy. As usual, we had a lot of fun."

"Glad you could make it."

"Why don't you come over to the house later for a game of pool and another nightcap," Nicholson suggested. "Shelly will be there, George and Kate, and the Butterfly told me she's coming over for a couple of final-final pops."

"I don't know, Gary, I'm already a little in the bag, and I have two liquor salesmen due at the bar about eleven tomorrow. Don't think I need another drink."

"Who cares if you need it or not? Come over and have one for the fun of it."

I thought for a minute then said, "OK, since you're on my way home. But right now, I need to get my clean-up crew organized. See you in an hour or so."

What I meant, of course, was that I was hoping to see Shelly in an hour or so.

And just thinking about the possibilities was mouthwatering.

Chapter Six

About eleven that night, driving up Red Rock Road toward Bear Creek Park just before reaching the Y that splits the old cemetery at the edge of the city limits, I turned left into a driveway lined with high shrubs. The driveway led me to the front of a modern two-story home. There were other cars parked in front, but I managed to find a spot under a pine tree.

I walked along the driveway to the side door near the back of the house and entered without knocking—something I had often done when visiting Gary. Once inside, I walked down the steps while listening to loud voices and laughter coming from the basement rec room.

There were half a dozen close friends huddled around the pool table—actually, a snooker table—while others sat at the bar with drinks in hand, a plate of cocaine in front of them. Five or six lines of coke had already been lined out, and a supply of straws awaited anyone inclined to indulge.

Playing snooker goes back to my teenage years when I would drop by the O. K. Pool Hall on Argonaut Street—Pop Hawkins' place. We often played a few games of snooker after school and, believe me, once you play snooker and acquire a feel for its subtleties, you'll never go back to regular eight-ball pool.

Snooker is played over in England more than here, and on a bigger table with smaller balls and smaller pockets than a regular eight-ball table. It's a point game—no eight ball to sink for the win.

Red balls count as one point and numbered balls, one through seven, have the same point value as the number imprinted on them. To keep playing, you need to sink one red ball and then sink any numbered ball you want. Miss any shot, or scratch, and your opponent shoots. Snookers official rules are far from simple, but it can be dumbed down to a simple game.

Once sunk, red balls stay down, but numbered balls—after they find their way to a pocket—are brought back up and put back in play. Then, once all the red balls are down, you must sink the numbered balls in sequence, receiving points consistent with the number on the ball.

A beautiful twist in the snooker game that I learned is the pink six-ball, which you can shoot anytime you choose. If you sink the pink six, you receive six points, and the ball is put back into play, but if you miss, six points are shaved off your score, and your opponent takes control of the table. This pink six option isn't in the official rules of snooker, but it's a nice twist to the game. The player with the greatest number of points wins.

Snooker can be a simple game and fun to play.

George's girlfriend, Kate, a regular at Bogart's and server at a popular restaurant in town, was at Gary's that night, as was Musette Parks—a/k/a Madame Butterfly, as she preferred to be called.

Kate was about five-five with wavy red hair, brown eyes, cute face, and a slender figure with small breasts. Well, maybe small compared to a lot of other women, but just right for Kate's frame and George's pleasure. She was hard on the outside, like a tortoise shell; a tough persona. If she had been born a male, he would have spent most of his time in bar fights trying to prove himself.

Musette/Madame Butterfly was tall, perfect breasts, great legs, and ass, about thirty-eight, with jet-black hair and dark eyes set back in their sockets with eyebrows suggesting just a hint of her Asian bloodline. Her skin was very white, very smooth, and she wore bright red lipstick and dark eyeliner. She was very pretty in a hard-but-pleasing way, but not the sort of woman most guys would even attempt to charm. Although she smiled if looked at, there seemed to be a "No Trespassing" sign hanging from her neck.

Madame Butterfly was known by customers at Bogart's and elsewhere to have a fast and sharp tongue that sometimes cut too deep into her targets. Along with Gary Nicholson, she was one of the main cocaine importers and distributors in town. But they didn't compete. Not at all. Rather, they conspired together to freeze out any competition. You've heard the expression "win-win?" That's what Madame Butterfly and Gary had going for themselves.

Except for me, everyone was fucked up from a long day of booze and cocaine abuse. I was only drunk—at least legally. I was a professional drinker, however, not an amateur who went into Irish bars on St. Paddy's Day to drink green beer until they puked on their shoes.

But this was July. It had been a great party at the ranch, and I was ready to relax for an hour or so then go home. But I was also hoping to rub elbows—or more—with sweet Shelly Summers.

Like the fictional little Alice Liddell, however, who fell through a rabbit hole and soon found herself in Wonderland with the Mad Hatter, March Hare, Knave of Hearts and other peculiar characters, I began walking toward Gary's basement bar unaware that I was about to stumble and fall into my own rabbit hole. My own Wonderland.

And if my aging memory cells are functioning as I type this anecdote more than twenty-five years later, I believe I heard the voice of Grace Slick coming from Nicholson's old eight-track tape player, singing:

"What are you drinkin', Adrian?" George asked when he saw me enter the rec room.

"A Heineken, thanks."

As I waited for my drink, I noticed Shelly was standing next to me.

"Adrian, right?"

"Adrian, it is...Shelly."

We exchanged smiles, then I said, "Whatta you say we shoot some pool?"

"OK, but not 'til I light up my nose."

Leaning over the plate with a small straw in one hand, Shelly quickly and expertly inhaled a line of coke, then rubbed her nose for a couple of seconds and smiled at me.

"By the way, Adrian, that's an English snooker table, not a pool table," she said with a wink, "but I'll be happy to shoot some snooker with you if you'd like."

"Well, then snooker it is, young lady."

When we reached the felt-covered table and began picking out a cue to use, George and Kate walked up and stood next to us.

"Tell you what, buddy, Kate and I will play you and Shelly for ten bucks a game but watch out for the mean six. I own that pink ball tonight."

"Let's make it twenty a game to keep it interesting," I countered.

"OK," George agreed, "and if you lose, I'll treat you to a line of coke. But just one."

"Come on, Davis, take the bet," The Butterfly said, butting into the conversation. "Who knows, buttercup, you might even learn to like it," she added with a knowing smile.

"OK, OK, I'm not worried," I announced. "Hell, Shelly and I can beat George and Kate at snooker anytime, so rack 'em and let's play."

The game took about an hour because the girls were not very good, and the pace of the game was not what George and I were used to. But as the numbered balls began dropping into the snooker pockets, the score was close. After I pocketed the pink six for extra points, only three balls remained on the table. George then sank the five to give his team a 22-21 lead, but I responded by sinking the six—permanently, this time—to take the lead at 27- 22.

One numbered ball remained—worth seven points. But I missed my easy shot at the seven and left George with a slam-dunk game-ender.

"Don't choke," I whispered as George leaned over the table to line up his shot.

"Choke?" George said without taking his eyes off the final numbered ball. "Are you kiddin' me? Chokes are for chumps."

Finally, with most of the crowd rooting hard for George, he calmly sank the seven ball in a side pocket and raised his arms in victory.

Final score: George and Kate, 29—Adrian and Shelly, 27.

As soon as the seven-ball dropped in the pocket, Madame Butterfly motioned for me to come to the bar. And I knew why.

"Hey baby here's a big fat one just for you," she said, holding out the coke plate and beckoning me with a come-hither look.

I hesitated, then reluctantly walked over to the bar, picked up the straw, bent down until my face was nearly touching the plate, and quickly inhaled the white powder up my nose.

Instantly, my nose burned, and I grabbed for it, hoping to lessen the pain. At the same time, however, a very pleasant feeling of euphoria swept over my body and mind. I liked it; there was no doubt about that. And I immediately knew that one hit would not be enough.

"Wow, that's nice," I announced to the applauding friends who had just watched me lose my virginity at the coke bowl. But I wasn't done having fun. Nicholson slid the plate back in front of me.

"Have another line, buddy. On me."

Without hesitation, I accepted the offer, and another line disappeared from the plate.

***

At about two in the morning, totally blitzed, I found myself sitting at Gary's bar with Gary, George, Kate, and the Butterfly. Shelly had her right arm around my shoulder, kissing me gently on the cheek and lips as her left hand rested inside my left thigh. I was trying to make sense of what had been happening since George pocketed the seven ball, but my brain wasn't running on all cylinders.

"Let's go," Shelly whispered, and that sounded good to me. I knew I was truly fucked-up, but in a way, unlike any fucked-up night I had ever known. My mind was racing in several directions at once, but mostly toward sex—especially with Shelly. I wanted her badly. All of her. Naked. Spread out on top of my bed, beckoning. At least that's what the throbbing between my legs was telling me.

"Good night to all, and to all a good night," I said to Gary and Madame Butterfly. "And if you see George and Kate before I do, tell' em they cheated."

"Cheated?" Gary asked with that big smile.

"They must have because there's no way I could lose to that asshole in a fair game of snooker."

"You'll get' em next time," Gary assured me as he steered Shelly and me up the basement stairs and outside.

Knowing we were fast becoming a newly bonded couple, we got in my gun-barrel grey 1976 Cadillac Seville. I backed out of the driveway on to Red Rock Road, then headed up the hill a mile or so to Bear Creek Park, where my home was located.

As I slowly drove up the hill, careful to keep the car on asphalt and not drift into the gravel shoulder, Shelly wiggled her tongue in my ear, gently squeezed my thigh and, despite the fact that we were in a moving car, in the dark, stoned, maneuvered her breasts on to my chest with adept skill.

I was a rock 'n' roll guy, not inclined to listen to twangy country stuff. But at that moment, with Shelly gripping my leg and licking my ear, I felt like singing a few bars of the Buck Owens song from the sixties, *I've Got a Tiger by the Tail*.

And what a tiger she was.

I turned off Red Rock Road onto a long, tree-lined driveway that led to a new four-bedrooms, 3-1/2 bath house with a private office, formal dining room, and a spacious great room with a modern kitchen. The backyard was enclosed, with a well- manicured lawn, large swimming pool and spa, and a built-in barbecue area—a playground for Tonto, my beautiful off-white, tan-spotted rescue dog.

We stumbled up the stairs from the garage to the pantry, and from there to the large main room where the bar was located.

"Nightcap?" I asked.

Shelly nodded while laying a bindle on the bar counter. "Gary gave this to me on the way out," she said.

I opened the bindle, took a credit card from my wallet and cut the cocaine into thin lines. Shelly noticed that for a rookie, I had the process down pat.

I then rolled up a hundred-dollar bill, and the two of us snorted coke and drank Amaretto for the next half-hour. Between sips of the almond-flavored Italian liqueur and trips to the coke plate, our tongues kept busy twisting and darting in each other's mouth while our hands explored each other's soft, warm spots.

I was about to suggest that we move from the great room to the bedroom, but Shelly beat me to the punch.

"Time for bed," she whispered after removing her delicious tongue from my mouth and giving my leg a gentle squeeze. "Show me the way."

I tried not to seem too anxious, but it took about twenty seconds for us to reach the bedroom.

Holding Shelly's body spread-eagled across the bed, I frantically removed her clothing. And as I did, she pressed her face against me, her mouth slowly moving down my chest toward my manhood that she softly held in her sensuous hands.

Our insatiable appetite for one another was clearly fueled by something more than normal desire. It was more than the booze, more than the coke, more than the normal giddiness of being in bed with someone new and different. It was more than all of that. Much more. There was a kind of mindless, uninhibited wildness that literally fed upon itself, continuing to escalate rather than gradually subsiding. I was surprised that such a young gal was so expert in love-making techniques, but this was no time to ask her how she knew what she knew.

I was torn between a giant climax or more sex. I chose more sex — at least for a few minutes.

"Come, please come," Shelly said as I continued to thrust inside her.

"You're still so hard. How do you do that?" she asked. "The sun's been up for hours and so have you. But I can't keep going like this, so please come, come."

As Shelly's hips swayed back and forth against my hardness, I could hold it no longer. And when I finally exploded, we shouted in unison, "Yes, yes, God yes!"

***

By noon we were in the kitchen, neither able to sleep. My scheduled meetings with liquor reps would have to wait. The heavy coke intake had left us jacked-up and wide awake but also exhausted. It had been an extraordinary night of bedroom gymnastics.

"I've had good sex," I told her, and it was the truth, "but that was flat-out over the top. You're an amazing young lady; that was fun, fun, fun."

"Ditto," she said, standing on her tiptoes to kiss me on the cheek. "I can't believe you stayed so hard for so long; you keep doing that, you're going to hurt me," she said, laughing as she rolled her eyes.

"No doubt about it, coke is great boner food. No wonder it can be so addictive."

Shelly cocked her head, raised an eyebrow and said, "So, you think it was only the coke that gave you that hard-on?" She looked up at me flashing her eyelids.

"Well, the coke sure didn't hurt, did it?" I laughed as Shelly gave me a faux glare.

I reached toward her, hands outstretched, looking for a hug.

Shelly took a step forward and collapsed into my arms.

"We ought to try that again sometime," I told her as a big smile flashed across my weary face.

"Try what? Another all-night marathon, or coke?"

"Both."

Sighing and reaching for her cup of black coffee, Shelly didn't take long to respond to my suggestion.

"Yeah, that sounds good to me. Really good, in fact," she said holding her coffee cup aloft and motioning as if toasting the decision. "And I hope it's soon."

"The love-making? Tonight, if we can," I told her. "But I'm not sure how soon I want to do coke again."

"Because?" she asked.

"Because there's a good reason some folks around here call it fool's gold."

As Shelly walked over to the kitchen sink to get a glass of water, I could feel my heart pounding and a light sweat forming on my forehead. I had fucked more women than I could remember, but this had been different. Very different. I wasn't sure what was going to happen, but I knew Shelly, and I would be spending a lot of time together.

At least a lot of nighttime.

Chapter Seven

It was a beautiful evening in the Gold Country, summer of 1983, as George Allen and I left Gold City on our Harleys and rode east on State Highway 20, headed for Lake Tahoe. The sun felt warm on our backs as the fading sunlight bounced off the tops of large pine trees on either side of the highway.

Highway 20 is one of the most picturesque rides in California—especially the final sixty-miles from Gold City to Emigrant Gap, where it connects with Interstate 80. Summer or winter, (unless it's snowing), the route is a favorite with recreational motorcyclists.

The twisting, two-lane highway leading east from Gold City has a steep, three-mile climb, then it levels off as the roadbed follows the contours of Hummingbird Ridge.

During the Gold Rush, when tens of thousands of gold seekers heard about the riches in Quartz County, they turned off at Emigrant Gap, above what is now Donner Lake, dropped down into Cougar River Valley, climbed back up the granite mountains, then zig-zagged their way west through heavily forested land until safely in Gold City.

Sections of the original wagon road can still be seen on either side of the nineteen-twenties-built two-lane state highway, and the trip from Gold City to Lake Tahoe takes just under two hours. In the early years of the Gold Rush, however, that same trip would have taken several days.

George was a few yards in front me when I heard him let up on the gas and point to his right, toward the Stage Coach Inn—an old roadhouse converted into a bar and restaurant. We were only ten miles from town but stopping for a beer was appealing.

The Stage Coach Inn is a two-story building, constructed in the 1890s as a stagecoach stop for passengers headed east or west. For eastbound stages, it was a good place to change teams and let fresh horses lead the way until they reached the Twenty Mile House. For westbound stages, it was the last place horses were watered and fed before descending those final, dangerous ten miles from four thousand feet down to twenty-one hundred feet of elevation.

When Gold City has a winter dusting of snow, you can be sure that a foot or more has fallen at the Stage Coach Inn. And if Gold City has its own foot of snow, then a trip east on Highway 20 is out of the question—even with four-wheel drive and chains.

Our planned ride for that evening, however, was during perfect weather; nothing to slow us down. At least that was the plan. Ride and daydream. Not a worry in the world.

Or so we thought.

We entered the old stage stop and found a couple of empty barstools. The interior reflected the building's age: wood walls, wood tables, and wood chairs. No plastic, no chrome. Nothing fancy, but good food and cold drinks. The tables had red and blue checkered tablecloths, and in the center of the bar area hung a large chandelier assembled from deer horns.

The place was busy for an early Tuesday evening, a small group of bikers playing pool in the rear of the bar while some sat at a table eating. One table had three bikers George and I had never seen before, but we nodded and smiled. They chose not to return the friendly gesture. OK, no big deal—just trying to be friendly.

As we settled in and began enjoying a cold beer on a warm night, a tall brunette who had been seated with her back to us at the table with the three bikers, suddenly rose and came over to George. Smiling, she tightly wrapped her arms around his shoulders.

"Hey, Paula, where the hell you been, sweet thing?"

"Don't give me that crap, Georgie. You always know where to find me—when you want to find me. My jugs are your jugs any time you want 'em; you know that." Paula said as she seductively looked down at her ample breasts.

George playfully hugged her at the waist and chuckled. "Not true, Paula; not true. Not since the night at Stoney's party. They were his jugs that night."

"Me and Stoney? Hell, man, that wasn't anything," she told him. "I was just hanging with him for some fun. His wife had left him, and I thought he needed a little pick-me-up. Know what I mean? It was some basic adult fun, nothing to write home about."

"Say what you want, but it was a shitty thing to do right there in front of me. Real shitty, in fact."

"Well, you pissed me off earlier at the party, so I got drunk and did something that pissed you off. No need for you to hold a grudge over a little thing like that, now is there?" she said as she leaned over and gave George a lock-lip kiss.

Adrian could see that the three bikers were watching the pawing and fawning. And they sure as hell weren't smiling.

"So, what happened to Stoney after that?   Did he go back to his wife?"

"How would I know? And who the hell cares, anyway?" Paula said as she shrugged her shoulders and moved even closer to George.

"Not me, ladybug, not me," he laughed. "I don't really give a flyin' fuck about Stoney's situation, but I'm glad to see you this evening and happy we've resolved whatever misunderstanding may have existed between the two of us."

George stood and faced Paula, brushing his chest against hers. "Now, about those amazing jugs of yours. Why don't we..."

Before Paula could respond, the table of bikers hollered for her to rejoin them. She nodded, gave George a peck on the cheek and left.

"An old friend?" I asked.

"Yeah, I play with her sometimes—or at least I *used* to play with her. She's a little nuts, doesn't give a shit about anything, but fucks like the sun will never come up."

"Sounds like fun, except for the part about her being a little nuts," I laughed as George ordered two more beers.

George could see over my shoulder that the bikers sitting with Paula were looking his way. Glaring, actually. A few minutes later, Paula got up and walked back to where George and I were sitting. She approached George and stood next to him. She didn't speak at first, but her body language was screaming. Then she took another step, put her hands around George's neck and pressed herself against his groin.

"What the hell are you trying to do Paula, start some trouble?"

"You bet sugar, just like the old days."

"I didn't mean that kind of trouble," he said as he pulled away from Paula's sudden embrace. "I meant the kind of trouble I see over at that table where you've been sitting. I don't know what you've been telling them, but they don't seem very happy to see us standing here together; especially that big dude with the shaved head."

"Ah, don't worry about it, sweetie. Me and Royce?   Hell, that's a big nothin'. We just know each other, that's all. We hang out sometimes."

Paula then turned to look at me. "So, who's your friend, Georgie?"

"Paula, meet Adrian. He owns Bogart's on Commerce Street. If you haven't been there since he remodeled Frank's old place, you need to give it a look."

I stood, like a gentleman ought to, extended my right hand and said, "It is a pleasure, Paula, truly a pleasure."

"Thanks...err, Adrian. Right?"

I nodded, smiled and gave Paula's hand a gentle squeeze.

"Nice meeting you, too, Adrian. I've been to Bogart's dancin'— fun place."

I looked over at the table where Paula had been sitting with the bikers. I had seen that "look" before. It was time to chug our beer and say goodbye. They seemed aching for a fight, and I wasn't in the mood. I won't back away from a fight, if unavoidable, but as I'd gotten older, I had learned that a strategic retreat was a hell of a lot better, and smarter, than getting clubbed, kicked and battered.

I think German general Erwin Rommel—the Desert Fox—said it best: "Don't fight a battle if you don't gain anything by winning." And there was nothing to gain by getting into a brawl with those bikers. Nothing whatsoever.

Before I could get George's attention; however, my instincts were confirmed when one of the bikers suddenly got up and approached. He was the tallest of the trio, six-five at least, and the most muscular. His arms were filled with tats, some appearing to have been carved into him during an extended stay at Folsom or the Q. His head was shaved, and he had a dark goatee with so much scar tissue around his left eye it seemed nearly closed.

And he wasn't walking toward us with a smile and friendly gait.

"So, you guys plannin' on leavin'?" The burly biker asked, staring at George. "Like real soon, maybe?"

"I've never planned nothin' in my life," George defiantly replied, "and so far, it's worked out pretty well for me."

"Is that right, wise guy? Well maybe you'd better start plannin' on your swift departure, or it might not work out so well for you this time."

"Nah," George shrugged. "Things never turn out the way you plan' em, so why bother planning. From where I'm sitting, that would be a waste of time."

"Well, little man, I think you might want to reconsider your philosophical outlook on life. Might be a healthy thing for you to do."

Paula realized that George's snarky approach was not working, so she decided to take a shot at being a peacemaker.

"Royce, this is George," she said. "He and his friend here, Adrian, they rode out here on their Harleys to have a couple of beers, that's all. So please go back to the table and be nice. I'll be right over, OK?"

"Don't give me that shit, bitch. I know what's goin' on here and so do you," Royce hollered as other patrons turned to look. "Do you think I'm an idiot?"

Then he looked over at me.

"Adrian, huh? That's a fuckin' girl's name," he said with a sarcastic laugh.

Instantly, George grabbed Royce by the arm and whipped him around so quickly that the biker didn't have time to react. In the blink of an eye, Royce was prone on the pool table, bleeding from a punch to the nose, while George continued pummeling the biker's face and body with his fists.

There was something swift and deadly about George's level of aggression, belying the fact that a smaller George seemed an easy target for the heavier and more muscular Royce. What he lacked in stature and muscular appearance, however, was more than compensated for by his kill-or-be-killed tenacity. It was a quality Royce, and the other bikers quickly recognized.

Royce had just been bloodied and beaten by a slightly smaller man, but he knew better than to pursue a fight he wasn't going to win. Instead, he motioned to the other two bikers, and the three of them left the Stage Coach Inn licking their wounds. And as they walked out, another table of bikers also got up and headed for the front door.

We could finally take a deep breath.

"Sorry about that, my friend, but I can only be pushed so far," George said, apologizing for having precipitated the short brawl.

"Hey, nothing to apologize for," I assured him. "Truth is, that was impressive; thanks for taking care of things."

"He had it coming. He talked to Paula like she was his slave girl and he insulted you."

"You were great, buddy, but next time I'll do the swinging, and you can do the watching, OK?" I responded with some dry humor.

"Promise?"

"Well...probably not, so don't hold me to it," I laughed, relieved that all the biker boys were gone.

We finished our beers and ordered another round, agreeing that we would ride back to Gold City and have a nightcap at Bogart's. The ride to Lake Tahoe would have to wait for another day.

"Not sure I ought to serve you two again," the bartender said. "We have a rule around here that if you take a swing, you take a walk."

I reached out to shake the bartender's hand and said, "Good rule. It's the same one I have at Bogart's."

"Bogart's, eh? You Adrian Davis?"

"Yep, that's me. Sorry, my friend got so riled up, but that guy was asking for it."

"Yeah, he was," the bartender said, looking out the window to the parking lot where the bikers were saddling up and heading east. "I cringe every time Royce, and his gang come in here. So, no loss there. Let's just consider that your friend here was my bouncer tonight and that he took care of a bad situation before it became worse. Sound OK to you?"

"Appreciate your understanding," I told him.

Uncontrollable aggression—vicious and relentless—was a side of George Allen that I had never seen before. George's street-fighting skills had been impressive, but I was thankful he had stopped before permanently injuring the biker. Or worse.

As we sat at the bar finishing our final beers, it was obvious that George and Paula were getting ready to hook-up for the night. And I knew that could be as dangerous for George as getting into a bar fight with a biker. Paula was trouble, but George was George.

Outside the Stage Coach Inn, sitting on our bikes waiting for Paula to finish in the restroom, I asked George, "What about Kate? She might be in town tonight?"

"Nope, I'm safe. Kate's in the Bay Area visiting her sister," he said with a laugh, "and she won't be back until tomorrow."

"First you whip the big dude, then this; it seems to be your lucky night, my friend."

With a shrug and smile Allen told me, "You know what they say: 'When she's away, it's time to play.'"

But nothing that happened after that was play.

Chapter Eight

When Paula walked out the front door of the Stage Coach Inn and over to George, she gave him a tongue to taste then climbed on his bike. George and Paula pulled out first, and I followed close behind. We headed west, back to Gold City for a drink or two at Bogart's while Royce and his boys headed east.

We moved swiftly along the highway, enjoying the openness and refreshing early evening air. But a mile or so from the Stage Coach Inn, I glanced at my side mirror and noticed the reflection of a row of headlights. Six, seven lights. Maybe more. I immediately realized that a small army of bikers was approaching.

After the fight, they had headed east from the Stage Coach Inn, but that had obviously been a ruse—a tactic designed to catch us off guard and vulnerable. They seemed to be hanging back on purpose, staying about a hundred yards behind us—close enough to watch us, perhaps waiting for the right moment to attack.

Riding up beside George, I gestured for him to look at what was behind us. He saw the bikers, still about a hundred yards away. He nodded and motioned for us to pull off the highway about thirty yards after taking a big curve that led down the steep grade to town.

With our bikes off the road, George and Paula dismounted, then he quickly reached into his saddlebags and pulled out a canvas sack. From the sack, he took out a Mini-Uzi with collapsible stock, clicked the metal stock into position, slipped in a 25-round clip of 9mm ammo, and looked back at the bikers—now moving slowly as they rounded the turn.

I stood next to my Harley—caught up in a situation, unlike anything I had ever experienced. And as the approaching pursuers revved their engines like bulls snorting before they charge a matador, black-and-white images of Marlon Brando and Lee Marvin facing off in *The Wild One* flashed before my eyes.

I was confused, not sure what George would do next. My heart was beating so hard I could feel blood throbbing in my temples. My buddy was a few feet away, holding a weapon normally associated with top-tier international security agencies and crazy terrorists. Then George said, "Watch this—it's about to go Western out here," as he walked out to the middle of Highway 20 to face the approaching bikers.

Calmly and defiantly, George released the safety, raised the Mini-Uzi and started to spray bullets at the asphalt in front of Royce and the others. He was careful not to aim higher—at the bikers. As he fired off the clip, ricocheting sparks lit up the highway while riders swerved, desperately trying to avoid the gunfire.

Some bikers escaped the fusillade but fell from their bikes when they collided with others. Two bikers purposely dumped their hogs on the highway then jumped into nearby bushes to avoid the spray, while a rider in the rear of the pack steered away and came to an abrupt stop.

George surveyed the scene with a big smile, then silently walked back to his bike, disassembled the stock and returned the Mini-Uzi to the saddlebag. After helping Paula get secure on the passenger seat, he hopped on and gave his Harley a crank. I did the same to mine.

As we began the final descent into Gold City, I stole a quick glance to the rear and saw at least half a dozen bikers and bikes in the middle of the highway. Some guys were in obvious pain; probably a few broken bones, some bad skin abrasions. Maybe worse. But it was getting dark, and I couldn't tell from that distance all the damage that George had done.

To our astonishment, the Highway 20 incident was never reported in the local newspaper, nor mentioned on the radio. I figured the bikers—some no doubt having outstanding warrants—decided to get back on their machines and leave the scene: no police report, no ambulances, no reporters.

As for the barroom brawl, George was merely performing the bouncer's job the bartender had assigned to him. After the fact, yes, but it still worked for our purposes.

All things considered, we couldn't have hoped for a better outcome.

***

A few days later, I was sitting at Bogart's talking with customers—when Mike Hodge—a jovial county deputy sheriff, dropped by.

Affectionately known as New Jersey Mike, the Garden State transplant had settled in Gold City in order to get away from the hustle and bustle of his home in Newark and follow the call of "go west young man." And although he had left New Jersey ten years earlier, his accent and mannerisms were ingrained in him.

Deputy Sheriff Hodge was about thirty-eight, medium height, and probably ate too many doughnuts during coffee breaks at the mini-mart. But with a full head of dark hair, great smile, and spellbinding personality, he was a babe magnet. Hodge enjoyed flirting with the gals, but he was a married man with a couple of kids and never strayed. That was a quality I admired.

As Mike worked the room like a politician campaigning for election—walking up and down the bar shaking hands, slapping shoulders and spreading goodwill—he motioned for me to meet him at the table next to the fireplace.

Once seated, I looked at Hodge with a cautious eye.

"What's up, Mike? I don't usually see you here in uniform."

"I wanted to ask you about that ruckus at the Stage Coach Inn the other night."

"What ruckus was that?" I asked, knowing that Hodge probably had all the details and all the names of those who had been involved.

"That fight in the bar area involving your buddy George Allen and that biker, Royce what's-his-name. I've got his last name here somewhere," Mike said, thumbing through loose papers in his shirt pocket. "But you know who I mean, right?"

"Yeah, sure, I know who you mean," I admitted.

"Near as we can tell from the rumors flying around, there was some nasty gunplay on the highway a few minutes after Allen decked that guy. No one's given us any details, so we're not sure what the hell happened," Mike said as he looked directly at me, "so I'm hoping you can fill me in a little, Adrian. The sheriff wants a detailed incident report, and I have a hunch you can give me what I need to make my boss happy."

"Well, first of all, you're right, Mike, there was a fight, and I was there when George slugged the biker. No need denying what you already know," I said, "but as for gunplay, sorry, I can't help you. I heard some stuff; probably the same barroom rumors you heard. But I don't know anything else. If I knew more, I'd tell you more."

"Just keep in mind that those guys don't fuck around, Adrian. They're bad dudes, OK?"

"Thanks for the info, Mike. I'll let George know the next time I see him."

"This is serious shit, my friend. They're a biker gang, not a bunch of good ol' boys out for a casual recreational ride. Our Gang Task Force knows them well, and I've been told they're never bashful about taking care of their own and getting even when one of them is hurt—or shot at."

"Yeah, I agree. They looked like bad guys up at the inn."

"They're worse than bad; they're mean, you hear me? I deal with a lot of bad guys, but this gang is way beyond mean, trust me," Mike said. "I'm here to say that you and your buddy George need to know that rumor is three of them got hit with ricocheting fragments, and a couple of others got busted up pretty good when they spilled their bikes dodging bullets."

"Sorry to hear that," I said, trying to hide my concern about possible retaliation from the bikers, "but I don't know anything about guns." I looked away from Mike and said, "Wish I could help you, I really do, but all I saw was a little tussle that lasted less than a minute. A few punches were thrown."

Hodge just stared, not believing a word I said.

"By the way, Adrian, I've heard some rumors about you and this bar," Mike said as he stood and prepared to leave. "Not saying anything illegal is going on in here, of course, but I think you'd better be careful. It's still a small town, you know, and rumors aren't good for business."

"I appreciate that Mike, but I'm not sure what you're hearing on the street that I should be concerned about. Nothing bad is happening here that I know of, but I'll keep an eye and an ear open. And thanks for dropping by; I always like seeing you."

We shook hands.

Deputy Hodge walked toward Bogart's front door, then paused and asked, "Tell me, Davis, how the hell did George get his hands on an Uzi?"

I didn't respond.

Hodge tipped his cap, smiled, and walked back to his patrol car.

Chapter Nine

Michael placed the manuscript on his lap and paused to consider what he had just read. He was amused by his father's description of the visit from Deputy Mike Hodge, but what happened at the Stage Coach Inn and on the highway was serious stuff. Bikers don't forget.

After resting his eyes for a few minutes, then gazing down at the patchwork Iowa farmland, young Davis put his wine glass back on the drop-down tray in front of him and returned to a story that continued to surprise him with every page he read.

A couple of Thursday nights a month, Madame Butterfly— Musette Parks—hosted a poker party at her home. I was invited to join the parties not long after I first experimented with cocaine. I assumed I was added to the invite list because the evenings revolved around the consumption of coke with the alluring mistress I had gotten to know from her visits to the bar, as well as her connection with our mutual friends, Gary and George.

Not only was the product consumed in quantity those Thursday evenings at Madame Butterfly's, but it also replaced cash for betting purposes. No chips, just quarter, half and full grams of the white powder. Twenty-five, fifty, and one-hundred-dollar bets with bindles representing cash value equal to their weight.

The games drew some interesting characters, and word circulated through the bar scene that the occasional card game was the hottest ticket in town. Getting an invitation was tantamount to my doorman, Wally, escorting someone into Bogart's while others stood outside in the snow waiting their turn.

We had a lot of snow at Madame Butterfly's, but it wasn't the kind that melted.

A Thursday night session in the fall of nineteen eighty-three had an especially elevated level of anticipation because one of the invitees was Gold City Councilman Vance Egan—a former mayor and self-absorbed prick. It was Egan's first time with our crowd of merrymakers, so we were all curious about how he'd react when the coke started flowing. He took his seat at the table with a lot of bravado, but it was obvious to all of us that he was one nervous bastard.

Others around the table that night, including me, were Gary Nicholson, George Allen, Madame Butterfly, her gay friend Asa Kalb, who called our hostess, Miss Fly—and a couple of Asa's friends visiting from Sacramento.

Kalb was in his late twenties with a movie star face. He was about six feet tall, slender, light-blue eyes with long blond hair that hung loose like a surfer, usually attired in expensive designer threads. He was clean-shaven with a sparkling smile and, with his All-American looks, was a popular waiter at two Gold City restaurants.

Word around town was that Kalb came from a well-to-do family in a high-end suburb of San Diego and received a generous allowance to stay away. He was part of the growing gay community relocating to the Sierra foothills in the 1980s to open antique shops, B&Bs, restaurants, and other businesses oriented for tourists and locals alike. Asa was a fun guy to be around, and his preference for sexual partners was not an issue with any of us. The Butterfly's house was located on Veterans Avenue, just across the street from Veterans Park, surrounded by pine trees and tucked away about a hundred feet from the street. It was a modest three-bedroom, two-bath house, ideal for Butterfly and her teenage daughter. She bought it in the seventies for a good price, and most were envious of her modest monthly mortgage payments.

The eight of us were seated at the dining room table just off the living room—a warm, cozy environment with a small fireplace a few feet away. As usual, the game started at nine that night. We didn't have a regular end time, but the games normally lasted until a couple of players went broke, or until we were all too fucked up on coke to play any longer. After too many lines, a three might be mistaken for an eight, and making that kind of mistake could be costly.

Our hostess was serving drinks when I walked in. She gave away buckets of booze because we purchased the bindles of coke from her—except, that is, for Nicholson and Allen. They had their own from their personal stash. Madame Butterfly figured the more we drank and snorted, the better chance she had of making multiple and profitable coke sales during the evening. And based on what I saw on those Thursday nights, she was a smart businesswoman who knew how to turn over her inventory.

In those years, I liked to wine-and-dine the young ladies, then get in their pants. Madame Butterfly liked to get in her guests pants as well; by first getting her guests high, then robbing their wallets and purses. The same concept, only one was legal, and the other wasn't.

I bought-in with three hundred bucks in cash, and Musette handed me a handful of bindles in different denominations along with a line of the white powder from a courtesy plate she held under my nose. She was generous with the coke at the beginning of our games but always got it back in sales before the night was over. As I said, she was a smart businesswoman.

Just before the game began, an attractive young girl came from a back bedroom. She was of medium height with long black hair flowing down her back. For a sixteen-year-old high-schooler, she had a striking figure, cute face with large lips, a bright smile and dark eyes, as well as her mother's body and perfect white skin. Standing there with tight jeans, pink tennis shoes, a white sweater, and a black parka coat, she was a hellcat in the making. And her mother knew it.

After glancing at the pretty bundle of jailbait, I went over to the large cooler that the Madame kept stocked with beer. I reached in the ice and grabbed a bottle of Heineken while the others played a silent version of musical chairs—looking to their left and right before settling into their lucky seat at the table.

As for me, I knew the chair didn't matter, only the cards.

"Mom, I'm going to Sally's for the night and need the car keys."

Her obliging mother reached down and picked up her purse from between her feet, retrieved the keys and, as she handed them to her daughter, said, "Bye, baby. Have fun, but be careful, OK? See you tomorrow morning before school."

"Okay, Mom, and you guys have fun, too," she said as she walked out of the living room and headed for the garage.

"Goodnight, Stacy," we said in unison.

"You better keep an eye on that sweet young thing of yours," George cautioned, looking at the girl's mother with a sarcastic expression evident to all of us. "If she brings someone home with her, you'd better get that shotgun out of the closet and be ready to use it."

"Come on, you guys, let's get on with the game, OK?" Egan announced as if he was calling a city council meeting to order. "I came here to play, clean your clocks and take home the bacon. So, let's get started," the asshole pleaded.

"And enjoy a few lines of nose candy while you're here, councilman?" Nicholson asked.

"That, too," the local politician said with a cocky nod of anticipation.

Like most Thursday nights at Madame Butterfly's, the clock moved at warp speed. When you're tooting coke and pounding booze, the time has a way of flying by. It was 2:00 A.M. before anyone knew it and looking around the table the winners and losers were obvious based on the stack of bindles in front of them. Or, in some case, the lack of bindles.

I was up some, George was up, and so was Asa. The big losers for the night at that point were the two visitors from Sacramento, along with Gary, Councilman Egan, and our hostess. At least in the card game, she had been a loser, but Madame Butterfly's cocaine sales actually made her the biggest winner at the table. It was another lively Thursday night that had turned into a coke-infused Friday morning.

"For Christ's sake Davis, I call your bluff," the councilmen said as he dropped two bindles in the center of the table and stared at me.

"When you have a good hand, there's no need to bluff," I answered without showing emotion; my stone-cold glare fixed on the cocky councilman.

The game was seven-card stud, nothing wild. Trying not to show any anxiety, I turned over two tens. And staring back at Egan was another ten and two sevens, face-up on the table.

"I believe that's known in casinos as a full house," I told him. "But here at Madame Butterfly's, on Thursday nights, we like to call it a *fucking* full house."

"Shit!" Vance blurted as he threw his cards on the table.

"Looks like my full house beats the hell out of your three queens, councilman," at which point I reached out and pulled the bindles from the center of the table and added them to the modest pile I had already accumulated.

Councilman Vance Egan sat silent, staring at his dwindling supply of coke. I smiled then turned to Asa.

"As I look at Vance's queens on the table, I'm wondering why you're not downtown tonight hustling some action with the boys of our fair town."

"No, not tonight, Adrian," Asa chuckled at the not-so-subtle comment. "Tonight's my night with you lovely boys," he said. "Besides, I have my buds from Sac here to keep me company."

Everyone at the table laughed at the suggestive implication of his remark.

"Plate break," George announced, leaning back and grabbing a platter with complimentary lines of coke on it. The plate was passed around with a straw so that everyone could partake.

Between the drugs and alcohol, all of us were fucked up—and Egan was the most fucked-up of all. It had been an expensive night for the councilman. He had shot his coke wad, easily four- hundred dollars, at the table and was headed home to his wife knowing he had to scramble for an excuse to explain why they would—once again—have to cut back on household expenses and credit card payments.

It was time for The Butterfly to make her move.

She walked up behind Egan and leaned over to whisper in his ear. He listened, smiled, then stood up and followed Butterfly into the kitchen while the rest of us kept playing cards.

We soon noticed that Madame Butterfly was holding Vance's hand, walking him toward her bedroom. As they walked past the living room, Gary said, "Well, folks, it looks like our genial host is going to take care of one of our town's illustrious politicians."

Then, cupping his hand and shouting in the direction of the hallway, Nicholson said, "Be good, Miss Butterfly, and City Hall will remember your generosity."

'I'm always good, as you well know," she said to Gary, looking back over her shoulder as the two figures disappeared from view.

"They say her mouth is as warm and soft as mink," Kalb told us. Then he turned toward the hallway and shouted, "Hey, Councilman, I'll suck that thing of yours, and when I get through, you'll never look at another woman."

All the guys laughed.

"If she's in the mood, she'll take a big loser to the bedroom for a blow job to keep them coming back," George explained to the other card players. "She won't fuck, and she doesn't give it away to anyone—everything is business to the Madame. Trust me; she's not an easy fuck, but, if she likes you, and she's in the mood, you better be ready for action," George said.

"The Butterfly has what we connoisseurs call a 'magic pussy'" he added. "And if it takes a few tries, don't give up. It's worth the wait," he chuckled, remembering a couple of nights when he had the pleasure of Miss Butterfly's company after a game.

"I'm not interested in her sexually, of course, but I'm confused," Asa said, looking around the table for some insight. "If a volunteer city councilman is blowing big money on coke and card games, where the hell does he get the dough? I thought he had his own feed, grain and farm supply store he inherited from his dad?"

"That he does," Nicholson said.

"Well, can he be making that much from the store?"

"A living, yes. But not much beyond that," I told him, "but he is bartender over at the Grizzly Bear Lodge, and it is rumored that the bar register has been coming up short lately."

"Sounds like a lot of loose change floatin' around, if you ask me." George laughed.

"No kidding," I said. "The guy lives way beyond his means from what I can see, and I hear he taps his wife's register for cash at the beauty parlor when he really gets short."

"So, what's going to happen to Vance if he's actually caught with his hand in the cookie jar over at the Lodge?" Asa asked. "You think he'll be arrested?"

"Arrest a seated city councilman around here? Not hardly," Gary injected. "If it's true, and he's caught, the Grizzly Lodge board will simply sweep it under the rug. They don't want the bad PR, and no one will be the wiser. I mean, who's going to have him arrested? The mayor? The police chief? Hell, they're all best buds."

"Maybe Madame Butterfly will get the truth out of him back in that bedroom," I joked. I paused, then added, "Hope Miss Butterfly is giving him the best head he's ever had because it might be the last time he'll be able to get out of the house after his wife finds out about this one."

"You're a real pisser, Davis; you know that?" George said.

"What the fuck is a pisser, George? I've heard you say that before, but what the hell does it mean?"

"Pisser is my way of saying you're OK, my friend. My dad used to say it to us kids, his friends, and those he approved of. It's a sign of affection."

"*Affection*?" I asked. "It sure doesn't strike me as a sign of affection."

"Guess it depends on how you say it," George explained as he gave me a hug and air kiss alongside both cheeks.

"Glad to hear that I'm an OK guy in your book," I told him as he gently broke the hug and stepped back, "but let's not get all mushy about it."

"Your turn to deal, Davis," Gary announced with more laughter and another line.

The evening had cost Egan between four and five hundred bucks, but he left smiling—at least until he got home and Gloria, his wife, saw how fucked up he was, as well as broke, and ordered him downstairs to the guest room. Again.

Whoever said, "Laughter is the best medicine," never lived through the cocaine-infested eighties.

Chapter Ten

As 1983 drew to an end, I felt great. Bogart's was packed nearly every night, and my bank account was growing in leaps and bounds. Unfortunately, my coke consumption was also growing in equal measure.

On balance, however, life was good. Money, sex, and coke were plentiful and, as with most aspects of my life, nothing seemed to stop me from doing exactly what I wanted. As I said earlier, live and let live—as long as you don't hurt anyone else. I tried hard to adhere to that credo but sometimes fell short. Hell, we all do.

I was thirty-four, full of piss and vinegar, with a head full of great memories and few regrets. I was lucky, and I was grateful. A lot of my high school chums were struggling, trying to keep the rent paid and their family fed. I had no responsibilities, except to keep Bogart's full of happy drinkers and dancers.

And I was doing a hell of a job handling that responsibility. Christmas was around the corner, and there was nothing Santa needed to bring me other than a steady flow of adult drinkers— along with a steady flow of women and drugs. But life sometimes has a way of jumping up and kicking you in the ass. Nothing stays the same, as I have said before, and was about to learn.

Christmas season in Gold City is special—more so than in most small towns. Thousands of twinkle lights outline all the downtown buildings, a large Christmas tree glows in the town square, holly wreaths hang from all the lamp posts, and most of the retail stores, restaurants, and bars have window displays celebrating the season of joy.

It was my favorite time of year. I loved the camaraderie, the family gatherings, gift giving, and the community's annual Dickens Christmas street fair. Strolling downtown on a cold winter night, gaslights burning and occasional snow flurries adding to the spirit of the season, was like walking through a 19th century Currier and Ives print.

On this particular night, the chamber of commerce was hosting the third of its five scheduled Dickens Christmas celebrations. It was a Friday, light snow collecting on vendor tents while several hundred-people enjoyed live Christmas music and carols. Craft artists and food vendors sold their wares and parents held hands with their children.

While Don handled the bar that night, I was having dinner at The Firehouse restaurant with George Allen and his girlfriend, Kate.

As dinner was ending and a bottle of 1980 Stag's Leap Cabernet Sauvignon was being emptied, George reached in his pocket and pulled out a large bindle of cocaine. He gently tossed it on the table in front of me and said, "Dessert time, ol' buddy."

"Indeed, it is," I said, smiling and stealthily pouring enough cocaine on my empty bread plate to create three hearty lines.

In addition to tables in the center of the dining area, The Firehouse had booth seating, where it was easy to snort coke with a degree of privacy. Besides, in those years coke was so common in public places that it was not unusual to have someone stop off at a booth for a dessert tasting of their own.

After a couple of lines of coke, George asked, "Want to take a ride out Highway 49? I have a collection to make; shouldn't take long."

"Sure," I said. "Don and Carla are taking care of the bar and Wally's manning the door, so Bogart's is in good hands right now."

"What about you, Kate?" George asked.

"No thanks, hon. Think I'll sit this one out and have a couple of drinks with the girls down at Adrian's place."

"Make sure Wally doesn't try to get a cover charge from you," I told her.

"I never pay a cover charge in this town," she said. "Wally always waves me through."

"Good," George announced, "let's go."

"How about the dinner tab?" I asked.

"I think it's your turn," he answered.

I shook my head and grinned, then put three U. S. Grants in the guest check holder handed it to our server and said, "Keep the change, Stormy, you did your usual masterful job of taking care of us."

"Wow, thanks," she said, looking at the money sticking out of the holder and realizing her tip was going to be more than thirty bucks.

While Kate walked down Commerce Street to Bogart's, George and I got in his Chevy Blazer and headed west, on Highway 49, driving along the state road for about three miles. At that point, George turned on to a narrow dirt road, drove another quarter- mile and stopped in front of a small house.

The roofline and windows were trimmed with flickering, multi-colored Christmas lights and a Christmas tree was visible through the living room window—as were two wide-eyed small children, curious about who was visiting them.

Parked in front of the house, George turned off the engine, opened the bindle of coke we had sampled at The Firehouse, scooped two big piles with a credit card and snorted the powder. Then he handed the bindle to me, and I did likewise.

George opened the door, pulled the seat forward and retrieved a baseball bat.

"Insurance," he said when I showed surprise seeing the bat in my friend's hand. "Everything's cool, buddy, trust me. This won't take long."

The porch light came on as we approached the house, and a tall, good-looking brunette greeted us at the front door. Joyce was about twenty-five, married to Scotty Peterson. She was wearing a bathrobe and slippers, hair pulled back, no make-up, and had a look of concern on her face.

"Hi, George, Merry Christmas," Joyce said, trying not to look nervous.

"Yeah, right, Merry Christmas," he responded with a snicker. "Get Scotty for me."

"I would, but he's not here right now."

"When's he coming home?"

"Later, but I don't know when. He's downtown having a little Christmas cheer with his work friends."

"If he has money for bar-hopping with friends, then he must have money for me, right?" an agitated George asked.

"Not that kind of money, no, but he's trying to get it for you, George, I swear."

"Swear, my ass. Get inside, Joyce."

George pushed on the door as Joyce backed up. In two seconds, the three of us were inside the Peterson house, standing in the entryway. And Joyce was getting frantic.

The living room was furnished in second-hand furniture: a couple of sofas, a recliner lounge chair, end tables, a cheap glass-top coffee table with lamps on each of the end tables. A television was in the corner near the Christmas tree, not far from the fireplace, and it was showing the Jimmy Stewart classic, *It's a Wonderful Life*.

To the left of the living room was a small dining room that led to the kitchen. Directly behind Joyce, and to the rear of the house, was a hall leading to the bedrooms and bathroom.

"Where are the kids?" George asked.

"I sent them to their rooms when I recognized your Blazer out front."

"Good," Allen told her.

"What are you going to do, George? We don't have the money tonight, but we'll have it soon, I'm sure of that."

"Listen, bitch, you two owe me a couple of grand, and that doesn't include the five bills you owe me that hubby boy doesn't know about."

"He can't find out about that, OK. Please. I'll pay you as soon as I can, but please don't let Scotty know about our side deal. If he finds out, he'll beat the hell out of me."

"I've been through this shit before with you two; it's always the same. I told Scotty many times, as politely as I could, there would be consequences for not paying. He knows I'm fair, probably too damn fair for my own good, but I'll only go so far before the shit hits the fan. Understand?"

George was pissed, and I was getting nervous. George could be a charmer when he wanted, but, as I witnessed at the Stage Coach Inn, he could be a raging wild man. Especially when pissed and coked up.

"All we need is one more week, please; one more week. It's Christmas, for God's sake. We need to take care of the kids; then we'll take care of you," Joyce pleaded.

"One more week? That's bullshit, lady, and you know it. You and Scotty have been one-more-weekin' me for too fuckin' long, and now you stand there begging for even more time? You must be kidding, lady."

"We don't have two thousand, George, much less the extra dough I owe you. There's no way we can pay you until after Christmas."

"I need a chunk of money tonight, no more delays," Allen barked as a spray of spit landed on Joyce's face. "Now, if you want to keep your IOU our little secret, that's fine, but you're going to have to pay me some interest," he said with a smile as he glanced down the hallway toward the bedrooms.

George looked back at Scotty's wife. She stood her ground but had a look of fear, wary of what was coming next. She tightened her bathrobe and began to walk backward, but quickly realized what was about to happen.

George took Joyce by the arm and began walking her down the hallway toward the master bedroom. She resisted and tried to break away from his grip, but he kept pulling on her arm as she pleaded, "No, George, please—not with the kids in the house."

When they reached the master bedroom, Joyce planted herself against the door jamb, careful not to scream and scare the children, but George was too strong. He gave one final jerk on her arm, pulled her inside, then closed the door. She knew the game and what was expected. It wasn't the first time she paid the interest on her coke habit. Paying the vig can sometimes be humiliating.

Walking over to the recliner, I sat and stared at the twinkling Christmas tree lights, patiently waiting for George to finish inside the master bedroom. I still had the bindle George had handed me in the Blazer, so I took a couple of hits. Then I got a beer from the refrigerator and returned to the recliner.

I wasn't comfortable with what was going on in the bedroom and wished I had never accepted George's offer to join him for a collection. I was no saint, mind you, but I didn't go around banging my friend's wife. Debt or no debt.

After twenty minutes or so, George walked back from the bedroom while Joyce lingered behind. George was smiling; Joyce was running her hand through her hair and pulling the robe back around her to cover her naked body.

"So much for the interest payment," he said with a sinister chuckle. "Now it's time to leave a message."

With that, George swept his right arm across a nearby bookshelf, scattering books and sending a vase filled with flowers into the middle of the room, where it shattered into little pieces.

He then walked over to the television and kicked-in the screen. I sat in the recliner watching my friend commit mayhem inside the Peterson home, recalling the rage Allen had displayed that summer night at the Stage Coach Inn. When bedlam struck at the Inn, I had stood and watched, neither joining in the fight nor trying to stop it. I had been a silent witness. And here, at the Peterson home, I was once again a silent witness.

I should have grabbed George and dragged him back to the Blazer, but I couldn't do it. My brain was telling me to get out of that house as quickly as possible, but the coke in my head had me jacked up and excited.

"Well," George said, looking over at me and motioning around the front room, "what the hell are you waiting for?"

I hesitated, then reached for the baseball bat that was leaning against one of the sofas. Gripping the bat as I had as a hard-hitting high school outfielder, I swung wildly and smashed a lamp, then another one. A moment later, I shattered the glass-top coffee table, then headed for the Christmas tree—swinging the bat at tree lights and stomping on presents waiting for the kids on Christmas morning.

For good measure, I also attacked the television George had bashed a couple of minutes earlier.

Joyce came running down the hall with her two small children and headed toward me, but George held them back as she and the kids screamed for me to stop. I had gone berserk and would not heed the cries coming from behind me, continuing to wield the Louisville Slugger for another fifteen seconds or so.

I was filled with uncontrollable rage, but even at that moment I realized the rage was not aimed at Joyce or Scotty; it was me thrashing at demons I had created. I was thrashing at my own failures, not at Christmas presents and a fucking television.

When I finally stopped swinging and put the bat down at my side, I was breathing hard, in a sweat, shocked at the damage I had caused. I could hear the children crying and Joyce screaming. George was mute, perhaps as shocked by what he had seen as I was shocked by what I had done.

As I tossed the bat aside and stood there in disbelief, still jacked from the coke, feeling sick to my stomach.

George walked over, picked up the bat, and told Joyce, "Tell Scotty I want the money by New Year's Eve. No dough by then and

I'll be back on New Year's Day. And I'll bring Adrian...with a bigger bat."

The two of us were quiet on the ride back to town, both looking straight ahead without talking. Finally, George said, "They're not exactly the All-American Family—more like Norman Fucking Rockwell on acid." He paused for a few seconds, then added with a laugh, "I've always said, 'Anything worth doin', is worth doin' to excess,' and I wanted to send a message, but I don't think we needed to bust up the kids' Christmas presents."

I didn't answer, reliving those horrible few minutes in my mind, but George chuckled lightly and said, "Even so, that was a pisser, my friend, and I bet I'll have my money by New Year's Day."

George spoke only that one time—and me not at all—but our silence spoke volumes. When we were back in town, I got out of the Blazer a few blocks from Bogart's and walked to my car. I wasn't in a mood to walk down to the bar, so I drove home. Alone.

When I got home, I opened a bottle of Cab and poured a glass, then opened the bindle George and I had shared a few minutes earlier. A few horrific minutes earlier.

I poured the remaining coke on the glass-top coffee table in my living room and thought about the glass-top table in Scotty and Joyce's house. I closed my eyes and saw myself smashing the table with the bat, then smashing the Christmas tree and presents intended for innocent children.

I sat there on the sofa for a long time thinking about what I had done inside the Peterson home—especially what I had done to ruin Christmas for those kids. Unable to purge visions of the onslaught from my mind, I tried to convince myself that I was watching someone else. It couldn't have been me, could it? But sadly, it was. Truth is truth. Was I addicted to cocaine or was I sick, in need of help? Or maybe both? I know the answer today as I write this, but I didn't have an answer that terrible night in December 1983.

Why did I do it? How could I have smashed that Christmas tree and the kids' presents? What was it that provoked me to become so hateful and vicious?   Hell, I didn't have any skin in the game; the Petersons' didn't owe me any money. In fact, I liked Scotty and Joyce. They often dropped by Bogart's for a quiet drink and friendly conversation. They were young and a little flaky, without any real direction in life, and they did way too much coke for their own good, but half the town seemed to be doing too much coke in the 1980s.

I have never forgotten that night and the senseless havoc I wrought. Images of my rage are burned into my brain. Even now, as I sit here years later typing this manuscript, I can close my eyes and see lamps crashing to the floor, shattered Christmas tree lights and ornaments bouncing off the walls, lovingly-wrapped Christmas presents smashed and destroyed, shards of the television screen flying through the air, and two young children crying while their mother screamed.

I'm ashamed to be writing this, I truly am. But I know I must.

Maybe by telling my story now, this demon from my past will go away. I sure hope so.

***

Michael closed the manuscript and stared out at the dense clouds that engulfed the plane. He was determined to finish his father's story before the flight touched down at Dulles International Airport, but it was becoming increasingly difficult to read.

He knew his dad had a temper, but….

Chapter Eleven

On a chilly January afternoon in 1984, three weeks after the senseless episode at Joyce and Scotty's, I was tending bar and looking forward to Don arriving at six to relieve me. It was about five when the bar phone rang. I figured it was probably another wife or girlfriend calling all the bars in town looking for their partner.

"Bogart's," I answered.

"Hey, buddy, come over for dinner tonight. I've got a couple of nice steaks for the grill, and the Forty Niners are playing Green Bay in the playoffs."

It was Gary Nicholson with an offer I couldn't resist.

"Sounds good," I told him. "I'll bring the wine and head over there as soon as Don gets here to relieve me."

"Good, see you then, pal."

Twenty minutes after I took off my bartenders' apron and Don put on his, I pulled up to Gary's house just off Red Rock Road. I walked up to the front door, opened it and announced myself as I entered.

"In the kitchen," Gary said.

We opened the wine, marinated the steaks and settled in to watch football with an occasional game of nine-ball on a pool table that Gary had conveniently set up in his dining room area. Nicholson didn't need a dining room table and chairs; he ate sitting on the couch or in his huge recliner. And if he had friends over, they were adults and could fend for themselves.

The carefree bachelor thought the space in his great room could be better utilized with a regulation pool table in the center, not a dining room table, and I agreed. Besides, what a great set-up: nine-ball upstairs, snooker downstairs. And a bedroom and full bathroom on each floor. What more does a bachelor need?

I handled grilling the steaks that evening while Gary mixed the salad and baked a couple of potatoes. Then we settled in for dinner and watched San Francisco crush the Packers 35-17.

"How about dessert, Davis?"

I smiled as Gary went out into the garage where he stored his special dessert in a hidden compartment on his eighteen-foot ski boat.

Returning with a small baggie of white powder, Nicholson grabbed a plate from the kitchen, brought it to the living room and placed it between us on the sofa. He opened the plastic baggie and used a teaspoon to scoop out a pile of the drug, carefully spreading it on the plate. Then he cut lines with his fingers, so we could share.

Between snorts, Gary asked, "Another game of nine-ball?"

"Sounds good—you break."

We shot some pool and snorted coke for the next hour or so, then the phone rang. Gary thought it might be a customer in need of some dessert of their own.

"Hello," he said. "Yeah, of course, I'm here. I answered the phone, didn't I?"

Gary listened for a few seconds then said, "Sure, come on over; Adrian's here, but he's cool. No problem. See you soon, gal."

After he hung up, Gary turned to me and said, "Got someone coming over."

"Want me to leave?"

"No, it's cool."

"He or she?"

"A she, and you know her," Gary answered. "Pixie Flowers, the FedEx driver."

"Sure, sure, I know her," I chuckled. "At Bogart's, we call her Crazy Pixie—but not to her face, of course. She comes in the bar, usually late at night after getting back from a trip, starts banging down drinks to get caught up with everyone else in the club, and then usually shows me a bag of coke tucked into her handbag. Then we go upstairs to my office."

"You've snorted with her; I take it?" Gary asked.

"Snorted and fucked," I told my friend. "Fucked her a few times upstairs after closing time and had an amazing threesome with her and Stubbs one night over at his house."

"At the *house*? Where the hell was his wife?"

"Annie was vacationing in Mexico with some gal pals."

"Well, Pixie's coming over here in a few minutes, bringing me a package."

Gary noticed my smile and understood my unspoken question.

"If you must know, she's my new connection to Southern California cocaine suppliers. I've known my Mexican boys since we were kids, so when I found out Pixie drives in and out of Southern Cal for her job with FedEx, I approached her, made her a good offer, and introduced her to my guys down there. She brings me about a kilo every other week, sometimes two, depending on demand."

"A kilo? Gary, my man, that's over two pounds."

"Tell me about it," he said with a smile.

"You're not going through that much shit every week, or so, are you?"

"Easily, as I said—sometimes more."

"So, how do you take care of the 'more' part between deliveries from Pixie?"

"Simple, my friend. I step on the kilo with a half-pound or so of filler from the get-go, usually baby laxative, because the coke's eighty percent pure. Then, presto! Out the door it goes, an ounce or more at a time, and I leave the bindle sales to George and Kate and other street dealers."

"Seems like half the town is dealin' coke these days."

"Not dealing, necessarily, but the whole fuckin' town's high on the stuff, especially during the holidays."

"No doubt about that," I said.

"Pixie's coming over with my allotment; then I'll get it ready for street sales as quickly as I can."

"Is she like the Avon lady?" I asked.

Nicholson stared, not sure what I meant.

"You know—does Crazy Pixie hand out product samples when she makes house calls?"

"Sometimes." And we both laughed.

Shortly after ten, the doorbell rang, and Nicholson ushered Pixie into the front room. She was still in her FedEx uniform, all jacked up and laughing, clearly in a mood to party. First, however, she took care of business with Gary. The package was wrapped in air-bubble cellophane and cinched tight with duct tape.

Gary handed Pixie a fat envelope then took the special delivery package out to the garage. Meanwhile, Pixie reached into her purse, withdrew a baggie much like the ones I'd seen at Bogart's when she and I went upstairs for pleasure. Then she poured a pile of blow on the same plate Gary and I had been using earlier.

Pixie was about thirty with tinted red hair falling below her shoulders—a statuesque five-ten with a thin frame and great legs. Her breasts were average, but no man ever complained. She had impish dimples on both cheeks, straight white teeth that produced a great smile, and deep brown eyes.

She was a very sexy woman who loved to fuck, but she was always in control of who she fucked and when she fucked them. And when she was partying hard, she came across as a little goofy, which led customers at Bogart's to stick her with the Crazy Pixie nickname.

Pixie had a boyfriend who worked in Sacramento—a nice guy, but way out of his league when it came to corralling her. I knew it was none of my business, but it was obvious that she wore the pants in their relationship, and pretty much did what she wanted when she wanted.

When Gary got back from the garage, Pixie pointed to the pile of coke and said it was time to party. She didn't have to say it twice.

She picked up the plate and snorted two big lines, then passed the plate to me. By this time, I was already high, as was Gary, so the conversation for the next couple of hours consisted of a lot of babble. Conversations on coke tend to be that way.

I can't tell you how many hours of cocaine-driven conversations I've had that were a total blank to me when I woke up the next day. But they sure seemed important at the time.

I do remember that as the three of us snorted our asses off, we talked about Gary's connections in L. A. and about him being behind a little with payments. Pixie brought the issue up because they had mentioned it to her, knowing it would get back home and into Nicholson's ears. We also talked about a couple of real estate ventures Pixie and Gary were looking to invest in. Real estate was a good place to invest drug money in those days. Still is, for that matter.

As the night got later and longer, it became difficult to be around Pixie and stay focused because she tended to walk around and around the room when she was out there on coke. She walked and talked, walked and talked. Always talking and walking.

All I wanted to do was fuck her, and she knew it.

Finally, at about two in the morning, Gary slipped away and went upstairs without saying a word. Pixie soon followed, saying she wanted to be sure he was tucked in. I figured the night was over for me, but I was mistaken. Boy, was I mistaken.

"Whatcha lookin' for?" I asked when Pixie returned downstairs and went straight to the kitchen.

"Baking soda," she said, "and I just found it, thanks."

"A little medicine for Gary?"

"No, not at all," she said with a wink and smile.

She then took the baking soda package and poured some of the contents into a glass, added warm water from the tap and said, "Get the plate of coke from the coffee table and we will do something I don't think you've ever done before."

I did as she asked and set the plate on the kitchen counter.

Pixie handed me the glass, "Now, take a mouthful of this, swish it around and spit it out," she instructed. "Then take your finger and press it on a line of coke, then place your finger and the coke on your tongue. Like this," Pixie said as she demonstrated for my benefit.

I watched Pixie's routine then I did the same thing with my coke-encrusted finger. Instantly, the coke went right to my head, causing an overwhelming euphoric reaction that quickly rushed to my groin.

It was a new sort of coke rush, and I loved it.

She laughed, filled the glass again with baking soda and warm tap water, picked up the plate of coke, then took me by the hand and escorted me over to the couch. After the second round of her magic elixir had settled in my head and between my legs, Pixie reached over and unzipped my pants.

"I absolutely want to fuck, but first I want to suck," she said as she pulled off my pants and positioned herself.

I was already hard from the coke mix and the excitement of knowing that Pixie was ready to be fucked. As usual, she was ready to give as well as receive, and I was similarly inclined. And when Pixie was fucked up, she could suck a golf ball through a garden hose. No exaggeration. Well, just a little.

***

Shortly before sunrise, I got in my car and began to drive home from Gary's. Like many other nights driving up Red Rock Road, headed back to my house, I was in a fog. Later, when I woke up in my own bed, I had no memory of the drive, but I could still smell Pixie's lovemaking.

It was that intoxicating smell that helped drive the desire for more sex, and cocaine was the catalyst for more sex. Yes, I liked the high I got from the coke, but it was the sex on coke that kept me going back for more of the white powder.

More coke equaled more great sex, and the more sex I was getting, the greater the consumption of coke I was inhaling. Eventually, I was psychologically addicted to both. It was not like being a heroin addict who needed a fix, but my appetite for coke and sex became insatiable. It was a vicious cycle, and I was a captive of my desires and not remotely interested in being set free anytime soon.

Chapter Twelve

Bogart's was not only drawing the white-collar courthouse gang, local business owners and beautiful women, it was also attracting a cast of characters suitable for a Damon Runyon story. Hell, we were Cheers before there was Cheers.

We had a local bartender and newspaper editor by the name of David Cantrell. He moved to Gold City in the seventies and over the years became a local politician and historian. If someone wanted to know about the history of Quartz County or Gold City, David was our go-to guy.

For a time, he worked forty hours a week walking the plank at the local hotel bar and another twenty or so hours attending public meetings and writing about them for a weekly newspaper. His diet was primarily bar snacks and beer, so by 1983—exhausted from long hours and without much real nourishment in his daily routine—he came down with a major bout of shingles.

His doctor told him it was Mother Nature's way of telling him to slow down and decide if he wanted to be a bartender or newspaper editor. But not both—at least not at the same time.

Cantrell chose to newspaper.

He lived in town, walked everywhere and had no need for a car. He came into Bogart's most days between two and four for a couple Budweiser's, some lively conversation, and whatever gossip he could pick up for his paper. Naturally, one or two Buds often became five or six, and conversations became longer and longer. He used to tell me it was "research," but I knew it was just an excuse to stay planted on his favorite barstool and drink.

David was in his forties then and divorced. He said no one could live with him for more than a few months, so he had pretty much given up on a second marriage. He stood a few inches over six feet, about two hundred pounds, with a receding hairline and expanding belt length. And, as the saying goes, had the map of Ireland spread across his face.

Fresh out of high school, he had played a little pro ball and used to tell people how he once pitched to the likes of Ted Williams and Willie Mays. Oh, he did throw to both, and other future Hall of Famers as well, that was true, but he admitted it had only been in batting practice—Williams at spring training in Florida and Mays at Candlestick Park in San Francisco—not in an actual game.

David's so-called minor league "career" was brief—very brief—but he was full of entertaining stories from his travels and experiences. When not drinking, talking or writing, he did what he could to help the community, including two stints on the chamber of commerce board of directors.

A couple of times he was asked to be MC at the chamber's annual installation and awards dinner, and we knew that meant the affair would last at least an hour longer than planned. But storytellers are, after all, storytellers. The night Cantrell received the chamber's Citizen of the Year Award, his acceptance speech took at least thirty minutes—thanking everyone in the hall except the janitor who stood ready to sweep the floor. It was the last time the chamber let him get within ten feet of a microphone.

In 1992, with the weekly newspaper bankrupt and David now employed as a night clerk at the local hotel, he was elected to the city council. He served sixteen years—including a term as mayor—and told me he wanted his obituary to begin with the following seven words: "David Cantrell, former mayor of Gold City..."

He wasn't ready to have that obit published anytime soon, of course, but his parents had died young, and David always figured his genes had a defect or two. His philosophy for happiness was to make enough money to keep a roof over his head, a burger in his belly, and a cold Budweiser in his right hand. He seemed set on that course for the rest of his life, but one night decided to look online for an old girlfriend—and found her. Quite a search tool, that Google, eh?

We lost our town historian and favorite barstool storyteller a couple years ago, but I was happy when he reunited with a flame from the 1960s and moved to Florida to be with her. Last, I heard, they were married, and he was doing well, for an old-timer.

***

At about the same time Cantrell settled in Gold City, so too did an interesting couple from San Francisco. I never did know their last names; everyone simply knew them as Peter and Perry, and that was all that was necessary. Frick and Frack didn't need first names and Peter and Perry didn't need last names.

They were a gay couple that bought an old four-story brick house on Miner's Hill—one of Gold City's five named hills. The Orange Brick Castle, as it was known, had been abandoned for years. In fact, as kids, we used to go there after school and on summer breaks and vandalize the place. Break out windows with our slingshots and set firecrackers off in empty rooms. Youth, what can I say?

Squatters sometime slept there, and empty bottles of cheap wine littered the place. We didn't have "homeless" people back then; they were called tramps or bums. Sometimes even worse. (And they would have called us "juvenile delinquents" if anyone had caught us trashing the stately old house).

Peter and Perry had an eye for class and fashion, and it showed when they completely renovated the Orange Brick Castle, turning it into Gold City's first bed and breakfast inn. The 1850s Gothic-revival mansion looked down on the center of town and quickly became a very successful inn. The two men lived there and had a reputation for welcoming their guests in true San Francisco style. Their renovation of the building came early during the town's 1970s and eighties renaissance and economic revival and showed others—including me—how it should be done.

Peter and Perry were very much part of the Gold City social scene. Peter was the flamboyant one, while Perry was more reserved and quieter—the intellect and money man. Peter was conspicuously gay, as in the most flamboyant; Perry not so much.

Peter was tall and thin, a full head of blondish hair, a great smile, and an infectious laugh. He was quick with his tongue and very critical of anything that wasn't quite right. Perry, on the other hand, had dark hair, a soft, smooth face, a little round in the body and usually had a calmer reaction to annoyances than did his bombastic partner.

The gay community in Gold City was growing in the 70s and early 80s, and they were great for the town and for Bogart's. Gays drank the best booze and most expensive wine and frequently filled our outdoor deck for an afternoon of drinking, snacks, laughter, and camaraderie. Although we still had a lot of rednecks living here in those days, gays and lesbians knew Bogart's was a safe harbor. I loved hosting them and looked forward to their visits.

Perry died in 2010. He had suffered a stroke some years earlier, and I remember his final months when Peter would bring him downtown for dinner at The Firehouse. He was very thin, very ill, and we all knew he would not be with us much longer.

After Perry died, Peter sold the B&B and eventually left Gold City. He sold the inn for a nice profit, bought a house on a small island off South Carolina, and opened a retail store catering to tourists. I'm told he's now retired and enjoying fine wine on the patio of his beachfront abode. Wish he was still in Gold City, but happy to hear that he's doing well.

***

Then there was the well-to-do retired businessman who lived up on Bridge Street in a big house built by one of the titans of the Gold Rush era in Quartz County. His name was Bernard Oldman, but everyone called him Bernie. He and his wife, Lois, would frequently come to town for lunch then drop by Bogart's for a couple of drinks. Usually three or more.

They loved their Manhattans and Bernie would tell stories about the "good old days" in Gold City until Lois couldn't take it any longer. Never bashful about how she handled her husband in public, Lois would pull Bernie out of Bogart's before it got dark and made sure they got back up Bridge Street safe and sound.

Bernie loved drinking and telling stories at the bar, but he also enjoyed having a few pops at home as well. And that sometimes led to peculiar behavior. When the weather was pleasant, Bernie would sometimes get a little tipsy at home after dinner and then, when Lois had gone to sleep, walk downtown in his pajamas, bathrobe, and floppy slippers. Most nights our local police cruiser took Bernie home after an evening of revelry.

One night, about eleven or so, when my brother was tending bar, and I was there enjoying a cold beer, in came Bernie in his bedroom attire—and in his cups. He sat down, ordered a Manhattan for himself and told Don to get everyone a drink. He didn't carry cash in his PJs, so he told Don to put it on his tab. We didn't run tabs, but when Bernie was on one of his nocturnal walks downtown, we made an exception. He was good for it.

The bar was busy that night, so no one paid much attention to Bernie after the round of drinks. They all hoisted their glasses and thanked him with a "Here's Lookin' at you Kid," but then went back to whatever they had been doing. A few minutes later, however, we noticed him at the far end of the bar in a lip-lock with a local named Gena.

Keep in mind, Bernie was an overweight, gray-haired man in his sixties and pretty much past his prime as a cocksman. Gena was a petite, cute woman in her thirties, who had worked at several local restaurants waiting tables. She had large breasts—which Bernie gently massaged while they kissed—and a slim body with dark hair. How in the hell those two ever got into a game of tongue tag was a mystery to all of us.

Suddenly, Bernie stopped kissing Gena, took a deep breath and upchucked his dinner all over the bar. Startled customers within twenty feet of the eruption stepped back from the bar, gagging and laughing at the scene. But it didn't seem to bother Bernie or Gena one bit.

Without so much as apologizing (or even blushing) for what he had done, Bernie took a long drink from his Manhattan, ordered another one, wiped his face and chin with a couple of bar napkins, and went right back to kissing and mauling Gena—who didn't seem to notice anything that had just happened.

My brother walked down to the opposite end of the bar, where I was drinking and laughing, waving his hands and muttering, "I'm not cleaning up that shit."

While Bernie and Gena went back to flapping each other's tongues, the puddle of vomit sat where it had fallen. Eventually, however, Don acquiesced and mopped up the regurgitated dinner that Lois had worked so hard to prepare for her husband.

Both Bernie and Lois died in the late 1990s, and I miss them. It was reported that upon his death, Lois said, "He had to go first because I wasn't about to leave him alone and unsupervised." And I suspect that that's exactly what she said to her friends.

If you ever wanted to meet a real character and a genuinely nice guy, it would be Andy Zimmer. Andy was about forty when I met him in the early 1980s, a well-built man, with long wavy brown hair, deep green eyes, and a handsome stubble face.

Zimmer was a painting contractor and good at his craft. He was a lady's man, to be sure, and just plain fun to be around— especially when he was drinking, which was much of his free time. He also occasionally indulged in cocaine. And when he combined booze with drugs, well—weird things happened.

I recall a mid-summer afternoon in nineteen eighty-four when Andy left his job site early and decided to devote the afternoon to recreation. In his dictionary, of course, the definition of recreation was a long day of uninterrupted alcohol and cocaine abuse. And, later, a pretty gal curled up next to him.

When he walked into Bogart's just after lunch that particular day, it was hot outside, and I had all the doors open to enjoy a light breeze and some fresh air. The bar and deck were full of regulars and tourist taking shade under the trees and table umbrellas. Naturally, Andy immediately made his presence known. He was, as they say, feeling no pain.

For the next two hours, Andy drank a steady flow of Cuervo Gold tequila shots with beer backs. He was legally drunk, I suppose, but if bar owners had to toss every customer who was technically drunk, there wouldn't be many people left to serve.

Since I was busy at the bar, unable to watch Andy at all times, I didn't realize that he kept sneaking up to my office to snort coke. And in between snorts and shots, he was getting louder and louder, although, for the most part, not disrupting the other customers. I knew I would have to keep him on a short leash, but for a couple of hours, at least, everything seemed fine. And everyone was having fun.

Finally, at about four o'clock, I convinced Andy that he had had enough. He was pissed when I grabbed his truck keys off the bar, but he was in no condition to drive. And I know he was smart enough to know that as well and I was really looking out for him.

He eventually got a little testy because I wouldn't hand over the keys, so I gave him the bar phone and told him to call one of his lady friends and ask her to come by Bogart's to give him a lift home. If he got lucky when she got him home, he could consider my offer a twofer.

About fifteen minutes later, one of his pretty party gals pulled in front of the bar in an old sports car with the convertible top down. She honked, and Andy reluctantly got off his barstool. Everyone cheered his departure (in a good-natured way, of course) as he swaggered out the front door and walked toward the car.

Zimmer then did the unthinkable. After walking up to the driver's side and appearing to have a friendly conversation with the girl, he suddenly took a step back, unzipped his pants and began pissing on the car's windshield in the middle of Commerce Street in broad daylight.

Not to be outdone, his ride home simply reached down and turned on the windshield wipers as Andy continued to urinate on her car window. The wipers did their job—spraying most of the piss back on Andy's body and face.

The impromptu sideshow stopped Commerce Street traffic for about five minutes as customers from Bogart's and several surrounding shops gathered in amazement, and applause, as Andy casually zipped up his pants, looked back toward the bar and blew us all a kiss. Then he climbed in the passenger's side, and the two of them rode off in the little convertible. Only Andy Zimmer could get away with this and come back to town the next day as though nothing happened.

Andy is now in his seventies, retired from painting and everything else that once made him one of Gold City's beloved characters. As I sit at my computer thinking of Andy and his ill-advised adventures, I lift my glass to his health.

***

There was a burly man of Polish descent in Gold City named Mick Malkovich—in his early seventies when I opened Bogart's–who worked in the local mines until they closed in the 1950s. After that, he was a logger and lumberman for twenty years. He was about five-eight and maybe two-twenty, all of it solid muscle. His hands were huge, and he could crush walnuts like I crush marshmallows. He had a full head of graying hair that he wore in a butch flat-top with a face that reflected decades of hard living.

Mick owned a hard rock mine up in the hills, in a nearby county, and, in mild weather, often went there for weeks at a time. Kind of a hermit, alone with his thoughts while he hammered away in his mine in search of gold-laced quartz. Then he'd come back to town, sell his gold, and return to serious drinking. And talking.

It was as if he had a lot of pent-up thoughts he wanted to share with others, so when he was in town and not at the mine, he would talk to bar customers until they either walked away or I had to suggest that he take a stroll to another bar. And in those days, there were plenty of bars to choose from.

He drank Jack Daniel's on the rocks and spoke in plain, blunt English. No one misunderstood his meaning or where he was coming from on any given topic. And he had an opinion on everything.

Mick had been permanently eighty-sixed from one of the local bars for having one too many and harassing some tourists who were frequenting the establishment at the time. But he was a good customer for Bogart's—at least most of the time. Mick meant well, but sometimes he came across in a threatening manner.

The term "86" has been part of bar and restaurant lingo for

decades. It means "no more service" for a bar customer who's gone beyond their limit or caused a disturbance, and "we're out of it" when shouted in a restaurant kitchen.

When the chef has cooked the last of the night's fresh salmon, he will tell the waitstaff, "Eighty-six the salmon."

And when a guy like Mick the Miner disturbs a group of tourists visiting Gold City, the bartender will tell him, "That's it, Mick, you're eighty-sixed for the day."

Mick drank during the day and walked from one bar to another, never staying too long at any one saloon. He didn't know it, but he was following a pattern that smart celebrities use. As long as an actor, politician or athlete spends a short time in any one place, a curious reporter who's tipped off that the celeb was seen drinking at, say, the Beverly Wilshire in Hollywood will be told by the bartender, "Oh, sure, the guy was here last night. Had a beer and left."

Mick went from place-to-place like a celebrity, but in his case, it was because he had either bored a bar customer to death or had gotten out of hand and received a one-day eighty-six. Either way, he spent most days walking up and down Argonaut and Commerce streets in search of a drink and someone who would listen to his embellished tales about mining for gold or working in the woods. It was not surprising, then, that by late afternoon he was often drunk, and his "personality" could be taken the wrong way if you didn't know him.

He had multiple run-ins with one particular bar owner—the guy who had permanently eighty-sixed him. So, one afternoon when that bar's proprietor, Sam Westin, was at Bogart's for a quiet Scotch and water, who walks in but Mick the Miner.

Having both at the bar at the same time made me nervous.

Sam was about forty-five, stood over six feet, and was a few pounds north of two-twenty. He had black hair, brown eyes, and fair skin, and most women considered him fairly handsome.

Unfortunately, he was an arrogant bastard and said insulting things to your face in what he considered to be a joking manner. Most people, however, failed to find any humor in his snarky insults and attempts at being funny.

I was bartending that fateful afternoon, and it wasn't long before Mick and Sam were in a verbal jousting match. Westin needled him about being eighty-sixed, and Mick grew increasingly angry by what he felt were insulting, embarrassing comments from Sam.

Westin was drinking Dewar's White Label Scotch with a splash of water. Mick was drinking Jack Daniel's whiskey on the rocks—without the splash. And neither man was merely sipping, which was not a good situation for a bar owner like me to be in when two men hold such disdain for each other.

I was about to step in and ask them to cool it when suddenly Mick hit Sam square in the jaw with his left hand. Not his left fist, but his open left palm. And Mick was right-handed.

Mick's hand speed was so fast I barely saw it, and Sam hit the floor like a proverbial sack of potatoes. Out cold. I had seen a lot of fights in my youth, and lots of boxing matches on television, but I had never seen a hand and arm move faster nor deliver a more lethal wallop than when Mick cold-cocked Sam that day at Bogart's.

As I looked at the prone bar owner, I was reminded of the Joe Frazier–George Foreman fight in nineteen seventy-four, when Foreman hit the then-heavyweight champ with a thunderous punch and announcer Howard Cosell shouted, "Down goes Frazier! Down goes Frazier! Down goes Frazier!"

It's one of the most memorable boxing calls ever, so seeing the KO'd publican on the floor, unresponsive, I was silently shouting to myself, "Down goes Westin! Down goes Westin! Down goes Westin!"

As Sam came to and tried to get up from the bar floor, dazed and holding his jaw, I called 911 requesting medical assistance. And as I talked with the 911 dispatcher, Mick calmly polished off his Jack Daniel's and walked out without saying a word. But he left a good tip, which was unusual for the old miner.

It took about five minutes before Westin was upright, but he wasn't talking and for a good reason. X-rays showed he had a broken jaw—in two places. His jaw was wired shut at the hospital, and for the next six weeks, Sam drank his meals (and his Scotch) through a straw. But, as I always say, things happen for a reason. Sam lost twenty excess pounds while he was healing.

Westin filed assault charges against Mick, who got a slap on the wrist with informal probation for a year and a $500.00 fine. Gold was bringing more than $300.00 an ounce at that time, and Mick usually had a nugget or two in his pocket to show tourists, so he didn't have a problem with the fine. Truth be told, he got far more than $500.00 worth of satisfaction when he put Sam flat on his ass. Knowing the judge as I did, I wasn't surprised that he went light on Mick. Westin had insulted the judge one night at a chamber of commerce social mixer, suggesting he must have received his law degree from a mail-order diploma mill. Mick's sentence showed us that His Honor hadn't forgotten the incident.

Sam could occasionally come across as a "bully." Back then we knew how to take care of bullies. Before all this "politically correct" crap came into fashion, if someone was bullying you, you could take care of it by one surprise punch to the face. Nothing like a broken nose, or jaw, to improve a bully's disposition. Period!

Mick died not long after his eightieth birthday and no one I knew ever talked back to him after word got around about the old-timer's pugilistic prowess. Also, he was never eighty-sixed by another bar owner. To eighty-six Mick the Miner, ran the risk of serious bodily harm. Westin's broken jaw and years of ongoing, expensive dental work was a testament to that.

***

Then there was our resident cartoonist Bobby Shrimp—the Shrimp

Man—who would sit at the bar with his pencils and sketching book nursing his beer. One afternoon Bobby drew the ultimate cartoon that pretty much defined the eighties drug scene in Gold City.

The drawing was of a male caricature sitting at Bogart's long bar with a fishing pole. On the end of the line was a bindle of cocaine—as bait—and the fisherman was casting the line with the bindle down the bar towards a group of women. Bob's drawing depicted the "ladies" at the other end of the bar as a fighting mob—pulling hair—and knocking each other over to get to the bindle of cocaine.

When the Shrimp Man showed the guys at the bar his creation, he all but put us on our knees with laughter.

The Shrimp Man is still creating wonderful gems of wisdom around Gold City with his creative and imaginative drawings and the stories that go along with them. I tip my hat to that creative, talented mind.

***

Most of Gold City's colorful characters in those days were men, but we had some memorable ladies as well. And when they dropped by Bogart's, there was no telling what might happen.

There were two sisters in particular that I recall—Amanda and Kendra Garber. They both worked as in-home care providers for the elderly and, to supplement their modest wages, they sold cocaine to locals.

They also had a thing for musicians—any musician. So, on weekends, when Bogarts had live music, the sisters catered to the bands by dispensing packets of sought-after white powder. Sometimes the coke was purchased with cash, and sometimes by partying with one or both sisters.

Strange, eh? They gave their product away in exchange for getting screwed or giving a musician a quick blow job. To my way of thinking they were getting screwed twice, but that was their choice.

They were our very own Gold City groupies, and the bands loved it.

The sisters weren't drop-dead gorgeous, but attractive in their own way. They were young, adventurous, tall, and shared the genetic marvel of large, solid breasts. And they loved to party. Oh, how they loved to party. A few pounds overweight, maybe, but virtual fucking machines with plenty of coke. And that made the bands very happy.

They were a mischievous pair, especially Kendra, who was given the nickname of Kinky by her sister. They were wild, but if you knew them, you could trust them. If you didn't know them, however, or they didn't know you, then hold on to your wallet.

I provided a room in the rear of Bogart's for band breaks. I gave them an ice chest filled with cold beer and only band members were allowed to be in there. The two sisters, however, didn't pay any attention to my rules and frequently spent entire evenings in the break room—servicing the band on their breaks to everyone's mutual satisfaction.

Naturally, out-of-town bands loved coming back to Bogart's. But because the sisters provided too many piles of free coke to band members during these frolicking evenings, they had to make up for it by cutting the product more than usual. Typically, they cut it with baby laxative—lots of it. So, if you got your coke from either of them, you'd better be near a toilet. That adulterated stuff would run through you like crap through a goose.

Local musicians knew about the thinned-out coke, so they would thank the girls for their generosity, put the bindle in their pocket, then tell them they were looking forward to a snort after the show. What many of them did, however, was flush the laxative-laced junk down a restroom toilet.

***

I could go on and on writing about a slew of Gold City characters from the nineteen eighties, but I can't end this aside down Memory Lane without mentioning Gabrielle Lightner, who, naturally, was called Gabby for short.

Gabby was what polite society would call a full-figured gal—Rubenesque in every way. She was about five-seven, a pretty face with a bright smile, long brown hair, large breasts, shapely legs, large hips, and plenty of derrière to hold on to when she was taking you for a ride. She was about twenty-seven, fast with her tongue, fun personality, and regularly partied from sundown to sunrise (and often longer).

One summer afternoon, around nineteen eight-five or so, she entered Bogart's wearing shorts and a tight tube-top. Her ample breasts tended to dominate the landscape, but her wide hips and prominent behind were also on display.

Everyone greeted her arrival with a friendly "Hey, Gabby" and offers of a drink. She was a popular gal, and men and women alike enjoyed her outgoing personality and gift of gab.

On the day I am referencing here, three guys I had never seen before were seated at the bar near the front door. So, when Gabrielle came in, and everyone greeted her by her nickname, one of the guys looking at her from behind said, "Gabby? Hell, they should call her Flabby."

Most customers laughed, but not Gabrielle. She was embarrassed and so angry you could see the fire in her eyes. She was normally a happy-go-lucky young woman out for a good time, but the insulting comment was too much for her to ignore.

She walked back to the wise guy—about five-eight, one-seventy, with a pockmarked face and long black hair. Without warning, Gabrielle reached up and grabbed the guy's hair at the back of his neck, pulled hard while twisting his head, and jerked him off his barstool. Once he was standing, she pulled him around by his hair about 180 degrees and smashed his face into the front door jamb, breaking his nose; followed by a gush of blood that covered the front of his shirt in deep red.

Not quite done with her work, she then dragged the guy out to the sidewalk and firmly smashed his head into a parking meter. Twice. Satisfied that she had repaid the insult with an appropriate lesson in good manners, Gabrielle left the bloodied smartass sprawled on the sidewalk. Then she came back inside the bar and sat down to total silence. My customers were speechless—stunned at what they had just witnessed. I was stunned as well.

The other two strangers went outside to help their fallen comrade and never returned to Bogart's. Probably never returned to Gold City. And take my word for it, no one ever said another derogatory word about Gabrielle's nickname.

We lost contact with Gabby when she moved to the Oregon coast to run a charter boat fishing company and tackle shop with her boyfriend, but I still laugh thinking about the day she slammed that unsuspecting guy's head against the bar door and then against that steel parking meter. I'm sure his manners improved considerably from that day forward.

***

Yes, life in Gold City was sometimes Looney Tunes in the nineteen-eighties, but deep down I knew I was one of the looniest with the least self-control. Each time I bent over and snorted a line, and then snorted again, I knew I had to find a way to break the senseless cycle. But that would come later.

Chapter Thirteen

My brother was a huge golf fan. From spring until fall, Don played as often as he could. He modeled his swing after Tom Watson's, but the only similarity between my brother and Watson was that they both carried MacGregor clubs in their bag.

In 1982, at Don's suggestion, we hosted the first Bogart's Invitational at the Quartz County Country Club, and I appointed him tournament director and master of ceremonies. It's a small nine-hole course established back in the nineteen-twenties when Bobby Jones was wearing knickers and dominating the sport.

The first two tournaments had been held in September, but for 1984 we wanted to do something different. So, Don and I decided to schedule the Bogart's Invitational for Halloween Day. As we prepared for the third year, players were affectionally calling it The Coke Open—a well-deserved moniker for our day with little white balls and large piles of white powder.

The 1984 tournament was scheduled for a shotgun start at ten with a full field of thirty-six golfers entered. It was a little frosty when we arrived at the country club just after 8:00 A.M., but the forecast was for a beautiful fall day, topping off at seventy degrees at high noon.

More than a hundred guys wanted to play, but the shotgun start limited entries to thirty-six—four to a hole on a nine-hole course. Naturally, we gave preference to those who had played in the previous two tournaments, so guys on the waiting list knew they had little chance of teeing it up that day.

The Open started with a buffet breakfast in the clubhouse, including Bloody Marys and Boilermakers (shots with a beer wash).

Also, a line or two of coke was offered to each player to help shake the cobwebs from those who had partied the night before at Bogart's while drawing the names to fill the foursomes.

At ten o'clock sharp, my doorman Wally fired a blank round in the air from his Remington Model 870 shotgun, and we were off to the races with about five hours of best-ball fun.

Nearly every player had a bindle or small plastic container with a spoon attached, containing a gram or more of cocaine. At each hole, as the last player sank his ball and the foursome headed to the next tee, the best-ball winner for that hole provided a toot of coke to any of the players in his foursome who wanted one.

By the end of the first nine-hole round, as players made their way to the clubhouse bar for lunch before heading back for the final nine holes, effects of too much coke and too many beers consumed along the way became very evident.

Joining the players at the clubhouse were several wives, girlfriends, and Bogart regulars. We always enjoyed having a few friends follow the players and join us for the afternoon festivities. Besides, players who had not been in the original field of thirty-six knew that some guys would be too fucked up for another nine holes. That would be their chance to step in as a substitute and play the second nine.

The clubhouse and outdoor deck were packed with players and non-players as Don tested the microphone and prepared to make a few announcements.

My brother began by announcing that a tragic accident had occurred during the first nine holes. He explained that on the third hole, a short par three, Mikey Fountain was hit in the head by Brian Barber's tee shot from over at the fourth hole. It had hit him square in the forehead and knocked him on his ass.

Dr. Ivis Rose, a proctologist, who was in the foursome just ahead of Mikey's, circled back in his golf cart to take a look. Doc Rose conducted some basic concussion tests on Fountain then cleared him to keep playing.

During the lunch break, Rose said, "I examined Mikey's brain and found nothing."

The group cheered as Mikey acknowledged the good-natured ribbing and adjusted the ice pack, he had fashioned out of an empty plastic baggie. Dr. Rose was proud of his brain diagnosis, considering it wasn't his normal area of expertise.

Don then announced that if any players were too drunk to continue, they needed to let him know so that someone on the waiting list could take their place. He also reminded everyone that a trophy presentation would be held at the clubhouse at the conclusion of the second round.

Eight guys raised their hands and said they were done, so the first eight names on the waiting list of invites went to their cars to retrieve their golf bags and take a few practice swings. I was one of the eight who withdrew. Enough was enough, and I needed to help Don prepare for the awards ceremony.

Taking a line from Hill Street Blues, my brother said, "Hey, hey, hey, let's be careful out there." And with that, thirty-six players—many of them ripped and wasted—headed back for the second shotgun start.

My brother Don never really got into coke. He told me that during our first "Coke Open" in eighty-two, he and a couple of friends were standing in the parking lot after the first nine and one of the guys had a bindle. He opened the bindle to share the coke with the other two but instead dropped it. All the coke fell out of the bindle landing in the dirt and gravel on the parking lot.

Don watched in amazement as his two friends got down on their knees and tried to suck the coke out of the dirt and gravel with straws. He said that pretty much cured him. As he walked away, he was saying to himself that he had enough trouble handling booze without that shit in his life—bravo for him. I should have been there that day; maybe I would have seen the light as well?

As the second round drew toward its merciful conclusion, several players had already walked off the course, too drunk and high to play golf, or drive their carts. Two carts ended up in the pond during a chicken drag race, and a couple of players threw their clubs in the pond on their way to the clubhouse for more drinks, sandwiches and a final line of dessert.

The trophy presentations followed for Best Team Score, Worst Team Score, Best Player and Worst Player. Mikey, of course, received a trophy for having the worst injury.

As with previous tournaments, several cars were left in the Quartz County Country Club parking lot, and Pinky's Taxi Service made a lot of six-mile roundtrips from the golf course to Gold City, ferrying players to their homes or Bogart's.

We made a hell of a mess, I'll admit it, but booze and beer had flowed for several hours at the country club bar. We had a good time, and they had a profitable day. And the five hundred bucks I paid the club manager to take care of dewatering and repairing the two submerged golf carts, was a small price to pay for all the fun we had on and off the course.

Chapter Fourteen

Halloween Day 1984 definitely had its share of wild golf to remember, and Halloween Night awaited those who could stay awake long enough—or sober enough—to enjoy it.

In Gold City, Halloween is celebrated as wildly as New Orleans celebrates Mardi Gras, and nineteen eight-four was no exception. By ten o'clock, Bogart's was packed, and Wally was trying his best to placate fifty or more celebrants waiting out on the sidewalk for a chance to have a drink or two and dance to our rockin' band. And while Wally handled the door, I listened to the cash register bell as it kept ringing.

Trust me; a ringing cash register bell is the sweetest music a bar owner can hear.

I was standing at the far end of the bar with the usual suspects—Gary, George, Kate, Shelly, Madame Butterfly, and Asa—along with other regular customers and friends. Don and my weekend bartender, Carla, were walking the plank, trying their best to keep up with the flurry of drink orders yelled at them by customers and our cocktail waitresses.

Most customers were in costume—some complex, some simple. When I saw George in regular street clothes, I asked him why he hadn't worn a costume. He said he had, and that he had come dressed like an off-duty Episcopalian priest. Well, he certainly had me fooled.

Then, from out of the blue, my weekday cocktail waitress, Michelle Fish, walked into Bogart's in the skimpiest Cupid Angel costume I had ever seen. And Michelle had the body for it.

In classical mythology, Cupid is a boy, but no one was objecting to

Michelle being a Cupid Angel for the evening. After all, it was Halloween and Cupid is the God of desire, erotic love, attraction, and affection. And no one ever fit the definition better.

Her costume was a two-piece, pink bathing suit. Adding to the look of authenticity, she had white wings attached to her back. Around her neck and shoulders, she had a quiver of arrows and a bow. She had painted a heart on each cheek in red and had pink sandals on her feet. Not dressed for warmth on a cool Halloween night, but, oh, what a sight.

Michelle was of Native American blood, and proud of it. She was a hard worker and kept to herself when her shifts ended. Guys hit on her all the time, but she was engaged and never seemed tempted to stray. She was twenty-five, tall, with long jet- black hair and beautiful dark skin. Her dark eyes, full lips, and an inviting smile were the kind of assets that led to guys being very generous when the time came to tip her, but her greatest natural asset was her body.

Michelle's breasts were solid and firm and stood straight out, complementing an outstanding ass and great legs. All of this was on display that evening when she walked through the door and joined us.

What was missing was her fiancée. Michelle was due to be married the next spring, so seeing her out on the town on Halloween, alone, was odd.

Shortly after she joined us and Don was able to deliver a round of drinks, George and I asked Michelle if she would like a line of coke. She said she would, but that she'd like to have it upstairs, in my office above the bar. She didn't have to ask twice.

After climbing the stairs and settling in on couches and chairs in the office, George poured a pile of coke on top of my desk, cut out some lines, and handed Michele a straw.

Considering what we had already consumed at the golf tournament, we were both way ahead of her, so we told her to take what she needed. And there was plenty to go around. She quickly inhaled four lines and sat down.

Then I complimented her on the Cupid costume. She looked down at her full breasts, and then down her legs to her toes, and said: "Not much to it, but at least it covers my Venus." I smiled; she winked.

Fortunately, George saw the teasing and interplay and told us he was going back downstairs to be with Kate while Michelle and I made the kind of magnetic connection that would hopefully lead to bigger, more exciting things.

Here I was, once again full of booze and coke with my little brain thinking for the big brain. But I couldn't help it—firm tits and a tight ass had been my weak-spot for years—coke or no coke.

We kissed and fondled each other; then she suggested we go back downstairs for some fun and return to the office later for more coke. I wanted to stay where we were, but everything worked out just fine because every half hour or so, she would whisper in my ear at the bar that she needed more coke.

That meant another walk upstairs, and another opportunity to advance our fondling to something more serious. As long as I kept feeding her coke, she kept indicating more interest in partying after hours. She also wanted George to join us at closing time. She liked George.

The next time we were at the bar, I told George about Michelle's request, and he quickly started an argument with Kate about something stupid. A few minutes later, Kate grabbed her purse, told George to fuck-off, and walked out of Bogart's in a huff.

George smiled at me, happy that he had cleared the deck for what awaited the two of us.

At closing time, as the lights went up and bleary-eyed Halloween partygoers filed out of Bogart's, George and I escorted the Cupid Angel back upstairs. She went to the couch in my office, and we began the process of removing what little she had on. She was a very willing participant.

When Michelle found herself sensuously naked, she stopped us and noted in mock alarm that George and I were fully clothed. We took the hint and stripped. She blushed when she saw two hard poles saluting her and inviting her loveliness.

As we stood in front of Michelle and gave her time to size things up, she reached up and took a shaft in each hand while George scooped out more cocaine from a bindle into a straw and put it under her nose. As soon as she had snorted, I suggested she get started doing what she came there to do.

And that was just the beginning.

George and I were still in our stud days in nineteen eighty-four, but the third time took longer. Fortunately, Michelle enjoyed the extra ride, and we enjoyed her amazing enthusiasm.

A little after six o'clock, as the sun was getting ready to reappear, the three of us left Bogart's, walked to our cars and drove home. I was spent—totally spent—and I belly-flopped on my bed without bothering to undress.

George and I later thought that Michelle came to town that night wanting to fulfill a repressed desire or fantasy and we were at the right place at the right time. But who knows?

All I do know is that Michelle Fish never returned to work, nor picked up her last paycheck. In fact, I never saw her again. I heard sometime later that she didn't marry her fiancé as planned; instead, she moved to Sacramento to attend school to be a veterinarian assistant, then moved to Reno and married a blackjack dealer.

When I close my eyes, I can still envision the multi-layers of sex from that night, and I have often wondered whatever became of the most beautiful Cupid Angel I ever saw.

Chapter Fifteen

Couple days before Christmas 1984, I was sitting in my upstairs office when one of the bartenders, Carla, buzzed to let me know Tommy Brice, manager of my local bank, was on line one.

"Hi, Tommy, good morning to you, my friend. What's up?"

"Adrian, I hate to start your day off with bad news, but I just received an order from the State Board of Equalization to take over fifty-six hundred from your account."

"For what?"

"For unpaid state sales tax, I'm afraid."

"Shit."

"Don't feel like the Lone Ranger, Adrian, the new guy managing the office is apparently trying to make an impression on his bosses in Sacramento."

I was too shocked to respond.

"Ever since Rusty retired, things have been different with the local state board office," Tommy advised me. "He was there for more than thirty years and understood the ebb and flow of seasonal businesses here, but the new guy's playing it strictly by the book."

"And it sounds like he's throwing that fuckin' book straight at me." I said, shaking my head.

"Looks that way, yep."

"So, taking fifty-six hundred pretty much drained my account, I suppose?"

"I'm afraid so," the bank manager told me. "As of this moment, you have exactly three hundred and ten dollars and forty-six cents to draw upon."

"Can you delay the attachment?"

"Nope, wish I could."

"Well, thanks for letting me know, Tommy. Guess I need to pay the new manager a visit."

"You can try, but from my dealings with him, the guy's a real bastard."

"That's OK, Tommy, I can be a real bastard as well."

The State Board of Equalization office was on Argonaut Street, a block from Bogart's. It had been in the same location for decades, and I was steamed as I walked through a heavy December rain to confront the new manager.

The State Board of Equalization operated from the ground floor of a two-story building constructed in 1903, located at the corner of Argonaut and South Oak streets—the busiest intersection in town and geographical center of Gold City when the first city limits were drawn up in 1866.

I took a deep breath, tried to calm myself best I could, then entered the office, walked up to the polished oak counter and was greeted by long-time office assistant Karen Kristin. Karen had been behind that counter for at least twenty years as Rusty's assistant and now worked for the new state employee assigned to Quartz County.

"Hi, Adrian."

"Just got a call from the bank, Karen. They told me you guys took over fifty-six hundred bucks out of my account. What the hell's going on?"

"I'm sorry, Adrian, I really am, but that's how the new manager wants to run the office. If you're more than sixty days behind in a scheduled quarterly payment, the money will be taken from your bank account."

Karen shrugged, but I knew she was just doing what she was told to do. My beef was with the new manager, not with Karen.

"Who is your new boss, anyway? Doesn't he know how Rusty always worked with us during the winter? I mean, this is bullshit; we both know that."

From the back office came a young man of about thirty, average height and weight, brown hair cut short, blue eyes with steel-rim glasses. He was wearing off-the-rack brown slacks, black shoes, a white shirt, and red tie, with an over-sized tweed sport coat.

In other words, he looked like a dork—nervous and out of place in Gold City.

"Hello, sir, I'm Frank Stuhltrigger, the new state board manager. Is there something I can help you with, or is Karen taking care of you?"

"Doesn't seem Karen's able to help me right now."

"Because...?"

"Because she's not the one who ordered my bank to garnish more than fifty-six hundred dollars from my account and give it to the State of California. You did it, not Karen."

Karen showed Stuhltrigger the paperwork she had on her desk. He looked it over and said, "Yes, we ordered the money taken from your account because you were late in paying your third-quarter taxes."

"Hell, I know I'm late, but what's up with the attachment?"

"It has been the State of California's longstanding policy to collect delinquent taxes in whatever manner is legal and available to us. You were late, so we did what was necessary—and legal—to bring your taxes current."

"Did you ever hear of the telephone?"

"I did what the law allowed—nothing more, nothing less."

"This isn't the way Rusty did things," I reminded him, clearly angered by what had happened. "Didn't you know he worked with all the businesses in town during the winter to help us out during the slow season?"

"That may well have been my predecessor's policy, sir, but it's no longer the policy of this office. Pay your taxes on time, or we'll take the money from your bank account."

"You're a real prick; you know that, buddy?"

"Call me what you wish, Mr...ah, Davis, but my boss in

Sacramento has instructed me to run this office the way it ought to be run, and that's what I intend to do."

With that, I reached over the counter, grabbed the manager by his tie and began pulling him over the counter. I was pissed.

"Well, fuck you and your asshole boss in Sacramento, Stilltrigger, or whatever the hell your name is. This isn't how we do things up here in the mountains, OK? This isn't fuckin' Sacramento."

As I continued pulling on the manager's tie, determined to jerk him over the counter, Karen held Stuhltrigger's waist and legs, trying to keep him on her side of the counter.

She yelled at me to stop as the young manager began choking, his face turning red as I continued pulling his tie.

Suddenly, I realized what I was doing and released my grip. The manager slumped against the oak counter, trying to regain his breath while I stepped back. I was embarrassed by what I had done and the scene I saw in front of me, and fearful that the guy might call the cops and have me arrested for assault.

I had once again reacted with anger. Extreme anger. Not as violent as that evening with George when I trashed the place and scared the hell out of those two young children, but at that moment, standing in the Board of Equalization office knowing that the money was gone, a rush of uncontrollable anger swept over me.

I stared at the bureaucrat's red face and bulging eyes, trying to make sense of my transition from carefree bar owner to out of control madman. Who was I? How did this happen? And why?

As a child, I had been about as normal as any youngster was in those days. It was an innocent time for the nation, and I was an innocent kid. My energy and thoughts were focused on sports and Saturday matinees where the Lone Ranger saved the pretty damsel in distress, fifteen-part serials where Flash Gordon saved the universe, and Elvis sang love songs to beautiful women on the beach.

Sure, I raised some hell in high school and did some dumb things, but I was never a violent or disorderly teenager. Nor had I been a violent or disorderly adult. Sometimes I drank too much, but that usually brought out my charm, not my anger.

This anger didn't begin that night in Gary's basement when I felt the first rush of cocaine going up my nose. This devolve into darkness has taken time, and many nights of abusing the "White Lady."

"I'm sorry," I said, looking first at Karen and then at the manager. But neither of them responded; they seemed as shocked as me by what had just transpired.

I turned and left the state board office and walked back to Bogart's. I was shaking and fully aware that what I had done was wrong. I knew my verbal and physical attack on Stuhltrigger could bring a tsunami of problems my way.

I once read somewhere that the male species is a human being chained to a maniac. I don't recall who said that. Maybe Socrates? Maybe Yogi Berra? It doesn't really matter, but I think I had just affirmed that those words were correct.

In my heart, of course, I wasn't a maniac, but my actions said otherwise. Were the wheels coming off the cart?

Chapter Sixteen

One of the great pleasures of owning a popular drinking establishment like Bogart's was meeting and greeting the people who came in on a regular basis for their favorite libation and conversation.

The nightly cocaine abuse, however, had beaten me up from the inside out. And by August 1985, I knew I had taken about all the beating I could handle. In fact, I hated the bar business. I kept smiling in public, but in private I was sad and withdrawn. I was also praying a lot, but He didn't seem to be listening.

Bogart's was a popular watering hole to talk local and national politics, catch up on daily gossip, and even start some. We were not considered a sports bar per se, a relatively new concept in the mid-eighties, but we had a couple of big-screen TVs, and sporting events were always on one set or both.

Until the sun went down each evening, we were a conversational bar, where friends could talk without loud music blasting away in the background. From the beginning, almost six years earlier, I had made every effort to design Bogart's look and feel for the women of Gold City—and that brought in the men. In droves. It was a time-tested formula that bar owners had been using since Cleopatra sat at a Cairo pub and winked at Mark Anthony.

And it certainly worked for us.

We were also a very popular watering hole for the many upper-middle-class, white-collar working folks: Realtors, attorneys, engineers, teachers, county and courthouse employees, health care workers and high-tech management types who lived in and around town.

High-tech companies had made a big splash in Gold City during the early eighties. They brought in a lot of good-paying jobs when they built their offices and plants here, and intelligent, talented professionals began to arrive as well. They enjoyed healthy salaries and knew how to spend it—especially when it came to be having a good time.

One of the more talented people I got to know from the high-tech community was a young lady named Stephanie Papadimitriou. Poppy, for short. She was a thoroughbred Greek, about thirty, and had an important management position with The Quartz Group—an electronics company that had relocated from Silicon Valley to Quartz County and brought their top-tier management staff with them when they made the move.

Poppy was smart, had a strong personality, was very outgoing with a beautiful smile, and men were immediately attracted to her. She had long, naturally wavy jet-black hair, dark black eyes, and eyebrows, along with full red lips that most guys fantasized about. And her naturally dark skin was the envy of every woman spending time at the local tanning salon.

In short, Poppy was a true Greek beauty—a living Aphrodite— who turned heads whenever she came into Bogart's. Women's heads as well as men. She wore expensive clothes and always looked fresh on Friday nights after work, as though her day was just beginning. And you always knew when Poppy had arrived because she was confined to a wheelchair.

The bar crowd would spot the wheelchair coming through the front door and make room for Poppy as she headed to either the fireplace area or, in good weather, the outdoor patio. And she never quit smiling.

Poppy was in a wheelchair because she had no legs, literally; they had been removed at birth, but her personal assistant, Gail, was always with her. Gail was also employed by The Quartz Group and drove Poppy to and from work each day. She also took her shopping, to the doctors, and wherever else she needed to go.

They didn't live together, but Gail was never far away from her friend.

Performing minor tasks that we all take for granted was impossible without Gail's help, but once in her wheelchair, at home or out on the town, she was able to take pretty good care of herself. She would pull her wheelchair up to a table at Bogart's or a local restaurant, and quickly blend in with the rest of the crowd.

I always looked forward to seeing Poppy on Friday evenings and special occasions or outings with her gal pals and co-workers. I enjoyed sitting with her at the fireplace, or on the outside patio in the summer, engaging in conversation with an intelligent woman.

And I enjoyed looking at her beautiful, captivating face; there was no denying that.

Seeing that she had wheeled herself out to Bogart's patio, I walked over to the table where she and Gail were seated and said, "Hi there, Miss Poppy. See any good movies lately?"

"I've seen 'em all." Poppy laughed.

"Any worth seeing twice?"

"None. I never watch a movie twice. It's a waste of time."

"Well, let's go in another direction. How are you on this beautiful evening?"

"In love with the dream, Adrian; always in love with the dream. And how are you, my friend?"

"Just fine," I answered. "So, what's new in the world of high-tech?"

"Well, as usual, we're moving faster than the speed of light," she told me. "We have just unveiled a device that'll increase the speed of capturing and showing instant replays for televised NFL games, and it will do it a hundred times faster than our earlier gizmo."

"Gizmo?"

"Sorry, Adrian, that's the kind of high-tech lingo they use in our Research and Development Department," she said with a big laugh. "In any case, it'll be ready to go for next season, and I bet you'll like that, eh?"

"Sounds great, Poppy. Anything you engineering geeks can invent that makes watching sports here, or at home more pleasurable, I'm all for it."

Drinks were delivered, so I decided to have a little fun at Poppy's expense.

"What else is new?" I asked. "How's your love life?"

I knew Poppy would respond to the question in the same spirit it was asked. I knew her well enough to know that she would not toss her drink in my face.

"Love life, you ask. What's that?" she chuckled looking over at Gail.

"You mean when a man and a woman spend time together, in private, and do things that bring bliss, satisfaction and a smile to each other's face? Is that what you mean by love life?"

"Seems like you know what I'm talking about," I said as I blushed.

We were laughing, but I sensed she wanted to change the subject. And I was right.

"By the way," she said, "I hear you're having a birthday next week."

"You've heard correctly."

"Well, how about coming over for dinner to celebrate. I'm a very good cook," she said confidently while cocking her head.

"I would love to, but I'm having a birthday dinner with my mom and dad. Maybe another night will work for both of us?"

"What about the next night, Sunday, September first? Say about seven at my condo off Beal Avenue? You know, those new units that were just built behind the school?"

"Yes, I do, and the first is fine with me," I told her. "Tell me the unit number, and I'll be there with bells on."

"I own lucky number thirteen, so just park in front of the garage and come to the door."

Poppy then handed me her business card with her home number written on the back. For emphasis, she included a smiley face below the telephone number.

"You'll be thirty-eight, right?"

"How'd you know?"

"I asked Don," she laughed. "Your brother's such a sweetheart."

"A good guy he is; that's for sure."

"Well, I look forward to you coming over for a second birthday dinner. This way you can celebrate it two days in a row."

"Sounds great," I said as I got up from my chair, said goodbye to Gail and reached out to shake Poppy's hand.

It was time to put on my proprietor's hat and circulate through the crowd.

It was Friday night, and the place was jumping.

Chapter Seventeen

At seven o'clock, the evening after a thirty-eighth birthday dinner and a few laughs with my mom, dad, and brother, I pulled up in front of unit thirteen at Stephanie Papadimitriou's condominium complex. The building was only five years old, in a great location, surrounded by tall pine trees and beautifully landscaped green space.

Gold City officials weren't too keen on giving the green light to large housing projects, but this was a perfect example of condos built in a way that preserved as many native trees as possible. Also, walkways were designed to weave their way through large rock outcroppings. It had a country feel—isolated from the hubbub of downtown.

Because of her special needs, Poppy had acquired an end unit, so a small ramp could be built from the walkway to her front door without creating an obstacle for other condo owners. It was a simple solution to a minor problem and allowed for easy access to her unit.

I walked up and rang the doorbell. It took a minute or so before the door opened, but when it did Stephanie greeted me wearing a stunning pink blouse and light-green shorts.

"Come on in, birthday boy," she said, her face filled with a welcoming smile.

I stepped in and closed the door behind me, then followed Poppy into the living room/dining room area. Her choice of furniture was primarily modern with a tan leather-and-cloth sofa, two matching chairs, glass-top coffee and end tables, and a chrome-and-glass dining table with five wicker chairs, not six.

The carpet was a soft grey, and area rugs were brightly colored, thick, with an expensive tight weave. Poppy had reproductions of Modern Masters on her walls, a couple of signed Dali's, and several original Peter Max paintings as well.

The kitchen was a bright white with light blue trim and special installed waist-high cupboards for Poppy's convenience. The bedroom and bath were off to the right of the living room, and there was a staircase leading down to additional bedrooms, which I assumed she made available to friends and family when they visited.

"Please," she said pointing to the sofa, "come in and get comfortable."

Once I was seated, she asked, "Glass of wine?"

"Thanks, red if you have it."

"Cabernet good with you? Your brother said it was," she smiled.

"Perfect."

After some wine and conversation, Poppy served a delicious dinner of peach halves over romaine lettuce with peach Champagne vinaigrette dressing, sprinkled with raisins and nuts, followed by chicken cordon bleu with scalloped potatoes and green beans, topped off with crushed pecan nuts. Perfect!

We drank two bottles of Cab during a leisurely dinner and talked about her having grown up in San Francisco as an only child— albeit a privileged only child. Her protective parents were wealthy, which made her unique childhood easier than it would have been had she been raised by parents without the same means and resources.

She asked what had brought me back to Gold City to take over Frank's Place and convert it into Bogart's, so I shared some family history.

We were at ease with each other, and our conversations flowed comfortably—as did the wine.

Between the wine, great dinner, and enjoyable conversation, a comfort zone had been established between the two of us. It was the first time we had been alone, without Gail or a bar crowd around us.

As I helped clear the table and loaded the dishwasher, Poppy asked, "Would you like Frangelico for an after-dinner drink?"

"My brother again, eh? Don told you I liked Frangelico?"

"As a matter of fact, he did," she answered, "but, fortunately, I like it, too."

Poppy got two stemmed snifter glasses from a chair-level cupboard, put them in her lap and wheeled toward the living room. I carried the bottle of Italian liqueur.

When she got to the sofa, Poppy lifted herself out of the chair and onto the sofa, patted the seat pad next to her and motioned for me to join her. I did. Then I poured Frangelico into the glasses and handed one to my dinner hostess.

"Happy days," I said as we clinked glasses and sipped the hazelnut liqueur.

"Sorry I didn't make dessert, but maybe this will be an adequate substitute," Poppy said as she reached over to the end table, opened the drawer and withdrew a large bindle. She held it out in front of her smiling face then passed it over to me.

"Well, well, my favorite kind of dessert. How did you know?"

"A little birdie told me," she replied, "and I was happy to hear that you partake because I'm a weekend user and this is Labor Day weekend. I love the high, and I like that it lets me escape reality—at least temporarily."

She looked down at her lap.

I pulled out my wallet and withdrew a credit card, then opened the bindle and scooped out some cocaine onto the card, I then held it under Poppy's nose, and she took a hit to each nostril. I scooped more coke on the plastic card and snorted twice myself.

"Do you want to talk about it?" I asked, knowing she understood the thrust of my question.

"I lost them within days of my birth," she answered matter-of-factly. "I was born with legs that didn't function; they were like strands of spaghetti. Doctors told my parents my legs would never develop and would be of no use to me because there was no muscle or tissue to develop. No bone structure whatsoever. In fact, my folks were told the deformed legs would be a burden to me if they remained connected. So, when the doctors recommended amputation, my parents decided to follow their advice."

"Looking back at what your parents decided for you, any regrets? Do you wish they had waited to see if the doctors were wrong and that, over time, your legs would have developed?"

"Nope," she said without hesitation. "I've been without legs since I was a few days old, Adrian, so it's all I've ever known. And as I've grown older and been able to research and understand the deformity I was born with, I know the doctors were right. So, I fully support the decision my parents made, and for thirty years they have done everything in their power to make my life as good as it can be, considering."

We talked for another two hours about her career, the challenges she had faced working her way up the corporate management ladder, her likes, and dislikes. And we talked about how it was for her to now be living and working in rural Gold City and not the urban, culturally sophisticated setting of San Francisco. Close to Palo Alto, Stanford, and her parents.

As we talked and shared insight about our respective lives, we continued to drink Frangelico and scoop coke into our head until a sizable dent in the bindle had been accomplished.

It had been more than three hours, so I was not surprised when Poppy slid over into the wheelchair and excused herself.

"Bathroom break," she announced.

When she returned, she again lifted herself onto the sofa and sat next to me.

"I'm so delightfully high and so glad to be here with you," Poppy said as she reached out and placed a hand on my arm. "I've always thought you were so good-looking and independent thinking, and I like that in a man."

Turning to face me, she asked, "Do you find me attractive?"

"Not just attractive, Poppy, you're flat-out beautiful. Stunning, in fact."

She looked at me and calmly said, "I want you to fuck me. You asked the other day how my love life was; well, it's not very good. I know it will be very different for you, without legs I can't move like other women, but I need sexual contact, and I want it to be with you."

I leaned over, kissed her deeply and found her mouth wet, open and eager with passion. As we kissed, I gently unbuttoned her blouse and bra, so I could kiss and feel her breasts. They were firm and perfectly suited to her frame.

Poppy was shaking, like a shiver from being cold. Then she pulled away and said, "Stand up in front of me, please. I want you in my mouth."

I stood, and she leaned forward, unzipped my shorts and let them fall to my ankles as I pulled my shirt over my head. I wasn't wearing undershorts, so my hard erection was within Poppy's immediate reach. She took my erection in her right hand, while simultaneously using her left hand to caress everything else. Poppy took her time and seemed to derive as much pleasure from the caresses of her hands and mouth as I did from being the lucky recipient.

"Thank you," she said when I finished, as she reached for her glass of Frangelico and took a sip.

"Your turn," I said.

"Are you sure you're ready to see me?" she asked.

"Absolutely, and I want to see all of you." I answered.

Her top and bra had already been removed during the kissing and exploring, so I got on my knees in front of her and removed her shorts. It was a perfect line below her midsection—two stubs where her thighs should have been, with a patch of hair perfectly and beautifully situated in the middle of her lap.

It was different for me—I'll admit that—very different than

anything I had ever seen or done. Yet, at the same time, very exciting. All I wanted to do was taste her. And I did.

Twenty minutes later, I was hard again and knew what to do about it. I reached under Poppy, lifted her to the front edge of the sofa, and slid inside her while on my knees.

After a couple of awkward attempts to create a rhythm to our lovemaking, I was able to meet her fully as her hips pounded against mine with each stroke I took. Once a comfortable position had been found, and the two of us were coupled in passion, it became clear to me that Poppy was ready to explode. And she did. And *we* did. Together.

And that proved to be just the beginning of the evening for the two of us.

I lovingly carried Poppy from the sofa to the bedroom, put her on her bed and spent the night with her soft hands and sensual mouth exploring my body. Every so often, as the passion grew between us, I would mount her in a missionary position for a few minutes, then slide down the bed to deliver G-spot arousal leading to a pulsating climax.

Then she would return the favor.

Later in the night, we lay there talking, and she said. "Have you always enjoyed sex with such passion? I mean I could really feel your passion, even your heartbeat."

"Always, clear back to high school. Sex is like oxygen to me. I adore women. In fact, I elevated the opposite sex to the highest possible pedestal right after the first time I had sex at age fourteen. And you have all been there ever since."

Poppy laughed and said, "Have you ever thought about therapy?"

"Ah, who needs it? This is a game to me, and I think I play it rather well."

"I agree," Poppy said, snuggling in closer to me, "but I've been noticing a change in you recently."

"Really? What kind of change?"

"I've noticed that your frown lines are getting deeper and your smile lines are hardly visible these days. Want to talk about it?" she asked.

"Nothing much to talk about; just the usual business worries and concerns," I told her.

"No, Adrian, there's something more bothering you, and we both know that, don't we?"

She was right, of course. I had always worn my heart on my sleeve, so I shouldn't have been surprised when Poppy confronted me with the truth.

"Can we save that conversation for another night?" I asked.

"Any night you want," she assured me. "Just call me and let me know you're coming over."

"I'll do that," I said, and I meant it. I needed a friend—a real friend—and maybe Poppy was the person who could fill that void. But tonight, was not the night for a serious conversation.

In the morning, after satisfying each other one final time, Poppy invited me to be her dinner guest whenever I wanted. She promised to keep a bottle of Frangelico in the cupboard, and I promised to call soon. And I did.

Chapter Eighteen

It was New Year's Eve 1985, and Bogart's was filled to capacity with revelers waiting to shout, "Happy New Year" and pop the bubbly. Soon it would be nineteen eighty-six—a better year for me, I hoped.

I was standing in my usual spot at the far end of the bar, near the restrooms and door leading to the outside deck. Sitting near me at the bar were Gary and George. As usual, Gary's ever-present pack of Marlboro cigarettes was sitting next to his drink. I knew if I ever wanted to screw with Gary's head all I had to do was take his Marlboros when he wasn't looking. If he reached over to pick up his cigs and they weren't there, he would go into major panic mode.

A few of us knew that Gary kept a self-consumption bindle of cocaine in his Marlboro box. If the box was ever found with the bindle inside, especially if found by law enforcement, Gary could claim it wasn't his. So, he always set it on the bar near his drink, within easy reach.

These days, of course, that wouldn't work—human DNA would be found inside and outside the pack, and on the bindle as well. But in 1985, ten years before the O. J. Simpson trial, DNA testing was in its infancy and not yet cutting-edge technology.

My brother Don, along with my main weekend gal, Carla, were working opposite ends of the bar, fixing drinks with highly-coordinated precision. New Year's Eve is always a madhouse, and only the best bartenders can survive the onslaught. Believe me, Don and Carla were the two best—not just at Bogart's, but anywhere in Quartz County

Suddenly, George and Gary began laughing as they looked

toward a young woman, obviously drunk, exiting the ladies' room with a long stream of toilet paper caught inside her pantyhose. The stream trailed back into the ladies' room, perhaps still attached to the roll. Gentleman George reached out with his left foot and stealthily stepped on the stream of toilet tissue as the young woman continued to walk past us, back to her table, with a trail of paper following behind.

"Amateur night," George said with a shrug and laugh.

"Looks like you two hit the jackpot tonight," I said, motioning toward the packed house.

"Yeah, the snow bunnies are out tonight, and business is good," George responded.

I laughed then stepped away to play saloonkeeper. Time to shake a few hands and slap a few butts, including a table with city councilmen Vance Egan and Danny Tobias, and others celebrating and bringing in the New Year. I sat with them and ordered a round for the group.

Egan and I were never close, and he was still smarting from the night we took his dough at Madame Butterfly's place, but he was cordial when I sat across from him. Tobias didn't need to pretend, because we were good friends, that went back many years of close family ties. I loved the guy and seeing Danny at Bogart's on New Year's Eve made it a better night for me than it otherwise would have been.

As we waited for the drinks to be delivered, Marilyn, one of my best cocktail waitresses, approached the table and said, "Adrian, we've got trouble on the dance floor."

"What kind of trouble?"

"It's Ralph Pittman, the police sergeant. He's drunk and up on the bandstand hassling the band and makin' a fool of himself."

"Thanks, I'll take care of it."

I looked around until I spotted Wally, my doorman/bouncer. Wally was about six-four, 240 pounds, and all muscle. He was from New Jersey and loved being a bouncer. He was a nice guy—unless you pushed him the wrong way. Then watch out.

I waved to Wally and pointed at the dance room. He nodded, and we met at the dance room entrance.

"Seems we've got trouble with one of our boys in blue," I advised my burly bouncer.

"You mean Sarge?"

"Right," I nodded, "and we need to get him off the bandstand."

"Want me to toss him?"

"Nah, no need for you and Pittman to have a public scuffle. Call the P. D. night number and have someone send a car to get him out of here. He's a pain in the ass sober, and a real prick when he's drunk—so let them handle him."

"Will do, boss."

It was a busy New Year's Eve for the understaffed department, but when Gold City police were told that one of their sergeants was the cause of the disturbance, they immediately headed for Bogart's. Five minutes later, two patrolmen walked in, met with Wally, then walked over to Ralph's table. They sat with Pittman for a few minutes then escorted him out the front door. From there, the two patrolmen took their supervisor home—not the first time they had performed that chore.

Live music in the bar business is a pain in the ass. Owners and their crews are always dealing with a drunk or two. Or else someone's wife is out on the dance floor, and the old man is pissed that she's dancing with another guy—especially a slow dance, which is really nothing more than a chance for breasts against chests and a feel below the waist.

And while customers are tough enough to deal with, there are the musicians. Ah, the musicians.

Musicians are a whole different breed of people. They think bar owners are always taking advantage of them. They want drinks on the house, take breaks when they want, not when it is best for the club, and they generally drink and do drugs to excess. There are the exceptions, however. When Bogart's first opened, I had some local talent play on weekends near the fireplace. We had many seriously gifted acoustical musicians in Gold City in those days, including George Xouza, Tom Mack, and Johnny Veredith. And bands like the Badlanders and Black Dog. We even had a brother team of Dom & Zink with lots of acoustical stuff to keep the mood mellow. These were the good guys then—and they still are!

But mellow ended once the dance room was in operation and electrified bands began to attract large crowds at night with pulsating boom-boom music that got folks dancing and drinking. The louder they played, the more the people danced and drank. And that kept the cash register ringing.

The upside of live music is that it brings in the women and is usually very profitable. The women drink, and they attract the guys—who drink even more. So, when you consider the cover charge collected at the door and the increased drink prices whenever there's live music, it's usually worth the aggravation and added heartburn that most club owners experience.

Not always, but most of the time. New Year's Eve 1985 was an example of everything that's good—and profitable—about live music in the bar. Wally handled each problem child with professionalism, and we got through the night without any fights or disturbances, except for our local GCPD sergeant making a fool of himself.

Chapter Nineteen

Michael's long flight from California to Washington, D. C. took his plane over the heart of Illinois. The Land of Lincoln was below him, and his father's amazingly candid memoir rested on his lap—many pages having been read; many more unread. And much to think about.

***

In early 1986, as I was trying my best to get straight and be a responsible business owner, Gold City hired Abel Kane to be the new police chief. He was personally vetted by the city's mayor Arthur Fenwick, and the city council had little say in the hiring.

The past chief had been popular with merchants and citizens alike. I never had an issue with Nick Snowden; in fact, I liked him, although sometimes I thought he was a little too full of himself like we all can be. Unfortunately, Chief Snowden was found in his patrol car, dead from a heart attack, just off Eagle Way one afternoon in late January of 1986.

Shortly after Snowden's death, Kane was brought on board with, as I was to later learn, a mandate from the mayor to rid the town of drugs and druggies—and, in the process, stifle its reputation for a special sort of nightlife.

Both the mayor and police chief were convinced that Bogart's was a major contributor to the town's perceived problems. They especially believed that I contributed to the drug trafficking by turning a blind eye when dealers walked in to have a drink and conduct business.

There may have been some wheelin' and dealin', I'll admit that,

129

but they had no evidence of any illegal activity on my part. Because there was none; if you ignored my personal bad habit.

Fenwick gave the new Top Cop authority to deal with Bogart's in whatever manner he thought would work best, and also gave Kane strict marching orders to close down Gold City's drug trade and nightlife. It was a tall order, but the mayor was a determined man on a personal mission.

I was told later that Fenwick believed there were too many bars in the small downtown area and too much outside influence coming in on weekends to party—an influence that contributed to Gold City's bad boy/bad girl reputation. He may have been right but undoing nearly a decade of rock 'n' roll would not be easy.

The hang-loose attitude of Gold City was deeply ingrained in its daily life—not to mention its nightlife—and I guess I had something to do with helping shape that attitude. Almost overnight Gold City became the one-night-stand capital of California.

Naturally, the new chief wanted to please the mayor, so he agreed with his boss that it was time to find a way to close Bogart's by any tactic he deemed legal—or not so legal—as long as it didn't reflect negatively on the city or expose the city treasury to a legitimate lawsuit.

Several years later I was told exactly what had happened and who had been the driving force behind the plan to bust me. But as I sit here at the computer more than twenty years after the world began caving in on me, writing my memoirs and recalling those dark days, here's what I know to have been the truth and had taken place at meetings inside the Gold City Police Department and City Hall.

***

Chief Kane sat behind his desk in the small City Hall office surrounded by stacks of paper, files, wanted posters, and city memos. The new chief was black and had just turned fifty- five. He was the first African American police chief in Gold City's history. Kane stood a notch over five-eight, a stocky two-twenty, and had a bulging paunch that made him look like a typical law enforcement lifer who ate and drank too much, got too little exercise, and couldn't have chased down a fleeing bad guy if his life depended on it. Prior to his career in law enforcement, he had been an Army Drill Instructor, Sergeant E-6.

Kane's father was Black Irish, career Army. He met his wife while stationed in South Carolina. Kane's mother worked at the base PX. Her maiden name was Abel, thus—Abel Kane.

Chief Kane had a full head of curly white hair with a full white mustache to match. His cheeks were badly pock-marked. His black eyes were set back in their sockets, and he wore blue-tinted glasses most of the time. His teeth were uneven and darkened by nicotine. He was not an especially attractive guy, but for reasons no one could understand, his wife was an attractive black woman, over six-feet tall, and several years his junior.

Kane had been police chief in Otter, another Northern California community the previous twelve years, where prior to that the twenty-five-year law enforcement veteran had advanced up through the ranks as a Sergeant with drug enforcement and eventually a Homicide Detective with the sheriff's office.

Across from him sat Sergeant Ralph L. Pittman, a transplant from Oklahoma, a Coast Guard vet, who had joined the force ten years earlier. Ralph moved here to be closer to his sister and was married to a local gal. He had three small children, and for the most part, was a naive small-town police officer who had never handled a serious case.

Pittman stood about five-seven, slender, 170 pounds with brown hair, brown eyes and was, according to most of my female customers, an ugly, pushy cop, that used his badge to charm the ladies. He wore jeans, black soft-soled street shoes, and his beige uniform shirt displayed three stripes on its sleeves. He was one of three sergeants on the force and, from Kane's perspective, needed more training and discipline. The Coast Guard didn't provide much of either, but he had tenure and had worked his way up through the department to the rank of sergeant.

Pittman had his eyes fixed on becoming a lieutenant—perhaps even chief when Kane retired or was fired—so he had to play the hand he was dealt, no matter how unpleasant or tedious it might be on any given day.

"So," Kane began, "I understand you had an altercation of sorts at Bogart's on New Year's Eve; even dropped your gun on the dance floor in your drunken stupor, is that right?"

"Yes, and I'm sorry about what happened and embarrassed by my behavior. Won't happen again, Chief, I promise," Pittman said, clearly uncomfortable.

"It better not," Kane shot back. "If we ever again need to send a squad car to retrieve your sorry ass from a bar, you're history. If it happens again, you'll be turning in your badge and handing me your weapon. You'll be lucky to get a job as a school crossing guard. Understood?"

"I hear you loud and clear, Chief."

"Do you have a drinking problem? Is that why you acted like an idiot at Bogart's?" the chief asked

"No, sir. It was just inexcusable stupidity on my part; that's all."

"And it isn't just the fact that you drank too much and made a fuckin' fool of yourself and this department, it's also where you were drinking. *Bogart's*? Are you kidding me, Sarge?"

"Whatever you say, Chief," Pittman responded without emotion.

"The word's come down about Bogart's."

"The *word*?"

"Yes, the word is to close Bogart's—permanently."

"Close?" Pittman asked with surprise.

"That's right. It's been suggested to me to find a way to close the place, and you're going to help me do it."

"You're the boss," Pittman said.

"And don't you forget it, Sergeant."

 Pittman nodded.

"What I'm about to tell you is strictly between you and me. Understood? No one else in the department will know about this scheme except us. We will call it Operation Dark Night."

"Scheme?"

"The word is that Davis is out of control—too much coke up his nose."

"I've heard the rumors myself, Chief. Maybe his fuse is a little short, but he seems to function just fine."

"He might fool you and others, but Bogart's is a hub for coke distribution and consumption. And he's a consumer, Ralph, make no mistake about it."

"If he's using that much, he sure hides it well," Pittman said.

"Sometimes he hides it, you're right," the chief told his sergeant, "but I've been hearing from some reliable sources that other times he doesn't hide it well at all."

"So, what do you need me to do?" Pittman asked.

"I want you to start pulling some night shifts. Alternate between the four-to-midnight shift and graveyard. Start looking for any unusual activity at Bogart's. It could be during operating hours or after-hours. I want to know anything you see of interest, especially anything related to drugs—and especially if it involves Davis. Understood?"

"Got it, Chief. I'll report to you every few days, in person, with a detailed report. I won't let you down," Pittman said as he stood up, shook the chief's hand and exited the office with an air of new-found importance.

Chapter Twenty

I was upstairs in my office one-afternoon going over inventory and accounts payable, recalling the first few years of owning Bogart's—when money was plentiful, and life was good—when a knock on the door brought me back to the present.

Those days, whenever I got engrossed in the business finances, I had a tendency to float out into space, hoping something might change for the better by the time I came back to reality. But, of course, it never did. For the life of me, I couldn't understand how I was falling so far behind in so many areas of the business; including my growing accounts payable and state and federal taxes.

After returning to the real world from my momentary haze, I said, "Come in."

Gary Nicholson stuck his head in the door. "It's me, buddy. Okay to come in for a few minutes?"

"Yeah, sure, sure," I told him.

Gary was, as usual, dressed in black jeans, black t-shirt, black tennis shoes and carrying his signature men's purse—black leather, of course. He sat across from me, opened the purse, then reached in and extracted a bundle of cash.

"Here's the ten grand you asked to borrow. I'm good with lending it to you till summer, but I expect you to pay it back by then; before the end of July at the absolute latest."

I took the cash without counting it nor thinking about what I would do when the loan came due. "Thanks for saving my ass," I told him. "I need this to get the tax people off my butt and be able to breathe again."

"Glad I could help."

"For sure I'll have it back to you by July because, as you know, in the summer, with good weather, my cash flow really increases. So, thanks again, my friend."

We shook hands, and the deal was sealed.

"No problem," Gary told me. "As I said, I can do it now, but I need it back in the summer—the earlier, the better."

Nicholson got up, headed to the door with a smile and waved as he made his exit and walked downstairs to the bar.

I sat there counting the cash, feeling relieved for the moment, knowing I could get some liquor bills paid and delinquent taxes brought current. What Gary didn't know—and continued to worry me—was that I had just gone back to my dad and borrowed another ten thousand dollars from him. He was not happy, but I was optimistic that all would be good once summer arrived. I told my dad the business would be jumping by July, just like I told Gary, and Dad agreed to the new loan—another ten thousand on top of the ten grand I had borrowed from him last fall.

Unfortunately, I promised him I would make good on at least ten grand by mid-summer; the same promise I had just made Gary. Now I had three loans total—thirty thousand in all—twenty to Dad, ten to Gary. Interest-free. How the hell did that happen?

I knew there was no way to repay my dad and Gary that kind of money so quickly, but what the hell. At least I would have a few months to think of an excuse for not repaying them. And I was getting pretty good at thinking of excuses for almost everything I did—or *didn't* do.

****

That night, to celebrate my new-found financial breath of fresh air for the business, I joined friends London and Paris Maxx for dinner at The Firehouse. We ordered our favorite bottle of Jordan Cabernet, French onion soup, salad, and teriyaki steak. We were there for about three hours—eating, drinking and talking—then headed over to their place for dessert.

Their home was on the edge of town, at the end of Fox Street above Bear Creek, surrounded by large pine and oak trees. The house was about five years old, set on two acres—which allowed for a lot of privacy. It was a two-story, three-bedroom, two-bath home. The spacious living room had a large fireplace that brought the kitchen and dining room into the living area. The large master bedroom and bath were upstairs in a loft, with two bedrooms and a Jack and Jill bathroom downstairs.

We gathered at a bar near the fireplace and filled a plate with a pile of fool's gold, as London liked to call cocaine. His nickname for the stuff was easily explained by saying the more one consumes the white powder, the more foolish one becomes.

Geologically speaking, fool's gold is nothing more than sparkling iron pyrite. It looks like gold, but it's worthless. Tourists visiting Gold City would sometimes stroll down to Bear Creek and see dozens of tiny pyrite pieces glimmering in the shallow water. They'd instinctively reach down to pluck them from the creek and, for a moment, feel their heart pound in anticipation of having stumbled upon a rich gold deposit. Then reality slowly sank in, and their handful of worthless pyrite was unceremoniously dumped back into the creek.

Although mineral fool's gold was worthless, there was nothing cheap about the price of cocaine in the mid-1980s. It ran about $120.00 a gram in Gold City—expensive even for a bar owner like me, who took in over a thousand dollars on a weeknight, and over three-thousand each weekend night at Bogart's. A bottle of beer was less than two bucks in those days, so one gram of coke equaled the sale of sixty-plus beers—not counting my cost for the product, or labor, utilities, taxes, and rent to my grandparents.

My margin was small, and the more coke I snorted, the smaller my margin became. The smaller my margin was, the more it led to more financial worries, which in turn drove me to more coke—and a further drain financially. Hell, I knew what was happening, but I was stuck on the merry-go-round and couldn't get off.

Just one night at the coke plate could make a big dent in the average day's profit, but I wasn't paying attention to the bottom line like a responsible business owner. I was in deep shit, but I kept smiling—at least in public.

And I was smiling that night with London and Paris.

London had been born and raised in Gold City, where his late father had once owned a grocery store. Paris was from Southern California, and they met at UCLA in the nineteen-seventies. In celebration of their first names they were married in London, England and honeymooned in Paris, France after college and settled in Gold City, where they bought a small antique store and owned some income property.

They seemed to be a perfect couple, but a lot of couples seem perfect to outsiders.

I had known London my entire life and considered him one of my best friends. They were a fun couple to party with, and we partied together frequently. We loved talking local politics, business trends, and hashing local gossip.

"You know what they're saying about Councilman Egan and the continuing bar shortages at the Grizzly Bear Lodge?" London asked.

"He's still doing that shit?" I asked as I took another line of coke from the plate on the bar. "He can't help himself; it's in his DNA."

"I hear the count is up there, Adrian. Seems the dollar amount is in the thousands that can't be accounted for. The lodge board may be serious this time about pressing charges. Who Knows? At least he's no longer bartending; that's a start."

London took another line of coke and shared some additional insight he had on Egan. None of it was good news for the honorable councilman—but it was time that someone in authority had the balls to do something about the councilman's indiscretions.

"His day will come," I assured London. "What goes around, comes around."

"Ah, such wisdom from a man who proclaims to know everything, yet sometimes seems to know nothing," London said with a big smile.

"Isn't that what Socrates said? That true wisdom comes from realizing that one doesn't know anything," I asked my friend.

"I think I read that a few years ago while at UCLA. But that's too philosophical for me to consider in my present condition," London said again, with a big smile.

London and Paris were an attractive couple. She was a petite, well-shaped sweetie with chestnut brown hair, blue-green eyes, a beautiful smile, great legs, small breasts, and a tight cute ass.

London stood about five-eight, a full head of wavy blond hair with brown eyes, glasses, thin features and was rumored to have a big dick. I had never asked him about it, so I had to depend on what the gals at Bogart's told me. And they were usually smiling when they described his attributes.

Our conversation, drinking, and consumption of cocaine continued until about 1:00 A.M. when we ran out of coke. We were all very high. None of us needed more coke, nor did we need more booze. Sleep became my top priority.

About then, London suddenly jumped up and said, "I want more coke, and I'm going downtown to get some before the bars close."

I told him that it was time to call it a night, but he grabbed his coat and headed for the door. "I'll be back soon, don't leave," he said as he headed out the door.

I looked at Paris and asked, "What the hell was that all about? When's he coming back?"

"He's not coming back, least not tonight," she said looking at me for a couple of seconds, then looking down at her lap. "He's going over to one of his girlfriends. He wanted to leave us here alone."

"Why?" I asked.

Paris looked me straight in the eyes and said, "Because he wants you to fuck me."

"Are you kidding? Why?" I asked.

"He wants us to fuck then have me tell him about it. He wants me to tell him everything I do to you while we're fucking. He's bored with our sex life. Hell, he's been fucking coke whores for months, and he wants me to fuck others, too, so he won't feel so guilty about his infidelity, and he can justify his stupid behavior."

"How do you feel about what he's doing?" I had known about his dalliances, being a bar owner, and had heard all the salacious gossip.

"I feel helpless, to tell you the truth. I want him happy, so I'm going along for now."

"So, you're going to start fucking other guys in order to keep London happy? Is that what you're telling me?"

"Hell, no, I don't want to fuck other men, but I'd fuck *you*," she said with a tantalizing smile. "He also wants me to be with another woman, so he can watch," Paris added, staring straight ahead and wiping her eyes.

"Anyone in mind?"

"His fantasy, for now, is on your main squeeze, Shelly Summers. I guess I'm curious enough that if the opportunity were to present itself, sure, I'd do it. But I'd want a lot of coke if it happens. I'd just want to lose myself and not think about where things are going."

I looked at Paris with a mixed sense of sadness and curiosity.

"Where are things going?" I asked, curious about the evening ahead of us—or if there was to be one.

Paris sheepishly smiled, took my hand and we walked toward the stairs leading up to the master bedroom.

"He wants to hear about us fucking," she said, "so let's give me something I can really brag about."

Fucking London's wife was the exception, not the rule. I had more than one wife of a friend approach me with their desires during the years I owned Bogart's. In fact, the wife of my best friend, came in the bar one afternoon while I was bartending and asked me to have lunch with her the next day at the Yellow Rose Cafe. We were good friends too, and she helped me with Bogart's interior design, so I said OK, see you at noon.

Almost immediately after we ordered, she made clear to me the real purpose of the lunch. She wanted to have sex right after lunch. Now. Seems my best friend had been treating her badly and she wasn't very happy. We both acknowledged that if it weren't for my best friend, we would have done something about our mutual attraction for each other long ago. I would have gone after her in a heartbeat because she was very attractive and very sexy. And what a body.

I must admit I was uncomfortable sitting there, but she wasn't taking no for an answer. On top of that, her husband was sitting not far away in the restaurant with a group of businessmen. He was pitching them on a project for some land outside of town and kept looking over at our table.

Finally, we finished lunch and the conversation. It was over, but she sure tried hard to convince me to see it her way. Just like other times, I just couldn't bring myself to betray a trust of friendship over a piece of ass.

Not long after that eventful lunch, my best friend moved his family to Southern California, and I heard later that my friend's wife eventually scratched that itch with her tennis pro. I'm not sure hubby ever found out. I learned early on that when a woman wants to play and is determined, they are relentless and put their desires above all else.

And they don't play fair. When it comes to the female sex, men will do about anything to look at, touch, taste, and/or penetrate the V of the female anatomy. Once the little brain takes over, and the big brain has lost control, forget about the male conscience. Never mind friendship, religion, or ethical barriers outweighing the desires for passion and sex. And absolutely forget about any hope of keeping a clear thought process while deliberating the pros and cons of such actions. Fact is, when a man gets his head under a skirt, stupid takes over.

Chapter Twenty–One

One of the joys of spring and summer in California's Gold Country is the weather. Unlike some parts of the state—especially the coastal and desert areas—the Sierra foothills enjoy four distinct seasons. And for me, the cusp of spring turning into summer was the best time of all.

It meant summer was right around the corner and Bogart's was about to experience a surge of business from tourists and day-trippers who like to leave the hot, humid valley floor in and around Sacramento and head up to Gold City for relaxation and cool, mountain evenings.

On a beautiful morning in May 1986, I removed the top of my light-blue Jeep Wrangler with its big V-8 engine and headed downtown on Red Rock Road with Tonto in the back seat enjoying the morning breeze rushing past him as only a dog could enjoy it.

As I came around a corner and passed the old cemetery about a half-mile or so above town, I saw Gary Nicholson with a handful of friends in front of his house, walking along the road as though they were looking for something. I honked and waved. Gary waved back and indicated with his arm movement for me to keep going.

A few hours later, he came to my office door and stood there waiting to be invited in. I motioned for him to take the chair in front of my desk and noticed he wasn't his usual jovial self. Something was troubling Nicholson, and I sensed he wanted to talk.

"What was going on this morning out in front of your place? Why were you waving me on?" I asked him.

"I got fucked really good today, buddy. You know I bury the bulk of my stash out in back of the house on that parcel of county property?"

"Yeah, you told me you had a hiding place away from the house."

Gary said he stashed his coke largess on the county land in case law enforcement came to his house with a search warrant. If they searched the house, they'd only find a small amount for personal use, if any. Meantime, his stash was safe and secure about forty yards away from his property line.

"So, what happened?" I asked my distraught friend.

"I was partying last night and ran out of my personal supply," Gary began, "so I went out back and dug up the stash to get some more. I took it in the house, cut out what I wanted and took the rest back and buried it at my usual spot near the big pine tree. This morning, I went back out there to check on it and be sure I buried it deep enough, but I guess I didn't. It wasn't there. Not a trace."

"So, what do you think happened?" I asked.

"I didn't notice anything unusual at first, but then I saw the digging pattern and dog tracks around the pine tree. Turns out my fuckin' neighbor's dog dug up the stash and hauled it away. We were out looking for it when you saw us this morning, hoping the damn dog had dropped the bag somewhere close to the house."

Gary looked up at the office ceiling for a couple of seconds, then at me, telegraphing the fact that the search party had come up empty-handed.

"The fuckin' dog took my stash home with him and dropped it at my neighbor's front door. The neighbor went out to pick up the morning newspaper, and I guess you can figure out the rest?"

"Doesn't sound good."

"Worse than not good, I'm afraid," Gary said, his head buried in his hands. "My neighbor called the sheriff's office and told them what the dog brought home."

"How do you know? Did the neighbor tell you?"

"Fuck, no. When the sheriff's narc guys got there, we saw them pull in the neighbor's driveway and park, so we went inside at that point. A half-hour later the cops came over and knocked on my door. Of course, I didn't know what they knew—was I going to be arrested, and taken to jail? Hell, man, I wasn't sure what the fuck was happenin.'"

"So, what did happen?" I asked.

"They just wanted to inform me what was going on in the neighborhood and that I should keep my eyes open for any suspicious activity. Can you believe that shit?"

"They were rubbing your nose in it, that's what they were doing, Gary. They couldn't prove it was yours, so they decided to play with your head. But they knew."

"Didn't seem like play to me," Nicholson said as he took a deep breath and tried to regain his composure.

"They couldn't bust you, so they gave you the middle finger," I told him.

"Well, if that's what it was, it was sure a big middle finger."

"How much did you lose?"

"Just under a kilo; worth about twenty-five grand."

"Fuck," I said.

"Yeah, for a guy like me that's a huge hit, and now I don't have the ready cash to square this with Pixie and the L. A. boys. Especially since I lent you that ten grand a while back."

I knew what was coming next.

"Any chance you can get me some cash? Maybe enough so I can at least make a partial payment?"

"No, Gary, wish I could, but I paid all the back taxes and outstanding invoices. Sorry, but I'm tapped right now."

That was not the full truth, but fairly close. I still had a few thousand from the combined twenty grand I had borrowed from Gary and my dad, but I knew if I gave any of it back, I would be scrambling for more dollars very soon. I wanted to help the guy but thought I'd better protect my own ass first.

"Shit, I'm in trouble, man—big trouble. I've got to get an advance on a kilo to sell so I can cover the loss. These guys don't fuck around when it comes to getting their money. I miss another payment date, and you'll be reading my obituary."

I knew he wasn't joking.

"I've got to go, Adrian. Get me some money as soon as you can, OK?"

"As soon as I can, you can count on it," I told him with a straight face.

I got up and gave Gary a firm man-hug, then he headed for the door and the staircase that led back to the bar.

The tsunami wave of bad news was continuing to lap at my office door. I just hoped it wasn't going to get any worse.

Chapter Twenty-Two

By the summer of 1986, the town was hopping, and the annual Fourth of July party for preferred customers and all employees was another big hit. Lots of food, booze and, of course, piles of coke. It was a tradition worth sustaining for as long as I could, but certainly not what my grandparents had in mind the first time I asked if I could have the gang over on the Fourth.

Women who came to the annual party understood that they needed to leave their inhibitions at the front gate. Most did. Others needed some encouragement.

Gary was at the party that year looking for some dough. Ten grand, to be exact. I didn't have it, nor had I been able to repay my dad even the first ten thousand, but I kept promising both of them that I'd soon be making a big dent in the debt. I never said how soon, nor how big a dent, and I suppose they knew it was a hollow promise, to begin with.

With more and more cash-flow problems arising and not being able to pay my loans back, sleeping at night was becoming increasingly difficult.

Many nights I was in bed, on my belly, clinging to my mattress, in a storm, hurricane winds blowing a gale as I held firm trying not to be swept away. Sleeping in the wind before being swept into Hell. And it took all my strength to keep from falling to the floor.

The dream—no, the nightmare—became more and more frequent, and I would awake with a lurch. Usually, about 5:00 A.M., sweating but relieved to be alive.

It was a tough time, but I held out hope that a busy summer would bail me out, get a line of credit reestablished with my major vendors, and then I could operate like a normal business owner. Most of all, I wanted to make good on the loans from Gary and my dad. Especially my dad. That was very important to me.

Little did I know, however, that by fall a plan would be hatched to set me up for using and dealing drugs. A plan designed to put a padlock on Bogart's and handcuffs on me.

It was only later that I learned the truth of how and why it happened.

***

Parked about twenty yards past Bogart's on Commerce Street at 3:00 A. M. on a foggy, cool, fall morning in nineteen eighty-six, was a Gold City patrol car with Sergeant Ralph Pittman behind the wheel. His eyes were trained on a light coming from an upstairs window at the back of the building. Pittman knew that the light was coming from my office.

Stepping from his car and quietly closing the door, he moved quickly and furtively toward a better vantage point.

The agile and athletic Pittman—in plain clothes, without his heavy service revolver, cuffs, mace canisters, radio and the other items he had stored in the trunk of the car—jumped a fence onto the patio of Bogart's. From there, he went around to the back of the patio and jumped another small fence that led to the rear deck of an Argonaut Street business.

Once on the adjoining deck, Pittman climbed to the top of the Bogart's walk-in refrigeration box—a large unit that bordered the deck of the Argonaut Street business. From the top of the large walk-in, Pittman was able to squat and creep over to my second- story office window.

The cop could hear laughter and loud voices coming from the office, so he knelt down and carefully looked through a corner of the window. I was sitting behind my desk, and three females were

147

sitting on the sofa and chair in front of the desk. The four of us were drinking, laughing, talking loud and clearly enjoying the private after-hours party.

Pittman observed what looked to be a pile of white powder on my desk and watched as I periodically took a credit card and made lines from the stack. We took turns leaning over the desk, grabbing a plastic cocktail straw, placing it in our nose and snorting the white powder. After a few seconds to get our bearings and clear our heads, the straw would be passed along to the next person in line.

Sergeant Pittman watched the office activities for about ten minutes then quietly lowered himself from the bar's walk-in box, climbed the fences in reverse order, and returned to his car. Once in the car, he drove back to the City Hall police station and prepared a report for Chief Kane.

Late that afternoon, Pittman and Kane met in the chief's office to discuss the sergeant's report, and here's what I was told occurred next.

"Good work, Ralph." the chief said, seemingly impressed—if not surprised—by the detailed report his young sergeant had filed. "You got what we need, that's for sure. He's obviously snorting coke and partying in his office, which I think is an extension of the bar's premises. We need to check with ABC on that. And based on what I read in your report, he's supplying the coke as well as snorting it."

"No doubt about it, Chief. Davis was putting the coke on the desk."

"Unfortunately, Ralph, you didn't have a warrant, so nothing you observed or included in your report is legal or would stand up in court. The judge would throw out your observations and testimony in a New York minute. You did a hell of a job, but we'll have to take a different tack if we're going to actually put the screws to this guy."

"So, what do you suggest? For sure, we're going to need a demonstrable cause for a judge to sign a search warrant and/or an arrest warrant. Especially for a well-known downtown merchant.

Hell, Chief, he's on the chamber of commerce board of directors, Gold City Rotary and the board of the Quartz County Business Association. So, it's not like busting some toothless meth-head without cause—a person no one knows or cares less about."

Chief Kane already had a plan all cooked up, ready to implement. And Pittman was about to learn that it would be up to him to make the plan work.

"Here is what I want you to do," the chief told him. "At some point over the next few weeks, I want you to force your way into Bogart's late at night, after closing, and after Davis has gone home, and move some things around. Make it obvious that he had a break-in. Bring a crowbar to rip out the office lock, scatter some papers."

"You're telling me to burglarize Bogart's? Is that what you're saying?"

"Burglary is the act of entering a building with the intent of stealing something," Kane reminded him. "I don't want you to steal anything, just make a mess. Leave a window open, ramshackle the office, move a few things around in the bar area, leave a file cabinet drawer open. And one more thing," he said, "I want you to do it more than once. We need to establish a pattern of break-ins at Bogart's, not an isolated incident. So, do it twice—better yet, three times—and a month or so apart."

Sergeant Pittman nodded, showing his boss that he understood the mission.

"Davis might let the first break-in go; maybe assume it's the work of a disgruntled customer looking to fuck with him. But if there are two or more burglaries, he'll no doubt report them to us," the chief said. "And when he starts coming in here to report what happened, we can put together a file documenting multiple burglaries. Then we can fatten the file by showing that I had you patrol the building after hours in order to hopefully catch the burglar in action."

"Makes sense to me, Chief. Shit, Davis will have no idea that the bad guy is me."

The chief continued giving Pittman instructions

"After we have a file confirming multiple break-ins, you'll need to make another observation at a future date that will again confirm his drug use and illicit activities at his business. Then we'll request a search warrant for all of Davis' properties based on what you witnessed while conducting a routine courtesy check—during which, of course, you hoped to prevent an additional burglary at his business. Naturally, we'll remind the judge that what you did was nothing more than the kind of extra protection we offer any business or homeowner who has been repeatedly burglarized. Nothing you did will seem out of place."

"'Preserve and protect,' right, Chief?"

"Right you are, young man. And because of the reported burglaries, you were merely checking out the office and, in doing so, observed blatant illegal activity. That will lead to a righteous warrant that will stand up to any challenges from his defense attorney."

"I like it," responded an energized and enthusiastic Sergeant Pittman. "I'll begin in a week or so and keep you informed of what's what."

"Please do," the chief told him. "Let me know when you hit the place the first time, and again when you bust in the second time. By then, I'll be expecting a visit from Davis."

"Will do."

Pittman got up from his chair, shook Kane's hand and said, "We're going to nail this asshole, Chief; we're going to really nail him."

"We'd better nail him fella because if the scheme goes south, I'll deny that this conversation ever took place. Understand?"

"You'd deny it?" Pittman asked.

"Deny *what*?"

Chapter Twenty-Three

My periodic liaisons with Paris Maxx continued through 1986. She would contact me when she wanted company—usually at my house, mostly in the afternoons, sometimes evenings. Evenings were the most satisfying because they would include marathon coke fests.

I would see London around town, and when he'd drop by Bogart's for a pop or two, but he was always the same ol' London Maxx. He never said anything to me or indicated that he knew or cared about me screwing his wife. Paris said he had continued to see other women in town, mainly his gaggle of coke whores, and I had heard the rumors as well. She also said he continued to want to hear about everything we did together. And she told him. In detail while sharing their bed.

After one of our acrobatic afternoon sessions, Paris asked if Shelly and I would like to come to dinner the Friday after Thanksgiving. She knew I celebrated the holiday with my family, so the Friday offer seemed fine.

"Besides dinner, what do you two have in mind?" I asked with a grin.

"London wants to take our conversation about me being with another woman to the next level. Shelly's my choice—if she's willing, that is—and London wants her to be the one as well."

"You sure you know what you're doing?" I asked.

"I think so, Adrian, but I guess I'll find out for sure after our dinner. What I do know is that London and I are drifting apart and getting further apart by the day, so I'm hoping I will bring him back to me if I can keep him happy during this crazy period.

"I hope that fulfilling his fantasy will be curative. And if I'm still here when things do return to reality, maybe we can put it all back together and be husband and wife again. At least that's my hope."

"Big if, Paris. You absolutely sure you want to do this?" I asked.

She slowly nodded while staring at the floor.

"If Shelly has enough coke, she's open to anything, but putting Shelly and London together could backfire, you know? He may like it and pursue her and not get back in sync with you."

"The relationship can't be any worse than it is right now," she sighed. "We don't fight, just exist—snort blow—and fuck."

"Well, if that's what you want, then that's what we'll do."

"You and Shelly come to dinner and see what happens."

"Okay, we'll see you next Friday for dinner at about seven o'clock," I assured her.

***

Paris had decorated the house in traditional fall colors, and the table was set with a mauve tablecloth, bright red napkins and a centerpiece of flowers and fall leaves. The ladies were dressed in slacks and pumps with bright, comfortable sweaters. London and I wore our usual Levi's and tennis shoes. I wore my favorite powder-blue sweater while London had a checkered flannel Pendleton shirt with a wrist button missing. Two sexy, snazzy women and two guys dressed for a night at the bowling alley.

We started off with drinks while we enjoyed a cheese fondue appetizer with fruit and bread that Paris had prepared. Then, about eight o'clock, we sat down for dinner.

Paris was a great cook. She served a fruit salad over hearts of palm, beef Wellington, and twice-baked potatoes. For dessert, she had baked a sensational apple strudel.

She may have been nervous thinking about the after-dinner activities, but nothing about the meal, nor our table conversation, gave a hint of what was planned for later.

By the time the cocaine came out, we had consumed multiple bottles of wine and were opening more. The conversation continued to be fun and light, sprinkled with some town gossip. And, believe me, in Gold City in November 1986, there was plenty of gossip to exchange.

By midnight we knew it was time for the bedroom adventure. A couple of days earlier I had shared the plan with Shelly, who was intrigued by the possibilities. She liked London and Paris and wanted to play with both. And she hardly blinked when I first mentioned the idea to her.

I reached over to Shelly, took her hand in mine and said, "Why don't you come with me?" We stood up and walked upstairs to the master bedroom. When we got up there, I helped remove her clothes and asked her stand on the far side of the bedroom, next to the nightstand, with the stand light on to show off her amazing body.

As planned, she would be the focal point when London and Paris entered the room—and a delightful sight she was. I was already growing envious of London, but I knew my turn would come later.

I then went back down to the dining room to join London and Paris who were still seated at the table snorting coke and drinking wine.

"Okay, guys, here are the rules," I announced. "When we get upstairs, you'll see Shelly. London, my friend, she's all yours for thirty minutes on the bed and not a minute longer. Understood?"

London smiled and nodded.

"Paris and I will watch and play. Then, after thirty minutes, London will get off the bed and Paris will join Shelly for the next half hour. We want this to be as natural as possible, so Paris will take Shelly's lead. She told me she wants you to enjoy it Paris, so relax and let things evolve; however, they evolve. Meantime, London and I will observe your new adventure."

"And what happens to me after thirty minutes with Shelly?" Paris wanted to know.

"At the end of your thirty minutes, London and I will join you two for the rest of the evening's festivities. Sound good?" I asked.

London and Paris looked at each other and nodded with big grins. "Good plan," London said. "So, let's have another line, then go upstairs and let the games begin."

After a hit of coke, we went upstairs and, of course, upon entering the bedroom the first thing London saw was the nude Shelly, standing by the bed flushed in light from the table lamp.

"I'm all yours," she told him, motioning for London to join her next to the bed.

London walked over to Shelly, who began by removing his shirt, then his pants, then his shorts. Then she gently pulled him onto the king-sized bed.

Once London ran his hands over Shelly's perfect body and ample breasts, and Shelly saw and felt London's largesse, Paris, and I stepped back into the shadows with our wine and plate of coke. We left them alone while we played with each other and indulged.

"Time!" I announced after thirty minutes.

They rose from the bed with big smiles, laughing as they uncoupled themselves from a position one of them must have found in a copy of *Kama Sutra*. I was impressed.

Shelly then came over to Paris and took her hand, walked her to the far side of the bedroom and began removing her top while whispering in her ear and flickering her tongue in Paris' mouth.

Once Paris was also nude, they fell onto the bed with very enthusiastic, animated passion. Shelly was soft and gentle with her hands and tongue and encouraged Paris to do the same. And she did. It took a couple of minutes for Paris to get in the flow of things, but once she got active, she got *really* active.

London and I watched with pleasure and amazement, and when the half-hour was up we got on the bed with our ladies—taking opposite partners at first; then taking one lady at a time while three of us took turns giving pleasure to whichever partner wanted it.

As the evening progressed, it became a case of mix-and-match, and it lasted until sunrise.

When we finally ended the sexual adventure and Paris went downstairs to make a pot of coffee, I looked over at Shelly, still naked on the bed, her breasts cast in a subtle orange glow from the rising sun. I wanted to crawl back on that bed for one more romp, but I knew my tank was empty.

She was gorgeous, as was Paris, so I smiled and quietly hummed a Frankie Valli song from the seventies:

> *I felt a rush like a rolling bolt of thunder.*
> *Spinning my head around and taking my body under.*
> *Oh, what a night!*

I had learned that owning a bar was somewhat akin to being a rock star. I can't remember the number of one-night stands I had in those years, nor can I recall all their names. It was in the dozens, many dozens, and nearly all involved drugs—mainly cocaine—or were strictly alcohol related. Or both.

I loved the game. They would tell me, "I've heard of your reputation." Or, "I'm not like the others; I'm not easy." Or, "Just because I go home with you for a drink and a line, doesn't mean I'm jumping in bed with you."

Yea, right! If they left Bogart's with me, they knew exactly what was going to happen.

If I got them home, I got in their pants. They wanted to bang me as much as I wanted to bang them, and usually, it was a lot of fun.

Sometimes, it was much more fun than I ever expected.

Oh, what a night!

Chapter Twenty-Four

If City Hall wanted Bogart's closed it was a well-kept secret—at least from me. I had no idea at the time that plans were already in place.

Gold City had a City Administrator to run the day-to-day operations of the city. City Administrators have no real power. Power remains in the hands of the council and the mayor. Mayor Fenwick had controlled much of that power for over a decade.

***

As I was to learn later on a chilly April morning in 1987, there was a meeting at City Hall between Gold City Police Chief Abel Kane and Mayor Arthur Fenwick in the mayor's office—with the door closed. Arthur Fenwick was pushing three-hundred pounds had large elephant ears, wore round thick glasses with rims that hooked around his large ears, a nineteen-fifties flat-top haircut, and had lost all his teeth to gum disease. He had a full set of false teeth, that would clack when he talked, so he had a tendency of removing them and placing them in his shirt pocket, which, in turn, would leave a wet horseshoe pattern on his shirt pocket from the saliva.

It was a clear day with temperatures in the forties, accompanied by a steady breeze. Cool enough to remind people that although spring was emerging in some places, it was still winter in the Sierra foothills.

Fenwick's office was on the second floor of City Hall—a building constructed in the 1930s with an exterior look consistent with the era. My grandfather was a city councilman at its dedication.

To the casual observer, City Hall appears to be a classic Art Deco building, but it was a product of the Depression-era Works Progress Administration—the WPA—so technically the design is Art Modern, often referred to as a poor man's Art Deco. Similar in many ways, but not as much attention to detail.

It was a typical small-town mayor's office: faux hardwood floors, a large desk at the far end that looked out on Argonaut Street, a framed map of the city behind the desk, two chairs in front, and a sofa-and-chairs combo with a coffee table at the opposite wall from the desk.

I was told later the meeting between Chief Kane and Mayor Fenwick, as they sat in the comfortable couch-and-chair portion of the office, had the following agenda: "Where are we at with Mr. Davis, Chief?" the mayor asked. "What's happening with our problem child on Commerce Street?"

"It's all coming together just like we planned, Art. I'm meeting with Sergeant Pittman this afternoon for an update. He told me he'd completed the field work and now it's time to prepare for the final observation to secure the warrants."

"Good." Said the mayor with a gleeful smile.

"And when we get the warrants—and I'm sure we will—we'll tear through his bar, house, and vehicles. We'll be thorough, believe me. If there's even a grain of coke, we'll find it."

"I don't want fuckin' grains, or even grams, Chief; I want ounces. Pounds, if possible. Understand? And you better be thorough. Very thorough. We're only going to get one bite at this apple. If the searches fail, our plan fails. And you're not going to let that happen, are you?"

"No sweat, Art. And unless you insist on hearing all the details, I'll merely tell you that we carried out your request without a hitch. Pittman has cooperated fully and is closely following my instructions about how to prepare his reports. With those reports, we will go to the courthouse, get the warrants signed, and arrest the bastard before he knows what hit him."

"The less I know, the better, especially if something goes wrong, so I'm trusting you to do what's needed. A good or bad outcome of this operation rests with you and Pittman, and it sounds like you have things under control."

"We sure do. We planned this like a clandestine military mission, and it went down without a hitch. To tell you the truth, I didn't think Pittman had it in him."

"I didn't either, but he proved us both wrong." Fenwick nodded and asked, "How many are in on this plan?"

"Just you, me and Pittman, and I intend to keep it that way."

"No leaks?" the mayor asked.

"No leaks, no drips."

"Then get the hell out of here and do what you have to do to get that fuckin' saloon closed and Davis in jail where he belongs. And don't diddle-daddle around, OK? Get it done."

"We should be able to initiate the warrant request soon, certainly in a few weeks."

"A few *weeks*? Can't you move in on him faster than that?"

"Too risky to move quickly. We've been going about this at a safe pace in order to camouflage what Ralph's been doing to create reasonable cause for the warrants. Fortunately, we're just about at the Finish Line."

"I suppose you're right," Fenwick conceded. "And as long as the warrant judge buys it, that's all that counts."

"We've put too much time and effort into this plan to have it crash on the rocks because of a technicality or by moving in for the kill-shot prematurely," the chief assured the mayor.

"Well, good luck—and remember to cross every t and dot every i before you go up to the courthouse to get the warrants."

Kane nodded.

"Anything else going on in our fair city I should know about?" Fenwick asked.

"Nothing as important as what we've been talking about."

"No shit." Mayor Fenwick came across as the jovial "fat-man" politician, but he reminded me of a guy who would piss down your back and tell you it was raining—with a big smile on his face.

***

Later that afternoon, in Kane's office, Sergeant Pittman was sitting in a chair opposite the chief's cluttered desk.

"I understand you've completed three break-ins since the first of the year and Davis has reported all three to the police department? Is that correct?" the chief asked.

"Correct. We've established a pattern of break-ins at Bogart's and, yes, Davis reported all three of 'em. In fact, he's insisting that we do a better job of preventing crime and less time at the Express Mart drinking coffee."

"Perfect," the chief said as he leaned back in his swivel chair and laughed. "The stupid, fuckin' doper obviously has no idea what we're doing. And that gives us the established authority to make the observations in his business to prevent further break-ins. What with his bitching about our lack of crime-fighting skills, he's asking us to do essentially what we need to do to complete our task.

"But my concern continues to be the date of your original office observation last fall. Obviously, it was before the first of your three break-ins. We now need to make sure that our request for a warrant is supported by your actual observations and facts you can swear to in court."

Pittman knew where the conversation was headed.

"So Sarge, the question of the day is: Are you ready to make another after-hours visit to Bogart's and use whatever illegal act you observe this time in the upstairs office as the official report of the incident? This will ensure that the report is legit and guarantee that we'll have search warrants that'll hold up in court."

Pittman was being asked to jump back over those fences, climb back on top of the walk-in box, and crawl over to the office window again without being detected. And once there, he had to find Davis, and maybe one or two others, snorting coke. But without a fresh incident report that could be sworn to in court, indicating an observation date after the reported break-ins, the chief's Operation Dark Night would prove to be a waste of time. And the chief had made it clear to Pittman that there wasn't much time left to do what was needed.

"If that's what needs to be done, Chief, then that's what I'll do," Pittman said with a smile.

"Good bo... man, Ralph, I knew I could count on you. And if you can accomplish your final mission as smoothly as you did it the first time, I think there's a few hundred in discretionary cash in the department safe that might find its way into your pocket as a bonus. The money is for undercover drug work, right?"

"Right."

"Well, that's what you'll be doing when you're peering in that office window, so I don't see anything shady about having a few bucks land your way."

"Appreciate it, Chief, and I don't think it'll be a wasted return to the scene of the crime," he laughed. "Since my first observation, I've noticed the light on in Davis' office numerous times long after closing. I'm certain that when I peek in that window, he'll be snorting, and he'll have others there with him. My sources tell me that coke has become a regular after-hours feature at Bogart's, so don't worry—I'll see something illegal that will cover us for the search warrant; no doubt in my mind, sir."

"Good, then do it. We want to make the arrest soon, so don't fuck it up now, OK?"

"You can count on me, Chief, you know that."

***

Pittman continued to observe my office for any after-hours activity. Finally, after six nights of stakeouts, he saw the office light on at about 3:00 A.M. and proceeded to retrace his journey back to the top of the walk-in box, then over to the office window.

It was like shooting fish in a barrel. It was all Pittman could do to hold back his excitement.

Pittman saw me sitting behind my desk with my friend, London Maxx. Two gals were sitting on the nearby sofa. The sergeant saw me opening a bindle and pouring the white powder on a plate. Then I used a razor blade to chop the apparent cocaine into lines. After I consumed a couple of lines with a straw, I picked up the plate and handed it to London, at which point London and the ladies took turns snorting the white powder.

With the sergeant's fresh observation of me consuming and providing a controlled substance and the fact that it occurred after I had reported the suspicious burglary activity, Pittman knew Chief Kane would now be able to obtain warrants for Bogart's from top to bottom, plus my home and automobiles.

It was like hitting the trifecta at Santa Anita.

Three days later, a request for a search warrant was submitted to the Quartz County Superior Court. The warrant, if approved by the judge, would give Kane and his department legal authority to freely search the bar, my home and my vehicles.

They would be looking for drugs and drug paraphernalia—especially a large quantity of cocaine in one or more of the areas described in the warrant. The more coke, the larger the newspaper headline and longer the prison sentence.

Inside City Hall, it was becoming a circle jerk. The mayor wanted to hang me out to dry and have me implicated in both sales and distribution. The police chief wanted to see a successful caper because he was looking for a raise and Fenwick controlled the council, thus controlled the votes and the funds. And as for Pittman, he was thinking about the dough Kane promised he'd withdraw from the department safe—a token of his appreciation for the sergeant's fine police work.

In other words, Chief Kane was Fenwick's stooge, and Pittman was Kane's stooge. They were Gold City's version of Larry, Moe, and Curly, but what they had in mind for me was no laughing matter.

***

This was not going to be a request for a simple drug possession warrant; it would be a warrant to establish me as a major player in the local cocaine distribution business. The warrant request would also note that the business was open for the purpose of maintaining and operating an illegal enterprise.

If only I had known about the trap, the Three Stooges were setting. Unfortunately, the chief had been right when he assured the mayor that there had been no leaks. I had some good sources inside City Hall, but obviously not good enough.

The warrant request was submitted to Superior Court Judge Joseph Heim, and he signed it without asking any questions. Ironically, Judge Heim was a regular at Bogart's, as were many other courthouse employees.

That would soon change.

PART TWO
Crash Landing

Chapter Twenty-Five

The text of his dad's manuscript was devastating enough, but the vision Michael Davis had of the mayor as the ringleader of the scheme to bust his dad—and put him behind bars—was shocking.

He recalled that his dad never had a kind word to say about Fenwick, but Michael knew a lot of people his dad didn't care for—and a lot who didn't care for his dad. Adrian Davis had been a man who always spoke his mind, and that can ruffle a few feathers. It can also put distance between people.

Gold City was a small town, barely 3,000 residents, so Michael knew of Arthur Fenwick. He often heard his dad speak ill of the man. He now understood why.

***

It was May 24, 1987—a bright, sunny spring day in Gold City, California; a day and time burned into my brain. It was also my brother's birthday.

Shortly after three that afternoon, as I was tending bar at Bogart's and exchanging dumb jokes with my customers, three patrol cars from the Gold City P. D. came down Commerce Street and pulled up in front of the bar. They were joined by a couple of cars from the Quartz County Sheriff's Office.

My first thought was that someone had just robbed the bank—located a couple of hundred feet from Bogart's front door. There hadn't been a bank robbery in town in decades, but most every small-town bank gets hit occasionally.

As blue, white and red lights flashed from the top of cop cars, a door opened, and Chief of Police Abel Kane squeezed his chubby body past the steering wheel, stood on the street, hitched up his baggy pants, walked toward our building, then stared through the large front window. As he was doing that, other cops and county deputies exited their patrol cars and headed for our front door and the gate to the patio area.

Once he opened the door and entered Bogart's, I smiled and asked, "What's all the excitement, Chief? Somebody rob the bank?"

He didn't answer.

"Please step down to the end of the bar, Mr. Davis," Kane said with the tone of a friendly request and not a demanding order.

I walked to the end of the bar, where a stoic Kane said, "We have a warrant for your arrest and to search the premises."

"Search? Arrest? For what?"

"Adrian Davis, you're under arrest for the sale and distribution of cocaine and maintaining a business for the purpose of operating an illegal enterprise. Please turn around and put your hands on the bar."

My customers looked on dumbfounded, in silence, as Sergeant Pittman patted me down, ordered me to put my hands behind my back and slapped on the cuffs.

"He's clean, Chief," Pittman announced.

"Before we go any further, Davis, I want to make sure you understand your rights. Sure, don't want to see this arrest and search nullified because of some silly technicality, do we now?"

I was in shock, not sure what to say or do. Kane pulled a card from his shirt pocket and read: "You have the right to remain silent. Anything you say can and will be used against you in a court of law. You have the right to an attorney. If you cannot afford an attorney, one will be provided for you."

Still calm and professional, he asked, "Do you understand the rights I have just read to you?" I nodded and answered yes.

"With these rights in mind, do you wish to speak to me?"

I stared at the chief in disbelief, then simply said, "I want to call my attorney."

"Okay," Kane replied, "then let's go upstairs to your office; you can call him from there."

Turning toward his sergeant, he said, "Sergeant Pittman, you search the bar area, dance room, patio, restrooms, and basement. Take as many officers as you need and be thorough. The warrant authorizes us to search for drugs, and drugs can be hidden in very small places."

Pittman nodded in agreement. Then glanced at me with a quick snicker.

To my customers, Kane announced, "Sorry, folks, but Bogart's is closed for the day—maybe longer. We apologize for disrupting your otherwise pleasant afternoon, but please grab your belongings and leave through the front door. Thank you."

Once we reached my office, I was allowed to call my attorney, Walter Bartell Nash, Jr. Walter's office was on Summer Street, two blocks over from Bogart's. Fortunately, he was at his desk. I told him what was happening and requested his presence at the bar to help witness the search and protect my rights.

Walter said he would be there in five minutes; he arrived in four. Limp, cane and all.

Over the next couple hours, as Nash watched, officers searched the office, the bar, the patio and all related areas for evidence of cocaine. Also present was a representative from the Marysville office of the State Alcoholic Beverage Control—taking notes and examining the evidence.

The search continued until about 5:00 P.M. and the evidence bag held six bindle papers with a white powder residue on them, believed to be cocaine, as well as four straws with similar white residue on them as well.

That was it. That's all!

Kane walked in Bogart's that day believing he would find a cache´ of coke, not just a few pieces of paper and a handful of straws. He was clearly pissed that the Search of the Century was so uneventful, but their entire theory was flawed from the start. There never was any large amount of cocaine in Bogart's, or my home, to be found. I was a user and abuser, never a distributor.

My coke friends used to joke that I wouldn't know an eight-ball from a curve-ball.

Chapter Twenty-Six

Walter Bartell Nash Jr. was in his mid-fifties—a slender, fragile man with certain feminine idiosyncrasies. He was not an especially attractive man. He had a shaved bald head, a rosacea skin condition that also created a dry, flaky scalp that fell off on to his suit like dandruff. Also, as a child, he had polio that resulted in his left leg being two inches shorter than the right. He supported his walk with a polished thick manzanita cane but could walk and maneuver as well as anyone on the street. Walter had a brilliant legal mind and had been a Quartz County District Attorney and Superior Court Judge in his early career. Although he never lost an election, he returned to private practice in the early seventies for reasons never made completely clear to his voting public.

While in private practice he remained very connected to the DA's office. He could get things done, and his phone calls were returned, which is why I called Walter when I needed the best. He was, according to his peers, one of the most respected jurists in Northern California.

He walked into Bogart's that fateful May day in 1987 dressed in an expensive grey pin-striped suit, blue shirt, pink and blue tie, and black wing-tip shoes. He looked every bit the legal pro that he was, and he kept a careful eye on the cops conducting the search. There would be no planting of evidence with Walter Nash on the premises.

After Walter witnessed the search at Bogart's, Chief Kane told him, "We need to take your client up to his home where the sheriff's drug investigation officers are waiting."

Walter nodded, knowing that the warrant included my home

and vehicles.

"No one's up at the house," the chief told him, "and they don't want to break down the door, so I need your client to let them in and be present when they search the house. You're welcome to be present as well, of course."

"Appreciate that Chief," Nash responded. "Very thoughtful of you."

I was taken from Bogart's in handcuffs, escorted out to Commerce Street and placed in the back seat of Kane's patrol car. Walter said his car was parked nearby and that he'd be right behind us. He reminded me to say nothing on the trip up to my house and that he would be there to watch as the search was being conducted.

We then drove to my home on Red Rock Road, where two deputy sheriffs were waiting. Detective Lieutenant Tom Sadler and Detective Sergeant Mark Evans were known around Quartz County as Batman and Robin, and word on the street was that they were thorough and relentless. If they didn't find what the warrant described, then the item wasn't there. Period.

When we arrived, I was taken from the back seat, cuffs were removed, and I unlocked the front door to my house. Sadler and Evans entered and began the search. And as he had promised, Nash arrived just as I was opening the front door.

Because my house was outside the city limits, Chief Kane and his officers remained outside. Kane and Mayor Arthur Fenwick, who was back at City Hall nervously awaiting the outcome, didn't want to do anything that might negatively affect the case they were trying to build. My house was outside the chief's jurisdiction, and a former district attorney and judge was present to observe the search, so the chief and his men leaned against their patrol cars, pulled out their packs of cigarettes, and waited.

In my bedroom, Lieutenant Sadler found an empty gun holster in the nightstand drawer and asked, "Do you have a gun that fits this thing?"

I walked over to the waterbed and began to reach down between the bed and the bed frame, but Sadler immediately stopped me.

"We'll get it, Davis, not you," he said, adding, "Is it loaded?"

"Of course, it's loaded. What good is an empty gun?" I said just as Sadler removed the snub-nose .38 Special from the bed, looked at it, then returned the weapon to the place where I kept it handy. The search was for drugs and drug paraphernalia, not a fully licensed handgun.

Batman and Robin searched the house for over an hour while I sat on the sofa in the living room and Nash bird-dogged the deputies. When the search was complete, nothing of substance had been found. White powder residue in a couple of places, but nothing to indicate or imply that I was a major drug dealer or supplier. Hell, they couldn't even prove I was a frequent user.

At that point, Kane came inside at Sadler's request and walked up to where Walter Nash and I were standing.

"We found enough in our search of the bar to implicate you in cocaine use and possible distribution, so we're going to book you and ask the judge to set bail at an appropriate amount."

I was stunned. Speechless. They hadn't found enough coke residue to create a pinch of the stuff, and I was going to be arrested?

What the hell?

"Will you be making the arrangements for bail, Mr. Nash?"

"Yes, I will, Chief," Walter told him. "In fact, I'll have it arranged by the time you finish with booking. But right now, I want to speak to my client in private; it will only take a couple of minutes."

"I guess we can grant you a couple of minutes, so why don't you two step out on the back patio where you can talk in private, and we can keep an eye on your client. He is, after all, a prisoner headed to the county jail."

"He won't be in there for long, trust me," Walter said as we walked outside.

"Take a deep breath and relax, Adrian. It's a bogus bust," he assured me. "They found nothing, and they're embarrassed. They realize the city and county could both be open to a civil suit, but they want you booked and in the system."

"Why?" I asked. "If I'm clean, I'm clean. Right?"

"The system stinks, Adrian, but we'll beat this thing."

From the look in his eyes, I was confident Walter was correct.

"Tomorrow they'll probably file a report for the DA's review; then we'll see what happens next. Might be a few days; maybe a week or longer. In the meantime, don't talk to anyone about this and I'll see what I can learn from my contacts. Be patient, be calm, and don't do anything to give them any ammunition they can load in their guns. Understand?"

"I do, Walter, but they really fucked up this time, and I want to even the score."

"Let me handle this," he said with an assuring pat on shoulders. "Go to booking with them, stay calm, be a gentleman, don't argue with anyone at the jail, and we'll talk tomorrow."

"Okay," I promised him. "We'll see you tomorrow."

"By the way," Walter added as we walked back inside the house, "You at least dodged one bullet."

"How's that?"

"The search has ended, you're going to be taken to the jail for booking, and they didn't bother to search your vehicles."

We both laughed, which puzzled Chief Kane and the two deputies who waited inside the house, out of hearing range.

It was one of the last good laughs I would have for a long, long time.

***

Three days later, I left the bar early and arrived home just after two o'clock in the afternoon. It was a warm Friday; weekend fun was about to begin, and I needed a nap before the sun went down and thirsty hoards stormed the door at Bogart's.

As soon as I got out of the car, I knew something was wrong. I'm no psychic, mind you, but I felt some bad vibes. Bad energy. A premonition. Call it what you want, but I knew something was wrong about the house.

I was walking toward the front door when I noticed a metal screen had been removed from a window and placed on the porch. Also, the window was open, so I knew someone had broken in. Then it dawned on me that since I was arriving home much earlier than normal, an intruder might still be inside.

I slowly opened the front door and immediately noticed that my camera was missing from a hook on the foyer coatrack. And when I walked in the master bedroom, a large glass container into which I dropped my spare change each night, was empty and on the bedroom floor. The container was huge and had been nearly full when I left the house that morning. It represented at least six or seven hundred dollars in coin, maybe more, that I'd been planning to cash-in at the bank.

Nothing else seemed to have been disturbed or missing. The house had not been ransacked nor searched. Only spare change and a camera were missing. An odd burglary, for sure.

Instinctively, I checked to make sure my gun was still secured in the bed. It wasn't. That was very strange because no one knew that I kept the gun in the bed. Then I realized that at least two other people did know: Lieutenant Sadler and Sergeant Evans from the sheriff's office. Maybe they told Chief Kane about it, or one of the other officers?

I didn't know who had taken the gun, camera, and coins, but

whoever did this was in and out very quickly—and knew exactly what they were looking for and where they could find it.

The camera and coins, easy. But the gun? Not so easy. Very strange.

I called the sheriff's office and reported the burglary. They sent a patrol car with a female officer who took the report and began snapping pictures of the scene. The deputy asked if I had any idea who might have broken in. I explained my theory about Sadler and Evans—the only two I knew with certainty who would have known where to find the .38 Special.

Maybe I should have kept my suspicions to myself because it was obvious that the comment had fallen on deaf ears. The female deputy sheriff standing in my house taking pictures of the break-in scene worked for the sheriff who sent Batman and Robin to search my house three days earlier. Was she going to tell her supervisor what I had said about Sadler and Evans? And was that supervisor going to tell the sheriff?

I wish Nash had been there that afternoon because he would never have let me point a finger at the two deputy sheriffs. Never.

***

By Labor Day 1987, I was persona non-grata in Gold City—the place of my birth. People who used to be regulars at Bogarts were staying away in droves. More than once I noticed "friends" cross the street as I walked toward them, pretending they didn't see me or had business to attend to on the other side of the street.

Sure. You bet.

Since the arrest, business at Bogart's had been reduced by half. No longer were the downtown business and professional clientele coming in after work or on weekends to meet friends and enjoy the great drinks. The lively atmosphere that Bogart's was famous for had turned dark and gloomy.

Not enough five-dollar bills were being collected at the door to pay the band. I didn't need the extra overhead, but I didn't want the public to think that anything was wrong, so I kept booking bands and smiling when I handed them a check that I hoped would get through the bank without bouncing.

The regular weekend business and dance crowd, as well as the out-of-town weekend business that used to pack the joint, began to dry up like a prune left to bake in the sun. In fact, the summer of 1987 was so slow I had to let half my staff go. I found myself working more and more shifts behind the bar, and they were, for the most part, lonely, depressing shifts.

Business sucked, and my cash flow was taking a big hit. I had no idea where I was going with the business—much less my ongoing legal problems.

One afternoon, standing behind the bar waiting for someone to walk in and maybe buy a pint of beer, or at least a soda, Walter Nash called, and we agreed to meet the next morning to discuss a plea offer from the District Attorney's office.

Maybe, I thought, just maybe, I could get my personal nightmare behind me and move on with life. Maybe the wind that howled while I struggled to sleep would turn to a light breeze.

Maybe the nightmares would end, and pleasant dreams would return? Or maybe it was time to pull the plug and move on.

Chapter Twenty-Seven

The next morning, right on schedule, I walked into Walter's office with a high degree of optimism. He greeted me in the reception area with a handshake and an offer of coffee or tea. I declined both.

Nash was wearing an expensive light-brown suit with powder-blue shirt and a blue-and-yellow striped tie. Very dapper. Very smart. He began talking as I took my seat in front of his desk.

"They're determined to nail you to the proverbial cross, Adrian, so I worked out a deal that will keep us out of court and keep this incident as quiet as such things can be kept in a small town. And I think it's the best we can hope for."

"Which is...?"

"You will plead *nolo contrendre* to a minor misdemeanor charge of 'being in a place where a controlled substance was consumed.' It isn't a felony, just a misdemeanor, and you won't be named as the user. I agreed to the lesser charge in order to protect your liquor license and put this behind you."

"I can't believe this shit, Walter. I thought you were going to tell me this whole thing was going away with a slap on the back of the hand."

Nash leaned back in his chair and shrugged, then threw his arms in the air as if to say, "That's the way it is, fellow; that's the way it is. And basically, this is a slap on the hand."

"It's been over five months since Pittman looked in my office window, over four months since the arrest, and what the hell did they get from the search? Nothing. A few straws and bindle papers with residue on 'em; that's what."

"I know, Adrian, I know. It was a bullshit bust, but they did find enough evidence to justify the arrest. Coupled with Pittman's observation, that's why we're in the predicament we're in today."

"What do you mean *we*, Walter? I'm the only one in what you could call a 'predicament'—not you. And we both know the search and arrest was one big set up."

Nash nodded in agreement and offered another "I'm sorry" shrug.

"As far as protecting my liquor license, it's been established that my upstairs office was never part of the premises covered by the liquor license. That area was beyond the scope of ABC's jurisdiction. So, from where I sit, it's a case of no harm, no foul."

"Wish it was that easy, Adrian, but this is not going away without a conviction for something. Believe me, accepting a misdemeanor charge beats the hell out of a jury trial that could result in a felony conviction and possible jail time."

I was pissed, and my attorney knew it. Nash had assured me that everything would be fine, but now he was telling me I had to plead guilty to a sham search and seizure. I was looking for help from Nash, and all I was getting were more problems tossed my way.

"So, what's the deal?" I asked.

"The DA has agreed to three years supervised probation, a thousand-dollar fine, and forty hours of community service."

"What? Hell, Walter, a first-time felony conviction gets softer sentences than that. You were DA for ten years, for Christ's sake. You're known around the county as the attorney who gets things done. And you're telling me you can't do better than this?"

Walter leaned forward; elbows propped on his desk.

"No, I can't," he said looking straight at me. "You've made some real enemies up in the courthouse since your arrest. You've been bitching about the search and critical of law enforcement. You've made some allegations about the break-in at your house that you can't prove. So, if you don't take the deal, the DA will file two felony charges against you. One, for distributing and supplying cocaine to others, and two, for maintaining a business for the purposes of an illicit enterprise."

I tried my best to keep control of my emotions but failed. "It's bullshit, Walter; total bullshit."

"Call it bullshit, horseshit, or chickenshit—call it whatever shit you want—but if you're found guilty on either felony charge, it's bye-bye liquor license. Also, you need to know that they have two witnesses who will testify that you supplied them with cocaine. Didn't sell it to them, mind you, but supplied it."

"Bullshit," I angrily responded.

"Maybe so, but I suspect that a conservative Quartz County jury will believe Kane and the rest of our local boys in blue—and that means they'll convict you."

"But, Walter, none of this crap is true."

"Doesn't matter if it's true or not. What matters is how a jury will see things and who they'll believe."

"Maybe we'll get lucky?" I told him.

"Hell, of a gamble, Davis. And as your attorney—and friend—it's not what I would advise," Nash said in a fatherly tone. I nodded in agreement. Reality was beginning to sink in.

"Okay, let's talk about another issue; let's talk money," Nash said. "If the DA files felony charges and you insist on taking this to trial, I'll need another twenty-five grand from you—to start—and maybe more down the road. Come on, Adrian, I know you don't have twenty-five-grand right now, nor will you have it anytime soon. And I'm sure as hell not going to take on a felony case pro bono just because you've shoved thousands of dollars up your nose and now, you're nearly broke."

He was right, of course, but the fact remained that this whole affair was a setup, with orders coming from City Hall to get me and put me out of business. Why? Because they could.

"Do us both a favor," Walter said. "Take the deal and put this thing behind you. Get on with trying to put your business back on its feet. Folks can be forgiving, in time, if you're at least a little bit humble about the error of your ways."

"What about the probable cause issue? Pittman had no business being up on my roof, in the middle of the night, looking in my office window without a search warrant."

"You're right, but Judge Barbara Worthington has already ruled on our motion to suppress based on an illegal search. Of course, the search was bogus, but you'll never convince a jury that the fuzzy-cheeked Ralph Pittman did something illegal."

"You mean, *you* will never convince them?"

"Whatever," the eminent attorney said, growing impatient with my resistance to the plea deal. "But because of the burglary reports you were filing with the cops; Judge Worthington ruled that Pittman had probable cause to check and see why there were lights on in the office of a closed business at three o'clock in the morning. She ruled that the sergeant's observations were valid, and no search warrant was needed to make the observation. Agree with it or not, it's final. And so, too, is the DA's offer."

"What burglaries? Give me a break, Walter. Pittman, or some other cop, conducted those break-ins in order to justify their bogus observation of my office. All done so they could seek a valid search warrant from a judge. They trespassed, for Christ's sake. *They* broke the law, not me. It's a fuckin' conspiracy."

"It might have happened just the way you say, but we can't prove it, can we?"

"Maybe we can't prove it, but this deal of yours sucks, Walter. Sure, it's only a misdemeanor, but is this the right thing to do?" I asked as my voice rose an octave and my anger continued to brew and boil.

Reaching into his desk, Nash pulled out a stapled set of documents.

"Here's how sure I am, my friend," he said, handing me the papers. "It's already been typed up. Go ahead, look it over and let me know if you have any questions. I'll be back in a few minutes."

Rising from his desk, Nash left me alone in his office while I studied the documents. There was a lot of legal mumbo-jumbo, but the bottom line was as Walter had described it: a misdemeanor *nolo contrendre* plea: In other words, guilty. *Guilty?* Guilty!

Nash nodded to his secretary as he reentered the office. Then, once seated at his desk, Walter leaned back in his chair and looked at me with a confident smile.

"So, what's it going to be, my friend?" he asked.

"Well, I hired you for the best advice and guidance I could get, so I'll take the deal. I'm pissed that this is the best you could do, but I guess I really don't have a choice, do I?"

"No, you don't."

Then he opened a side drawer of his desk and pulled out a bottle of 12-year-old Glenlivet Scotch. He set two water glasses on the desk, poured a generous shot into each glass and handed one to me. Then he raised his glass in the fashion of a toast and said, "May the Lord keep you in His hand, and never close His fist too tight on you."

I held my glass high and replied, "His fist is already too tight. It's around my fuckin' neck."

The Glenlivet tasted great, but the plea agreement was foul and sour.

"I'll take care of everything," Nash assured me. "Don't worry; just get on with your life and stay out of trouble."

I nodded, slowly rose to my feet, then reached across the desk and shook Walter's hand. But as I started toward the door, I paused and looked back.

"About the plea bargain, Walter. I do have a question."

"Okay, what is it?" he asked.

"It's right there in paragraph thirteen," I said, pointing at the signed document he was about to take to the district attorney.

"Something about violating the conditions of the probation. It says if I violate any condition—any condition of the probation agreement—the deal is dead, and the DA can file the felony charges against me at their discretion."

"That's a standard condition; nothing unusual about it."

"Maybe so, but I thought the whole purpose behind taking this, or any plea bargain, was to make certain I'd never have to deal with it again?"

"And you won't," he replied. "You have nothing to worry about, I promise."

Walter was smiling, but not me.

"That's easy for you to say, but if I were to violate any of the conditions I just agreed to, this whole nightmare could come back to bite me in the ass again. Right?"

"Nothing's going to come back to haunt you, Adrian. I'm on top of this and, like you said when we first discussed the case, you're paying for my experience, guidance, and knowledge."

"I remember saying that, sure, but at the time I was confident you were going to make it go away. Forever. Now I've got a litany of things I can't do or else they'll bust my ass and haul me off to jail again. That's not what I had in mind when I said I was looking to you for guidance."

"Trust me, it's over," Nash assured me once again. "Go back to work, sleep well tonight, start fresh tomorrow. In a couple years, we'll sit at Bogart's and have a good laugh about this whole fiasco—and the money you saved by taking their offer."

"Don't forget the thousands I paid you already, OK?"

"Sure, it was expensive, but all things considered, I got you a hell of a deal. It was money well spent."

I turned back toward the office door, gave Walter a quick wave, then returned to Bogart's. Yes, I was a free man, and there would be no trial, but what had I just signed?

Was I going to keep dancing with the devil? Time would tell.

Chapter Twenty-Eight

Visiting and having dinner with Poppy became a frequent escape for me. Her condo was my secret getaway pad—a safe house of sorts—where I could relax, confident the cops wouldn't be knocking on the door with handcuffs at the ready. It became almost like a second home, a hideout. And to keep it that way, our friendship and the personal relationship had to remain a well-kept secret.

On the night I'm about to describe, she answered the door with her usual big smile, as beautiful as ever. She was dressed in a yellow skirt and light-green turtleneck top. I had on my usual jeans, tennis shoes, a dark-blue V-neck pullover sweater and my favorite teal coat.

We enjoyed a couple of bottles of fine cabernet with our dinner of rigatoni pasta laden with my family recipe for Bolognese sauce. Also, Poppy fixed a fantastic Caesar salad. Then we settled in on the sofa with a gram of cocaine for dessert and a full bottle of Frangelico liqueur.

The dinner entree would change from time to time, but dessert always remained the same.

We talked about many topics during these marathon dinner/dessert evenings. No one knew we were together, hidden from downtown Gold City and wanting nothing but our own company.

I wasn't ready to visit a psychologist, much less a psychiatrist—a professional who could help—but being together, talking for hours, was so fulfilling that I began calling her Doc Poppy. She had become my therapist; my confidante.

She was beautiful and sexy and smart to a fault. In fact, her intellect and insight were almost scary. She once told me, "A women's beauty is a disguise. Intellect is what matters." On this night, for some reason, we began talking about God and how our belief in His existence, or not, had affected our respective lives. It wasn't the kind of conversation I had anticipated we'd be having with our coke and liqueur, but if that's what she wanted to talk about, it was fine with me.

After she told me about her longtime abiding faith in God, I asked, "Have you ever been mad at Him because you were born without legs that functioned? Mad that your life has been so physically difficult and challenging?"

"I've never looked at myself as being disabled, Adrian. My parents wouldn't allow it, and neither would I. Sure, there were times growing up when I wanted to cry—and I did when I couldn't go out and play or do what the other kids were doing. But my parents made sure I had other things to fill my life, such as playing the piano, singing lessons, and private tutoring to improve my education."

"Well, Poppy, they sure did an excellent job of that."

"Yes, they did. And they played different games with me after dinner: monopoly, chess, and cribbage, to name a few. They insisted I take care of myself without their help as best I could, knowing that someday I would need to be on my own, fending for myself. Dad even taught me to shoot a gun to protect myself, and I have a licensed twenty-five caliber semi-automatic next to me in the wheelchair at all times, even now."

"I would never have imagined you as a modern-day Annie Oakley, and I sure can't picture you with a gun in your hands."

"And I'd use it if I had to," she said.

"You'd shoot someone who looked to harm you?"

"Without blinking an eye, big boy, so don't try to take advantage of me, OK?" she laughed. "I'm a good shot, and I aim low if you know what I mean."

She stared below my belt as both of us laughed at the implication.

"What about you, Adrian? Do you believe?"

"I believe deeply," I told her.

"Why?" she wanted to know. Just like a kid who is never satisfied with a simple yes or no answer, she had to ask, "Why?"

"I've always said that I've been lucky all my life. But, truthfully, I believe God has been watching over me, especially during some of the dumbed-down days when I did stupid things or made bad personal decisions. Great combination, Lady Luck, and God. I even have proof of Him watching over me."

"Proof?" she asked.

"Proof, at least in my eyes and in my heart, and that's all that matters, right?"

"I'm curious," she said, cocking her head ever so slightly and looking at me in a quizzical sort of way.

"I've never told this story to anyone before, and only one other person knows about it."

"Who else?" she asked, knowing I probably wouldn't tell her.

"The guy who shared the adventure with me," I answered. "It was an agonizing seventy-two hours for both of us, but eventually there was a resolution beyond any expectation."

We both took a drink of our hazelnut liqueur and snorted another line of coke.

I was comfortable in Poppy's presence and had never been bashful about candid, open conversations with her.

"It was early May 1964," I began. "A Friday."

"You actually remember the day of the week?" she asked. "I'm impressed."

"And I'm serious," I told her.

Poppy nodded, and I began to explain how I found God. It was not our usual after-dinner banter, that's for sure.

***

It was a beautiful spring day about a month before Quartz Union High School graduation. I was a junior, and many of us cut school that day, mostly juniors and seniors, for a keg party at the Yuba River.

About the time school was ending for the day we had enough beer and sun and thought we would head for the A&W Root Beer joint near campus, meet some classmates and tell them what they missed by not attending the all-day beer bash.

Brad Hamell, son of a respected Gold City dentist, had driven his blue-and-white 1955 Chevy Bel Air coupe to the party but was too drunk to drive home. He decided the smart thing to do was get a ride with his girlfriend.

Jeff Hutchinson—Hutch for short—told Hamell not to worry, that he and I would make sure his pride and joy got home safely. I drove because Hutch was drunker than I was.

Everything seemed normal enough, but I knew something Brad and Hutch didn't: My driver's license had been suspended for too many moving violations. I knew I shouldn't have been driving, but my rationale was that although I didn't have a valid license, at least I wasn't as drunk as my buddy Hutch—proving once again that teenage reasoning should never be confused with smart, logical reasoning.

Once in town, taking a short-cut and not paying attention to the speedometer, I was flying along on a narrow, residential street, oblivious to the fact that a family was casually playing in their front yard: mom, dad, two small kids and a fluffy white dog—off-leash.

As we neared the family, the dog darted out into the street, directly in front of me. It was too late—especially at the speed we were traveling—and the dog was struck full-force by the car.

Seeing the lifeless canine rolling end-over-end down the street in the rearview mirror as I drove on was an image I'll never forget.

The entire family immediately ran into the street to comfort their dog, but I assumed it was hopeless. The mixed-breed family pet wasn't moving as I watched in the rear-view mirror.

The parents waved and yelled at us to stop, and the kids screamed when they saw their beloved white dog—bloody and still—on the black asphalt. Hutch started screaming at me to turn around and go back to the scene of the accident. That would have been the right thing to do, I know, but I wasn't about to go back.

No way.

A few minutes later, still headed to the A&W in after-school traffic, Hutch and I spotted a 1962 Corvette approaching on the other side of the street. As I looked at the Corvette, my attention was drawn away from the car in front of me—a late-model Cadillac Eldorado being driven by a woman. There was a little girl in the passenger seat. Bam! I ran smack into the rear of the Cadillac at about twenty miles per hour.

The women pulled over to the side of the road and, as she did so, I spotted a big dent on the trunk of her car as I pulled on to a side street. Maybe a foot or more in length, and it was deep. Since I had hit her from the rear, I knew I would be held accountable for the accident and the damage.

Naturally, the woman's attention was focused on her daughter. I'd seen enough, so I punched that blue-and-white Chevy, and we began speeding away down the side street. Hutch hollered at me to stop; said I was totally nuts and that we were in big trouble. He was right—on both counts.

I heard Hutch, but I kept my foot on the gas and ignored him. I drove up over Rattlesnake Ridge to the other side of Gold City, to Hamell's house, and dropped off the Chevy in his driveway just as we had promised. Despite the rear-ender, there was no visible damage to Hamell's front bumper or grill. Back then, of course, bumpers were steel, not plastic. Hutch spotted a small splotch of paint that had transferred from the Caddy's trunk to the Chevy's grill, but it came off with a stiff rub.

We walked home from Hamell's place and swore to each other to keep our mouths shut about the afternoon. The entire afternoon.

I didn't sleep that night. In a matter of hours, I had cut school, had two hit-and-run accidents in less than fifteen minutes of each other, was driving on a suspended license and, to top it off, I was drunk.

I wasn't sure what would await a sixteen-year-old, hit-and-run drunk driver who had killed a dog and banged into a Caddy, but I knew I was in deep shit. And knew I would be buried in that shit if I got caught.

I was facing arrest, probably lockdown time at Juvenile Hall, suspension from high school, fines, damage costs, insurance problems, continued suspended driver's license till God knows when, my dad's scorn, and... The list went on, and I knew that unlike my other episode with the law, the previous year, I wouldn't get out of this one. This was serious stuff.

I had a weekend job at a local grocery store in those days, so I went to work the next morning as if nothing had happened. Hutch popped in about noon, and we agreed that only a miracle could save our asses at that point. Surely, there were witnesses; kids were getting out of school. And once the cops knew what to look for, how many blue-and-white '55 Chevy Bel Air coupes could there be in our small rural county.

I needed to talk to someone, but who? Who could I go to with the truth? Who would listen to my explanation? Better yet, how would telling anyone help get me out of this mess?

So, very early Sunday morning, I crawled out of bed and headed for the one place I knew I could tell my story without recrimination or scorn. I hadn't been to church since Catechism.

I walked down to the Episcopal Church on Bridge Street, not far from my home. Sunday services would not begin for two hours, so I walked into the church, got on my knees, alone and frightened, and prayed for the miracle of a lifetime.

I prayed for forgiveness. I prayed for help. I didn't know exactly what I was praying for and couldn't even imagine the kind of miracle I needed at that moment. I just said, "God, only you can get me out of this. How I don't know. I probably don't deserve it, but please help me anyway. Please."

With that, I got off my knees, left the church and walked back into the morning sunlight. Talking with God had brought some relief, but I nevertheless felt an unsteady peace as I headed home back up Bridge Street.

How long would it be before I would know if God had been listening? And even if He had been listening to my plea, did I deserve His merciful grace?

Those were questions only God could answer, and He wasn't talking. At least not at that moment.

Chapter Twenty-Nine

Michael Davis knew his dad had an abiding faith in God, so going to a church to pray early on a Sunday morning in 1964 didn't seem unusual. But the reason for his prayers was a real shocker—something he had never heard about. He did know, however, that his dad's wild ride on a spring day was the sort of youthful folly that needed spiritual intervention. He leaned back in his first-class seat, California far behind him, and continued reading.

***

"So, what happened?" Poppy asked when I finished telling her my story of the worst day of my teenage years.

"What happened was a miracle—no other way to describe it," I explained to Poppy that the miracle began the next day.

Monday morning. Hutch and I were standing around on campus just before the first-period bell rang when someone told us Brad Hamell had been in an accident on his way to school.

After we heard where it had happened, we decided to cut school and check on Hamell's condition and, of course, the baby-blue Chevy. Not being sure if he was still with police at the scene of the accident or at the hospital with injuries, we jumped in Hutch's car and headed toward where the accident had occurred. When we got there, we could see it had been a head-on collision—apparently caused by Brad. No one appeared hurt, but both cars had extensive damage.

"The bizarre thing was, Hamell wasn't driving his Chevy," I told Poppy. "Turns out he had been driving his sister's 1958

Plymouth.

She was home for the weekend from San Jose State College, so Brad 'borrowed' his sister's car and was driving it to school when the collision occurred."

"So far this sounds like teenage idiocy."

"It was Poppy, but even idiots get lucky sometimes, or are blessed with miracles."

"And the miracle was...?"

"Because his sister's car was going to be out of commission and probably totaled, Brad agreed to give her the Chevy to return to school. So, she drove Brad's Chevy back to San Jose State that afternoon, never again to see the light of day in Gold City. Later that summer, Dr. Hamell bought Brad and his sister newer cars to replace the Chevy, and the totaled Plymouth."

Poppy shrugged, not sure of what I was telling her.

"It meant the cops were never able to locate that blue-and-white fifty-five Chevy in or around town. And that meant that as long as Hutch and I kept the mess to ourselves, we were home free."

"Did you?"

"Sure did," I laughed without trying to make what we did seem a joke or trivial, which it certainly wasn't. "For the remainder of May, until summer vacation, Hutch and I watched police cars routinely drive through the student parking lot. They were looking for a certain fifty-five Chevy, but we knew it was in a student parking lot at San Jose State and not the lot at Quartz County High School."

"What luck," she said.

"Luck or Providence?" I responded.

"Amen." Poppy laughed.

"The day after Brad's sister left town with the evidence, Hutch turned to me after school and said, 'Buddy, that must have been one hell of a prayer.' I looked at him, and we began laughing, then we laughed even harder as we drove out of the school parking lot on to Prospect Road." We had escaped the madness and laughter felt good despite the seriousness of our foolish escapade.

I then told Poppy about another classmate of ours, Janette Town, who drove a blue-and-white 1955 Chevy, just like Brad's, except she drove a sedan and Hamell's car was a coupe. For a month following the accident, Janette told us she was getting stopped by every cop, highway patrolman and sheriff's deputy in the county. They would look at her front bumper, checking for a dent, some paint smears or some other sign that it had been in an accident, then let her go without any explanation.

"You know what the ironic part of the story is, Poppy? All the police had to do was ask Town—or almost any other kid in school – –who else drove a fifty-five blue-and-white Chevy and they would have told them that Brad Hamell owned such a car. But no one ever asked."

"Adrian, other than hitting that poor dog, your story of finding God seems redemptive and honest, and I believe you're serious about your faith."

"I'm very serious about there being a higher power," I told her. "Maybe there a isn't God as described in the Bible, but I believe there's something out there that watches over us because only something God-like could have performed such a miracle in so short a time. So, yes, I believe and have put my faith and hopes in His hands ever since that horrific day many years ago. He doesn't always answer or respond, but I know He's there."

"And He's been there for both of us," Poppy said as she reached for the Frangelico.

Our decision to drink and do drugs might have represented a gross violation of everything God wanted from His followers, but Poppy and I were mortal humans, and He wasn't.

He gave all of us free will, and we were merely taking advantage of His gift.

Chapter Thirty

Two nights later, about 3:00 A.M., I was alone, sitting at the bar pouring myself a shot of tequila from a bottle I was quickly emptying. Bogart's was closed, and the dark, dreary atmosphere of the place matched my own desolate mood.

I knew I had to shake the cobwebs and get reasonably straight before driving home, so I unlocked the front door and stepped outside into a refreshing rain. As I stood on the sidewalk, enjoying the downpour, I could see a police patrol car coming down Commerce Street.

Seeing a cop car slowly headed toward Bogart's made me nervous, but then I noticed Sergeant Tom Cooper was behind the wheel.

Cooper was a twenty-year Army veteran—an MP before retiring and joining the Gold City Police Department in the late seventies. He was a tall, slender man with a full head of hair, a wrinkled face that showed the years of military service, and a snarly smile that struck fear into the heart of anyone he stopped for running a stop sign or staggering home after a night on the town.

I had always gotten along fine with Cooper. I didn't consider him a friend, mind you, but I could talk to him, relate to him, and have a pleasant, respectful conversation.

Having recognized Cooper that rainy morning, I stepped out onto Commerce Street to get his attention. Cooper saw me, pulled closer, then stopped and rolled down his window to talk.

"Seems a little wet out here, eh, Tom?"

"Yeah, Davis, and you've been drinkin' a little heavy, haven't you? Got a way home?"

"Yeah, sure, planned to sleep in the office for a couple of hours then drive home. But why should you care?"

"We've always gotten along, Adrian. Your lifestyle might be a bit different than mine, but that's OK. You do your thing, and I do mine. I just don't want to see you in any more trouble."

"Well, my *thing*, as you put it, has gotten me in a shit load of trouble, hasn't it?" I laughed, my clothes drenched and the rain pounding down hard on my head.

"Yeah, lately you've had your head up your ass, but I know what they did to you, and I doubt your life will ever be the same."

"They fucked me, Tom, that's what they did. They wanted to hurt me, and they succeeded. Your boss, the DA, and that fuckin' mayor—they flat-out fucked me."

I was full of anger and bitterness and began to pound the top of the patrol car with my fists while continuing to yell at Sergeant Cooper.

"They fucked me, Tom, they fucked me. You know it, and I know it, and there isn't a thing I can do about it. And they're going to get away with it, aren't they?"

I was drunk and knew it and should have had the good sense to go back inside Bogart's, but I kept shouting, over and over again: "They fucked me, Tom, they fucked me!"

Cooper patiently sat in the patrol car and let me vent the rage and frustration I was taking out on the car's roof.

"You know what they found with that search warrant, Tom? Do you know what they found?"

Cooper nodded. He had read Pittman's report; he knew it had been a sham bust.

"Nothing. Nothing, that's what they found. Then they conspired to cover Chief Kane's ass after the search warrant proved to be a bust. They got me, man—and the bad publicity is killing my business. Just killing it."

By then it was difficult to know whether it was rain or tears running down my face, but I knew I looked like a mess to Cooper.

He knew I was drunk. Too drunk to drive legally.

Cooper looked up and said, "Yes, Adrian, they did a number on you. But we can't erase what has happened, so get in and let me take you home."

"No, I can get home all right, I really can, but thanks."

"OK, but I'll follow you to the city limits. After that, you're on your own."

I went inside the bar, turned off everything that needed turning off, then locked the front door and walked up the street toward my Jeep. I needed sleep; I wanted to get home and go to bed. I wanted a woman as well—Poppy, Shelly, Paris, the Cupid Angel, or anyone willing to deal with me while I was in such a pathetic, brooding mood. But for now, I guess I should be happy just to get home and hopefully surrender to deep sleep.

Sergeant Cooper did what he said he would do. He kept me in view as I drove down Commerce Street and headed up Red Rock Road. When I reached the city limits, Tom flickered his headlights then turned around and continued his night shift while I went home to a cold, empty bed.

But I couldn't get to sleep. All I could do was stare at the ceiling and think of how I had ruined my life over this expensive white powder. Expensive fool's gold served up on a platter.

"Just say no." That's what Nancy Reagan said. If only I would have continued to say no—no—no.

Chapter Thirty-One

Next morning, sober but still in a rage over the situation I was in, I stormed into Walter Nash's office without an appointment. He was at his desk when I brushed past his secretary and stood in front of him.

Walter reacted cautiously, rather than in a retaliatory or alarming way.

"Hey, Adrian, guess it's my turn to buy lunch, eh?"

"Screw lunch; I want to file a lawsuit. And I want to file it today, not tomorrow or next week. Understood?"

"File a suit? Who or what do you want to sue?" he calmly asked.

"The city. The county. And every son-of-a-bitch involved in this stinkin' deal."

Nash got up from his desk and walked toward me with a fake smile on his face.

"OK, I hear you," my attorney said, "so just settle down and tell me what's got you so upset."

"Hell, Walter, don't you know? Can't you see what's going on? The other day a city cop stopped me as I was coming down Bridge Street and took me to jail for a urine test. They said my probation officer had ordered the city to pick me up as soon as a cop spotted me. Can they do that kind of shit?"

"I know you're upset, Adrian. But, yes, they can pick you up and test you at random. And they can knock on your door whenever they want and search your home without a new warrant. I told you all that the day you signed the plea agreement. It's part of being on fully supervised probation."

Then he looked at me for a couple of seconds before asking, "You haven't done any drugs since you agreed to probation, have you?"

I lied and assured him that I was as clean as the parish priest. I drank too much, I admitted to him, but no drugs. No coke.

"Being as clean as our beloved parish priest may not be good enough," Nash laughed. "Father Sheehan likes a little pot with his evening brandy, so it's best you not use him as an example of drug abstinence."

I didn't laugh.

"I didn't sign on for this crap, Walter. I want to sue 'em. I want to sue 'em all."

Before Walter could respond, I raced out of his office, slamming the door behind me.

***

Years later, I learned that after our argument, Walter Nash picked up the phone and dialed a familiar number.

"Our boy's not cooperating," the esteemed barrister told the person at the other end of the call. "He's still flying off the handle, out of control, demanding I file suit against everyone but the City Hall janitor. I think he's still using and not thinking very clearly. It's time for an unannounced visit from his probation officer and make sure the guy finds what he's looking for. Hit him hard, OK? Knock Davis down for good."

When the former Superior Court Judge hung up the phone, he had a confident smile on his face—satisfied that everything would be taken care of.

"A conspiracy is everything that ordinary life is not," author Don DeLillo once said.

Three days after my visit to Nash's office, I was awaked very early in the morning with loud pounding on my front door. I glanced at the clock on the nightstand; it read 7:17 A.M. I stumbled out of bed, pulled on a pair of pants and went to answer the door. As quickly as I unlocked the door, it was forced open by several individuals. I was pushed aside by three uniformed police officers, then my probation officer entered and began looking around.

My PO's name was Gary Weddle, a short man with a textbook Napoleon Complex. He had a pale complexion, dark mustache, and wore black-rimmed bifocal glasses. His hair was quickly receding, so he used lots of hairspray to create a lacquered combover he must have thought looked good. It didn't. Weddle was forty but looked at least fifty.

"Okay, Adrian, it's time for another bottle sample. And while we're here, we'll take this opportunity to have a look around."

"Jesus, Gary, I'm clean. It's only been a couple of weeks or so since my last test."

"True, but we can test you whenever we want, as often as we want. And we can search this house whenever we want. You know that, Adrian. I'm sure Mr. Nash has explained that to you."

I didn't respond, except to shrug.

"You have a late night or something?" Gary asked.

"Yeah, I tended bar until two and got back home a half hour later. Any problem with that?"

"Nope, no problem. I'm just doing my job, Davis; just doing my job. So, go pee in the bottle."

Grabbing the plastic bottle from Weddle's hand, I headed toward the bathroom to give them the sample. An officer followed and stood behind me at the toilet as I filled the small bottle.

I was not going to pass this test without a miracle, and I figured I had used up many of my allotted miracles back in May of sixty-four.

This time, God wasn't listening.

The following week after pissing in a bottle and having the results come back positive, I was back in Nash's office, pacing the carpeted floor like a caged tiger. Walter sat at his desk, tapping a pencil against the corner of his empty coffee cup while telling me what was going to happen next.

"Anyway, that's it," he concluded. "Since the last two piss tests came back positive, the district attorneys reevaluated your case and is filing additional charges. Wish I could help, Adrian, but you apparently thought you were bullet-proof and could snort coke without getting caught. That was your decision, and filing additional charges is the DA's decision."

"This is B. S. Walter; I'm being railroaded, and we both knew this would happen. It's that paragraph thirteen in the plea agreement you had me a sign. It's come back to haunt me, although you said it wouldn't. You said everything was taken care of. Bullshit! You messed this up Walter; you gave me bad advice. Having me on this supervised probation is equivalent to a death sentence."

"I gave you the advice any competent attorney would have given, don't you understand? I did my best to keep you out of jail, but you had to go and screw it up—not me. If you want to shout at the guy who screwed things up, shout at the dumb ass you see in the mirror when you shave."

"What I know is, you helped them by letting me play right into their hands. They had control over me, and it was inevitable that they would get me sooner or later. I'm done. Finished."

"Give me a break, Adrian. They didn't control you; you controlled yourself. And look what happened. So, calm down and relax. You're only making things worse by losing any sense of self-discipline—something that's evident from your continuing use of cocaine."

"Fuck you, Walter," I shouted with contempt.

"Curse me if you want, but the local law enforcement community takes your cavalier attitude about cocaine as a personal affront. It's like you're laughing in their faces. So, this time it will not be as easy to negotiate with them. They want blood, and you're only making things worse."

"Worse? How the hell could things get any worse?"

Chapter Thirty-Two

That evening, angry but hungry, I walked from Bogart's to The Firehouse restaurant for dinner. Good food, good wine, and fantastic dessert options.

Although there were some small, two-top tables available, I decided to sit at the bar. I liked the camaraderie of having others to talk with, and especially enjoyed a stool at the bar when my favorite bartender, Stanley Church, was working.

When I approached the bar, Stan greeted me with a big smile. "This one has your name on it," he said, pointing to a stool at the end of the bar while pouring a glass of my favorite Cabernet Sauvignon and placing it within easy reach.

"How's it going, my friend?" Stanley asked.

"So, so," I told him, trying to force a friendly smile. "So, so, I guess. I think I'll have a little dinner to go with this glass of Cab."

"Pepper steak, medium, potatoes au gratin, and mixed vegetables?"

I smiled, more relaxed than when I first walked in. Stan knew my routine.

"Dinner salad or French onion soup tonight?"

"Think I'll have the soup tonight, thanks."

"Sure thing, buddy."

For the next hour or so, I enjoyed a great meal, a third glass of Cab, and had some innocuous conversations with customers on either side of where I was sitting. Some were regulars at Bogart's —or, in a couple of cases, former regulars—and some were part of the normal evening clientele for The Firehouse.

Some wanted to talk shop and ask how things were going with

the arrest, and others just wanted to say hello and move on with whatever they had planned for the evening. A few, who hadn't stepped foot in Bogart's since the search and all the bad media coverage that followed, tried every dodge they could think of to avoid passing by me on their way out, to include walking from the bar into the dining room and exiting from the dining room door.

Over the years, I have had a few good friends and a regiment of acquaintances. When a person goes through the kind of experiences I had, it's easy to see who the friends are and who the acquaintances are. So be it. I've always said, don't be a hypocrite. If you don't like me, stay the hell away from me, and I'll do the same for you. Life's too short for backstabbing hypocrites.

After finishing my meal, Stanley came over to top off my glass of wine and asked, "That do it for tonight, or would you like some dessert?"

"Dessert? Yeah, thanks, I need it."

I watched as Stan stepped out from behind the bar and walked down the hall to the restrooms. When he returned, I handed him my Gold American Express Card, and Stan quickly wrote up my bill. The guest check had the charges for dinner and wine. On the line where the customer usually writes in a tip amount, Stan had entered $120.00.

The $120.00 paid for the dessert. Some would say an excess amount for a tip, but Stanley always delivered in a timely fashion. "To ensure promptness" is, after all, where the term "tip" originated—and Stanley was always prompt.

I signed the receipt, nodded at Stan then got up and headed for the men's room.

When I got there, I locked the door and opened the cabinet under the sink. When I spotted the Ajax cleanser container, I picked it up and reached for the bindle with a gram of coke Stan had placed under the cleanser.

I opened the bindle, took my American Express Card from my shirt pocket and scooped out a pile for each nostril, then a second hit in each nostril. Then I wet my fingers in the sink and wiped the excess coke off my nose. I stared into the mirror, looking at myself and wondering when—*how*—I would have the self-discipline to stay away from the white powder and move on with my life.

On the one hand, I was depressed with life in general and worried that the district attorney was going to nail me to the cross. But on the other hand, I was feeling the buzz of coke and my attitude was changing by the second. I even had a smile on my face.

As I wiped my nose at the sink and brushed some residue off the front of my shirt, I had to laugh at what I saw in the mirror.

"Only in America can you charge your cocaine habit on your American Express card," I said to the smiling face I saw in the mirror. For sure, Karl Malden telling us, "Don't leave home without it," had a very different meaning for me than what the suits on Madison Avenue had in mind when they created it.

I then unlocked the men's room door, walked past the bar, said goodnight to Stan, and headed back to Bogart's to relieve Carla.

It was a typically slow night. No one stepped foot in the place after midnight, so I closed early, turned off the interior lights, and started drinking tequila and snorting more cocaine. Bernard Shaw once said, "Alcohol is the anesthesia by which we endure the operation of life." Obviously, Ol' Bernie never snorted a gram of cocaine in one sitting.

About four o'clock in the morning, I was still sucking on lime wedges and popping shots of tequila. I had just finished the bindle of coke Stanley had supplied me with at The Firehouse.

Bogart's, the business I had built, was on life support. Everything I ordered—beer, wine, booze, janitorial supplies, even bags of lemons and limes—were sent by suppliers with instructions to their drivers that it was strictly COD. Cash or cashier's check, or no delivery.

Checks drawn on the business bank account were no longer being accepted by vendors. Most of my credit cards were maxed out.

It was a pain in the ass, but I understood why I had to pay cash. I'd bounced a lot of checks, and no one had confidence in my ability to pay. I had cavalierly snorted thousands of dollars of cocaine up my nose, so having to pay cash for supplies was the sort of penance I could expect.

The truth was, the devil had knocked at my door, and I had let him in.

Now, coked-out, drunk, tired and confused, I began talking to myself. Actually, rambling more than talking. It was probably 4:30 A.M.—maybe later. What the hell did I know, and what the hell difference did it make?

"I know they're out there," I said to myself as I peered out the windows fronting Commerce Street. "Play it cool. They just want me to fuck up again."

Hearing a sound that I thought came from just outside the building, I jumped up from my barstool and raced to a window to see what was happening. I looked for two—maybe three—patrol cars, lurking in the dark, cops ready to storm the place.

I knew they were out there, waiting for me to unlock and open the front door to go home. I knew they wanted to bust me again for something. *Anything*. They were out there just waiting.

"You'd like to get me, wouldn't you?" I shouted. "I know you're out there, coppers. You can't-fool me. If you want me, come in here like real men and quit hiding in your cars."

I rubbed my face with both hands. I shook my head, trying to get my bearings. It was all so fucking hopeless. And worst of all, I was lonely. I had never been so alone.

I walked back to the bar and poured another tequila gold—a double—then I began shouting aloud again. I was beginning to yell like James Cagney in *White Heat*, standing on top of that storage tank shouting at the top of his lungs, "Look at me, Ma. I'm on the top of the world!"

Cagney's character suffered from paranoia—and, in hindsight, I realize I was suffering from the same thing. Hell, paranoia of a reasonable potency is an essential survival tool. Every drug addict eventually suffers from it and, in the haze of my paranoia, I was sure that the end was near. Very near.

If I screwed up again, I knew I would end up in a cell—and for a long time. That fucking mealy-mouth attorney of mine was a joke; a fucking joke. "Everything's going to be okay," he assured me. Bullshit! Meanwhile, I knew the cops were out there on Commerce Street that morning, waiting for me. Well, they weren't going to suck me into their dirty little trap. Not me. No sir, no way.

I blotted my face with a bar napkin then dropped my head on my right arm. The sound I uttered as I drifted off to sleep is difficult to define; it was a cross between laughter and unintelligible mumbling, mixed with tears. But at least I was asleep.

At 8:30 A.M.—with people walking by Bogart's on their way to a normal nine-to-five job—I was still asleep with my head resting on the bar, still convinced that my days of freedom were running out. My own stupidity? Yes, but I had lost control and was in need of help. Immediate help.

My ship was sinking, and not a life raft in sight.

***

A few days later, sitting in Nash's office, Walter said, "They're not budging, Adrian. You're going to need to plead to the probation violation-misdemeanor possession. They got you on a dirty piss test; you're toast. If you do that, they'll once again drop the two original felony charges of maintaining a place of business for illicit purposes and supplying a controlled substance to others. Otherwise, my friend, we will need to prepare for trial, and you'll somehow have to find thirty-five grand to pay for my services."

"I thought you said it would be twenty-five grand, not thirty-five?"

"It's getting more complicated by the day, Adrian, and you're not helping matters."

"If we went to trial—and I'm only saying if—how could a jury convict me of any of these charges? The DA's office has shit, Walter. They have nothing from the search that points to a felony, and so what if I pissed dirty. No big deal. Who cares?"

"Maybe you weren't listening last time we discussed this, Adrian, but I told you long ago that a conservative Quartz County jury would probably convict you in a heartbeat. You've had too much negative publicity, not to mention the whisper rumors going on behind your back."

"Why the hell have these charges been so hard to beat? I don't understand it, Walter. I just don't understand it," I shouted in frustration.

"It's because of your continued use of cocaine. You keep laughing in their face, so this whole thing continues to have a drip, drip, drip effect. People believe you're guilty of *something*."

"What about the drug diversion program I've heard about? I'd be willing to..."

"Sorry, guy, but that's only offered to first-time offenders. That ship has sailed."

"Well, then why didn't you get me into the diversion program after the first arrest? I needed help then and...I need it now; maybe now more than ever."

I was nearly screaming when I demanded, "Why didn't you get it for me when I needed it? Why are you telling me now that it's too late?"

"Because it wasn't offered," he said. "I tried to get you into the program, but the DA put the kibosh to it. It's as simple as that."

I looked at him, wanting to jump across his desk and strangle the bastard. I said, "I'm tired, Walter, and I want this to end. All of it. All the shit. Cut a deal so that these additional charges, whatever the hell they are, will all be misdemeanors, and the hell I'm living will go away."

"I think we can do that, Adrian," he said. "Take their offer; it's a violation of probation, not a big deal."

"I want to leave—get the hell out of Gold City. I want to get on with my life. They won, OK? I can sign the bar over to my dad and brother, and they'll do fine with it. I know where I can go to get my head straight and start over, but you've got to get this done for me. No felonies, or no deal. Understand, Walter."

Nash looked at me and said, "I'll try my best. I promise you."

"You need to do more than try, Walter," I pleaded. "You need to get a deal signed, sealed and delivered—and quickly."

"Leave it to me," he said as he rose to shake my hand and send me on my way.

And his final, hollow words still ring in my ears: "Trust me."

Chapter Thirty-Three

A few miles north of Gold City is a place called North San Juan—a wide spot in the road, really—a former gold mining camp that flourished in the nineteenth century and is now nothing more than a handful of old buildings on a stretch of State Highway 49 that leads to Downieville, in adjoining Sierra County.

In the daytime, North San Juan is quiet, but at night it can get pretty rowdy—especially inside a bar known as Casey's. The sheriff's office knows most of the regulars and the problems they bring with them from time-to-time.

Drugs were a big part of the culture on the San Juan Ridge in the eighties. So, too, were motorcycles outside Casey's—mainly Harley's—and bikers inside with their girlfriends.

On a cool, November evening in 1987, George Allen and his girlfriend Kate were seated at Casey's enjoying their final beers and some laid-back country music coming from the jukebox. They had ridden up from Gold City on George's Harley earlier in the day and were talking about riding back to town.

The atmosphere in the bar that evening was typical of a biker bar: lots of camaraderie, lots of loud laughter, loud music, and a lot of empty glasses scattered around the bar and nearby tables. Casey's had two pool tables, dirty wooden floors and, for the benefit of spectators and those waiting their turn to play pool or shuffleboard, some old chairs surrounding two sides of the pool tables.

Behind the old bar was a large mirror and bottles of booze in no particular order. The bar top was old, splotched and stained from years of alcohol abuse and covered with burn marks from hot cigarette butts that missed the ashtrays. It was definitely a beat-up saloon, not a cocktail lounge. And the barmaid, although young, looked old and well-worn herself.

Several of the bikers who George had mixed with inside and outside the Stage Coach Inn a few years earlier, including skinhead Royce, began drifting into Casey's for a beer and some pool, so George and Kate kept to themselves at the bar. George didn't want trouble; he just wanted to finish their beers and ride back to Gold City.

Suddenly, however, Royce put down his pool cue, walked over to the bar, stood next to George and slammed his fist on the bar top.

"Remember me, pal?" he shouted.

"Yeah, sure, I remember you," George calmly answered. "Not that I want to, but you have this certain distinct smell that follows you around."

George knew he had just lit the fuse to a keg of dynamite, so to avoid a sucker punch from the drunk biker, he immediately got off his barstool and faced Royce.

"You want some more of the same, like the last time we met?" George asked with defiance and confidence.

Royce stared at George, then at Kate.

"This your new girl?" he asked with a snarky smile. "Not bad for an old fuck like you, but too bad you won't be around much longer to enjoy her."

With that, Royce turned and walked away.

"Who the hell was that and what did he mean by a new girl?" Kate asked, unaware of what had happened a few years earlier when she was out of town, and George had strayed.

"I don't know, hon; the guy's drunk and not making sense."

"Then let's get the hell out of here before it gets too dark," Kate said as she grabbed her purse, got off her barstool and headed toward the door with George.

Safely outside Casey's without further incident, George and Kate got on the Harley, he cranked her up, and they headed back toward Gold City. And like most riders and passengers in those days, including myself, neither wore a helmet.

About a mile outside North San Juan it was nearing dusk as George and Kate were rolling along a two-mile straight stretch of Highway 49 toward home, a string of lights appeared from behind. Seeing the lights closing in on him, George increased his speed until he was going nearly ninety. The pavement was smooth, he knew the stretch well, and no cars were on the road. But he knew he would need to slow soon to navigate a series of turns that lay ahead.

As expected by slowing, the other bikes had drawn up next to him and behind him just as the straight stretch of pavement was ending. Now several twists and turns lay ahead, but George opened the throttle wide to stay in front as the biker gang continued to pursue him.

As they headed into the first wide turn, Royce suddenly pulled up next to George, laughing and whooping, then raised his right foot and with his heavy boot kicked George in the thigh. George's Harley swerved off the pavement on to the gravel shoulder and sailed through the air. The bike came down in a large graveled turnout and immediately slammed into a row of pine trees that bordered the highway.

The force of the crash sent George and Kate flying into the large trees, killing them both. I can only pray that death was instantaneous.

Royce and the other bikers came to a stop and looked back at the cloud of dust left in the wake of the deadly crash. The gang leader paused long enough to laugh and spit in the direction of the bodies, then gave the word to the others to keep going to Gold City without bothering to check on the condition of George and Kate, crumpled and broken in the trees.

As a final gesture of contempt, Royce aimed his middle finger toward the wreck and extended his arm to offer several one-finger salutes. Then he and most of the gang continued toward town while a couple of the thugs, who lived in North San Juan, rode back toward Casey's.

Ten minutes later, a motorist came upon the horrific scene and rushed to Casey's to call 911. He stood at the public pay phone describing to the emergency dispatcher what he had seen and where he had seen it. No one at the bar seemed surprised when they overheard the motorist explain why emergency services were needed.

***

A week later, just before Thanksgiving, under dark, ominous clouds and a slight drizzle, we had a private memorial service for George and Kate out at the ranch next to the pond. It was a chilly afternoon, but we built a large bonfire and gathered around, telling stories about our two friends who had been taken from us so suddenly and brutally.

Later, I learned the truth of what had happened out on Highway 49, but at the time of their death, most of us assumed that a mix of booze and speed had been responsible. So, too, did investigators from the sheriff's office, even though they had heard rumors of foul play and a biker gang involvement.

We had heard the rumors as well, but we didn't know for sure when we stood in the drizzle to say our goodbyes to George and Kate.

On that miserable November day in 1987, their deaths were considered the result of an accident caused by heavy drinking, speed and cocaine use, as determined by the medical examiner. The sheriff's office knew that they had been at Casey's. When asked, the bartender and some of the regulars confirmed it, but

211

nothing substantive came of it. No one seemed to know anything, and there was no mention of the incident between George and Royce.

Sheriff investigators were aware of the brawl between George and the bikers up at the Stage Coach Inn, and of the Uzi incident on the highway following the fight, but that had been a few years earlier. Because of the gang involved and reputation for revenge, they believed there was a connection between that incident and the crash that killed George and Kate, but there was no direct proof. As the rumors continued, however, the picture became clearer, and rumors became truth.

Besides, with George dead and the case deemed closed, law enforcement could shrug and go about their jobs knowing there was one less drug dealer to contend with in Quartz County.

Chapter Thirty-Four

The day after we celebrated George and Kate's short life, I went over to George's to look around and have a private conversation with whatever spirit of his was still hovering around on the property. As I walked through the house, I was drawn to a pad of paper on the end table next to his bed. I picked it up and began thumbing through a few sheets until I came across what looked like a poem hastily scribbled on the pad:

Beware, my friend; my name is Cocaine, Coke for short.
I entered this country without a passport.
I've been hunted and sought by junkies, pushers, and cops.
But mostly by users that need a quick shot.
I'm more valued than diamonds, more treasured than gold.
Use me once and you to will be sold.
I'll make a schoolboy forget his books.
I'll make a beauty forget her looks.
I'll take a renowned speaker and make him a bore.
I'll take your mama and make her a whore.
I'll make a schoolteacher forget how to teach.
I'll make a preacher not want to preach.
All kinds of people have fallen under my spell.
Just look around, you'll see the results of my hell.
I've got burglars robbing the Lord's house.
I've got husbands pimping their spouse.
I'm the King of Crime and the Prince of Destruction.
I'll cause the organs of your body to malfunction.
I'll cause your babies to be born hooked.

I'll make you rob, steal and kill like a crook.
When you're under my power, you have no will.
Remember, my friend, my name is Big C.
Although White Lady is what some folks call me.
And now that you know, what will you do?
For if you jump in my saddle, it'll be the end of you, too!

When I finished reading the poem, I sat on the edge of George's bed, very sad and teary-eyed. I realized that the poem—true in every respect—could have been written for me.

Was it an omen, foretelling my future?

Did George know something I didn't know? Was it too late to heed the warning?

When I regained my sense of composure, I folded the sheet of paper with George's poem and put it in my shirt pocket, then drove over to Gary's place and walked in the front room without knocking. He was sitting on the sofa smoking a joint, watching TV dressed in his underwear and a bathrobe. Between hits on the joint, he was sipping on a glass of milk.

"Some farewell yesterday, eh?" he said.

"He had a lot of friends, Gary. He was a crazy bastard, but I loved him like a brother."

"Yeah, me too," Gary said, turning away from the television. "I'm going to miss his laugh. I've never known anyone who could make a place come alive the way George could."

He took another sip of his milk and a hit from the joint.

"They still haven't got anything that proves they were run off the road that night, even though the word is they were," I said. "Something's not right about the accident; if it was an accident. I talked to New Jersey Mike with the sheriff's office, and he said there were a lot of tire and skid tracks near the crash site. George wouldn't have missed that turn. Hell, he'd driven that road at night a hundred times, and he knew that curve came after the long straight stretch."

Gary heard me and nodded. "You know that; I know that."

"The ironic thing is, Kate, ends up dead—not that Paula chick that caused the problem years ago at the Stage Coach Inn. It just doesn't make sense to me," I told him.

"Death is a commodity no one wants, yet everyone gets, sooner or later. I've heard for years there was going to be payback for that bullet spray. There was lots of damage done that night."

"Yeah, you don't have to tell me," I nodded. "It was crazy-time what George did with that fuckin' Israeli bullet blaster. He was lucky no one was killed."

"No shit," he said. "Christ, I told George to watch himself, that Royce and the boys would be gunnin' for him—in more ways than one—but, hey, George was George, right? Never any regrets. The guy really thought he was invincible."

"They say the closest thing to immortality is youth, and the most bitter of all emotions is regret," I told Gary. "George never thought about dying, and he never had a regret." I paused for a moment then asked, "Have you ever considered that our lives are mostly chaos?"

Gary looked up at me with a smile and said, "You know what they say about chaos? It's nothing more than disorder waiting for direction."

"Talk about chaos." I took the poem out of my pocket and placed it on the sofa next to Gary.

"What the hell's this?" he asked as he reached for the paper.

"Something I found at George's; I think you'll find it interesting.

Gary picked up the notebook pages and began reading— quickly at first, it seemed, but then he appeared to be reading each line very slowly.

"A philosopher and a poet was George Thomas Allen? Wow! Who knew?" Gary said when he finished reading.

"Yeah, who knew?" I whispered.

"Looks as if he knew what we all know, but seldom care to acknowledge."

"Which is?" I asked as Gary took another hit on his joint.

"Verily a polluted stream is man," Gary said, gesturing with his arms as if standing in front of an audience quoting the author of the statement. Then he stared at me, apparently looking for a response.

"Shakespeare?" I suggested.

"Nope, Friedrich Nietzsche," Gary said.

"Should have figured," I laughed as Nicholson handed the poem back to me and I headed for the front door.

"Any other words of wisdom before I leave?" I asked.

"A man cannot be comfortable without his own approval."

"Nietzsche again?"

"Mark Twain."

Chapter Thirty-Five

Looking back at all that happened during those tumultuous years, my "Come to Jesus" moment was at the home of Musette "Madame Butterfly" Parks on Christmas Eve 1987.

I ran into Musette and Asa at The Firehouse after closing early, so we shared a booth for dinner and conversation. After dinner, we did a few lines for dessert then she invited me over to the house for more. This was how so many nights started: A line or two to take the edge off and, before you knew it, it was daylight.

For me, a known drug user under the watchful eye of my probation officer and every cop in town, it was especially foolhardy to snort even a line, much less get myself into an all-night session at Madame Butterfly's—a house no doubt under periodic surveillance.

Poppy's condo was my safe house—not Musette's—but self-discipline and avoidance of hedonistic pleasures was never my strong suit.

When I arrived at Musette's, they were already pouring wine and cutting lines on a plate sitting on top of the kitchen table. It started out like so many other nights had during the previous half-dozen or so years; then came the surprise. It was a choice I had never faced before. While the three of us were sitting at the kitchen table, Asa pulled out a small baggie of white powder that resembled cocaine. I knew it was heroin because I knew he and the Madame were users along with a small but growing heroin group in Gold City.

He then got a spoon and a candle from the kitchen and dripped wax on a plate after lighting it to stand the candle upright on the plate. Also, from the kitchen, he retrieved a small piece of aluminum foil and, after laying it out on the table, spooned some of the heroin out of the baggie on to the foil.

"Want to try something really special, Adrian?" Musette asked. "It's the heaven you've never seen before, and it's on me. A Christmas present to heaven."

"Don't think so, but thanks for the offer. I think I'll have a couple more lines and call it a night."

"Well, then, I'll sure as hell take you up on that offer," Asa enthusiastically told our hostess as he added a drop of water to the foil.

Asa put the foil over the candle flame, and when smoke started to rise from the foil as the heroin began to liquefy, he put a five-inch plastic tube shaped like a straw in his mouth and inhaled the smoke into his lungs.

He immediately closed his eyes and rolled his head back, repeatedly moaning, "Oh, fuck!"

"You sure, Adrian? Let's do it together," Musette suggested.

She then repeated Asa's steps and handed me the inhaling device as the smoke rolled off the tin foil.

I looked at the waiting inhaler and thought about Len Bias, the great college basketball star who had died the previous summer. Bias had been a star at Maryland and was the second player chosen in the 1986 NBA draft. Twenty-two years old and the world at his feet—an instant millionaire—and what did he do? He OD'd on a cocaine/heroin mix and died two days later.

I knew the dangers of coke, of course—much less heroin—but I was sick and unwilling at that point to admit that my sickness could someday be fatal.

Despite my trepidation, I reached for the inhaler and began taking the white-gray smoke from the foil into my lungs. It was instant euphoria. Instant. And, yes, I thought I was in heaven. But I didn't want God to see me in that condition.

I had truly gone over the edge. And, unfortunately, I liked it. My friend London Maxx once told me never to try heroin because I would like it too much. He knew what he was talking about.

After the Butterfly took her turn with the plastic inhaling device, she moved us over to the sofa for more coke snorting and some playful groping. It's a fun thing to do when you're a hedonist at heart, as I seemed to be, but maybe not a good thing after "Chasing the Dragon" —as it was called back then.

The next thing I knew, I was naked, in Musette's bed, and she was on top of me.

"You like what I do for you, baby?" My smile gave her the answer.

"OK, then take a hit of this popper as the chaser," she instructed me, "cause Momma Fly has something else new for you tonight."

She whispered in my ear and nodded toward Asa—who was standing next to the bed, nude. He leaned over and kissed her as he joined us. Then we all took another hit from the popper.

***

When I awoke, it was just after noon. I got up, dressed, stumbled into the bathroom and splashed cold water on my face—lots of cold water. I couldn't remember ever feeling worse, and the face I saw in the bathroom mirror truly frightened me.

Who was that sick, strung-out man I saw staring back at me? When I came out of the bathroom into the hallway and walked past the living room, into the kitchen, Miss Butterfly was at the stove, scrambling eggs and drinking coffee.

"Hey, baby, we were beginning to think we killed you last night. How about some coffee? Maybe something to eat?" she asked.

"No, gotta go, gotta go now," I said with obvious nervous agitation. Grabbing my coat from the sofa, I walked past the two of them and started for the front door.

"Thanks, Musette," I told her with the best smile I could muster at the time. "I'll see you soon."

"Don't thank me entirely for the enjoyable evening," she said.

"It was both our pleasure," Asa chimed in.

I looked at both, too groggy to know for sure what their references meant, or what the hell had really happened last night.

On my way home to shower and put on fresh clothes for Christmas dinner with my parents, I drove past the bar and saw that my brother had it open for business. Knowing that Bogart's was in good hands with Carla behind the bar, I continued driving toward my house.

Suddenly, however, I was overcome with tears and emotion. I pulled off to the side of the road, folded my arms across the top of the steering wheel and began to curse myself. Then I asked God to intervene.

"You've got to stop," I shouted at the reflected image in the Jeep's front window. "If not, you'll die, just like George. God help me to stop my destruction."

But I knew that talking with the image in the window was not going to do any good. I had to speak to someone else.

By the time I got home, a steady stream of tears was running down my face. All I wanted to do at that point was go to bed and stay there.

As the phantom wind blew and I held on to the edge of the bed, I finally fell asleep. In fact, I slept through the rest of that day, Christmas dinner, and all that night. And when I finally rose, I knew what I had to do to move on with the rest of my life.

God had talked with me throughout my long sleep. He had given me guidance, and He had given me comfort.

After a shower and shave, I called my mom and dad to apologize for missing dinner; I told them I had taken too much NyQuil for a nagging cold and fallen asleep on the couch. Then I drove into town and once again stopped at the Episcopal Church on Bridge Street. I entered the church much like I had done more than twenty years earlier when I asked God for a miracle to get me out of my teenage troubles. Now, here I was again on my knees, in need of another miracle—an even bigger miracle.

The church was cold and dark, but a beautiful structure—small, with a feeling of warmth and the certain presence of God.

I entered one of the pews and got down on my knees.

"God, you know I've been talking to you for the past year or so, and I know you haven't been listening to me because I've been asking for help in the wrong way, for all the wrong reasons. Yes, I've been a sinner in some very sinful ways. I've not been a good person lately. Maybe not for years. But now I really need your help, God, and I'd like to make a deal with you if it's OK."

I took a deep breath and continued, my knees aching, but knowing I shouldn't rise until I was through with the conversation. It was going to be the most important conversation of my life, and I knew it.

"I know you're not in the deal-making business, God, but I've got to try because I don't know where else to turn or what else to do. Many years ago, in this very church, you listened to a scared teenage boy pray for a miracle, and you came through for me. It proved beyond all doubt that you have the power to help when you want to.

"God, I need your merciful intervention more than ever. Today, I promise you I will never again touch cocaine or any other illegal drug. I ask that if I make good on my promise, that you show me the way back to a positive, productive life. Show me again how to be a happy, productive person and make my family—especially my dad—proud of me. Please, God, show me the way. I beg you."

Then I said, "Amen" and glanced up at Jesus on the cross, looking down at me from His place high up on the church wall.

I left the church with a feeling of spiritual satisfaction and genuine accomplishment. I left feeling as though I knew I could do what I had promised God if only I had His power helping me. I would succeed with my pledge and promise. I was sure of it.

My wise old friend, and mentor—Jerry Walser—once told me that none of us get through this life unscathed. At the time, I wasn't sure what he was talking about—now I know.

The next step would be deliverance—my deliverance.

Chapter Thirty-Six

February 1988, exactly forty-six days, after I knelt on my knees at the Episcopal Church and prayed for God to guide me through my pledge and promise, I signed a second plea agreement with the Quartz County District Attorney.

I pled to a misdemeanor count of violating probation and paid a thousand-dollar fine. By doing so, I agreed to remain on informal probation for another two years. The informal probation was a real bonus because it meant I was not required to report to a probation officer. Additionally, if I had no further arrests or violations during my probationary period, both misdemeanor convictions—my first for being in a place where a controlled substance was consumed, and the probation violation for a bad piss test—would be expunged from my record.

Without a tether between me and the legal system, I was free to leave Gold City and start a new life. A life, I hoped, that would bring me all the joy I had been dreaming of for years.

I said my goodbyes to friends and relatives and gave my brother Don all the keys I had for various doors and locks to Bogart's. The liquor license was transferred to my brother's name, and I essentially walked away from the broken business. Don gave me a brotherly man-hug and wished me luck. I appreciated the gesture, but luck would play only a small part of my new life. I knew if I began making good choices again and didn't stray from my promise to God, the rest would take care of itself. Of that, I was certain.

Before driving out of town, I turned off Lion Road onto Eagle Street, passing the old Gold City Hospital where I had been born more than forty years earlier. It was time to say goodbye to my parents, who lived in a country home at the end of the street.

They were waiting for me in the dining room when I entered the house. Parents—we are all so busy growing up, we often forget they are busy growing old. Love your parents!

"Good morning," I said.

They rose from their chairs and hugged me. "I love you," I told them both.

"And we love you, son," Mom answered as she brought me a cup of tea.

"Do you know for sure where you're going and what you're going to do?" Dad asked.

"Heading to Phoenix, Dad. My old friend from the rock 'n' roll tour days, Jerry Walser, has a guest house he's not using, and said I could move in there till I get settled and find a job."

"Any prospects?" he asked.

"Fortunately, Jerry is the manager of the Phoenix Coliseum and says he's made a couple of inquiries about me getting a job with one of his vending companies. We'll see," I shrugged, not sure exactly what to expect once I reached Phoenix. "Gotta get there first, Dad."

"Then what?" he asked in an uncertain voice, not wanting to seem pushy about my future plans.

"Well, here's the good news. I've been accepted to Arizona State University Law School, and I start in the fall if I can pass my LSAT exams, which I'll begin studying for when I get to Phoenix."

Having graduated from San Francisco State in the late sixties, I had my undergrad degree, but my father seemed surprised at what I had just told him. And he had some concerns.

"How are you going to pay for it, Adrian? And how the hell can you be an attorney with a criminal record? It doesn't seem like the kind of background that would endear you to law firms."

"As for money," I told him, "I sold the house and got a decent price. That money alone should pay for school. And I sold the Jeep for a few thousand, but I'm keeping the Caddy. I'll need a job to pay for living expenses, which is why I'll be at Jerry's office door in a couple of days looking for work."

My dad seemed satisfied with the financial part of my plan, but he wanted to know how my record would impact my chances of becoming an attorney. That was a fair question.

"You can't be an attorney with felony convictions, but misdemeanors don't count," I assured him. "I have two misdemeanors, sure, but that wouldn't prevent me from practicing law. Hell, Dad, we both know attorneys in Gold City who have been popped for driving under the influence and for minor drug possession, and they still practice law. I'll be okay, I promise. Besides, the convictions go away if I stay out of trouble for the next two years. So, by the time I graduate, there won't be a record of any arrests or convictions."

I knew I was leaving without paying my father the money I owed him, but he never raised the subject that morning at the house—nor did I. I needed to get back on my feet again and wasn't able to pay Dad—nor Gary, for that matter—what I owed them. But I was leaving with confidence that better days were ahead.

"When will we see you again, sweetheart?" Mom asked with the kind of sad eyes that a mother saying goodbye to her son would have.

"Without a doubt, I'll be here twice a year to see you, Dad and Don; I promise you that."

We talked a while longer, then I hugged and kissed my parents and gave Tonto a firm scrunch under his chin. It killed me to leave my dog behind, but I was grateful my parents were willing to take him in. They would give him the love he needed, and he would give his love right back to them—double.

I could tell Tonto was heartbroken not to be with me as he had been for the past eight years. I could see from his eyes that he was asking, what did I do? Why can't I go with you? My years with him had taught me that dogs needed no words to console you. Dogs are the ultimate practitioners of unconditional love and the therapy of touch and hugs. Dogs know and accept the hard realities of life that humans cannot sense or acknowledge.

Dad walked me to the car, where he gave me a hug and put a few hundred-dollar bills in my hand. Actually, ten hundred-dollar bills, but I gave them back to him and told him he had done enough, and I was going to be okay.

"Son," he said, "what you're about to do is going to be hard, but because it's hard to do, it usually means it's right to do. Never forget—the harder you work—the luckier you get."

I never forgot those words. Honestly, until I brought this tragic path of destruction upon myself, I had found very little in life to be difficult. Now we will see what I'm really made of.

I drove out of Gold City with relief, knowing that a huge weight had been lifted off my shoulders. I had no interest in looking in the rearview mirror as I passed the city limits sign and headed south. The bible says, "Pain is its own teaching," and by this time I had had a life's lesson in pain, and I got the message.

A Greek philosopher, whose name escapes me right now, had it right when he said, "You cannot step in the same river twice. The water flows by, and life moves on." And I was definitely moving on.

What I did not leave behind, however, was unabashed hatred toward those who went out of their way to hurt me. I wanted a form of justice, which can also mean revenge. However, revenge can sometimes be a crime—and usually is. First, you find the truth; then you take revenge. *Sweet* revenge—best served cold.

I was about to learn that hatred can be a great motivator—and so can revenge. I would use that internal hatred for the next few years to propel me forward and drive my ambitions.

***

A couple of days later, I wheeled my seventy-six Cadillac Seville into Phoenix. It was early February and the weather was a perfect seventy-six degrees.

I met Jerry at the Coliseum about four that afternoon, and we went to his home. It had been years since I had seen him, but Jerry didn't hesitate when I had contacted him from Gold City. He invited me to join him in Phoenix to start over, and I was very appreciative.

He knew a few things I had done to screw-up my life, but he didn't know everything. And I planned to keep it that way. Friend or no friend, there was no need to burden him with my tales of tawdry mistakes.

The guest house was a small building in the backyard, near the pool. It was all I needed. It had a small bedroom and bath with a combination living room/kitchen. Nicely furnished.

To conserve my cash reserve, I drove taxi during March, April, May, and June—twelve hours a day, six days a week, from dawn to dusk. I took Sundays off and made an average sixty-five bucks net each day—in cash, no taxes. That paid for what little overhead I had, and it put some spending money in my pocket.

Meanwhile, I had to park the cab occasionally to appear at job interviews and take the LSAT. But when I wasn't preparing for the next step in my new life, I was driving hack until my ass ached.

Actually, driving a taxi turned out to be very useful. When parked, waiting for my next fare out in Scottsdale, I could study for the LSAT. Also, it provided me with a world I had never seen before and exposed me to the kind of people I had never met in previous life experiences.

Anyone who says you meet every kind of person when you own a bar never drove a taxi—at least not in Phoenix, Arizona.

Chapter Thirty-Seven

In mid-June 1988, as temperatures soared, and the taxi's broken AC was blowing hot air in my face, I managed to escape the daily grind when I was hired as Clubhouse Manager for Phoenix Greyhound Park—a new dog racing track near the airport.

The air-conditioned Clubhouse included the upstairs restaurant and bars for high rollers. I worked six nights a week, Tuesday through Sunday, from 4:00 P.M. until 10:00 P.M.—off on Monday. It paid well and allowed me to get my own apartment on the east side of Phoenix.

I got the job because of Jerry Walser's connections and his introduction of me to the district manager for Sports Service, the food service company at the Coliseum, which happened to also own the race track. I went through the interview process and all that, but thanks to Jerry's influence, I had the inside track. It always pays to know someone who knows someone who makes the final decisions.

During my tenure at Phoenix Greyhound Park—and thanks to my bartender and good friend Bob Roloff—I learned the secret to betting the trifecta. Bob taught me how to place and bet the numbers and, as usual, I pushed the knowledge and took home the bacon.

There are no guarantees at the track, but Roloff's insight and advice helped narrow the risk. I tore up a lot of losing tickets, sure, but I cashed in more than enough winners. That occasional win helped with school expenses and plane tickets home to visit my parents a couple of times a year.

Thanks to Bob, I cleared an extra few thousand each year that I worked at the track. These days, my friend Bob is affectionately known throughout Arizona as The Arizona Duuude.

My new furnished apartment was small, a living room with a kitchen in front, and a bedroom and bath in the back. Fortunately, it was located next to the pool so that I could sit outside during the day and study by the pool. It wasn't luxury living, but it was all I needed.

I was thankful for what I had and the path I was on. And, best of all, I was drug-free for the first time in years. I'll never forget getting up at Jerry's at about 6:00 A.M. one morning and walking out to the pool with my cup of tea and sitting on the diving board. It was my twenty-first day in Phoenix and well over two months since the last time I consumed cocaine. I sat there thinking: Wow, what a fool I had been. My head was clear for the first time in years. I could see clearly the mess I had made of my life and the destruction and chaos I had left in my wake. And for what? It was all a colossal waste of time. I had wasted valuable, productive years in my thirties…years I could never get back. I had made a deal with the devil, and then with God. So far, God was upholding His end, and so was I. I was alive again, and never going back.

I aced the LSAT and had a hectic schedule, finding myself dashing from the ASU campus to the dog track several times a week. But I always kept my focus—getting that valuable sheepskin and then getting my revenge.

Arizona State University in Tempe is a beautiful campus, for the desert. Not on the level of Dartmouth, Duke, or Princeton, nor most of the Ivey League Universities, but still very nice. I began school in the fall of eighty-eight and had classes three or four days a week, depending on the semester.

However, because I worked full-time, I didn't finish law school in the usual three years. I needed another semester, but I didn't mind that at all. I loved going to school, and I loved learning more about the law—especially criminal law, which I intended to practice. And I knew exactly where I was going to hang my shingle.

I typically spent three days in school and three days studying, but Mondays were always kept clear for whatever combination of activities I could bundle together to be with Kathy Edal.

Kathy was a fellow ASU student and former Playboy bunny. We met on campus and hit it off right from the start. She was just over six feet tall, natural blond hair, deep green eyes, and a body to stop a clock with legs as powerful as an Olympic swimmer.

She was a stunning woman and a joy to be with—over a cup of coffee at the campus cafe, a beer at our favorite Mexican restaurant, or sharing a bottle of wine on her back porch. She loved to laugh, and that made me laugh as well. It had been a long time since I had good, honest laughs, but Kathy changed all that.

Kathy learned much about life being a Playboy bunny and often told me little antidotes of what she called bunnyism. She once told me, "A girl who believes every guy she meets wants to fuck her, is almost always right." How could I argue with that piece of wisdom?

The one I could really relate to was, "You could see the Grand Tetons, marvel in their majesty and take it off your bucket list, but everyone wants the next orgasm."

Kathy was working toward a master's in education and at night tended bar at my favorite neighborhood steakhouse. The two of us lived with cramped, busy schedules, but we made a point of being together on Mondays—and sometimes for Sunday brunch. We didn't see each other all that much, so our time together became very special.

And special, indeed, was one particular evening. We had dinner out and enjoyed a couple of bottles of wine then returned to her house. We spent the night together, and when I awoke in the morning, I knew I had just had one of the most exciting sexual encounters of my life.

At first, I thought it was a dream. I told Kathy about the dream, and she looked at me with her sexy, green eyes and said, "It was no dream. We had sex—great sex in our sleep."

We were both sound asleep and made love to each other. When sex is at its best, it's a team sport, and together we were bedroom all-stars.

*****

I graduated in the spring of 1992, just short of my forty-fifth birthday. I may not have been the oldest ASU graduate that year, but most of the young men and women who walked across the stage that day were young enough to be my children.

Determined to again succeed, I graduated magna cum laude and made the Dean's List each year. Hell, all I did for four years was study, work and occasionally saw Kathy. The law had become my life, and I loved the idea that I was on a clear path to both financial and personal satisfaction. And I was on that clear path with a clear head—something I had been missing for a very long time.

For nearly four years I had been driven by the past—and now I was going home a changed man. I had come to learn there is nothing you can do about the past, except keep it there. I had a lot to prove and thank many of my family and friends for sticking with me. I was determined to do right by them and my second chance at a new life.

*****

In the summer of ninety-two, I hunkered down in my Arizona apartment, preparing for the California Bar Exam. I could have taken the Arizona exam, but I knew I wasn't going to live or practice law in the Southwest. So, I took the California exam at UCLA—a five-hour drive in my Caddy.

I was warned that it would be a grueling process, and it was. Essay questions, problem-solving tests, hypotheticals involving both criminal and civil law, and much more. But those countless hours spent cramming in my apartment paid off in the fall of ninety-two.

In those years, more than forty percent of the men and women who took the California bar exam failed, some taking it for the second or third time—which was typical. But I'm proud to say I passed the exam on my first try.

I returned home just in time to celebrate Christmas with my family and share some New Year's Eve bubbly with friends. Some of the guys wanted me to share a few lines with them, but I was done with that crap—done with turning my brain into mush.

Then, on January 20, 1993, I proudly hung a sign—my "shingle," in the classic legal vernacular—outside my law office in downtown Gold City. And what a great location it was.

I rented an old law office on North Oak Street, directly across from the front door of the county courthouse. The building was owned by the Baker's—one of the most respected families in town. Mr. Baker had been a very successful attorney in Gold City, and Mrs. Baker had been my first-grade teacher back in the fifties.

Her husband had recently passed away, and the office was vacant, so Mrs. Baker was happy to rent the space to me. She knew my mom and dad, as well as my grandparents, and said she was happy to see what I had done with my life. I had left town in disgrace but returned like the prodigal son—the wayward lad described in Luke 15: 11-32, who comes home and is forgiven by his father.

I had kept my promise to myself and God, and He was blessing me in ways I could not have imagined a few years earlier when I was living in life's gutter, a druggie in denial.

My practice was entirely criminal law. The first year I won more cases than I lost and plea-bargained many clients to a resolution that satisfied them and added to my growing reputation as an attorney who could get things done. By the fall of 1993, business was brisk, and the drug trade was busier than ever in Gold City.

It hadn't taken long for word to spread that if you got busted for drugs, or any felony, and needed an attorney who would fight for you and get results, all you had to do was call Adrian Davis, Esquire. (I always loved adding "Esq." to my signature).

In fact, my first client was none other than my old pal Gary Nicholson, busted for possession and sale of cocaine. I still owed Gary ten grand, so I took the case pro bono and pled him out with a slap on the wrist. He was thrilled to stay out of jail, and I was very happy to have helped my old friend. Gary wanted to celebrate with dinner to show his appreciation for what I had done, but I knew it was best to decline the offer.

The truth is, I found myself declining a lot of offers of appreciation those first few months as an attorney, and my will was stronger than ever. Eventually, word spread through the local drug community that I loved winning felony and drug-related cases, but there was no way in hell I was going to get my nose anywhere near another line of coke. It wasn't going to happen.

I occasionally stopped by Bogart's to see my brother and have a beer. Don was doing fine, and the business was solidly back on its feet with him at the helm. I enjoyed sitting at the bar, talking to old friends and trying my best to show by example that the coked-up guy who had sold his worldly possessions and left town a few years earlier was, indeed, a changed man.

No more shots of tequila and no more Myers's rum and OJ; just a bottle of beer or a glass of wine. But neither of them to excess.

Occasionally, sitting at the bar, I connected with someone who would later be a client. I always needed clients if I was going to be as successful as I knew I wanted to be. From Day One, I wanted to beat the Gold City cops, the district attorney, and the Quartz County court system every chance I got. In particular, I wanted to stick it to Chief Kane, Sergeant Pittman and, whenever possible, to Mayor Fenwick—still holding the gavel and controlling City Hall.

Since my return to Gold City, I had been able to confirm with certainty that Fenwick had been the one to spearhead the effort to bust me both personally and financially. First the truth, then the revenge.

Winning cases was the kind of therapy I needed, and I was good at what I did.

I mostly stayed to myself, went to the gym and ran a lot—had an occasional date, but nothing serious. My mind and soul were healthy, but I wanted to be sure my body was fit as well. I didn't socially interact with other attorneys, but I met one that interested me. Her name was Sandi Stassi.

She was beautiful. She stood five-five, trim, stylish short jet-black hair, the darkest black eyes, full lips, perfect teeth, and a perfect figure as well. When Sandi smiled and tilted her head ever so slightly, she reminded me of actress Natalie Wood. Almost breathtaking, in a ballerina way.

In addition to her drop-dead good looks and womanly charm, she happened to be a firecracker of a defense attorney. Sandi was a bulldog who could rip a prosecution witness to shreds.

Her specialty? Criminal law.

Chapter Thirty-Eight

It was June 1994—a full eighteen months into my career as a defense attorney—when I received a call from Gary Nicholson. My secretary, Mandy, announced the call to me on the intercom and I took it in my office.

"Hi, Gary, how you doin,' buddy?" I asked. He was still a friend that I had an occasional beer with at Bogart's, and one of the most interesting guys I knew, so I was happy to hear from him.

"Not so well. Just bailed-out this morning. Got popped again last night driving home from downtown. I need to see you; it's way fuckin' serious this time."

"I'm clear till after lunch, so come on over. But I definitely need to be in court at one."

"Good, then I'm on my way," Gary said, relieved that I could see him so quickly.

He arrived at my office a little after ten wearing faded green sweats and paint-stained running shoes. He was unshaven, hair pulled back in his signature ponytail, and a concerned look on his face. More concerned than I had ever seen him.

"What happened?" I asked.

"I fucked up," he began, slumping in a chair and shaking his head in disgust. "I was downtown yesterday for my usual four o'clock cocktail at Bogart's and, stupidly, kept drinking until after nine."

"You've put in longer sessions at the bar than that," I reminded him.

"Maybe so, but Don was pouring heavy, and I had no self-control whatsoever. Anyway," he continued, "I was waiting to take possession of a kilo from the boys down south from my new connection. As you know, Pixie got popped a few years ago, so I had to make new arrangements to get it from there to here."

Gary told me the delivery went down without a hitch, but then he made the mistake of casually tossing the bag of coke in the trunk of his car and started for home.

He didn't get far.

Two blocks from Bogart's, he saw the flashing lights in his rearview mirror and knew it was all over. He was drunk, which has never been much of a crime in Gold City, but he was carrying a heavy load of cocaine in the trunk. And that *is* a crime.

He wouldn't have passed a breath test, so he refused. And to stall for time, he requested a blood test. They cuffed Gary, placed his drunken ass in the patrol car and walked the department's drug-sniffing dog in a circle around his car.

It only took a few seconds for the well-trained dog to freeze and stare at the trunk. Gary knew there was no hope, so when the cop asked for his keys, he handed them over without an argument. He was fucked—upside-down and inside-out—and he knew it.

But more worrisome to Gary was the situation he faced, again, of paying the boys down south for coke he no longer had in his possession. A few years in jail would be a walk in the park compared to what the Mexican gang suppliers in Los Angeles would do to him. He was especially concerned that they might take it out on his new connection. Even though it had been ten years since the dog incident at his house, not paying what you owed on time was still serious.

When he finished telling me about his predicament, I acknowledged that this time he was in deep shit—very deep—with both the law and the suppliers. I told Gary I might be able to get the evidence thrown out because the cop lacked probable cause to stop him in the first place. Plus, there was no reason to suspect him of carrying a kilo of coke in the trunk, and they had not acquired a search warrant. But I told him there were no guarantees, and the judge wouldn't be inclined to rule in our favor.

I suggested he go home and stay home—don't come to town. His job was to get his head right and let me handle the legal stuff. I told him I would continue to take the case pro bono and apply it toward the five-grand balance I still owed him, but this case was going to have billing hours and research well beyond five-thousand dollars, even if I settled it before it was scheduled for trial.

I considered the extra time as interest earned during the several years the loan had remained unpaid.

Over the next few months, I vigorously defended Gary and his arrest with numerous motions to suppress or quash the arrest and the search. Hell, I even suggested the cocaine had been planted in his vehicle by the police. I asked the DA why Gary had been stopped that evening without probable cause? He wasn't speeding or driving erratically; there was no reason for the traffic stop.

The DA said that the Gold City cop who made the stop and bust claimed Gary had crossed the yellow centerline turning on to South Oak Street from Argonaut Street. Maybe he had, but that was an after-the-fact excuse for the stop. It's what cops do to cover their ass.

I remembered the stormy nineteen sixties and early seventies when anti-war and civil rights protestors were tear-gassed and attacked by police slinging their heavy batons. When an arrested protestor filed a charge of police brutality, the cop would file a counter-charge of resisting arrest. Then the accommodating courts would schedule the resisting arrest charge first, to be followed by the police brutality charge.

That usually meant that the citizen protester, faced with two costly trials, not just one, would withdraw his charge of police brutality. And the cops would then withdraw their resisting arrest charge.

Hell, you can't beat 'em, both Gary and I knew that.

As further evidence that the search was going to stand and be allowed as evidence in court, every one of my motions was rebuffed by the DA's office and denied by every judge I appealed to. It was not going well, and it was going to get worse.

While I continued to fight as hard as I could, we met several times away from the office. Just Gary and me, at his house—either on my way home in the evening or on my way to work in the morning. Gary had moved from Red Rock Road to near the Oak Street bridge to be closer to downtown.

During the early years of my law practice, I rented a condo on Beal Avenue, the same condo units that Poppy had lived in years earlier—a half-dozen or so blocks from my office and not far from Gary's place. When I was arrested many years earlier, I too lived up on Red Rock Road, beyond the city limits, in an area policed by the county sheriff. But now both Nicholson and I were Gold City residents, under the watchful eye of Chief Kane and his boys.

As I mentioned before, I had stayed away from coke as well as from people who still partied with it, Gary being the exception. And my only alcohol intake was a glass of cab with dinner, or an occasional beer when I stopped in to see Don at Bogart's. I was focused entirely on my law practice.

I thought to drop by weekly to have a quiet talk with Gary was as innocuous as the Episcopal minister dropping by his neighbor's house for a cup of coffee and some kindly fellowship.

But little did I know that those innocent visits to Gary Nicholson's house were about to throw me into the legal fight of my life.

Chapter Thirty-Nine

When Michael's plane landed at Dulles International Airport shortly after sunset, he collected his luggage and walked outside the terminal to catch a cab for the twenty-five-mile ride to his Georgetown apartment. It was a cool Sunday evening, and he wanted to get home as quickly as possible. He wasn't due back in class until Monday afternoon—plenty of time to finish his dad's account of life in Gold City during the eighties and nineties.

Of course, Michael knew about the arrest and trial for murder because that's where his mother and father met and soon after married. But he didn't know the trial details as he was about to learn them.

Michael Davis would soon learn about his father's biggest legal battle, and he would not be able to set these pages down until he had finished every word of it.,

***

One rainy morning in November 1994, I was at home having a cup of tea, reading the local newspaper. On the front page was a story about the murder of drug dealer Gary Nicholson.

My buddy—my client—was dead. Murdered.

To say Gary's murder was the talk of sleepy Gold City during the fall of ninety-four would be an understatement.

His body had been found November third by his girlfriend, Roxanne "Roxie" Meyers—a local party girl who had a smartass mouth and quick tongue she took pride in using to verbally assault you when she had no other defense at her disposal. Roxie was a tall, attractive woman, about thirty-five, a good figure, with short naturally curly dirty-blond hair and light blue eyes. She had a faint thin scar that ran down the right side of her upper lip, just below her nose, from a childhood accident. Gary had genuine warm feelings for her, and I always thought Roxie had similar feelings about Gary. He said she was good for him.

Not sure they would have made much of a married couple, but at least they cared for each other. And as I grew older, having someone genuinely care for me remained an unfulfilled dream.

I was thinking to myself how sad it was that his life had been snuffed out in an instant, never having taken his innate intelligence, charm, and personality in a more positive direction. His was truly a life wasted. I spoke to him many times about leaving the garbage at the front door and moving on—moving in another direction with his life. But he was too far gone; too involved in the illegal drug trade and drug use in and around Gold City.

You can't start your day—every day—smoking a joint as soon as you roll out of bed and expect positive results in your work or your enthusiasm for life. It's akin to an alcoholic grabbing for the whiskey bottle on his way to the bathroom in the morning. It's a dead-end street.

I was also thinking about how—in a macabre way, of course— that the murder had been convenient. I was getting nowhere with his case and felt he should be getting mentally prepared for prison. Hard time. State prison. At least five years, maybe more.

Gary would not have done well in prison. He's was tough and would have survived, sure, but not well.

My thoughts and prayers for Gary were still floating around in my head when I heard the doorbell ring. Eight on a Saturday morning? When I opened the door, Chief Kane and three stern-looking officers faced me. And they weren't selling tickets to the annual Blue Light Ball.

"Good morning, Mr. Davis," the chief said with a slight tip of his cap as he held up a courthouse document. "We have a search warrant for these premises. We also have a warrant for your office, and other city officers are currently there conducting a search."

"What the hell is this about?" I asked as he handed me the warrant.

"As if you don't know?" Kane snickered. "Read the warrant. Your client, Mr. Nicholson, was murdered with a .38 pistol and we're looking for that .38 pistol. You own one, don't you?"

"*Used* to own one, you mean? You know I had a .38 when you searched my house years ago, but it was stolen during a burglary a few days later. The sheriff's office would probably still have the theft report on file."

Kane didn't respond, but his glare spoke volumes.

"Come on; you don't really believe I had anything to do with Gary's murder, do you? What possible motive would I have to kill him?"

"Motive?" he responded. "You were with him the night of his murder, and a witness tells us you were the last to see him alive. And you two were arguing about money."

I was in shock and lapsed into dumbfounding silence as the officers continued to search my home. I sat on my sofa, nervously raking my fingers through my hair. This was one search Walter Nash would not be bird-dogging.

Couple minutes later, an officer came out from my bedroom and announced, "Well, lookie here Chief."

The officer was holding a snub-nose .38 special revolver.

"Nicholson was killed with a weapon just like that one, Davis," Chief Kane said.

"Where'd you get it?" I demanded.

"Out of one of your bedroom closets," the cop answered, "in a suitcase."

"That's bullshit!" I yelled. "My gun was stolen years ago."

"Really?" the chief responded.

"Yes, really. That can't be my gun; somebody else put it in that suitcase, not me."

"Yeah, you bet," the chief said pointing toward another officer who was holding up a light teal jacket I wore frequently in cool weather. It was one of my favorite coats.

"What's that on the front and along the sleeves?" Kane asked his patrolman.

"Looks like blood stains, Chief," the officer said with a smirk and a smile.

I was standing there in my living room in disbelief. This couldn't be happening—no way my .38 magically found its way back into my house. No way. Couldn't possibly be true. And the jacket? The jacket with bloodstains? Where the hell did that come from?

"Okay, that's enough," Kane said, gesturing for me to turn around to be handcuffed. "Mr. Davis, you're under arrest for the murder of Gary Nicholson."

"Read him his rights, Ralph, not that this smartass lawyer doesn't already know 'em," the chief said to Sergeant Pittman.

No—No—No. This can't be happening.

Chapter Forty

Needless to say, my world was turned upside down the day I was arrested for murdering one of my best friends. My law practice was put on hold, and I spent much of the next week meeting with family and friends, reassuring them that I did not kill Gary and I would prove it. Also, I needed a good criminal defense attorney to assist with my defense, so a few days after my arrest I met with Sandi Stassi.

As I sat in Sandi's reception area waiting for her to finish with a client, I admired the plush office that obviously had the touch of a woman with good taste. The colors were pastels of beige and brown, with light green in the sofa and chair fabrics, dark hardwood floors, and a large dark-green area rug.

When the door opened to Sandi's office, she came out to greet me wearing a classy teal suede jacket, black pants with a white blouse and black heels. A very professional look. She looked to be barely thirty-five if that—and what a joy to look at.

When Sandi spotted me, she motioned to come into her office and said, "It's good to see you again, Adrian, but I wish it were under better circumstances."

"Can't really think of worse circumstances, can you?"

"Not really," she said as we sat down. "How did you arrange bail? I heard it was half a million."

"My dad put up the ranch as collateral," I told her, "and that saved fifty grand that the bail bondsman would have taken."

"Nice dad."

"The best," I said, knowing he and Mom were worried sick.

"After you called yesterday, I spoke with the DA. As a courtesy to me, the assistant DA went over the evidence against you—sort of an informal discovery without actually showing me."

"And what do you think?"

"I have to admit, they have a significant case, what with the murder weapon—which is registered to you—having been found in your home. Then there's your jacket with Nicholson's blood on it, and statements from his girlfriend saying you were the last one to see him alive. As for motive, it seems you still owed him ten grand, or so they say."

Sandi reached for a yellow legal pad and began to take notes. She also contacted her secretary and told her to hold all calls and not to disturb us.

"Why don't you start from the beginning and tell me the whole story going back to when you first got to know Gary Nicholson."

***

About an hour later, mentally exhausted from explaining some of the details of my friendship with Gary, the conversation drew to a close. Some things were still touchy. I explained that the ten grand I had owed him was now paid in full for my legal fees for services rendered following his latest drug arrest. In fact, he now owed me, but I hadn't planned to bill him anyway.

I didn't kill Gary and sensed Sandi believed me. Someone was setting me up, but at this point, I had no real proof as to their identity. I needed more time for my own investigation.

"I've been clean for years, Sandi. I've put my life back together with a good practice, as you know, and the bottom line is, I would like you to help me with my defense."

"By helping, you mean co-chair?"

"Correct," I said. "I'm a damn good attorney, but you know the old saying: 'Anyone who defends himself has a fool for a client.' I've seen you in action at the courthouse, and you can be a real bulldog for your clients. And I need a bulldog—one that can growl and bite."

"I give my clients the kind of defense they deserve, but thanks for the compliment."

"Sandi, I need someone to make sure I'm not missing anything. And to correct me when I get too deep into the weeds and the minutia—which I find myself doing when I get too personally involved. Also, I remember what they did to me in the eighties. I need your expertise, knowledge and criminal law experience. This is a conspiracy theory defense all the way, but I have to prove it or, at the very least, deflect it and give the jury reasonable doubt."

"I've been reading up on your previous arrests. Interesting. Nothing seems to be what they say it is."

"Nothin' ever is, Sandi. And I keep wondering why here, why me, why now?"

She looked for a long minute at me before responding. "Think we can work together?"

"I do," I answered without hesitation. "And I promise to listen to you and take your direction."

"You'd better," she laughed.

Seeing her smile was reassuring, and the smile broadened when I handed her a retainer check for thirty thousand dollars.

"Do you understand the DA's case against you?" she asked.

"Yes, I do understand the state's case against me. It's textbook prosecution. They believe they have the motive and opportunity to convict me and then some. I know that technically it doesn't matter whether or not you believe I'm innocent; your job is to defend me. But it does matter in this instance because it matters to me."

Sandi was listening, not just pretending to listen, and that was encouraging.

"Let's set aside the legal bullshit, OK? It's critically important to me that my attorney believes that I didn't do this. So, when—not if—I'm acquitted, it's important that people know beyond a shadow of a doubt that I did *not* kill Gary Nicholson."

"Adrian," Sandi said leaning back in her chair, "how are you handling this arrest and murder charge?"

"Not well. But don't worry, I haven't touched drugs in years, and I rarely drink anymore. But there are times when even drinking too much is not enough; if you know what I mean?

"We had a professor in law school who told us about a theory called the 'ten percent factor,'" I told her. "He said if you can keep the mistakes, misfortunes, and troubles in the many categories of life—those being personal, business, marriage, etc., not to exceed ten percent—it serves to ensure that ninety percent of your life is going very well. And you can't ask for better than ninety percent, which should guarantee you are living a happy life."

"Makes sense," Sandi agreed.

"Since he told me about the ten percent factor, I have strived to live my life within those parameters and, sure enough, I have found it really works. Now, with this hanging over my head, going forward, all my energy will go toward beating this misfortune that now far exceeds the ten percent theory. When I have succeeded in beating this bum rap, I will once again return to living my life within the ninety percent of happiness I'd gotten to know and appreciate."

From the way Sandi nodded her head, I knew that no further sales pitch was necessary, and she understood exactly where I was coming from. She rose from her desk, and I rose from the chair. She then extended her hand, and we sealed the deal with a firm hand-shake.

The manner in which we regarded each other was in the form of a salute.

***

Next up was the arraignment the following Tuesday. It was a routine hearing intended to put our plea on the record and to start the clock to meet the state's speedy trial requirement. Because I was already free on bail, we would be waiving a speedy trial. The arraignment also served the purpose of us getting an empathic "Not Guilty" on the record.

The arraignment and preliminary hearing judge would be Superior Court Judge Robert Corso. The preliminary hearing would be a rubber-stamping of the charges as I would undoubtedly be held to answer for Nicholson's murder. The case would be assigned to another Superior Court judge for the actual trial.

In the preliminary phase, the trick for District Attorney Thomas J. Penrose would be to present just enough evidence to the judge for a preponderance and get his nod without firing off all the arrows in his quiver.

There is little doubt that the prosecution's burden of proof is little burden at all. Though the preliminary hearing is to provide a check on our system and make sure the government doesn't run over the individual rights of its citizens, it is still a fixed game.

The California Assembly streamlined the process after much frustration with seemingly interminable delays with our criminal court system and defendants' speedy trial. The preliminary hearing went from a full airing of the prosecution's evidence to little more than hide-and-seek and lets-make-a-deal. Few witnesses had to be called other than the lead investigator, hearsay was allowed, and the prosecution need not offer but half of its evidence, if that. Just enough to get by, thus avoiding giving the defense any advance on their trial evidence or strategy.

The result was that it was very rare that a case did not meet the preponderance measure and did not proceed to trial on its merits. Still, there is some value to the defense in these proceedings. We get a chance to see some of what is to come and to raise questions about what evidence was presented and what witnesses will testify to.

We were not interested in a plea offer or deal, although, at this point in the proceedings, Penrose had indicated to Sandi that a Man One offer was on the table. I was innocent and not interested in hearing about any manslaughter plea deal, so we were well on our way to a May or June trial.

Also, during the past week of proceedings, Judge Corso had ruled against our motions to suppress the search warrant of my home and business on the grounds of selective prosecution and evidence against me that didn't justify search warrants being issued at that time.

Sandi and I would not present any defense tactics during the preliminary hearing. Penrose would put Chief Kane on the stand, and he would walk the judge through the investigation, findings, and suppositions and sidestep any weaknesses in the case.

Kane was considered the lead investigator for the prosecution. Normally, there is a lead homicide investigator in this role, possibly from the sheriff's office, but the murder took place within the city limits of Gold City, and Chief Kane—once a homicide investigator with the Otter County Sheriff's office, before retiring as Otter Police Chief, and being hired as Police Chief of Gold City—was appropriately named lead. Penrose would also probably put on the medical examiner and a forensic expert. No one else was needed for a prelim.

It was all strategy and games at that point, and I had to admit I loved this part of the trial. The moves made outside the court were many times more important than those made during the trial in the courtroom. Most of the moves inside the court were prepped and choreographed, but I preferred the improvisation done away from the courtroom.

It was time for the two of us to march into battle as a team. A damn powerful team.

Chapter Forty-One

By June 1995, more than nine months after being arrested for Gary Nicholson's murder, Sandi and I were continuing to work hard putting together a defense aimed at leaving reasonable doubt in the minds of the jury. We wanted total acquittal, not a hung jury and a second trial.

Our defense strategy was simple: Because we did not at that time know who actually killed Nicholson, we needed to do the ol' razzle-dazzle and present the jury with a number of alternative theories. By doing that, we would plant in their mind's other possible options and persons that may have had a stronger motive than me to kill Nicholson.

By the time the trial was ready to begin, we had assembled an impressive list of potential witnesses. We might not have to call them all, but the DA knew we were ready to go to the wall to prove my innocence.

Sandi and I decided to have dinner at The Firehouse the night before the trial started. We were seated in a large booth at the back of the bar area enjoying the last of our wine.

"I don't know about you, but I think we're ready," I said.

"As ready as we're ever going to be, I guess," she responded. "Besides presenting alternative theories and suggesting who might have killed Gary and their motive for doing so, we definitely need to get your past arrest and conviction into this trial. It's not going to be easy, because the DA knows we want to go in that direction. He'll fight it all the way, so our best hope is for the DA to make a mistake, then pounce."

"And pounce we will, right?"

"Like a panther on a rabbit," she laughed. "Also, we must convince the jury that the burglary at your home really did happen and that your gun, the murder weapon, really was stolen at that time. We can explain the jacket being at Gary's; you were wearing it that night, took it off and left it there when you went home. It got blood spatters on it during the shooting, and the killer knew it was yours. They took it and planted it along with the gun in your home. The pieces fit together, but somehow we've got to convince the jury that there was a conspiracy against you— then and now."

We both knew that proving conspiracy was difficult but raising that possibility with the jury was one of the best hopes we had for an acquittal.

"As you know," she continued, "a defense lawyer is responsible for the distort and destroy method of criminal defense. That is, you only need one juror to have questions or discrepancies to raise doubt in the prosecution's case. A lot of their positives can be turned into negatives. It's a dance; we trade punches. But, ultimately, they usually land more punches than we can block and that's why it's always good to have an alternative theory. We give the jury another explanation as to why Gary was killed and, if possible, by someone else other than you."

Sandi took a sip of wine and said, "I have learned through experience that when defending murder charges, it helps raise reasonable doubt if you can actually point to another person who might have committed the murder. Not just be able to say anybody else could have done it, but actually give the jury a name, a motive, an opportunity, and why they should be seriously considered, instead of the defendant."

That was the other best hope. If we couldn't prove a conspiracy, then we needed to provide an alternative suspect who could have committed the murder. We had some people in mind, but we knew a wild shotgun approach would not persuade the jury. We needed to figure out who the hell murdered Gary, then unload on that person with laser-like accuracy. And if we guessed wrong, I knew I might be spending the next twenty-five years of my life inside the walls of San Quentin.

"Remember," she added, "the DA offered you Man One to plea this case, which tells us they really didn't want to go to trial on Murder Two charges. Then, too, there was all the commotion we caused around town with our subpoenas, and that tells me there are a lot of nervous folks out there waiting to see what we're going to do.

"Adrian, they say you have three lives—public, private and secret. If you go forward with this trial that secret life of yours goes very public. Are you ready for that?"

"Yes, I have no choice. They have left me no choice." I paused with thought, then said. "Unrelated subject, are your thoughts about me testifying still the same? You know that most juries, especially in a murder case, want to see the accused get up there, answer questions, and say they didn't do it."

"True, but the last thing we want to do is give them the ammunition they may not otherwise have gotten by you not testifying. More importantly, we don't want to give the DA a shot at you in a cross-examination that's not necessary. So, let's see where we are as the trial moves along, then we'll make that decision together."

"Sandi," I said looking down at the table. "Until I fell apart and lost everything, I lived a life of discipline. I think I can say, with hindsight, that I would never do it again. I have real remorse about the pain I caused so many. I've apologized to those I hurt, but sometimes it doesn't feel like enough. The truth is, I almost didn't make it."

She smiled with a pause, then said, "You know, it's hard to measure *almost* because almost doesn't matter. I may be out of place here, and maybe even wrong, but you seem to be giving permission for everyone to punish you, including yourself—as if that will make up for the value you have attached to your devastating experience. Stop wasting energy beating yourself up. Other people are standing in line to do that for you. I think it's time to move on, stop saying 'I'm sorry,' and take advantage of what you have learned and the second chance you've earned."

We both fell silent. I looked at Sandi and said, "You're right, and thanks for being honest."

"This is going to be a tough time, Adrian, so if we're not honest with each other, we might not achieve our goal. Understand?"

"Understood. And thanks for keeping me focused so that we're in a position to offer the jury a credible and viable defense."

"That's my job."

"I know, but over the past six or seven months, well, to be honest, my feelings have been playing games with me. I've thought that maybe, somehow, this could become more than a job—more than a professional relationship."

"I know, Adrian," she answered as if she had expected my suggestion. "I feel the same way, and I'm glad you said something before the trial started. But we can't allow anything to distract us right now—especially personal feelings."

I nodded, encouraged by her words.

"Let's win this damn case, OK?" she said, "Then we can talk about us."

She looked deep into my eyes, gave a knowing wink and said, "And I really look forward to having that discussion—very, very much."

"I also look forward to that day," I said as I put my hand on Sandi's hand in a gesture that clearly revealed both my gratitude and growing feelings toward her.

We then got up and headed for the front door, saying good-night to each other outside on the sidewalk: no kiss, but a quick, gentle hug. Then we went our separate ways.

Both of us needed a good night's sleep, and I needed to mentally prepare for battle. Scenes of examination and cross-examinations. I was laying out my suit and imagining the positions and arguments I would make to the jury. The case was coming alive inside me, I had momentum and motivation, and that was a good thing. I had the conviction that I would not lose.

I didn't know what happened to Gary Nicholson, or what actions he had taken that might have brought his demise, or who was responsible for it. But I had the wind at my back, and this sail wasn't coming down until I hit the shore and got out of the storm.

I knew we were prepared to do battle, we were confident of that, but the words of General George Armstrong Custer ran through my brain as I laid my head on my pillow for some much-needed sleep: "There aren't enough Indians in the world to defeat the Seventh Calvary."

As I thought of those words—among the good general's final public utterances—I prayed that the district attorney wouldn't appear in court the next morning dressed like Chief Crazy Horse.

PART THREE
The Trial

Chapter Forty-Two

At 10:00 A.M. on Monday, June 16, 1995, I was seated with Sandi Stassi in Quartz County Superior Court Three in the old courthouse in Gold City. Above the courthouse entrance a sign reads, A PUBLIC OFFICE IS A PUBLIC TRUST. And if ever I was looking for public trust, it was in jury selection. We had spent the previous week selecting a jury, legally referred to as *voir dire*, and in their hands and hearts rested my fate.

By this time, life had taught me that everybody lies. Cops lie. Clients lie. Lawyers lie. Even jurors lie. In law school, you learn that in criminal law there is a belief that every trial is won or lost in the selection of the jury. I was never all-in on that commonly held belief, but I've always been convinced that for certain trials— especially murder trials—few things are more important to the outcome than the selection of the twelve citizens who will decide your client's fate.

And in this case, it was *my* fate.

Selection of a jury may also be the most complex part of the trial reliant on whims, fate, and luck—and being able to ask the right question to the right person at the right time.

Since Murder Two in California includes a possible life sentence, we were entitled to twenty peremptory challenges. We used them wisely, as did the district attorney with his twenty preemptory dismissals. The prosecution managed to get a couple of gun-control lefties seated over our objections, but, all in all, we felt we had a serious jury that would carefully listen to testimony and rely on the evidence.

And that's all any attorney—or client—can ask for.

Sandi was dressed in a navy-blue coat over a light-blue blouse with matching navy skirt and navy shoes. I had on a new grey pinstripe suit, white shirt, dark blue-striped tie, and cordovan dress shoes. We both looked sharp and confident, and that's how we wanted the jury to think of us.

Seated at a table to our right was District Attorney Thomas J. Penrose, along with two of his staff. Penrose had come up through the ranks as an ADA under now-Superior Court Judge Barbara Worthington and had been in office for about five years. He was telling friends that he was going to run for another term and putting me behind bars would help cinch that next election.

Penrose was a short man with a pocked face and very pasty, unhealthy complexion. He wore thick glasses and had one of the worst comb-overs I had ever seen. He was truly an unattractive man and his personality reflected his looks.

"All rise," instructed the bailiff as Superior Court Judge John J. Campbell entered the courtroom and took his position on the bench. Judge Campbell was a striking figure of authority right out of central casting. A John Forsyth double with a full head of white hair—a tall, thin man who moved with the ease of a gazelle.

He pounded his gavel and said, "Order, order please. Mr. Penrose are you ready to proceed?"

"Yes, Your Honor," the DA replied, using a deep voice in an attempt to sound as if he was in full control of the situation.

"Miss Stassi is the defense ready as well?"

"Yes, Your Honor, we are."

"At this time, then, are there any further motions for my consideration from either of you?" Judge Campbell asked.

Penrose and Sandi indicated they were ready to proceed.

"Good, then please bring in the jury, Officer DePhillips."

The bailiff nodded and opened the door to the jury room. The jury consisted of seven men and five women. There were also four alternates. All were Caucasian, which is not unusual in Quartz County, often called the whitest county in California. They ranged in age from mid-thirties to early seventies. Probably sixty percent retired.

The jury came out in single file, much like your favorite team taking the basketball court. They weren't all dressed in the same uniform, but there was a feeling of anticipation and some tension in the air. They carried pads and pens and assumed the same seats they had occupied when the final jury was selected the previous week. Two rows. Six up and six down, plus four alternates. Judge Campbell insisted on four alternates, not the usual two, because it was a murder trial, and he didn't want any jury problems to be the cause of a mistrial.

The courtroom was filled to capacity with spectators, press and friends, as well as a few lawyers with a keen interest in the case. My mom, dad, and brother were seated right behind us, and I was happy they were there.

Judge Campbell began by saying, "I want to admonish the courtroom. I will not tolerate any outbursts, laughter or talking during these proceedings. And if any of you have a beeper or cell phone, please turn it off. If I hear any beeping or ringing, I will have the bailiff take your device and keep it until you leave this courtroom. And if it happens twice, you won't be coming back."

Cell phones were just coming into widespread use in 1995, but beepers were pretty common. So, as Judge Campbell made his announcement, a dozen or so spectators reached for their device to make sure they were on mute.

Then came the judge's instructions to the jury. He told jurors that the trial would begin with opening statements from the opposing attorneys. "Ladies and gentlemen, remember," Judge Campbell said, "opening statements are not evidence. It is up to these attorneys to back up their opening statements during the trial with facts to corroborate their statements to you. I see many of you have notepads. Good. Please take copious notes and pay attention to these opening statements and look to corroborate those statements with the facts during the trial.

"Mr. Penrose, you may proceed with your opening statement," the judge announced.

It was like getting the green flag at the county drag strip. And away we go!

Judge Campbell had told us during the pre-trial session that we would be required to stay at our tables or use the lectern centered in the courtroom when addressing the witnesses during testimony. However, during opening and closing statements, we would be allowed to address the jury from any position within the courtroom that was within site-line of the jury, including in front of the jury box. This sweet spot was known to veterans of the court as the "proving grounds." It was the only time, other than closing arguments when the lawyers spoke directly to the jury and they either made their case, or they didn't.

Rising to his feet, Thomas J. Penrose walked over to the jury box and looked at the jurors with an earnest, somber expression. Then he turned sharply on his heels, pointed an accusing finger at me and said, "That man, Adrian Davis, murdered one of his best friends, Gary Nicholson. The evidence you will hear in this courtroom will clearly show that Mr. Nicholson was shot four times in cold blood—Mr. Davis having been motivated by money, greed, and, oh yes, also anger. When a person has been shot four times, it's usually by someone who knows the victim and by someone who is very angry and filled with hate or vengeance. One fatal shot is murder, of course, but four fatal shots show a personal connection."

Penrose paused to let that last point percolate with the jury.

Because the prosecution is first to address the jury with their opening statement, it was Sandi's practice to never take her eyes off the jury while the prosecution was presenting its case. She listened closely, observing each juror's expression as Penrose spoke, and ready to object to anything out of context. She wanted to see how the jurors reacted to Penrose and if her observations about them were correct.

Of course, Penrose spent most of his opening warning the jury about what he called the defenses' "smoke and mirrors." Confident in his own case, he looked to tear down ours.

"The defense is going to try and sell you a bill of goods," Penrose continued. "Big conspiracies and high drama. This murder is not complicated; in fact, it is simple. Don't be led astray. Watch closely. Listen closely. As Judge Campbell already told you, make sure that whatever is said here today is backed up with evidence during the trial. Evidence to substantiate and prove what has been told to you.

"The evidence will clearly show that Mr. Davis was the last person to see the victim alive. We will show that the murder weapon was registered to the defendant and found in his possession. We will show that at the time of death the defendant was on the premises where the murder took place and that the murder victim's blood was found on the defendant's clothing and his gun, which will be proven to be the murder weapon. These facts will unvaryingly point in the same direction—to the defendant, Mr. Adrian Davis."

Penrose paused to look at his notes then again pointed toward me.

"The direction to which guilt points is right there," he said as he wagged his finger in my direction. "The defendant was at the victim's home late that night, drinking alcohol while cocaine was being consumed. A witness will verify these facts and also testify that the defendant and victim were arguing about money related to the victim's defense in another case. You see, ladies and gentlemen of the jury, Mr. Davis, a lawyer here in Gold City, was defending the victim in another matter, and our witness will testify that Mr. Nicholson was not happy with his defense, telling the defendant in a loud voice of his displeasure.

"I have willingly accepted the prosecution's obligation of proving to you that this man, Adrian Davis, is a murderer beyond any reasonable doubt. A cold-blooded murderer. After you consider all the testimony and both sides present their closing arguments, it will be your obligation to follow the letter of the law as explained to you by Judge Campbell and find this defendant guilty as charged. Thank you for your patience and attention."

Penrose returned to his seat without any facial expression or body language. He was a pro, and we knew we had a tough fight ahead of us.

The DA consumed almost the entire allotted time for his opening statement seemingly leaving no secrets about his case against me. He showed typical prosecution arrogance; putting it all out there and daring the defense to contradict his findings. Being the eight-hundred-pound gorilla in the room, the prosecution was so big and powerful it didn't need to worry about arrogance, or if their statements were one-hundred percent correct, or not. They just painted everything they said with a wide brush and hung it on the wall with the finesse of a sledgehammer.

"Miss Stassi?" Judge Campbell said.

Sandi stood and said, "Your Honor, the defense wishes to reserve its opening statement until such time as the prosecution has finished presenting its case to the jury."

"Mr. Penrose?" Judge Campbell asked as he looked at the DA.

The DA rose and now both attorneys were on their feet.

"Your Honor, the defense is obviously playing games with this court and this jury, attempting to take unfair advantage through this request. Although opening statements are not admissible evidence, if the defense is permitted to hear our case prior to addressing the jury, it will allow them to address specifics which they may not presently be aware of or specific elements of the case that this court would consider unimportant. Finally, such a procedure is highly unusual in a murder trial and later could be interpreted as grounds for appeal. As the People's representative, I strongly object."

The judge looked over at the defense table. "Miss Stassi?"

"Your Honor, while we realize this is an unusual request, it is not, as you know, precedent-setting. And in our judgment, the defense would be better served with a later statement to the jury. If the prosecution has a case strong enough to convict, delaying our opening statement will have little or no impact upon the jury. In any case, Your Honor, the jury will hear all the facts, my client will have been well represented, and justice will have been served."

Judge Campbell paused for a moment looking over at the jury, then back at Sandi. "Prosecution's objection denied," Campbell ruled without further comment.

"Thank you, Your Honor," Sandi said as Penrose quietly steamed.

At that point, Judge Campbell asked the DA to call his first witness.

Caught off-guard by our strategical legal move, Penrose asked if he could begin after lunch. Judge Campbell grumbled a bit but agreed that, based on Sandi's unexpected announcement, the court would be adjourned until 1:30 P.M.

Chapter Forty-Three

That afternoon, shortly after 1:30 P.M., District Attorney Thomas Penrose called his first witness. There were very few empty seats in the courtroom, and a couple of Sacramento reporters were seated at a special press table.

There is an unfair advantage for the prosecution in every trial. The advantage being, the state has the power and presumption of right on its side. It also comes with an assumption of honesty, integrity, and fairness. The assumption is, we wouldn't be here if the smoke didn't lead to a fire.

"I call Gold City Chief of Police Abel Kane," Penrose said with an air of confidence.

Chief Kane rose from his seat in the rear of the courtroom and walked to the witness stand—to the left of Judge Campbell and to the right of the jury—where he was sworn in by the court bailiff.

In a murder trial, the main witness for the prosecution is always the lead investigator. There are no living victims to tell the jury what really happened, so it falls on the investigator to paint the picture for jurors. He puts everything together and makes his case clear and sympathetic to the jury. It is his job to sell the case to the jury and, like any other sales jobs, it often comes down to who is selling the goods to be sold. Does the prosecutor seem more like Elmer Gantry or Elmer Fudd? Style and confidence can often swing a juror's opinion.

Penrose called the case's lead investigator to the stand right after the noon lunch break. It was a stroke of genius and master planning on his part. Chief Kane would hold court through the afternoon session and into adjournment for the day. This would give the jurors the evening to think about his testimony, and short of a few objections here and there, we could do little else. Even with Sandi's cross of the chief, his testimony ensures that the first day of trial will end "15-love" for the prosecution.

Penrose took a sip of water, shuffled through some notes, then paced in front of the witness in his characteristically somber demeanor. After going through the chief's credentials and law enforcement history, he said, "Chief Kane, will you please explain to the jury and the court what you saw when you arrived at the victim's home on the morning of November third of last year?"

"Of course," the town's top cop answered. "Upon arriving at the murder scene, I checked with my officers to confirm that the outside perimeter had been secured. I was also told that the medical examiner was already in the house. I entered the victim's house and saw Mr. Nicholson on the living room floor with what appeared to be multiple gunshot wounds to the upper torso and head."

Chief Kane was a seasoned veteran and a solid witness for the prosecution. In his precise and sometimes droll delivery, Kane described arriving at the scene and determined that the victim's death was a homicide. Through Kane, the crime scene photographs were introduced and displayed in detail on the overhead flat screen in front of the jury. The photos, more than any testimony from Kane, established the crime of murder—a requirement for conviction.

Sandi and I had argued with marginal success during pretrial about the crime scene photos. We had objected to use of the overhead screen for their display, as well as the use of easels and large images because they would be prejudicial to me. Photos of real people murdered are always shocking, and its human nature to want to punish those responsible for another person's death. Photos of harsh death can easily turn a jury against the accused, whether the evidence backs up the accusations, or not. And for jurors, the larger the photo, the more shocking the murder scene becomes.

I knew we wouldn't win elimination of all the photos and Judge Campbell split the difference by allowing seven of the dozen or so photos the prosecution wanted to display, and he allowed the use of the overhead screen as well. It was still more of a win for the prosecution than the defense, but we took what we could get, scored a few points, and let them know that we weren't sleeping at the defense table. Naturally, Penrose chose the most graphic and bloodiest of the photos for his display to the jury.

"Thank you, Chief, for walking us through the crime scene photos with such precise detail, as uncomfortable as they may be to view."

He looked toward the juror box for their reaction, then asked, "What happened next?"

"I talked with the assistant county medical examiner, Marcus Kopp, and he confirmed the apparent cause of death. He told me the approximate time of death was between one and three A.M. I then did a walkthrough of the house with Sergeant Ralph Pittman, who informed me that no murder weapon had been found, nor were there any witnesses that we knew of."

"Who discovered the body, Chief Kane?"

"Mr. Nicholson's girlfriend, Roxanne Meyers. She arrived at the home about ten that morning to pick up Nicholson and take him to breakfast. She was pretty shaken up."

Penrose paused for a moment then turned back to the chief. "Did Mr. Nicholson's house look as if it had been trashed or torn apart as if somebody was searching for something? Any signs of a robbery?"

"No, sir. It was relatively clean and neat."

"Were you aware of any apparent motive?" Penrose asked.

"No, not immediately. But because of Mr. Nicholson's drug activity and arrests for drug sales and distribution in the past, we felt it may have had something to do with illegal drugs."

"So, you were aware of the victim's involvement with drug sales?"

"Oh, yeah, we knew. In fact, Nicholson had been recently arrested for the second time for cocaine sales and distribution by my officers, and his lawyer for both arrests was the defendant, Mr. Davis."

"Did you find any cocaine or other drugs at the victim's home?" the DA asked.

"We found a small amount of cocaine, about a gram. And we found a small amount of marijuana. The amounts represented what we would consider personal use."

"Chief Kane, were you aware that the defendant and the victim were close friends?"

"Yes, sir, we were aware that their relationship went beyond a normal attorney/client relationship."

"Were you also aware of the defendant's violent temper?" Penrose asked.

Sandi jumped to her feet to object, requesting, "Sidebar, Your Honor."

Judge Campbell waved both counsels to the right of his bench for a hushed discussion.

"Your Honor," Sandi told the judge, "this alleged incident that the DA is referring to was an isolated incident and has nothing whatsoever to do with this case. It was a long time ago, and it had to do with my client's business taxes that were allegedly owed at the time. The district attorney is trying to backdoor a way to bring suspicion on my client by alleging a bad temper that he may or may not have, to conclude that he must have been involved in this murder."

"Not true, Your Honor," Penrose protested. "The chief has specific information about an attack on a state employee by Mr. Davis some years ago, and I contend this information would help in showing the jury that Mr. Davis can be provoked when confronted."

There was a pause by Judge Campbell then, "Mr. Penrose, rephrase the question, or move on." The judge then asked both attorneys to step back.

"The jury will disregard the district attorney's last question," Campbell told the jury. "Mr. Penrose, do you have any further questions for Chief Kane?"

"No further questions, Your Honor," the DA said knowing that to pursue the incident at the Board of Equalization—something that had happened nearly ten years earlier—would again be objected to by Sandi, and again sustained by the court.

"Your witness, Miss Stassi," Judge Campbell announced.

As Sandi and I conferred for a moment, muffled audience voices in the courtroom became louder. Judge Campbell's resounding gavel, however, quickly brought an end to the chatter.

Sandi got up from her chair and entered the well of the courtroom, then walked up to the podium.

On cross, she decided to zero-in on one photo and try to get the jury to think about something other than the gore presented to them in the other photos. By planting questions with no answers, she felt she was doing her job while hopefully planting seeds of doubt in the jurors' minds. With the judge's permission, she used the projection remote to eliminate all the photos except one.

"Chief Kane, I want to draw your attention to the photo on the screen. I believe it is marked People's Exhibit Ten. Can you tell the jury what that is in the foreground of the photo?"

"Yes, it's an open briefcase."

"And is that how you found it when you arrived at the scene?"

"Yes, it is."

"It was sitting there open like this?" Sandi asked, pointing to the open briefcase.

"Yes."

"And did you make any inquiry of any witness or anyone else to determine if someone had opened the briefcase after the victim was discovered?"

"I asked Roxie Meyers, who had called 911 if she had opened it, and she confirmed that she had not, and that's how she found it."

"Being the veteran homicide detective that you are, and Gold City's police chief as well, what did seeing that open briefcase mean to you?"

"Nothing, really, it was just part of the crime scene."

"So, your experience didn't cause you to think there may have been a robbery involved in this murder?"

"Not really," the chief smirked.

"If robbery was not a motive in this crime, why would the killer take the time to open the victim's briefcase?"

"There is no evidence that the killer, in fact, opened the briefcase. It may have been open before the victim was killed."

"True, but it also may have been closed and, in fact, been opened by the killer looking for money or valuables that could have been in the case. Isn't that correct?"

"Objection, your honor, argumentative, and assumes facts not in evidence." Penrose was on his feet. "Miss Stassi is fishing here, Your Honor. There is absolutely no evidence that that briefcase has anything to do with this case and she knows it. To expect the police chief to speculate on such a hypothetical question is irresponsible, to say the least."

"Objection sustained. Move on Miss Stassi," Judge Campbell directed.

"Chief, did you have the briefcase dusted for fingerprints?"

"Of course, and only Mr. Nicholson's prints were found on the briefcase."

"What about blood? Any blood splatters from the victim's gunshot wounds?" Stassi asked.

"Yes. We found blood from the victim on the briefcase. A small amount on the inside and considerably more on the outside shell." Kane answered.

Defeated on that point, Sandi looked down at some notes that had nothing to do with anything she was addressing at the moment. Not as a stall, but for effect. She felt confident she had planted the question about a possible robbery in the jury's mind as a motive for the murder, but she didn't want to leave it at that. She decided to try a bluff. If you're killing birds, you might as well get two for one.

"Chief Kane, at any time during this investigation have you discussed with any other investigator or any other law enforcement officer the possibility that the murder of Gary Nicholson was the result of a robbery attempt?"

"No, I have not."

"Are you sure?"

"Quite sure."

Sandi scribbled something on my notepad, again having nothing to do with anything—just more theater for the jury.

"Chief Kane, I'd like to address another point of interest that we believe is a blatant flaw in this investigation. How many suspects have you had in this murder case? Or, for that matter, how many have you even questioned as possible suspects?"

"Just one," he answered with another smirk. "The defendant."

"Is this normal procedure in a murder case? Only one suspect? Settling for the first possible suspect?"

"I don't know about normal, 'cause there's nothing normal about murder, but we had the murder weapon registered to the defendant, found in the defendant's possession, and the victim's blood on the defendant's jacket. What else did we need?"

"Your Honor," Sandi said, "would you please remind the witness that attorneys ask the questions, not witnesses."

"Point taken, Miss Stassi," the judge replied as he admonished Kane.

"Chief," she continued, "did you recover any of the other clothing that Mr. Davis was wearing that evening? And if so, were you able to test it for the victim's blood, or gunshot residue, as you did with the defendant's jacket?"

"Yes, the defendant gave us a pair of Levi's, a pair of sneakers, and a shirt he said he was wearing that evening. We had them tested and found no blood on them from the deceased, nor any powder residue."

"What was your conclusion from that?" she asked.

"We dismissed it as not relevant because Davis could have given us clothing that looked similar to what he had been wearing that night. Nicholson's girlfriend, Miss Meyers, had given us a general description of what Davis was wearing, but we could not verify with certainty that they were the same clothes. Her description and what he gave us were similar, but we couldn't prove it positively."

"So," Sandi asked, "to confirm for the jury's benefit, the only piece of clothing that belonged to the defendant that had blood spatters on it was his jacket. This jacket, marked as Prosecution Exhibit Three, is the same jacket which you and your officers say they found at my client's home. Correct?"

"That's correct," Chief Kane answered.

"Thank you, Chief, that's all for now," Sandi said. Then she addressed Judge Campbell. "Your Honor, Chief Kane is on our defense witness list as well as the prosecution's, so I want to be clear with the court and the DA that we reserve the right to recall this witness during our defense presentation, should that be necessary."

"So recognized, Miss Stassi."

Turning his attention to Kane, he said, "Chief Kane, you will remain available for the defense should Miss Stassi request you be brought back. Is that understood?"

"Yes, sir," the chief answered.

"Mr. Penrose, any redirect?" Judge Campbell inquired.

"Yes, Your Honor," the DA said as he got up from his chair and walked toward the lectern.

"Chief Kane, would you be good enough to tell this court exactly why you were inclined to concentrate your attention on Mr. Davis in the process of seeking out a suspect in the murder of Gary Nicholson?"

"Certainly," Kane answered. "According to a reliable witness, Mr. Davis was the last person to have seen the victim alive."

"Objection, Your Honor, the question assumes facts, not in evidence," Sandi quickly countered. "The last person to have seen Mr. Nicholson alive was the murderer, and it's yet to be proven that my client is that person."

"Sustained."

"He had been drinking at Mr. Nicholson's home according to the same witness," the chief continued, "and that witness is Mr. Nicholson's girlfriend, Roxie Meyers. She also referred to reported cocaine use and an argument that subsequently ensued between the defendant and the victim concerning money the defendant owed Mr. Nicholson—some ten thousand dollars."

"And that information, from a reliable witness, is what prompted you to request a search warrant for Mr. Davis's home and office. Is that correct?" Penrose asked.

"Yes, sir, that's correct," responded the chief with a slight smile.

"Thank you, that's all," Penrose said as he returned to the prosecution's table.

Chief Kane was excused, and Penrose called one of the paramedics who responded to the 911 call and confirmed that Nicholson was dead at the scene. He was on and off the stand in fifteen minutes as we had no cross for the witness.

"Although it's just after four o'clock, I think that is enough for today, so we will adjourn," Judge Campbell announced. "We will convene again at nine o'clock sharp tomorrow morning. I wish to remind the jury that you are not to discuss this trial with anyone outside this courtroom or amongst yourselves."

And with that, a firm whack of the gavel signaled the end of the first day of the trial.

Sandi had done her job that first day, and I was beginning to think that maybe—just maybe—justice might actually prevail.

I was working to control my paranoia. I had to trust Sandi. And I did, I think. Someone had once told me that controlled paranoia was a survival mechanism and uncontrolled paranoia could end up being a greased chute into madness.

Frankly, I couldn't afford any more madness in my life than I'd already experienced, so controlled paranoia was my only option.

Chapter Forty-Four

At exactly 9:00 A.M. the following morning, as Sandi and I exchanged some last-minute thoughts about the next witness, the bailiff called for all to rise as Judge John Campbell entered the courtroom and took his place at the bench.

It had been a long night for me; I didn't rest well and already felt fatigued. And I knew the day had just begun.

"Good morning," Judge Campbell announced. "I trust we're all rested?"

I tried my best not to look the way I felt.

"Let the record reflect that we are all present and the jury is seated, so please call your next witness, Mr. Penrose."

"Thank you, Your Honor," Penrose said as he rose from his chair. "We call Salvatore DeMauro to the stand."

The Quartz County Medical Examiner walked to the witness stand and was sworn in. Then Penrose went to the lectern in the well of the court.

"Mr. DeMauro, you are the Quartz County Medical Examiner, correct?"

"Yes, that's correct."

"Your job is to determine the cause and time of death and to examine the body for any peculiar or out-of-the-ordinary things within a deceased body that both the prosecution and the defense should be made aware of. Is that correct?" Penrose asked.

"Well, sir, my scope of responsibilities actually exceeds that definition, but your description covers it pretty well for the purpose of this proceeding," DeMauro responded.

"Now, then, Mr. DeMauro, according to your official report, the time of death has been established to be between one and three in the morning, is that correct?" the DA asked as he handed People's Exhibit Thirteen to the medical examiner.

"Yes, it was determined at the crime scene by my assistant, Marcus Kopp, and later confirmed by me, that Mr. Nicholson died sometime between those hours of four gunshot wounds to the head and upper torso. One to the head, two to the chest, and one in the shoulder; fired at point-blank range."

"How do you know it was point-blank?" Penrose asked.

"Size of the entrance and exit wounds. You see, the further a bullet travels the more it wobbles and the bigger the wound holes. Nicholson's body had smaller bullet wounds in both entrance and exit."

"And the cause of death was...?"

"The cause of death was from multiple gunshot wounds to the torso and head. Any three of the four bullets that hit Mr. Nicholson could have killed him. The one head shot would have killed him instantly, and the one shot to the heart could have killed him as well. Actually, the shot to the upper chest—the one just below the throat—could also have killed him. Take your pick. The fourth bullet hit his upper right shoulder, which was not a kill shot."

"Did you conduct a toxicology analysis on the victim?"

"Yes, I did; a standard procedure."

"And what, if anything, did you find?"

"Mr. Nicholson had a very large amount of alcohol in his blood, along with cocaine and marijuana. All in amounts that would be considered excessive."

"Did you find anything else of interest, or what you would consider unusual?"

"Yes, Mr. Nicholson was also afflicted with the HIV virus. It was in its infancy, but surely something that would have developed into full-blown AIDS very soon."

"Nothing further, thank you Mr. DeMauro. Your witness," the DA said as he gestured toward us.

"No questions, Your Honor," Sandi announced as she looked over at me. We were not surprised by the reference to AIDS as we had prior access to the prosecution's discovery. But the HIV announcement was definitely a surprise to the court.

Caught off-guard by Sandi's decision to not cross-examine DeMauro, the DA hesitated for a moment then said, "I call Sergeant Dennis Miller to the stand."

Miller was the ballistics expert for the sheriff's office. Like DeMauro, he came in from the back of the court to be sworn in, then took his place in the witness stand.

Penrose approached and asked, "Sergeant Miller, please explain to the court what you do as a ballistic expert."

"We mainly deal in firearms; their calibers, their ownership, their destruction, their capabilities, bullet analyses, that sort of thing. Generally, most any question having to do with firearms, ammunition, and ballistic comparisons that comes to us, we can get an answer."

"Thank you, sergeant. Did you or your office have occasion to work on the murder of Mr. Gary Nicholson? And if so, what were your findings?"

"Yes, I was involved in the murder investigation. Mr. Nicholson was shot four times with a thirty-eight-caliber revolver. Three of the four slugs were retrieved from his body by the medical examiner. The shoulder shot passed through the body and lodged in the wall behind the victim. We retrieved that bullet as well. We successfully matched one of the spent bullets to the gun owned by the defendant, Adrian Davis."

"That is the same gun found at the defendant's home. The same gun purchased by and registered to the defendant, correct?" the DA asked.

"Yes, that's correct," Miller answered.

"Sergeant Miller, did you do a Seraphim Test, or otherwise known as gunshot residue, or GSR test, on the hands and clothing of Mr. Davis shortly after his arrest?"

"Yes, as ordered by your office we performed the test on both of his hands, his face, the jacket the police found at the defendant's house, and tennis shoes, pants and shirt the police identified as being worn the evening of the Nicholson murder. And we tested the murder weapon."

"Please tell the court what GSR is and its meaning if found on tested items," Penrose asked.

"When a gun is fired, the gunshot residue particles, small particles produced during the gunpowder explosions, are emitted from the back of the weapon and the muzzle. These particles fly onto the skin and clothing of the person holding the gun. They contain elements that result from the propellant and primer decomposing, as well as from the bullet coating or jacket, cartridge components, and previous residues in the barrel. Characteristic elements include antimony, lead, and barium. Some special types of ammunition also can contain titanium and zinc. These elements cannot be completely removed by normal washing or cleaning, and samples of the particles can be taken from suspects with adhesive collection devices for further examination."

"Thank you, Sergeant Miller. What, if any, gunshot residue did you find on the items you tested belonging to the defendant?"

"We found substantial residue on the murder weapon and the jacket found at the defendant's house. We also found residue on the defendant's shoes, a pair of Levi pants, and the shirt the police identified as being worn by the defendant the night of the murder."

"Finally, Sergeant Miller, in your professional opinion and expert knowledge on this topic, what, if any, conclusion is to be drawn from your testing of these items?"

"All the items that tested positive for gunshot residue did, in fact, encounter gunpowder at some point, and some items, like the gun and the jacket, were very close to a gunpowder explosion."

"Thank you, sir; nothing further."

Sandi stood and calmly asked the witness, "Sergeant Miller, let's go back to the bullets retrieved from the body. Didn't the bullets you retrieved from the victim's body have extensive damage to them?"

"Yes, they were pretty mashed up from hitting bones in the body, and the bullet lodged in the wall had hit a nail. The best-preserved bullet was the one that lodged in the victim's heart."

"So, even with the extensive damage to the bullets you were still able to identify and match these bullets to the defendant's gun?" she asked as she walked back toward our table.

"Yes, as I said, the one bullet retrieved from the heart had little damage to it, so we were able to match it positively to the defendant's gun."

"OK, now Sergeant Miller let's talk about that GSR test you performed. How many days after the murder of Gary Nicholson did you begin the GSR tests on my client and his clothing?"

"I believe it was six days after the murder."

"Were all three elements found in all your tests?"

"Yes, antimony, lead and barium."

"And did you get particle counts from all the items?"

"Yes," Miller answered.

"What does the particle count represent, or mean to this jury?"

"The higher the count the closer the item was to the gun explosion."

"What is considered a high count?"

"Any count of a thousand to two thousand, or higher, is considered significant."

"Did any of the items have these higher counts?"

"Yes, the gun and the jacket. The jacket was just over thirteen hundred and the gun over two thousand."

"And my client's clothing? What were their counts?"

Miller checked his notes and said. "The shoes, pants, and shirt were all less than one hundred."

"One hundred? That's almost non-existent." Sandi said.

Miller did not respond.

"As an expert in your field, what does such a low count tell you, Sergeant Miller?"

"That these particular items had significantly lower exposure to the gunshot residue."

"And how could that be if my client was wearing these items on the night of the murder and, in fact, fired the murder weapon that killed Mr. Nicholson as the prosecution is claiming?"

"In this case, more of the residue could have ejected from the barrel of the gun than from the cylinders to the rear. Thus, the high count of residue came down on the gun and the jacket that was laying on the couch under the gunshot."

"Yes, that sounds possible, but did you find any residue on my client's hands or face?"

"No, we did not."

"Can you explain that, Sergeant Miller?"

"No."

"Isn't it a fact that GSR lasts nearly forever? It can land on anything and stay there indefinitely. Isn't it possible that my client's clothing contacted the very low GSR count by being placed in the back seat or trunk of a patrol car on its way to the lab for the GSR testing?"

Miller shrugged, not sure how to—or whether to—answer the question.

"Because police shoot their weapons frequently for practice and qualifications, residue on their clothing from those shootings could have remained in the patrol cars and been transferred to my client's clothing just by being placed on the same seats, or in the trunk, of cars that have GSR residue in them. Isn't that possible, Sargent Miller? Could that explain the low GSR count on my client's clothing?"

Miller didn't immediately answer, then said, "Yes, what you have outlined is possible."

"Isn't it a fact," Sandi continued, "that the ability to contaminate is just one reason there is such a limited degree of conclusions that can be drawn from gunshot residue? And experts have testified in other murder cases that neither prosecutors nor defense attorneys should ever make a statement that says gunshot residue shows for certain that someone fired a gun. Isn't that correct, Sergeant Miller?"

"Objection, Your Honor, the question calls for speculation and a conclusion from the witness about a fact not familiar to the court." Penrose was on his feet knowing Sandi had shot several holes in the testimony of his firearms witness. "Sergeant Miller is not familiar with defense counsel's references to other experts and their statements, or conjectures. He can only testify to his findings, knowledge, and expertise."

"Thank you, that's all for this witness," Sandi told the judge before he ruled on the objection.

"Then let's break for lunch," Campbell said. "Court will reconvene at one-thirty."

***

After the lunch break, District Attorney Thomas Penrose called his next witness. "We would like to call Mr. Clayton Lingo to the stand, Your Honor."

Lingo, wearing a traditional suit and tie, walked to the witness stand with an air of confidence that came from many years of testifying in court.

"Mr. Lingo, as the county sheriff's fingerprint expert, did you have occasion to visit the Nicholson murder scene and, if so, what were your findings regarding fingerprints at the scene?"

"Yes, I was brought in the morning of the murder after the body had been removed and I could take charge of the house. I found many different fingerprints in Mr. Nicholson's home."

"Did any of prints match the defendant, Mr. Davis? And if so, where did you find them?"

"Yes, we found the defendant's prints in the kitchen, in the downstairs bathroom, in the living room, on pool sticks, the pool tables, on the front door, and on two empty beer bottles. We also found the defendants prints on the deceased boat in the garage."

"You say you found many prints from the defendant. Would this indicate that the defendant had made numerous visits to the defendant's home, or would you say he left them there all in one visit?"

"No, there were so many fingerprints matching the defendant's that I feel comfortable saying that they were left there over a number of visits to the home, not just on one occasion."

"That's all, Your Honor," Penrose said as he returned to his chair.

"Your witness, Miss Stassi."

Sandi rose and walked toward the jury box carrying some notes in her hand.

"Mr. Lingo, in your analysis of my client's prints, can you tell this court when they were left in the home and how old these prints were? Were they left there the night of the murder? A week earlier? A month earlier?"

Lingo looked down and said: "No, I can't tell the court that. I can only say for sure that they belong to the defendant."

"So, as you indicated, my client's prints were probably left there over many visits and not necessarily left there on the night of the murder, correct?" Sandi asked as she reviewed her notes.

"Yes, that's correct, as I said to the DA."

"Mr. Lingo, did you find the defendant's prints on the murder weapon?"

"No, I did not."

"Whose prints did you find?"

"There were no prints," he answered. "In my professional opinion, the gun was wiped clean at some point."

"Did you find any prints on the telephone receiver, Mr. Lingo?"

"No, the receiver appeared to be wiped clean as well."

"What about the base of the phone?" Sandi asked while looking at the jury.

"We found several sets of prints on the base of the phone."

"Did you find the defendant's prints on the base of the phone?"

"No, I did not."

"So, the receiver was wiped clean, and the base was not. What do you conclude from that, sir?"

"Objection, Your Honor," Penrose barked. "Calls for speculation, not a conclusion."

"Sustained," Judge Campbell ruled, but Sandi pressed on.

"Mr. Lingo, is it possible the murderer could have gone into Mr. Nicholson's home, shot him with my client's gun, made a phone call to someone, then wiped the phone receiver clean before leaving? Also, upon leaving, taking the gun with him and later wiping it clean of prints?"

"Your Honor, please, same objection."

"Withdrawn," Sandi said. "Nothing further of this witness."

We knew that questions about the phone receiver represented a red herring, meant to cloud the fingerprint issue with confusion. No prints on the gun, no prints on the phone receiver?

Judge Campbell looked up at the wall clock and said, "Because of the late hour, we will recess for the day and reconvene at nine tomorrow morning."

Another good day for us, but you can never second-guess a

jury.

Orson Welles had been correct years ago when he told a reporter, "Nobody gets justice. People only get good luck or bad luck."

Recently, in my defense of other clients, I had told several of them to keep that bit of wisdom in mind as their trials progressed.

But this time I was talking to myself.

Chapter Forty-Five

The following morning, back in Judge Campbell's courtroom, the third day of testimony was about to begin.

"Please call your next witness, Mr. Penrose."

"Your Honor, at this time I'd like to call Mr. Brendon Walsh."

The bailiff stepped out into the hallway and called for Walsh, who came into the courtroom, took the witness stand and was administered the oath. He was in his mid-forties, medium height and weight, brown hair, glasses and carrying a small briefcase. The DA then introduced a mock-up floor plan of the victim's living room, which he positioned so that Walsh and the jury, as well as Judge Campbell, could see it.

"Good morning, Mr. Walsh. As our expert in blood patterns, I requested that you visit the crime scene at Mr. Nicholson's house, correct? And does this mock-up accurately represent the floor plan as you saw it?"

"Yes, you did request that I visit the murder scene, and this does represent the floor plan quite well."

"What, if anything, were you able to determine from your examination of the Nicholson residence?"

"I determined that Mr. Nicholson was standing in front of his sofa when he was shot point-blank. I determined that the assailant was no more than three feet away when the victim was shot."

"Anything else, sir?"

"Yes. I also determined by the blood patterns on the wall behind the victim that the assailant was standing directly in front of the victim."

Walsh used a pointer to indicate areas of the room that he was talking about.

"Could you determine the approximate height of the assailant?" Penrose asked.

"My best guess is between five-ten and six-two."

"Did you determine if blood could have splattered from the victim back toward the assailant?"

"Yes, I determined that the assailant was no doubt hit by blood on their chest, arms and hands. Most likely from the gunshots to the head, rather than from the body shots."

Penrose then returned to the crime scene mock-up board and indicated where the assailant would have been standing in front of the victim.

"Have you studied the blood patterns on the defendant's jacket? And was there blood found on the murder weapon?"

"Yes, the victim's blood was found on the murder weapon's barrel and cartridge revolver. And there was blood on the front of the defendant's jacket consistent with a spatter pattern coming back from the victim's head wound."

"Why are you specifying the head wound?"

"Because we retrieved small bone fragments from the jacket consistent with the bone fragments from the victim's head."

"Mr. Walsh, can you determine whether the assailant was right or left-handed?"

"No, not with a hundred percent accuracy. However, I can usually calculate correctly by the angle of the bullet entry."

"What is your best guess in this case?"

Sandi jumped to her feet. "Objection, Your Honor, speculation, and assuming facts, not in evidence. Guessing and conjecture lend nothing to the accuracy or truth in this case."

"Sustained," Campbell agreed.

"Let me put it another way, Mr. Walsh. Do you know if the defendant is right or left-handed?"

"Yes, right-handed," answered Walsh.

"In your professional opinion, are the bullet entry wounds in

Mr. Nicholson consistent with a right-handed or left-handed person?"

"Right," Walsh answered.

"Thank you, Mr. Walsh. Your witness."

Rising to her feet, Sandi approached the witness stand.

"Mr. Walsh, if I understand you correctly, you're stating, in your professional opinion, that the assailant was right-handed and approximately six-feet tall. Correct?"

"Yes, ma'am; about six feet—give or take a couple inches."

"Which means that the suspect would easily be anyone representing at least half the male population of the United States, correct?"

Muffled laughter was heard coming from the audience, prompting Judge Campbell to pound his gavel.

"Order!" he shouted. "There will be order in this courtroom."

Pointing to the area on the mock-up exhibit, Sandi asked, "Mr. Walsh, could my client's jacket have been laying on the wing or back cushion of the sofa and still received blood spatters that are consistent, as you described, from the victim standing in front of the sofa, as I'm indicating to you at this time?"

Walsh studied the diagram and Sandi's pointer then said, "Yes, it's possible."

"Mr. Walsh, can you or any of your tests positively confirm who fired the gun that killed Gary Nicholson?"

Walsh again paused for a moment then said, "No, ma'am."

"Thank you; that's all I have of this witness, Your Honor."

"Without objection, we will reconvene at one-thirty," Judge Campbell announced.

Upon returning from the lunch break, DNA expert Jacob Schrammsberg and several assistants were assembling color charts with plastic overlays. They were also placing a slide projector and videotape projector on a side table near the jury box. Sandi leaned toward me and said, "Be prepared to be bored the rest of the afternoon. That's their DNA expert, and he's going to take us and the jury through his lab analysis process while he explains the scientific basis behind it. That guy Schrammsberg puts on quite a show, even if it is boring, and it should eat up the rest of the afternoon."

A murder scene is a map. If you know how to read it, you can sometimes find your way. The lay of the land can sometimes tell you the murder victim's response to their death—the angle, and views of light—and the victim's blood. The spatial directions and geometric definitions are all elements of the map.

At about four o'clock, following an exhaustive explanation of DNA's relevance to the case, Penrose got up from the prosecutor's table and approached the witness.

"That was an impressive demonstration, Mr. Schrammsberg." The witness acknowledged the compliment with a slight nod. "At the conclusion of your DNA testing, sir, were you able to conclude, positively, that the blood found on the defendant's jacket and the murder weapon were that of the victim, Gary Nicholson?"

"Yes, our testing confirmed that beyond any doubt," he answered.

"Thank you, Mr. Schrammsberg. Your witness," the DA said looking at Sandi.

"No questions, Your Honor," she replied.

"In that case," Judge Campbell announced, "this court is adjourned until nine tomorrow morning. Jury, please remember, no discussions regarding this trial."

After the judge gaveled the afternoon session to a close, Sandi whispered, "Good job, Adrian; you managed to stay awake the entire time."

I had known Jacob Schrammsberg for many years. His son Carl once wrote a poem about a river and its correlation to life. He dedicated it to the Yuba River. The Yuba River ran through Quartz County. For now, my River of Life was in the hands of the jury.

The River of Life

We start out as a spring in the River of Life, high on a mountain top,
born of the heavenly snows.
As we flow into the stream, we grow bigger, stronger and faster, to
become a river.
We race through life around boulders, through steep canyons, then
turbulent white-water rapids,
to serene pools of quiet water.
On and on we flow……down into the valley where the waters slow to a
rambling, drifting pace.
Until at last, we reach the end, the end of the River of Life, to the Great
Sea, where all life begins.

Chapter Forty-Six

When Judge Campbell called the court to order on Thursday morning, District Attorney Penrose stood and announced, "Your Honor, my final witness is Roxanne Meyers—Mr. Nicholson's girlfriend."

Beginning on Day One of the trial, Penrose had been carefully rolling out his case, easily handling the known and unknown. For the past two days, he had been tying all elements of witness testimony and evidence together with unbreakable findings of scientific fact—much of which is hard for the defense to contradict. But Sandi and I felt we made some valuable points along the way and poked holes where we could. As Roxanne's name was called, we knew Penrose wanted her testimony—the last witness he would present—to have a lasting effect on the jury.

Roxie, who had been sitting in the back row of the spectator section, walked to the witness stand and was administered the oath.

"Miss Meyers," the DA began, "please tell the court in your own words what took place at Gary Nicholson's home at approximately eleven o'clock on the night of his murder."

"Well, after we left Bogart's about ten, Gary, Adrian and I went to Gary's place for some drinks and shoot pool. After we got there, Gary started complaining about all the people who owed him money, including Adrian. Davis was saying he didn't owe Gary any more money. Gary was also mad at Davis because he was saying that it was going to cost Gary more money to defend his latest arrest, especially if they went to trial. Gary thought Davis should defend him and take care of his defense at no charge. They were friends, and Gary had helped in a pinch with a loan to Adrian back in the eighties; now it was time for Adrian to help Gary. They were still arguing about the money when I left around midnight."

Sandi immediately rose and said, "Objection, Your Honor. The answer is calling for a conclusion on the part of the witness as to what constitutes arguing and what is merely a discussion."

"Your Honor," Penrose countered, his arms outstretched in frustration, "the witness was there, and I'm sure she knows an argument when she hears one. She's merely stating a fact she witnessed."

"Overruled. I'll allow the answer."

"Were any drugs being used that night at Mr. Nicholson's?" Penrose asked.

"Yes, I smoked a little marijuana and Gary was inhaling a lot of coke."

"What was his demeanor?"

"Well, he was mad as hell and pretty drunk, and he sometimes over-did the drugs when he was agitated."

"Did you see Mr. Davis use any cocaine?"

"No, but based on his past, and how much he used to take advantage of Gary's generosity, I'm sure by the time the night was over he would have had his share," Meyers said with sarcasm.

If ever there was a response from a witness that cried out for an objection, this had been it. But Sandi sat mute, face stoic. Even Penrose was surprised by her silence, but he continued.

"Exactly what do you mean?" Penrose asked Roxie.

"Well, Adrian was a heavy user of cocaine. In fact, a few years back he was even arrested for a number of cocaine offenses, and he made some claim of a police conspiracy or some such thing."

Judge Campbell looked at the defense table, waiting for an objection as Sandi reached over and grabbed my fist. I too knew that we finally had the break we were waiting for.

"Miss Stassi am I going to get an objection from you related to the answer this witness just offered?" the judge inquired.

"No, Your Honor. No objection."

"Very well," he sighed. "Counsel, in my chamber. Members of the jury, we will recess for fifteen minutes."

Sandy and I exchanged a quick glance at each other then walked silently toward the door behind the bench. Courtroom spectators, clearly confused about what was happening, began murmuring and talking to each other.

In the judge's chamber, Campbell sat behind his desk, still in his robe, while Penrose, Sandi and I stood to face him. He seemed more frustrated than angry.

"I just want you to know Miss Stassi, you're not going to get a mistrial from me by not objecting to the referencing of your client's prior offenses; thereby laying the groundwork for a prejudiced jury. That's not going to happen; do you understand?"

"Your honor, as an officer of the court I can assure you that it isn't my intent to seek a mistrial. Far from it," Sandi calmly explained. "I intend to introduce evidence and witnesses to substantiate Adrian's past arrest and convictions, and to connect those past arrests with the present murder charge."

"Your Honor, where is this going?" Penrose wanted to know. "The defense is trying to hijack this murder case and take us in a completely unrelated direction. The defendant's past arrests involving cocaine abuse and his allegations of a conspiracy having been waged against him have nothing to do with the charges now pending against him in this case."

Penrose was steaming. He knew Roxie's testimony had been potentially damaging to his case and he was trying his best to scramble out of a bad situation.

"Your Honor," Sandi responded, "Mr. Penrose knows exactly where this is going, and he doesn't want the jury going in that direction because he knows the prosecution's case is a house of cards. He knows his case could be in peril if the jury hears about my client's previous arrest and we can make a connection to a conspiracy by law enforcement."

"But, Your Honor..."

"Enough, Mr. Penrose. You opened the door to all of this yourself when Miss Meyers took it upon herself, with a little help from your questions, to reveal all this information about Mr. Davis in open court. I can't take back what the jury has already heard, especially when there is no objection from the defense."

The district attorney stood in front of Judge Campbell, his shoulders slouched, not happy with his witness, nor the judge's decision.

"You're no doubt familiar with the phrase, 'You can't put the toothpaste back in the tube,' Mr. Penrose?"

"Yes, Your Honor, I'm familiar with the expression."

"Then let's get back out there and resume this trial," Campbell told the three of us.

Once court was back in session, Judge Campbell instructed Penrose to continue questioning his witness, with no mention of our in-chamber conversation.

"Miss Meyers, in your sworn deposition, before this trial, you said Mr. Nicholson had at least twenty-five thousand dollars in cash and about ten to twelve ounces of cocaine hidden in his boat, in the garage, at the time he was killed. Is that right?"

"Yes."

"Are you aware that no money or cocaine of that quantity was found by the police when they searched the house after you discovered the body the next day?"

"Yes, I'm aware of that, because you told me during some of your questioning sessions with me, when you asked what I knew about the murder; and any possible suspects or potential motives that I was aware of."

"To the best of your knowledge, did the defendant know where the cash and cocaine were hidden?" Penrose asked.

"Objection, Your Honor."

"Sustained. And watch yourself, Mr. Penrose."

"Miss Meyers, when you left the house at about midnight, what was the condition of both the deceased and the defendant?"

"Objection. Asked and answered," Sandi noted.

"Sustained," Campbell announced.

"Miss Meyers, when was the next time you saw Mr. Nicholson?"

"The next day, when I found him. I came back around ten that morning to get him up for breakfast. I opened the door with my key and walked into the living room."

"What did you observe at that point?"

"It was awful. There was blood everywhere. When I saw that he'd been shot, I started to scream and cry. I ran outside and called nine-one-one from my cell phone. And I've never been back to the house."

As Meyers began to cry, the district attorney granted her a moment to regain her composure. Then he held up a teal jacket and approached the witness with a sympathetic, fatherly smile. Holding the blood-stained jacket so the jury could see it clearly, the DA asked his final question.

"Miss Meyers, have you ever seen this jacket before?" The DA was holding Prosecution Exhibit Three.

"Yes, I have. It's Adrian's, the defendant. He was wearing it on the night of the murder."

"Nothing further, Your Honor," Penrose said as he looked at the jury to see how they had responded to Roxie's emotional testimony.

It was now a few minutes past noon; time for lunch.

Sandi and I grabbed a sandwich at a nearby deli and discussed strategy for the afternoon cross on Roxie Meyers. Roxie's response to Penrose's questioning had opened a door that we needed badly.

It was a huge door, and Sandi was ready to walk through it with both guns blazing.

When the court reconvened, Meyers was asked to return to the witness stand. A minute later, Sandi stood in front of her, ready to do battle.

"Miss Meyers, referring to the night of the murder, didn't the defendant and Mr. Nicholson have dinner at The Firehouse alone to discuss Mr. Nicholson's ongoing drug case before you joining them at Bogart's?"

"Yes, I believe they did."

"Miss Meyers, can we establish that you were drunk and maybe also high the night of the murder?"

"Yes, I already said I was," she answered.

"You testified that you did not see Mr. Davis use any drugs that night, is that correct?"

"Yes, but..."

"Miss Meyers, you said Mr. Nicholson was mad that night about money that people owed him. In particular, the money you say was owed by the defendant Mr. Davis. Correct?"

"Yes, that's what Gary was saying."

"Did Mr. Davis remind Mr. Nicholson that the earlier loan had been paid back in-kind by legal services performed in defense of Mr. Nicholson's two drug arrests?"

Roxie sat still, looking at the courtroom floor, hesitant to answer.

"Miss Meyers?"

"Yes, I recall something like that being said by Adrian in his defense, but Gary wasn't buying it. He didn't want to pay any more for his latest drug bust. He wanted Adrian to do—how do you say? Pro-something?"

"That would be pro bono. Meaning services at no charge," Sandi said.

"Miss Meyers were you angry with Mr. Nicholson when you

left his house that night?"

"Angry? What do you mean by that?"

"I mean, didn't you normally spend the night with Mr. Nicholson after an evening out?"

"Yes, usually," Meyers answered.

"So, why didn't you stay that night?"

"Well, Gary and Adrian were arguing and..."

"Isn't it a fact that Gary told you to leave? To get out. He wanted to talk to my client alone and told you to go home. Isn't that what happened?"

"Yes," Meyers responded, visibly annoyed by Sandi's line of questioning.

"Miss Meyers," Sandi asked as she held the blood-stained jacket in front of the witness, "you testified this morning that you saw the defendant wearing this jacket on the evening of the murder. Is that right?"

"Yes."

"Did you see him take it off at any time that evening?"

"No."

"Could he have taken it off while at the house without you noticing?"

"Objection!" Penrose shouted.

"She was there in the house, so I will allow the question," Judge Campbell said.

"I don't know; I suppose he could have," Roxie answered.

"You don't *know*? Miss Meyers is it possible that Mr. Davis removed his jacket after arriving at Mr. Nicolson's house and in your drunken, drugged state, you simply failed to notice?"

"Objection, Your Honor. Asked and answered, and defense is badgering the witness."

"Overruled," Campbell said. "The witness will answer the question."

"Miss Meyers is it possible that Mr. Davis removed his jacket that evening, either while you were still there, or after you left, and you simply didn't notice?"

"Yes, it's possible," Meyers said in a low, mumbling voice.

"I'm sorry, but I don't think the jury could hear your answer."

Clearly frustrated and angry with Sandi's cross-examination, Roxie barked, "OK, yes, it's possible!"

Sandi was clearly trolling here. She knew that on cross-examination one of the keys to success was to continue at the same pace and with little change of expression or voice inflection.

"Miss Meyers, do you like Mr. Davis?"

"No, not really. I always thought he was arrogant and too full of himself," she responded sarcastically.

"Miss Meyers, you were Mr. Nicholson's girlfriend. His trusted companion. Correct?

"Yes, I loved Gary. He took care of me, and I took care of him."

"I see. Miss Meyers are you familiar with the phrase, 'Get out of Dodge?'"

Meyers was slow to answer. "Yes."

"Have you ever used the phrase in passing?"

"Yes, I guess, once or twice," she said, again responding reluctantly.

"What did you mean when you referenced this phrase?" Sandi continued.

"Usually I said it when I was thinking of getting out of Gold City for a little R&R."

"By R&R did you mean a trip down to Fremont, to your hometown, to have sex with your cousin?"

"Objection, Your Honor! The question is inflammatory, irrelevant and beyond the scope. Where is this going, Your Honor? Penrose asked, "and what is the relevance of this line of questioning?"

"Miss Stassi, what is the purpose of these questions?" Campbell asked, seemingly amused.

"Your Honor, Mr. Penrose has painted Miss Meyers as a loving and devoted companion to Mr. Nicholson, but it has come to our attention that she was having an affair for many years with a member of her own family that we are sure Mr. Nicholson knew nothing about. This goes to the character and credibility of this witness, Your Honor."

"Your Honor, Miss Meyers' personal life is not on trial here, and rumors or innuendoes about her sex life are completely irrelevant. For all we know, Mr. Nicholson knew about this dalliance, or for that matter any other affair she may have had, or not, and simply didn't care."

"Objection sustained. Move on Miss Stassi," the judge commanded.

Sandi did some damage to Meyers credibility with her questions. Juries don't like witnesses who hide things. Sandi loved poking holes in witnesses' credibility, especially with juicy tidbits.

"Miss Meyers, you testified that you had a key to Mr. Nicholson's house and that you knew where he kept his cash and cocaine, isn't that true?"

"Yes." Meyers was pissed; she knew she got caught with her pants down. Literally.

"So, for all we know, you could have come back to the house that night after Mr. Davis left and robbed Gary Nicholson of his cash and cocaine—or for that matter robbed him the next morning—after discovering the body, and before you called the police."

"Objection! Objection! This is badgering, Your Honor, and again beyond the scope. Defense counsel is throwing everything against the wall hoping something will stick."

"And since you were angry with Mr. Nicholson, how do we know that you didn't return and kill him yourself later that night after my client left the house?" Sandi continued before the judge could rule.

Louder than before and now standing, District Attorney Penrose shouted, "Objection, Your Honor! Objection!"

Before the judge could rule on the objection, Sandi said, "I withdraw the question," and walked back to our defense table. In front of a jury, Sandi had perfected the "eight percent theory" — not that we thought we would need it.

The eight percent theory is simple enough. Eight percent represents just one juror of the twelve sitting in the box, and that is all that is needed for the defense to ensure a hung jury. Her goal was to be so persuasive that at least one juror would be convinced of my innocence, no matter the evidence.

Sandi had a mesmerizing courtroom presence and a full bag of tricks to boot, and her cross-examination of Roxie Meyers was pure magic. I was smiling on the inside but trying to remain stoic on the outside.

As the audience began to chatter, Judge Campbell pounded the gavel with force.

"That's all, Your Honor," Sandi announced. "I have no further questions of this witness."

"Redirect, Mr. Penrose?" the judge asked with an obvious level of frustration.

"Yes, thank you, Your Honor. Miss Meyers, before today, had you ever been exposed to the defendant's blood-stained jacket or the murder weapon? Both of which belong to the defendant and were found in his home?"

"I've seen the jacket worn by the defendant numerous times. But as for the murder weapon, no, I had never seen it before today in this courtroom."

"Miss Meyer's, one last question," stated Penrose. "Have you ever been in the defendant's home?"

"No." Roxie responded emphatically.

"That's all, Miss Meyers; thank you for your candid testimony. You were close to Mr. Nicholson, and we realize this has been difficult for you."

Once Roxie left the witness stand and returned to the audience, Penrose spoke the words we were waiting for: "The prosecution rests, Your Honor."

"Very well," Judge Campbell said. "Then we will take a long weekend, and this court is adjourned until nine o'clock Monday morning, at which time the defense will, as we ruled earlier, begin with their opening statement."

It was difficult to gauge the jury's reaction to Meyers emotional testimony and Sandi's riveting cross-examination, but we left the courthouse that afternoon with renewed confidence that reasonable doubt was being established in ways the jury would not be able to ignore.

Sandi was terrific—a pro. I could not have been prouder of her. She did her part.

But we both knew that on Monday when we began to present our side of the story, the district attorney would be ready to cross-examine our witnesses just as strenuously as Sandi had cross-examined his.

Such is the nature of trials—especially murder trials in a small town.

Chapter Forty-Seven

Friday morning broke clear and warm, so I invited Sandi to take a ride with me on my Harley. We left Gold City about ten and went out State Highway 20, then on to State Highway 49, toward Downieville and Sierra City. It's a beautiful drive, crossing all three forks of the Yuba River, with numerous places to stop for a dip along the way, or just sit and relax. It was a welcome change from the long, dreary hours we had been spending at the Quartz County Courthouse.

A trial is like a sporting event, and occasionally, there's need for a timeout. Today was our halftime break—a chance to temporarily forget all about the DA's evidence and the second half of a contest that would either put me in prison for twenty years or set me free to practice law.

Over the weekend, we would knuckle down and focus on next week's defense, but not today. Today was designed for peaceful relaxation—a perfect escape from reality. I had spent too many years escaping reality, but those days were in my rearview mirror, and I wasn't about to look back.

We arrived in Downieville just before noon and went into the Old Town Inn for a beer. Downieville, a one-street town with a population of just under three hundred, hasn't changed much since William Downie founded the place during the California Gold Rush.

Downieville is at the confluence of the Downie River and North Fork of the Yuba River, an area that became known as Tin Cup Diggins because miners who worked the claims were paid daily by having their tin coffee cups filled with nuggets and gold dust.

As we relaxed with a cold beer, Sandi jokingly mentioned a murder trial held in Downieville in eighteen fifty-one. And while she may have been joking, it was the kind of gallows humor that brought me back to reality. She and I were out in the country for a day, but what happened in Downieville in eighteen fifty-one was a reminder of what awaited us back in Gold City on Monday morning.

On the evening of July 4, 1851—the first Independence Day for the new State of California—a popular miner named Jack Cannon got drunk and tried to seduce a woman known as Juanita. He was unsuccessful, but about sunrise on July fifth, Cannon went to the cabin Juanita shared with her boyfriend.

According to which version you want to believe, Cannon either politely knocked on the cabin door, wanting to apologize to the woman for his rude behavior the previous night, or—more likely—he kicked in the door and started to approach Juanita with rape on his mind.

Juanita grabbed a large knife, killed Cannon by driving the knife deep into his chest, and was tried for murder that same day in the town square. Needless to say, self-defense was out of the question for the Mexican woman, and she was found guilty of murder. An hour later, she was hanged from the bridge that spanned the Downie River.

Images of Juanita dangling from the noose filled my head as we completed our brief stop in the county seat of Sierra County. It was time to get some distance between us and the legacy of the only woman ever hanged in California, so we headed east toward Sierra City, twenty-five miles up the road.

Sierra City has even fewer buildings and people than Downieville, but it's a charming wide spot in the road with the towering Sierra Buttes serving as a backdrop for the town.

From Sierra City, we rode to Bassett's Station—a grocery store and local sandwich shop just outside of Sierra City—and turned north, toward the many lakes that surround the Buttes.

We stopped at Little Sardine Lake, where Sandi spread out a blanket and served a nice lunch she had prepared. We opened a bottle of wine, sat in the sun, and talked about the next week in court. A make-or-break week and one in which I would begin to play a key role, becoming very active in the questioning of our witnesses.

But at that moment, thoughts of Juanita dangling from a bridge had moved on, and I was now—finally—alone with Sandi.

After lunch, we went for a walk along the lakeshore and, to my surprise and pleasure, Sandi gently took my hand in hers. We didn't talk much, but we were definitely communicating. As we walked around the lake, we would, from time-to-time, stop to kiss, each time with more passion. Yes, there was passion in both our lips and our touch, and I was buoyed by her willingness to become affectionate before the trial was over.

We continued our ride up to Grey Eagle, back down through the Feather River Canyon and over to Highway 20, then headed home. Back in Gold City we had dinner at the Yellow Rose Cafe and talked more strategy until late that night.

For the next two days, we met at Sandi's office and continued to discuss strategy and questions for our witnesses. By Sunday night, we were confident we had dotted every "i" and crossed every "t." We were not going to create reasonable doubt. Not us. That wasn't our goal. We were going to remove *all* doubt.

We were ready for Monday morning. I was ready to rise up as a defense attorney and be the kind of attorney I was trained to be. Sandi had set the bar pretty high, but I was confident I would make her as proud of me as I had been proud of her.

"Bring it on!" Sandi said with a smile. I had come to appreciate her meaning more and more when she had told me, "Life is a smile."

Chapter Forty-Eight

Monday morning, with prosecution and defense teams seated and ready, the jury was brought in. As expected, it was an SRO audience when Judge Campbell called the court to order.

"Miss Stassi, your opening statement, please," the judge requested.

Your Honor, defense's opening statement will be delivered by my co-counsel, Mr. Davis." Sandi informed Judge Campbell.

The judge seemed perplexed, and Penrose seemed confused as well.

Good. We had the DA off balance, determined to rattle him even further.

The person on trial is presumed innocent until proven guilty. However, anyone who has ever stepped into a courtroom, as lawyer or defendant, knows that presumed innocent is just one of the idealistic notions they teach in law school. There was no doubt in my mind that everyone associated with the trial assumed me guilty—except Sandi, of course. I had to find a way to either prove my innocence by proving the state's case against me was based on malfeasance and/or corruption or introduce a viable alternative to convince the jury that I was not the killer.

I rose and walked toward the jury box. I wore one of my best suits—Italian-made, dark-blue single breast, white shirt, with a blue-and-yellow tie. For extra points with the jury, I had stuffed a yellow, silk handkerchief in the suit's breast pocket. Also, I made sure to shine my black shoes until I could see my reflection bouncing off the leather.

"Ladies and gentlemen of the jury," I began, "to date you

haven't seen much of me, other than sitting over there at the defense table. My esteemed colleague and co-counsel, Miss Stassi, has been the lead for the defense through the prosecution's case, but starting today, both of us will be counsels of record, and I will be actively involved in representing myself against these charges."

I reminded the jury that I was an attorney licensed to practice law in the State of California, and I spoke without notes, hoping jurors would be more responsive to a free-form approach. I didn't want to deliver a speech—I wanted to have a candid talk with the men and women who would decide my fate.

"I stand before you today both humble and confident," I began. "Miss Stassi has advised me that it's important for you to like me. I agree, but I think it's also important that you get to know me, and eventually trust me. The prosecution has presented a competent circumstantial case, backed by scientific facts, with a lot of supposition attached. Beginning today, we will tell you the rest of the story. You will be hearing the truth of what happened the night my friend Gary Nicholson was murdered. No more speculation from the DA—just the facts from us.

"We agree with Mr. Penrose that this crime was brutal, violent and cold-blooded. No one should have taken Gary's life, and whoever did should be brought to justice. Although there should never be a rush to judgment, that's what happened here, and we will prove it. The investigators of this murder saw the little picture, and I was an easy fit for their purposes. But they missed the big picture. They missed the real murderer."

From behind, I heard Penrose's voice. "Your Honor, may we please approach the bench for a sidebar?"

Judge Campbell frowned, but then signaled us up to the bench. Sandi and I followed Penrose to the side of the bench, already formulating my response to what I knew he was going to object too. We spoke softly so the jurors wouldn't hear us as we huddled at the bench.

"Judge, forgive me," Penrose began, "I hate to interrupt an opening statement, but this doesn't sound like an opening statement. Is defense counsel going to hit us with facts his case will prove and the evidence he has, or is he just going to talk in generalities about some mysterious killer that everyone else involved in this case somehow missed?"

Judge Campbell looked at me for a response. I looked at Sandi, then responded.

"Judge, I object to the objection. I am less than five minutes into an allotted thirty-minute opening, and the DA is already objecting because I haven't put anything on the table. Come on, Your Honor, he's trying to show me up in front of the jury, and I request that you deny his objection and not allow him to interrupt me again."

"I think Mr. Davis is right, Mr. Penrose," the judge said. "Way too early to object. I'll carry it now as a running objection and step in myself if I feel a need. Meantime, please go back to your table and sit tight."

He rolled his chair back to the center of the bench as Penrose, Sandi, and I returned to our positions. Then Judge Campbell announced to the jury that he had overruled the objection.

"As I was saying before being interrupted," I told the jury without trying to show my anger at Penrose, "there is a big picture to this case and the defense is going to show it to you. The prosecution would like you to believe that this is a simple case of me killing my friend over money during a moment of anger. But murder is never simple. If you look for shortcuts in any investigation or prosecution, then you are going to miss some things, important things, including the real killer. I had no motive to kill Gary Nicholson, and the motive presented to you by the district attorney was false. A motive is like a rudder on a boat. You take it away, and the boat moves at the whim of the wind. And that's what's driving the prosecution's case. A lot of wind."

As I spoke, my eyes washed across the jury like Hollywood klieg lights at night. I remained calm and felt a certain rhythm in my thoughts, a cadence to my speech, and I knew I was holding the jury's attention. They weren't in the palm of my hands—at least not yet—but they were paying attention to the direction the hand was going.

"I know that in society we all want our law enforcement officers to be honest and the best they can be. They are, as we know, the thin line between order and disorder. We want them to be the best, but sometimes they step out of order and become a disorder, and we all know this to be true. I believe that while presenting my side of the story, I will show you—in fact, prove to you—that this happened in my case. We believe that some law enforcement officers thought that they were above the law and, as we will prove, even colluded and conspired to present a false murder case against me.

"The evidence will show—and I mean from the prosecution's own evidence and testimony—that from the start the investigators focused on only one suspect. Me. The evidence will show that once I became the prime suspect, all other considerations were tossed aside. All other avenues of this investigation were halted and never pursued. Once I was their prime suspect, and what they believed was a motive with opportunity, they never considered another possibility. I was it, and that was that.

"Ladies and gentlemen, this case is about tunnel vision. The focus of law enforcement was on me and no one else. And I promise that when you come out of the prosecution's tunnel, and your eyes get adjusted to the light—the light that I will be presenting to you—you will once again be able to see clearly. And when that moment arrives, you will be wondering where the hell their case is and why I was ever charged in the first place.

"We have subpoenaed over twenty witnesses. While each

person has something important to share with this court, some testimonies would undoubtedly prove repetitive. Because of that, I'll only call those who can be the most enlightening and who will have the greatest impact and provide the most information to you and for the defense."

I paused, put my hands in my pockets, looked up and down the jury box and said, "I am entrusting you with my future, perhaps the rest of my life, and I am confident that you will take this responsibility seriously. Please hold your judgment until you have heard all the evidence and arguments, and until the judge has fully explained the law. If you do, I believe you will have no choice but to find me not guilty of this murder charge."

I stood at the jury box for a long pause, looking each juror in the eyes, wanting my words to sink in, then I thanked them for listening to my opening statement and stepped away.

"Very well," Judge Campbell said, "please call your first witness, Mr. Davis."

Our defense strategy was simple: Blaze a path that would lead the jury away from me as the only suspect and shine the spotlight on other possible persons that could have killed Gary. Also, we needed to counter the prosecution's allegations as to why my gun and coat were involved in this murder. My first witness was one of the steps on this pathway to freedom.

"Your Honor, I call Miss Barbara Human."

Miss Human came forward and was sworn in by the bailiff. She was in her mid-thirties, short, thin, frizzy blond hair, designer glasses, and cute as a button by any standards. She wore her uniform—that of the Quartz County sheriff's office.

"Miss Human, you have been with the sheriff's office for about ten years, is that correct?" I asked.

"Yes, eleven years, actually."

"Going back to June nineteen eighty-seven, you were the deputy dispatched to my home following my report of a burglary, isn't that right?"

"Yes, it is."

"Please describe to the court what you witnessed and observed at my home that day."

"Upon arriving at your home, I searched the premises to determine if there was anyone in the house other than the two of us. Then I made notes and took pictures of the screen that had been removed from the front window, which indicated to me that entry had been made through that window."

"What was the condition of my home's interior when you entered it that day?"

"Your home had not been ransacked nor disturbed. You informed me that your snub-nose thirty-eight pistol, a large container of loose change, and a camera had been taken. And that is what I entered on my report."

I walked over to the defense table and picked up a document, then handed it to Miss Human.

"Is this your report of that investigation, Miss Human?"

"Yes," was her response after reviewing the papers I handed her.

"May I please enter this as Defense Exhibit Eleven, Your Honor?" I asked.

Judge Campbell so ordered.

"As a deputy sheriff, Miss Human, how many burglaries have you investigated?"

"Oh, easily over a couple hundred."

"Two hundred and twenty-three, to be exact," I told her as she blushed. "With your years of experience, would you say that a burglary did, in fact, occur at my home on that day?"

"Objection, Your Honor, calls for a conclusion," Penrose claimed.

"Your Honor," I countered, "I'm sure you would agree that this witness, having personally investigated more than two hundred burglaries, is qualified to make such a conclusion."

"Yes, overruled."

"Thank you, Your Honor. Miss Human?"

"From all available evidence, and based on my experience, it appeared to me that a burglary had taken place in your home," she told the jury.

"Thank you, that's all I have of this witness," I said.

"Mr. Penrose, your witness," the judge announced.

Rising to his feet, Thomas Penrose addressed the witness from the prosecution table.

"Miss Human, could you tell this court unequivocally and with certainty that this alleged burglary was not set-up or staged?"

"No, not unequivocally or with one-hundred percent certainty."

"Thank you, that's all," Penrose said.

"Redirect, Your Honor?" I asked.

Judge Campbell nodded.

"Miss Human, do you believe that what you observed, and as you reported, was anything other than the crime of burglary?"

"No, I believe your home was burglarized," she answered.

"Thank you; that's all."

Turning to the bench, I said, "Your Honor, at this time I would like to call Lieutenant Tom Sadler to the stand."

Sadler, who was in his late forties with twenty years at the sheriff's office, was an experienced witness. He had a calm demeanor and spoke in a matter-of-fact tone. He was skilled at not revealing the hostility that almost all cops carry for defense lawyers.

"Lieutenant Sadler, on June 4, 1987, you and your partner, Sergeant Evans, now deceased, were dispatched to my home with a search and arrest warrant, isn't that correct?"

"Yes, that's correct."

"The arrest warrant was for me. What was the purpose of the search warrant?"

"It indicated that we would find quantities of cocaine and drug paraphernalia consistent with a drug-dealing operation," Sadler said, with confidence.

"Please tell the court what you found."

"We found what we believed, and was later confirmed, to be residue from cocaine on a coffee table and on a kitchen plate."

"Anything else?"

"No, nothing else," Sadler said, not pleased at having to answer the question.

"From your observations and your professional experience, was there anything found during that search to connect me to a professional drug-dealing operation?" I asked.

"No, but that doesn't mean it was never there, or you didn't clean it up before we arrived."

"Objection," Sandi said from the defense table faster than I could get the words out of my mouth.

"Sustained," Judge Campbell ruled. "Strike Lieutenant Sadler's last remark from the record and the jury will disregard the answer."

I love it when cops improvise on the stand and go off-script—when they try not to give the obvious answer and make themselves look bad in the process. It was hard not to smile at Sadler's wild speculation.

"During the initial search, did you also find a snub nose thirty-eight pistol in my home?"

"No, not during the initial search," an irritated Sadler answered.

"Why didn't you find it during your initial search?"

"I don't know; I guess because it was pretty well hidden."

I held up the package the murder weapon was in for Sadler and the jury to look at and asked, "How did you learn of this gun's existence?"

"We found a holster for a thirty-eight revolver in your bedroom nightstand, so we asked you where the gun was."

"And did I show you?"

"Yes, it was between the mattress and the frame of your waterbed."

"When I showed it to you, you looked at it, then placed it back in the bed, correct?"

"Yes, that's right," he responded.

"So, if I hadn't told you where the gun was located, you probably wouldn't have found it, correct?"

"Probably not, but with enough time...well, maybe," Sadler answered.

I could tell Sadler was about to blow his cool. He wasn't getting any help from Penrose, who, without any valid objections, was hunkering down in his chair waiting for my questions to end and the damaging testimony to finish.

"Lieutenant Sadler, how do you explain the fact that three days after your search a burglar entered my home, went directly to that same spot where my gun was kept, and stole *the* gun you couldn't find without my help?"

"I can't explain it, as I don't pretend to understand how the criminal mind works," Sadler sarcastically answered.

"Thank you, that's all. But I'd like to reserve the right to recall this witness later, if necessary, Your Honor."

"So, noted," he said as he gaveled the morning session to a close.

To his credit, Sadler didn't lie on the stand. He didn't like my questions, but at least, for the most part, he answered them. Sandi said it was a good morning—and we hoped for an even better afternoon.

Chapter Forty-Nine

Jury trials have always made me hungry. Something about the energy expended, thinking about the prosecution's next move and worrying about whether I will successfully counter that next move. It's chess, played out in public. For the loser, it can be very costly. And I have never enjoyed losing.

By lunch break during trials, I wasn't thinking about soup or salad; I was thinking about a juicy, five-napkin cheeseburger with a mound of fries. Or pasta, or even a steak. Something heavy to get me through the next round.

On that particular day, I went with a rib-eye steak sandwich and fries, with apple strudel for dessert. And I was *still* hungry. Sandi, the sensible one, had a tossed salad with grilled salmon and a cup of fruit. We both had lemonade, but the wine list sure looked tempting.

When the afternoon session started, Penrose looked very relaxed and refreshed, and I began to wonder if perhaps he had had a pop or two during the break. Maybe that aloof thing of his was more about covering an alcohol problem? I wasn't sure, but I knew he had never been a Bogart's customer.

Sandi and I had a plan for our next witness, Sergeant Ralph Pittman of the Gold City P. D. We decided to use him as an early witness in order to set the stage for the other witnesses scheduled to follow. My case was a daisy chain of interlocking witnesses, where we hoped one could be used to build the path to the next, with the aim of establishing a conclusion that would lead the jury in our desired direction.

I stood and called Pittman to the stand. And when I

approached him, I held papers in my hand.

"Sergeant Pittman, in January nineteen eighty-seven, per this written declaration to Judge Heim, you undertook an investigation of me shortly after receiving orders to do so. Isn't that true?"

"Yes," Pittman answered, showing that he was uncomfortable being put on the spot as a witness for our defense.

"What was the purpose of this investigation and who asked you to undertake it?"

"The investigation was to gather evidence that you were involved in the use and distribution of cocaine. My instructions came from Chief Kane."

"Sergeant Pittman, on the night of May 19, 1987, at or about three A.M., you were on the roof of Bogart's walk-in refrigeration box outside of my office window, correct?"

"Yes, I noticed a light coming from your office window, and because of the recent burglaries at your bar—burglaries that you reported to us—I decided to investigate."

"Exactly what did you see from your vantage point outside my office?" I asked as I stood in front of the witness.

"I saw you, another man I identified as London Maxx, and two women that I did not recognize."

"And after recognizing me as the owner of Bogart's, also London Maxx, and confirming that there was no burglary taking place, did you continue to look through the window?"

"Yes, I did." Pittman matter-of-factly answered.

"Did you have a search warrant?" I asked.

"No, I did not," Pittman answered.

"Tell the court what, if anything, you subsequently observed."

"I saw you and your guests inhaling lines of white powder off the top of your desk through a straw."

"Lines of white powder? And what was the white powder?" I asked.

"I believed it to be cocaine."

"Cocaine, you say. Tell me, sergeant, how did you determine it was cocaine from where you were kneeling outside my office window?" I asked as I turned for effect and glanced toward the jury box.

"It was a supposition on my part, sure, but what else would you be snorting up your nose at three in the morning?"

Visitors to the court laughed out loud to the sergeant's answer, and the judge gaveled for quiet.

"Fair enough," I said with a smile. "How much white powder was on the desk?" I asked without waiting for quiet.

"Not much; a small pile. It came from a bindle I saw you pour from and put on the desk."

"In other words, not a bag full of white powder. Correct?"

"No, not a large amount," Pittman said. "Nothing like that."

"Did you report your observations to Chief Kane?"

"Yes, the next day," Pittman answered.

"And what you reported having observed on May nineteenth is what led to the issuance of an arrest and search warrant of my properties five days later. Is that correct?"

"Yes, I suppose so," Pittman answered as he shifted uncomfortably in his chair.

"Stop me if you think I'm trying to put words in your mouth, sergeant, but if I understand you correctly, you climbed on the roof of my walk-in box at three in the morning, knelt and looked in my office window without a search warrant, ostensibly to investigate an alleged burglary. Right?"

"Right."

"And in so doing, you observed me and three others inhaling some white powder through a straw. Is that correct?"

"That's correct."

"Assuming the powder was cocaine, you reported what you saw to Chief Kane who, in turn, got a search and arrest warrant, which alleged that I was a drug dealer in possession of a large quantity of cocaine. Is this your sworn testimony here in court today, sergeant?" I asked with a slightly higher pitch to my voice.

"Your Honor, the defense is mocking the witness," Penrose insisted.

"Thank you, Sergeant Pittman. That will be all," I announced.

"Cross, Mr. Penrose?" the judge asked.

"Just one question, Your Honor."

"Sergeant Pittman," Penrose began, "is it your testimony that the evening you were on the roof of Bogart's walk-in box looking in the window of Mr. Davis' office, you observed the defendant, and three others, inhaling a white substance into their nose? And that you were there initially checking on a possible burglary at Bogart's because Mr. Davis had reported numerous burglaries at his business prior to your observation. Isn't that correct?"

"Yes, that's correct. When I saw the lights coming from the back of the building, near the office area, I went up on the walk-in roof to make sure the place wasn't being burglarized again, as previously been reported by Mr. Davis."

"And to be crystal clear, you observed Mr. Davis provide the white powder to his guests from a bindle that he possessed. Correct?"

"Correct," the sergeant responded.

"No further questions for this witness," Penrose said, happy to have the nervous cop off the witness stand.

And since it was late in the afternoon, Judge Campbell adjourned court until the following morning with his usual admonishment to the jury.

***

That night, Sandi and I went to Lumberjack Steakhouse for dinner. It's a casual sort of bar and restaurant on the outskirts of

Gold City. Inexpensive steaks and chops, and always a friendly crowd.

As we entered the restaurant, several people turned in our direction and greeted us with a friendly smile or stared with suspicion. It was something we had grown used to since my arrest.

"The trial's making you famous, Adrian. Or do you actually know all these people?" Sandi asked.

"Yeah, I know most of them. Remember, I was born here; my roots go back a long way. And the Lumberjack is definitely a bar and restaurant for locals."

As we picked up our menus, I saw Madame Butterfly, and she saw me. I tapped Sandi on the shoulder and said, "In fact, there's somebody here tonight that I want you to meet. C'mon, I'll introduce you."

When I got to Musette's table, she rose, and we gave each other a short hug. When I began to introduce Sandi, Musette interrupted and said, "No need to introduce us, I know this lady. And from what I hear, you're just what our friend Adrian needs."

Sandi and I glanced at each other, not knowing exactly what she meant. Musette smiled, not missing the awkward exchange.

"What I mean is, Adrian needs a good attorney to help him and, from what I've heard, you're just that attorney."

"Thank you, Miss ....."

"Musette Parks, but my friends call me Madame Butterfly or just Butterfly."

Sandi turned to Adrian and said, "Maybe Musette would like to join us?"

"Oh, no," she responded, "I'm waiting for someone, but thanks for the invite."

"Well, if it's your daughter, Stacy, she can join us," I said, wanting to gracefully return to our table.

Suddenly, Musette's smile disappeared. I was puzzled. "What is it?" I asked.

"Adrian, you couldn't have possibly known about Stacy, what with everything that's been going on in your life. And you were still in Phoenix at the time."

"Know what?" I asked with concern.

"I lost her, Adrian. She died three years ago."

There was a short pause, then Musette said, "It was a painful death, but I was with her right to the end."

I lapsed into momentary silence. I had no idea Stacy had died, and I didn't know what to say, except, "Musette, I'm so sorry."

"It's okay. Adrian, we'll talk later. I hope before you call me to testify later in the week, although I'm still not sure why you subpoenaed me. I don't I know what I can contribute to your defense."

"As I told you a month ago, I just need you to confirm some details and loose ends regarding Gary," I answered. "I'll call you tomorrow after court and give you a heads up on some of the questions."

The Madame looked concerned, but said, "Yes, please call when you can. I'll be home all day."

When Sandi and I were seated back at our table, I looked over at Musette, seated alone at a large table. She was fidgeting with the beautiful gold nugget necklace she so often displayed. It had been a gift from someone from her past, and she cherished it. The nugget came from the Yuba River and was set by one of our local goldsmiths, at a business known as The Unique Stone. Truly a beautiful and unique gold nugget in the shape of Africa—or the human heart. Take your pick, but it was a dandy.

Sandi wanted to know why Musette was called Madame Butterfly.

"Do you know what divination is?" I asked.

"Predicting the future," Sandi answered.

"Yes, but not entirely. It is also a tool for uncovering the unknown, or hidden knowledge by supernatural means. Musette seems to believe she has some supernatural powers, akin to witchcraft. Voodoo shit. She likes to project that sort of image, and along the way, the nickname Madame Butterfly seemed to fit.

"As you can see, she also has a certain Asian look to her," I continued. "Her eyes, her make-up, her jet-black hair, and the cut. Her flour-white skin and red lipstick. A very mysterious look. Also, she almost always wears black, and that accentuates the Asian side of her."

I looked away from Musette, toward Sandi, who was nodding.

"When you put it that way, the name Madame Butterfly fits perfectly," she said.

"Bottle of Cab to start?" I asked the woman for whom I had become a bit more than just smitten.

She winked in approval.

Chapter Fifty

When court reconvened the next morning, I called Chief Abel Kane back to the stand—this time as a defense witness. He was attired in his snazzy dress uniform, four brass stars on each shoulder.

"Chief Kane, you heard the testimony of Sergeant Pittman, in which he testified that you ordered an investigation of me. Are you in agreement with his testimony?"

"Uh, yes...essentially," he slowly answered.

"Then you no doubt agree with his testimony that you found nothing in your investigation or the subsequent search of my properties to substantiate your suspicions. Isn't that correct?"

Before Kane could answer my question, it triggered an objection from Penrose and a three-minute exchange of arguments at a sidebar with the judge. Once again, the DA was arguing that my past arrest was irrelevant to this case and that I was using smoke and mirrors to confuse the jury.

This is one of the few places in a criminal trial where the defense has an advantage. Everything about a criminal trial is stacked against the defense, but the one thing no judge wants is a reversal on appeal due to their procedural error. Most judges will bend over backward and allow some latitude to the defense to proceed with its case—as long as it stays within accepted lines of evidence and decorum.

It did not surprise me, then, that the DA's objection was overruled, and I was able to continue questioning the police chief. First, however, I requested that my unanswered question be read back by the court stenographer.

"Quite the contrary," Kane confidently replied after hearing the question repeated. "What we found very definitely indicated drug use."

"You found cocktail straws and some small papers with cocaine residue on them at Bogart's, and cocaine residue at my home on the coffee table glass and a plate. Correct?"

"Yes, correct," Kane replied, looking over at the jury.

"Was any of this material found on me or, as they say, on my person?"

"No," Kane answered.

"So, anyone who ever visited my home or frequented my bar could have been responsible for that material being present. Isn't that true?"

"I guess so," he said with a shrug. "Yeah, I suppose it's possible."

"Exactly. Now then, Chief Kane, to what do you attribute the failure of your search to find large quantities of cocaine that would have indicated sales and distribution as the warrant stated?"

"I was never sure; maybe you were tipped off in advance that we were coming with a warrant."

"Or, a better explanation could be that there was never anything there to find in the first place. Isn't that possible?" I asked.

"Well..."

"Did you ever stop to think that that might have been the explanation for what you found that day? Or, rather, what you did *not* find?"

There was no response from the chief, so I took a quick glance at the jury then moved on.

"When the search provided so little evidence, what did you do next?"

"I placed you under arrest for possession and distribution of cocaine," the chief said.

"Chief Kane, without any real incriminating evidence to support such an action, why did you have me arrested and booked?"

"I felt there was enough to warrant it based on what Sergeant Pittman witnessed through your office window. He saw you giving your friend and the girls a white powder he believed to be cocaine, so we had reasonable cause for the search and reasonable cause to arrest you."

I walked over to our defense table where I poured a drink of water, gave Sandi a wink out of view to the jury, and paused for a moment.

"Really?" I said, turning back toward Kane. "On nothing more than what I would call circumstantial evidence, you arrested me on two felonies, had my name and arrest splattered on the front page of the local newspaper, publicly embarrassed my family, ruined my business, and destroyed my life as I knew it?"

I paused again for effect, then asked, "Are you really saying all that I have just described was warranted based on the flimsy evidence you just shared with this jury?"

"Your Honor asked and answered," Penrose said, "and again, I strongly object. Where is the foundation for this line of questioning and this unrelated evidence being presented in this trial?"

"I think Mr. Penrose may be right this time, Mr. Davis," Judge Campbell said from the bench, "so please get to the point of this line of questioning or move on."

"Yes, Your Honor," I said, thinking, *well so much for the defense advantage.*

"Chief, do you know what the Quartz County Drug Diversion Program is and how it operates? If so, please explain it to the court."

"A person convicted of a first-time drug offense is given the option to enroll in a drug diversion program as an alternative sentence to jail, or probation, or the like. If they complete the program and have no further drug-related problems for a set period of time, their arrest and convictions are usually expunged from the court record."

"Thank you, Chief, I appreciate your very concise and accurate description of the program. So, do you know what my plea bargain sentence was?"

"Yes, if I recall correctly. I believe you were sentenced to three years supervised probation, with drug testing, a fine of a few thousand dollars, plus community service."

"Correct again, Chief. But do you have any idea why I wasn't allowed to participate in the diversion program? Based on your own description, I was rightfully entitled to the program and, in fact, needed it at the time."

"I have no idea," he responded. "I'm not part of the sentencing process after a conviction or plea bargain. In your case, I believe the DA's office and Probation Department worked out the plea with your attorney, Mr. Nash."

"Chief Kane, were you part of a conspiracy aimed at getting me a harsher sentence? One that could conceivably prove to be detrimental to my future?"

"Absolutely not!" the chief bellowed in a hurried huff.

"Chief, who is Arthur Fenwick?" I quickly asked.

The chief paused momentarily, then said, "He's a past mayor of Gold City and presently sits on the city council."

"To that extent, as mayor, he was also your boss and the person who, because of his recommendation to the full city council, was instrumental in you being hired as chief. Isn't that true?"

"I suppose so," Chief Kane reluctantly answered.

"Did Arthur Fenwick have anything to do with your instigating the investigation of me, or with my harsh sentencing for a misdemeanor back in 1987? Remember, Chief, you are under oath, and other witnesses, including Mayor Fenwick, have yet to testify."

"No, Mr. Fenwick had nothing to do with your drug investigation beyond my normal weekly recap to the mayor about on-going investigations."

The chief looked uncomfortable, and I aimed to make him wiggle even more.

"With all due respect, Chief Kane, before this trial is over, I believe I'll be able to call you a liar. And you will have perjured yourself."

I began walking back to the defense table for some notes as DA Penrose immediately rose from his chair.

"Your Honor, please. The defense is again calling to question and harassing his own witness. In this case the Chief of Police and a decorated public servant."

"Sustained," Campbell said with emphasis. "Time to move on, Mr. Davis."

"Chief Kane, perhaps you could explain to the court why I was the only suspect in Mr. Nicholson's murder?"

"Because we believed you had the opportunity and motive to commit the murder. Also, after we found the murder weapon and the blood-stained jacket in your possession, there was no reason to look any further. As you know, Mr. Davis, that is what we call MOM in police talk: Motive, opportunity, and means."

The Chief's cocky smile and facial expression suggested that he was very satisfied with his answer. I needed to wipe that sarcastic smile off that smug face.

"Didn't you find any of these evidence discoveries to be...shall we say, rather convenient?" I asked.

"No, not at all. They were strong pieces of evidence implicating you and found legally with a warranted search of your property," the chief responded.

"After my arrest and booking, you questioned me about these

items, and I explained that I had left my jacket at Gary's that night and that my pistol had been stolen in the reported 1987 burglary of my home. Did any of these explanations sound plausible at the time? Did you or your investigators even check the plausibility of my statement, or did all of what I just said fall on deaf ears?"

"Is that a question?" the chief asked.

"No, but this is," I answered.

"Chief, you heard in previous testimony from Miss Meyer's that Mr. Nicholson had about twenty-five thousand dollars in cash and multiple ounces of cocaine in his home the night he was killed. Did you find any cash or cocaine from your search of my home or office after the murder and the day you arrested me?"

"No," the chief replied.

"Why do you think that is, Chief Kane?"

"Can't explain it. There could be numerous answers as to why the cash and cocaine weren't found. You could have sold the coke, or used it yourself, and hidden the cash. Or, hidden the cash and the coke for all I know. Take your pick. But we thought you were guilty then, and we still do."

"Chief Kane, have you ever heard of reverse discrimination?" I asked looking directly at him.

"Objection, Your Honor," Penrose yelled while coming out of his seat.

"Withdrawn," I said immediately.

"Be careful Mr. Davis," warned Judge Campbell. "Chief Kane is a respected law enforcement officer."

"Chief, you heard testimony from Miss Meyers that Mr. Nicholson was ingesting cocaine on the night of his murder, and she believed that I was as well. Did you have me tested for cocaine use when you arrested me for Mr. Nicholson's murder?"

"No," Kane said.

"Why not?" I asked.

The chief stared at the jury, then at the floor, but didn't answer the question. I didn't push him, because his silence roared like a hungry lion.

"That's all for this witness, Your Honor. I think the jury can plainly see the pattern in the first police investigation and its parallel to this murder investigation and draw the proper conclusions."

"Objection," Penrose said jumping up from his chair. "Mr. Davis is trying to deliver his closing argument to the jury, and he is out of order."

"Withdrawn," I said, "and I have no further questions of this witness, Your Honor."

"Redirect, Mr. Penrose?" Campbell asked.

"No redirect, Your Honor."

"Court will reconvene at one-thirty," Judge Campbell announced.

I didn't like making the reference to reverse discrimination with the black Police Chief in open court, but I was fighting for my life. And with an all-white jury, I couldn't let it pass without drawing attention to the possibility that it may exist.

Chapter Fifty-One

Sandi and I ordered chicken burritos for lunch at a downtown Mexican takeout, then walked over to a bench in the town square and finished them off with a soda. We felt good about how the morning had gone with Kane, and overall how our defense strategy was coming together.

We still had the best part of our game to come, and I had been contacted by someone well-placed in law enforcement assuring me that he had some interesting information to share and wanted to testify on my behalf. I informed Sandi that I would be meeting with him that night.

***

Back in court, I called as a witness my former attorney, Walter Nash. Walter had aged considerably since my 1987 arrest. He was walking slower, still with his cane and slight limp, and his head was still bald and flaky. His glasses had thicker lenses and were tinted a yellowish color that made him appear even older.

I stood and addressed the court.

"Your Honor, I'd like permission to treat Mr. Nash as a hostile witness."

"Objection, Your Honor!" Penrose shouted. "Mr. Nash is a defense witness, and before he has been given an opportunity to answer even one question, the defense wants to treat him as a hostile witness. This is out of the ordinary and, I might suggest, out of order."

"Your Honor, some of the questions I'm prepared to ask this

witness might make him uncomfortable, and even cause him to take the Fifth rather than answer. Thus, I make this request, and I make it in good faith to this court."

Judge Campbell paused for a moment then said, "Objection overruled; let's see where this goes, Mr. Penrose. But be careful, Mr. Davis, your witness, is a highly respected officer of this court."

The DA slumped back in his chair, clearly upset at the judge's ruling.

"Mr. Nash, you were my attorney in nineteen eight-seven when I was arrested for cocaine possession and distribution of cocaine, correct?"

"Yes," Nash answered calmly.

"Since I now understand the law better, and I've had time to understand what happened during those proceedings a few years ago, I believe you and the then DA—now Superior Court Judge Barbara Worthington—concocted a misdemeanor crime for me to plead to. Is that correct?"

"Objection. Privilege, Your Honor. The witness, by answering may be exposing himself to self-incrimination and/or divulging attorney/client privilege."

"Your Honor," I countered, "this witness, as an officer of the court, has sworn to tell the truth, and I release him from any attorney/client privilege he may have with me, or had with me, in order to get to the truth."

"Mr. Nash," the judge asked, "as an officer of the court, you are aware of the objection and defense rebuttal. Are you comfortable answering Mr. Davis' questions going forward?"

Nash paused for a moment, looking at the jury, then said, "Yes, as I'm here as a witness for the defense and to clarify my actions."

"Very well, please proceed, Mr. Davis," Campbell ordered.

"Do you need the question read back, Mr. Nash?" I asked.

"Yes, please."

The court reporter read back the question to the witness. Nash looked at me and said, "Correct, we arranged a plea agreement for your benefit; a misdemeanor offense that eliminated any need for a criminal trial on a felony charge."

"And that concocted crime was, 'being in a place where a controlled substance was consumed.' Is that correct?"

"Yes, as I recall," Nash responded slowly.

"And the incentive you repeatedly used for me to take the plea was the threat of losing my liquor license should the DA convict me of a felony. Again correct?"

"In a manner of speaking, yes, you're correct. We devised a plea agreement that we felt best fit your situation at that time. We considered the circumstances and drafted a recommendation for you that we felt would accomplish both your and our considerations for a satisfactory plea."

"And did I more than once express my reservations over the severity of the sentence being imposed for this first-time concocted misdemeanor, not to mention the fact that this was my first offense of any kind? I had never been arrested before as an adult, correct?"

"Yes, as I recall, you expressed concern. And yes, it was your first offense."

"Even so, you used your persuasive powers and my ignorance of the law to convince me that the plea was a great deal and that I had better take it or felony charges would be filed against me. And if convicted of a felony for providing cocaine to my guests that night in my office, I would lose my liquor license. Do you recall that?"

"Yes, I recall those conversations."

I took a breath then said, "Mr. Nash, why did you work so hard to convince me to take that plea agreement?"

Walter Nash paused, then calmly said, "Because the DA's office wanted you on probation."

"Objec..." was all Penrose could muster before deciding to sit back down in his chair.

I moved over to the defense table, picked up some documents and walked back to the witness stand.

"Mr. Nash, I have here a copy of the plea agreement you had me sign in nineteen eight-seven. Will you tell the court the purpose of a plea agreement?"

"Well, usually its purpose is to save the state the manpower and cost of a trial by having the defendant plead to a lesser crime than originally charged. In most cases, it's a way to dispose of a matter to the mutual satisfaction of both the defendant and the state."

"Isn't it also the function of this plea agreement to ensure against double jeopardy—that is, being charged twice for the same crime, further ensuring that the matter is considered closed?" I asked.

"Yes, it usually accommodates all those things," he answered.

"Mr. Nash, do you recall what paragraph thirteen in the plea agreement stated in regard to the probation terms?"

"Yes, generally," Walter replied. "To paraphrase, it basically stated that if you violated any conditions of your probation, the DA could come back and file the original felony charges against you."

"So, that being said, will you now tell this court how you, despite my objections, allowed me to take such a plea bargain, knowing full well that because of paragraph thirteen in the agreement, this whole episode would undoubtedly come back to haunt me?"

Nash paused with his head lowered, not wanting to look at me and not wanting to answer, but knowing he was under oath, to tell the truth.

"I was pressured by the DA's office to make a deal with you."

"Did you know I was physically and mentally sick from

cocaine abuse when you misrepresented me and sold me out?" I asked accusatorially.

"I did not sell you out," Walter said with some anger in his voice.

"Did you know about my cocaine dependency? Yes or no?"

"Yes," Nash responded looking away from me.

"And did you also know that as a first-time offender I was entitled to a drug diversion program as an alternative sentence? Not only because it was the law, but also because I really needed it."

"Yes, of course, I knew."

Nash was becoming increasingly agitated, and his demeanor was becoming less professional.

"And, of course, the DA's office knew, right?"

"Yes, they knew," he answered.

"So, did the DA and you conspire to make my sentence harsher than it should have been?"

Walter sat silently until Judge Campbell finally said, "Please answer the question, Mr. Nash."

"I think conspire is too harsh a word. The DA simply did not offer any diversion program as an alternative sentence. She insisted, at the very minimum, that you be placed on supervised probation for the innocuous misdemeanor charge you pled to."

"Did you just say that my misdemeanor charge was innocuous, sir?" I asked with my arms open.

"Yes, that's what I said," Nash said, again looking away from me.

Finally, the answer I had been waiting for since 1987 that confirmed my suspicions.

I asked Nash, "To what purpose and end did the district attorney want me on supervised probation?"

Again, a long pause, and again the judge had to direct Nash to answer.

"The DA contended that because Chief Kane had bungled the search, having you on probation while still using cocaine would make it easier to get you the next time. By inserting paragraph thirteen into the agreement, it meant that once you provided a dirty urine test, they could charge you again with a felony. A felony conviction would vindicate the police department and Chief Kane, even the DA's office, and they could say, 'Look, we told you so,' and it would eliminate any liability they might have been exposed to should you have proceeded with any lawsuits."

"I appreciate your candor," I told him, "but I could have used it a long time ago."

Nash shrugged and once again looked away.

At that point, I didn't know who needed a break more—me or Walter. I looked at the jury, scanning eyes and body language. Then I walked back to the defense table and took a slow, long drink of water from my glass. I then shuffled through some of my notes and took a deep breath to kill more time.

Finally, Judge Campbell said, "Mr. Davis, do you have any further questions for this witness?"

I turned back to the witness and said: "I only have a couple more questions, Your Honor. Mr. Nash, what did the DA have on you that would compel you to misrepresent me so severely?"

Nash sat up in his chair, turned toward the bench and said, "Your Honor, at this time, I wish to invoke my Fifth Amendment rights and refuse to answer any further questions. Mr. Davis is on trial—not me."

"Walter, thank you for being so candid this afternoon, but if I were you right now, I wouldn't answer either," I told him. "Whatever it was, it must have been so egregious that I'm sure you don't want this court or anyone else to know."

Walter Nash froze, not wanting to show any emotion.

"I have nothing further for this witness, Your Honor."

Thomas Penrose got to his feet and addressed the court in a

tone intended to convey his mounting impatience with the crux of my argument.

"Your Honor, I have no questions for this witness. Once again, however, I must object to the defense's use of these irregular tactics in an effort to cloud this murder trial with the hypothetical theory that Mr. Davis' past arrest somehow relates to the charges now under consideration by this court. I continue to look for this connection, Your Honor, but as yet I have been unable to connect the dots. If ever I have witnessed a courtroom fishing expedition, it has been the just-completed examination of one of our most esteemed attorneys and citizens. And for that, Mr. Davis should be ashamed of himself and admonished by the court."

Penrose sat down, and I rose to address his objection.

"Your Honor, I would remind the court that the prosecution's case rests directly on my jacket, my gun, and lots of supposition. Our goal is to show this jury and the court, with the aid of additional witnesses, that if local law enforcement was capable of conspiring against me in nineteen eighty-seven, they are capable of it today. In addition, the murder weapon, in this case, is inexplicably connected to my eighty-seven arrest, and if allowed to proceed we believe we can connect those dots. We ask for the court's indulgence in allowing the jury to decide once they have heard from all of our witnesses and all the testimony."

Judge Campbell paused and leaned forward before speaking. "Because of the late hour, I will make my ruling on Mr. Penrose's objection tomorrow morning at nine o'clock."

Looking at Nash, still in the witness stand after the jury had filed out, the judge said, "Mr. Nash, I want to inform you that I will be contacting the California Bar Association with a recommendation for disciplinary actions against you based on your testimony this afternoon. I am truly astounded at some of the testimony I heard from you today—especially your admitted lack of competent counsel for Mr. Davis in nineteen eighty-seven when he obviously was depending on your experience and advice."

Walter sat at the witness stand, unwilling or unable to look at the judge. He appeared a broken man.

Judge Campbell slammed his gavel. "Court is adjourned." The stealth squeeze I felt on my arm from Sandi told me that she thought things had gone well. I shared her optimism, but I wasn't sure how Judge Campbell would rule the next morning.

I knew I had pushed the envelope as far as an attorney could push it, without being admonished.

I hoped I hadn't pushed it too far.

Chapter Fifty-Two

That night, as Sandi and I enjoyed dinner at The Jake's Bistro and planned for the next day in court, she asked about Walter Nash's odd behavior as a witness. She said that when I asked him about possible pressure from the DA in 1987—enough pressure to make things tough on me in order to protect Nash in some way—he had turned beet red and began to sweat visibly.

He had hidden his emotions best he could, not wanting the jury to see that he had been rattled. But turning red-faced from embarrassment and sweating is an uncontrollable human reaction.

I explained to Sandi that it was never clear, at least to the public, what had happened. But the rumor was that in the early seventies when Walter was Quartz County Superior Court Judge, he went to a judge's conference/seminar in Seattle and, while there, he was busted in a hotel suite partying with other judges, DA's, and law enforcement officials, and some happy hookers.

It was a sting, and Walter was arrested along with the other mix of law enforcement officials from around the country.

The Quartz County sheriff was contacted by the Seattle P.D. and arrangements were made for Walter's release and quiet return home. The charges were eventually dropped, but Walter was pressured by local judges and attorneys alike to resign from office and return to private practice.

"No wonder he reacted the way he did," Sandi said after I finished telling her about one of the most scandalous skeletons hanging in any Quartz County judicial closet.

"He knows that I know, so when he suddenly clammed up and

took the Fifth, I had to smile."

"But how did you know?" Sandi asked.

"A family friend and city councilman told me the story back when I hired Walter to defend me. It was just an FYI at the time, and my source knew the story to be true because his dad was the county sheriff in the early seventies when the Seattle incident occurred. Obviously, the sheriff knew the details."

I told Sandi that to most of the community—outside of the legal community, that is—Walter was a devoted husband and father. But to some, they knew he had his skeletons, and he was able to dance in the closet with those skeletons because of who he was and the position he held.

For someone like me, with a history of drug abuse and unrestrained sexual indulgence, it was not my place to pass moral judgment on Walter's behavior. That was between Nash, his wife, and his God. But he should never have been so careless as to get himself into such a compromising situation.

Morality is one thing, but the law is another—especially when you are a Superior Court Judge pontificating about the sordid character of men and women you are judging. Walter had a brilliant legal mind and was a hell of a judge, but he succumbed to carnal temptation one too many times. And no one knew more about succumbing to temptation than me.

"Truth is," I told Sandi, "Walter helped me back when he was DA, prior to him being elected to the bench and representing me in the eighty-seven-drug arrest."

"How so?" she asked with a curious eye.

"Well, it was a long time ago, when I was in high school. There were actually three incidents that he was instrumental in that helped me, my brother, my cousin, and several other kids, walk away from certain prosecution. You want to hear about these all-but-forgotten escapades?"

"Please, I have nothing but time."

I began explaining that when I was a sophomore in high school, one of our classmates, who was a year older than the rest of us, had a driver's license and was lucky enough to have a 1957 Chevy with a 327 V-8 engine and a Hurst three-speed floor transmission that he and his dad had re-built.

One Saturday night in the fall of sixty-three, five of us got in Fred's Chevy and headed to Marysville to see the Beach Boys at the Civic Auditorium. A couple of us had flasks of Kessler Bourbon, and we all sipped the alcohol during the ride. Needless to say, we were feeling no pain by the end of the concert. We were parked in downtown Marysville on the main street in front of a men's retail store and, when we went back to the car after the concert, one of my friends spotted a display of Pendleton shirts in the store window.

Back then, Pendleton shirts were the premium men's winter shirt, but they were expensive, about thirty bucks each. A lot for a shirt in the sixties. Someone suggested we break into the store and take the Pendleton's, then sell them to our friends at school. Seemed like a good idea at the time.

So, that's exactly what we did. We went around behind the store and kicked in the back door. It was easy. Fortunately, there were no alarms to deal with, so we were in and out in about ten minutes with over forty Pendleton shirts.

For the next week, we sold the Pendleton shirts out of Fred's car trunk in the parking lot of the school for ten bucks each, a fiver for a good friend. Many got shirts, but many didn't. So, the next weekend we headed to Oroville to another men's store that someone had scouted. Too cocky for our own good, we broke in and stole even more shirts than we took in Marysville.

Over the next several days we sold all the Oroville shirts in the parking lot to the students, but this time school officials notified the sheriff's office about our activities. Naturally, they had been alerted to the burglaries by their counterparts in the neighboring counties, and we were arrested and charged with burglary and grand theft. That was the beginning of October.

By Thanksgiving, the neighboring county DAs had dropped all the charges against us, and all record of the arrests had been expunged. Turns out Nash had negotiated a settlement with the other two DAs with both Yuba and Butte counties. The settlement agreed to was that our parents would pay the store owners retail price for the shirts and damages done to their stores. That was it. It all went away—dozens of kids and a few teachers wore their new Pendleton shirts to school that winter and all was forgotten. Poof!

"How much did the settlement cost your parents?" Sandi asked.

"If I recall correctly, I believe it was about five or six grand. Split between the five families it was cheap, considering the alternative—not to mention what we damn fool kids were facing had prosecution gone forward."

Then, I told Sandi about the other incidents involving Nash, that seemed even more inconceivable.

In early May of sixty-five, on a warm spring Saturday night during my senior year of high school—and my brother Don's junior year—he and a bunch of friends went to a place called "The Pizza Factory" on the old Gold City highway. It was a teenage nightclub, of sorts. A place for us kids to hang-out, a place to gather, dance—or "slop" as we called it—and stay out of trouble. At least that was the intent behind its origin. As the name implies, they served not so good slices of pizza for a buck. The place closed in less than a year.

Don and his friends had been drinking Country Club Malt Liquor in the parking lot before going in, and they were in their cups when they entered the club. A high school dropout by the name of Dodi Woods started hitting on him and wanted to go to the parking lot and drink beer in Don's '59 Ford convertible. Dodi was a few years older than Don and had a reputation for being promiscuous. She was only five-foot two with long straight blond hair and deep green eyes. She was built like a female gymnast with a solid muscular body, yet a body to admire. Don told the other guys what was up, and they followed him to his car in the parking lot behind the club.

When they got her in the car, she slammed down three or four malt liquor beers, while acting provocatively, so they asked her to show off her body by taking her clothes off. She did and laid down in the back seat of the convertible, with the top down. Dodi then called for Don to get in the back seat with her. He did, and they did the dirty thing. Then she called out for another friend of his, and he did his thing.

Throughout the affair, all the other guys were standing around the car, watching the action. In all, four guys got in the back seat with her and rode her like a pony.

By the time the fourth guy finished it was just after midnight and the club was closing. A couple dozen guys, and a few girls had watched the action in the '59 Ford convertible. It was time to go. Everyone there was sworn to secrecy, pledging to keep their mouths shut about that night's event. Oh Sure!

By the end of the next day, everyone had heard about the "Saturday Night Gang Bang" at the Pizza Factory. The name quickly changed to the "Pussy Factory."

Soon after that, the DA heard about the incident and contacted the sheriff's office to request an investigation of that evening's activities. Following the investigation, the DA, Walter Nash, chose not to charge my brother and his friends with anything. Once his investigators confirmed that the sex was consensual, Dodi was essentially calling the shots, and she was over the legal age of eighteen, the matter was closed.

What happened to Dodi, I have no idea, but a few years later she shows up again in Gold City and becomes involved with my older cousin, Mark Davis.

Just outside of Gold City was a place called Lake Olympus, a shallow pond really, but a lake to us. In the middle of the lake was a roller-skating rink on pilings that you walked to from shore on a long wooden bridge. During the forties and fifties, it was a popular place for dances and to hang out and skate or celebrate birthdays and such.

The place closed in the early sixties and sat dormant for a couple of years. At the same time, there was a group of wealthy businessmen and community leaders that met every Friday for lunch and an afternoon of drinking and embellished storytelling.

Around 1963 four of these businessmen bought the Lake Olympus building and converted into a restaurant and night-club/bar. It was the hottest place in town, and the restaurant served the best steaks around. It became the new hangout for many in the community. They called it the "Lake Olympus Steakhouse and Lounge." Always good food and on weekends they had a band for dancing so the ladies could dress-up and the guys would throw fewer punches. On many nights someone ended up in the lake after a fist fight on the bridge outside the club.

They hired my cousin, Mark, to manage the place and it was an enormous success. Then around sixty-eight Dodi Woods came back to town. Now over twenty-one and a regular at Lake Olympus Lounge she was back to her old tricks. Literally!

I was gone by then, away at college, and my cousin was living in a forty-foot trailer just off the Lounge parking lot, in the trees, near the water. He moved Dodi in with him and began pimping her out to the businessmen, politicians, and professionals that frequented the Olympus Lounge for a hundred bucks a pop. Business was brisk.

So good, in fact, my cousin bought a new baby-blue Cadillac convertible from the local car dealership for three-thousand-dollars. Cash. I'm not sure what Dodi was getting out of the deal, but something tells me Mark was doing better.

Anyway, all was going well until one day Mark gets a phone call from the DA, Walter Nash, telling him that he was aware of what was going on in the trailer and to knock it off. Now!

So much for a good thing. Once again, Dodi disappeared from the scene, and not long after that, the Olympus Lounge burnt down to the pilings. My cousin was out of a job, and the rumor for years was that the club was torched. Of course, that was never proven, and life around here went on as usual with the powerful in charge.

I never heard another word about Dodi Woods until the early eighties when I was told she was beaten to death by her pimp in the Fillmore District of San Francisco. Life's choices—sometimes they end with a sad story.

When I finished my tale, Sandi had a question.

"So, to be clear," Sandi said, "Nash looked the other way at your brother's gang-bang and negotiated with two other county DAs to get your charges dropped for burglary and grand theft. He kept your cousin out of jail for pimping, and turned a blind eye to a bunch of businessmen paying for sex? Unbelievable!"

Sandi was dumbfounded by how the law had once worked in Quartz County.

"Yep. And to this day I have never understood how it all really happened. I never spoke to Walter about it, nor have I ever questioned my dad about it. All I can figure is that we had the power on our side. My dad was mayor of Gold City, the Davis name was fourth-generation, Grandpa was a large contributor to local politics, and most of the other guys that were involved in these adventures had parents that were the business and professional leaders in the community—with deep roots here. Back then, that's how things worked around here. And a few businessmen paying for sex—no big deal."

"Hell," I said with a laugh, "in the good ol' days, the lifeguard at the Gold City swimming pool was elected to serve as the Municipal Court Judge. In fact, around here prior to the nineteen sixties, when the law was eventually changed, you didn't even need to be an attorney to be a judge on the Municipal Court. Just being a 'good ol' boy' was all that was necessary to qualify."

"So, when Walter Nash testified today at your murder trial, he unwittingly once again became a star for your defense. In fact, he was, without a doubt, the best witness we have presented," Sandi rightly proclaimed.

"It seems so, at least so far," I said with a smile while shaking my head at the irony.

Chapter Fifty-Three

The next morning, when Judge John Campbell entered the courtroom and settled in at the bench, he was prepared to rule on Thomas Penrose's objection from the previous day. Understandably, he kept the jury out of the courtroom, not wanting to influence their thoughts or decisions regarding future witnesses and their testimony.

"Mr. Penrose, I've thought long and hard about your objections regarding counsel's referral to his past arrest and its relevancy or, as you stated, its connection to this murder case. After yesterday's testimony from Mr. Nash, I am curious to see where Mr. Davis and Miss Stassi are going with their defense and what else we might learn in the way of testimony from the few remaining witnesses. With that said Mr. Penrose, your objection is denied."

Turning to his bailiff, the judge said, "Please bring in the jury."

Penrose showed his frustration with Judge Campbell's ruling but did not respond.

I called Dr. Cynthia Rubin to the stand. She was the psychologist I turned to for help beginning in 1988 and periodically through law school in Phoenix. Cynthia was a petite, attractive woman with a strong personality. She was about sixty, a shade under five feet and always dressed in beautiful designer clothes. She had short, stylish black hair, deep brown eyes, and skin so white and perfect I doubt it had ever seen the Arizona sun.

Cynthia took the stand and was sworn in.

"Good morning, Doctor Rubin," I began. "As a practicing psychologist, perhaps you could briefly explain to the court the basic differences between psychology and psychiatry?"

"Certainly," she answered. "A condensed definition would be that Psychiatry deals with disorders and/or sicknesses affecting the mind, while psychology is a science dealing with the mind and its mental and emotional processes. It is most commonly known as the science of human and animal behavior."

"So, when I came to you for advice and therapy in nineteen eighty-eight, it wasn't a mental disorder but rather a behavioral concern that I asked you to analyze. Correct?"

"Yes, correct."

"We had numerous sessions together from eighty-eight through ninety-one or so, is that correct?"

"Yes, we did. If I recall correctly, it was usually when you could afford to pay me," she said, eliciting light laughter from the spectators and smiles from the jury.

"And what were your findings, specifically, during my addiction period?"

"I found that your personality fits perfectly into the addiction dynamic. You have hedonistic tendencies; that is to say, tendencies to seek out those things that you desire or find enjoyable. The more cocaine you consumed, the more you craved its pleasure, until, finally, the pleasure cells of your mind took complete control, leaving you helpless in the face of your desire to consume more and more cocaine. Ultimately, what was most striking to me was that you seemed to have such an intense longing for something missing in your life, and then with your drug and sex addiction, you seemed to believe that you had found what was missing."

"Going back to my eighty-seven arrest, how did I react to it?"

"Quite typically. You felt shame and guilt at the realization that you had hurt your family and friends—and your failed business, of course. As you began to lose everything that mattered to you, you also began to learn more and more about your arrest. The more you learned, the more you felt you had been unfairly treated. You believed that your own attorney had not done well by you and, along with other revelations, you began to realize that a grave injustice had been perpetrated at your expense."

"Doctor Rubin, in your professional opinion, and observations, how do you interpret the fact that I did not revert to a violent form of revenge—especially with your understanding of how much anger and hatred I was harboring inside me by the time I left Gold City for Arizona?"

"It demonstrated to me that when in a normal state of mind, which in your case would mean no longer under the influence of cocaine, you do not have violent tendencies which would cause you to revert to violence to vent your anger or seek revenge."

"Doctor Rubin, from your experience and study sessions with me, do you believe I have the capacity to commit murder?"

"Objection! Speculation and calls for a conclusion the witness is not qualified to render, Your Honor."

"I'll allow the question, Mr. Penrose," Campbell ruled.

"Everyone has the capacity to commit murder," Dr. Rubin began, "but evidence of restraint was shown by the direction you chose after your arrest and humiliation. You left Gold City and went back to school to better yourself, rather than seeking some violent means of revenge against those that you believed had done you wrong. Your choice of revenge was to better yourself, get your law degree, and return to the 'scene of the crime,' if you will, and practice criminal defense law defending others against the same court system and prosecutors that so blatantly abused their power and positions against you in and around nineteen-eighty-seven."

"I most strenuously object once again, Your Honor," Penrose told the judge. "The witness is delivering a speech, not testimony."

"She was asked for her professional opinion," Campbell responded, "so her answer will be allowed."

I continued my line of questioning.

"To summarize, Doctor Rubin, in your professional opinion, am I now normal? And would you state professionally that for me to have committed murder would surprise you—having known me in my past life, and who I am today?"

"Yes, I would state without hesitation that for you to have committed murder would not fit with the person or personality I have studied, counseled and gotten to know."

"Thank you, Doctor Rubin. That's all the questions I have for you."

"Your cross, Mr. Penrose," the judge said.

Rising from his table, Penrose walked over in front of the jury and asked the witness, "Miss Rubin, can you professionally and categorically state that it is virtually impossible for Mr. Davis to have murdered Mr. Nicholson?"

The doctor paused, then said, "No, I can't, however..."

"That's all, thank you," Penrose said interrupting her.

"You're excused, Doctor Rubin," Judge Campbell said as he called for a ten-minute break. We stood as the jury left the courtroom and Judge Campbell stepped back into his chambers.

Cynthia hadn't been just photogenic; she was telegenic. She was articulate and confident but never came across as arrogant. The one word to describe her was the one word every lawyer wants for a witness: likable.

Ten minutes—time enough to confer with Sandi and press onward.

Chapter Fifty-Four

Following the brief break, I stood and called my next witness.

"Your Honor, at this time I would like to call Pixie Flowers." Pixie, dressed in a bright yellow sundress with flower prints, and soft blond hair bouncing on her shoulders, made her way to the witness stand.

"Miss Flowers, we know each other, do we not?"

"Yes, we do," she answered. "Some would say that we know each other intimately?"

Light laughter came from the back of the court as I continued.

"Back in the day, in the early eighties, we consumed cocaine together and had sex, to put it bluntly. Is that correct?" I gently asked.

"Yes, that's exactly what we did."

Again, there was some laughter, but Judge Campbell was quick to react.

"During that time, as I recall, you were a FedEx driver, frequently driving round-trip between Sacramento and Southern California. Correct?"

"Yes, I was," she answered. "And yes, I drove that route frequently, sometimes into San Francisco as well."

"I first met you at Bogart's, the bar I owned, in the early eighties. Is that right?"

"Yes, I think that's right."

"Then, later, we would occasionally see each other at Gary Nicholson's house. Correct?"

"Yes, that's right," she said.

"Are you still driving or working for FedEx?"

"No, I'm not." Pixie answered.

"Please tell the court why you are no longer a FedEx driver," I asked as I leaned against the lectern.

Pixie looked down and then answered hesitantly, "Well, the truth is I was fired for transporting cocaine between LA and Sacramento in my delivery truck."

"How long ago was that?" I asked.

"I was caught in nineteen eighty-eight and fired after my plea conviction the following spring."

"But you were bringing cocaine into Quartz County on a regular basis for many years prior to your arrest, correct?"

"Yes," she said looking away from me.

"And who were you getting the drugs from in Southern California?"

"A Mexican cartel called El Bandito, out of Torrance."

"And they were importing, or smuggling, the drugs from Mexico. Right?"

"Yes."

"Pixie, who was your connection in Gold City for the drugs?"

"Gary Nicholson."

"How did this connection between you and Mr. Nicholson and the Mexican gang come about?"

"Gary approached me in late nineteen eighty-two with a proposal to transport the coke, and then he introduced me to Paz Vega in L.A. to set up the how, when and where details for making it happen. And that began in eighty-three. Everything went as planned until I got hooked and addicted to the stuff, then things started to spiral out of control, and I got caught. I was fired, then Gary and the cartel blamed me, and things got very ugly after that."

"They got ugly because Gary owed the cartel a lot of money, didn't he?"

"Yes, Gary was behind about forty thousand dollars at the time

I was fired in eighty-nine."

"And he couldn't pay it back because, without the continued supply from you, Gary was always behind at least one shipment, sometimes two."

"Yes, he was."

"In other words, it was almost like a Ponzi scheme, in that the cartel would advance him one or two kilos—about two-to-four pounds—and he sold that to pay for the previous shipment. Correct?"

"Yes, Gary was his own worst enemy because he was not a very good businessman. He consumed and gave away too much of his own product."

"Did Gary ever tell you that Mr. Vega, or any other member of the Bandito cartel, ever threaten to kill him for not paying the money he owed them?"

"Objection! Hearsay, Your Honor."

"Overruled, Mr. Penrose. Miss Flowers and Mr. Nicholson appear to have been business partners—of a sort—and I want to hear this answer. Please continue, Miss Flowers."

"After my arrest and the relationship between the cartel and Gary abruptly ended, Gary told me he was under constant threat from them to pay his tab. He took it seriously because these El Bandito dudes were bad guys. Really bad guys. I learned later that he eventually patched things up with Paz and the cartel began deliveries again from L.A., but it was all COD, and Gary would occasionally send additional money to be applied toward the past-due amount owed. But it didn't make a dent in the IOU because they were charging him a very high-interest rate to carry the debt."

"Pixie could Gary have been killed by the El Bandito cartel for not paying the IOU?"

"Your Honor! I again object to this speculation, and the question calls for a conclusion from this witness she can't possibly know," Penrose shouted.

"Sustained. The jury will disregard the question and its implications. Move along, Mr. Davis."

It was clear that I had gone as far as I could with Pixie, but I thought I got in a few good licks and possibly planted another theory for Gary's death. The jury seemed mesmerized by her account, and I knew that would work in my favor.

"Thank you, Miss Flowers; I have nothing further."

"Mr. Penrose?" the judge asked.

The district attorney got up and walked toward the jury box.

"Miss Flowers, could you possibly explain to the jury how the El Bandito cartel could have gotten their hands on the defendant's gun to kill Gary Nicholson? That is, of course, if this alternative defense theory was even possible in the first place."

Pixie looked at me, then at Penrose, and said, "No, I have no explanation as to how that could have happened."

Penrose turned and looked at the jury, letting Pixie's answer sink in. I had to admit that he had just scored a few points with the jurors, but creating alternative theories is one way to create reasonable doubt.

"Thank you, Miss Flowers, that's all."

Judge Campbell excused Pixie and told me to call my next witness.

"I would like to call Musette Parks."

I didn't know what any of this was getting me, but I felt the jury was getting tired of listening to speculative testimony. It was time to open the window and let some fresh air in the courtroom. It was time to attack.

Musette was looking pretty spiffy in her all-black outfit—black slacks, black sweater, and black pump shoes. Around her neck was the beautiful gold nugget necklace she so often wore. The necklace was even more pronounced today because of its contrast against her black sweater.

I walked up to the lectern, looked at Musette and said, "As was the case with Miss Flowers, we also know each other from past years. Correct, Miss Parks?"

"Yes, I would say we have a history."

"We used to do a lot of drugs together, didn't we Miss Parks?"

"Yes, we partied some, I guess you could say."

Musette looked away from the jury and answered with caution, not sure where I was headed with my questions. We had talked in advance of her appearance in court, but I had been coy as to the directions of my proposed questions.

"Like me, you were also good friends with the deceased, Gary Nicholson. Correct?"

"Yes, he was a good friend," she answered, again with some hesitation.

"In fact, he was a connection for you to acquire drugs, especially cocaine when other sources of yours could not get your supply to you? Isn't that right?"

Musette stared back at me, then said, "By the tone of that question, you're implying that I am, or was, a drug dealer. Therefore, I'm reluctant to answer anything along that line of questioning."

"Miss Parks wasn't our friendship, and the fact that we even knew each other, have everything to do with your direct connection to drug dealing, and the fact that I used to purchase cocaine from you?" I asked with a direct, unblinking stare.

"I'm not comfortable answering these questions. In fact, I refuse to answer, and I wish to exercise my Fifth Amendment right against self-incrimination," Musette said as she looked over at Judge Campbell.

The judge hesitated but did not comment, deciding to see where my questions of this witness were going. So, I continued.

"Miss Parks isn't it a fact that you owed Mr. Nicholson a considerable amount of money for cocaine that he advanced to you, for you to sell, and you had yet to pay him for that cocaine at the time of his death?"

"Again, I refuse to answer on the grounds of self-incrimination."

The Butterfly was pissed.

Musette Parks was clearly flustered and uneasy with my questions and my tone. She stared back at me with daggers in her eyes—something I'm sure the jury could easily detect.

"Let me take you in another direction, and maybe you'll feel more comfortable."

"That would be nice," she said in a voice laced with sarcasm.

"Miss Parks, do you know two county narcotic detectives by the names of Sadler and Evans?"

I was fishing at this point, but I had nothing to lose. She stared at me with outright hate in her eyes.

"Again, the same answer. I exercise my Fifth Amendment rights."

"You mean you have never heard their names before, not even in passing, or maybe read about them in the newspaper?"

She sat silent, looking directly at me with real contempt.

"If I recall correctly, Mr. Evans was murdered about five years ago," I reminded her. "Articles about his death and the subsequent investigation appeared in local papers for months. Are you sure you have never heard of the men, or, for that matter, actually knew them?"

"Objection. Defense counsel is mocking and badgering his own witness. And again, Your Honor, where is this going?" Penrose demanded.

"Sustained, Mr. Penrose. Mr. Davis, do you have any further questions for this witness that she would not consider self-incriminating?"

I paused, then looked up at Madame Butterfly and said, "No, Your Honor. I'm finished with this witness."

"Mr. Penrose, any cross?"

"No questions, Your Honor."

The judge excused Musette and, as she quickly walked toward the doors at the rear of the courtroom, she was staring at the floor, softly cursing. I took a shot, but she had stood her ground. She had been wounded, perhaps, but not mortally, and if you didn't knock the Butterfly out—she would surely live to fight another day.

I had the advantage, however, of knowing what my next witness was going to say. We had met a couple of days earlier, and his discovery that I would present to the court would change the direction of the trial. But I still needed to connect some dots for the jury to conclude that I was innocent and, in the process, determine who might be responsible for Gary's death.

I said to the court, "Your honor, at this time I would like to add an additional witness to my list for tomorrow."

"Your Honor, the defense and I exchanged witness lists long before this trial began," Penrose responded in the form of an objection.

"Your Honor," I said, "this witness came forward just a couple days ago with information that I had to verify before I could comfortably request that the court allow him to testify. However, I feel sure that you will not object to this witness once his name is revealed to the court."

"OK, I'll bite, Mr. Davis. Who is it?" Judge Campbell asked, his head slightly cocked.

"Your Honor, I wish to add retired Quartz County Sheriff Samuel Chaffy to my witness list."

Judge Campbell looked at the DA and asked, "Any objections, Mr. Penrose?"

Penrose requested a sidebar and Campbell waved us up to the bench.

"Your Honor," Penrose told the judge, "I haven't a clue as to what former Sheriff Chaffy will testify to, but I will not object to this last-minute addition to the witness list as long as his testimony has some substantive value and is not a continuation of Mr. Davis' wild attempt to cloud this case with his arrest from the past."

Judge Campbell looked at me for a response.

"Your Honor, what Mr. Chaffy will testify to is very relevant to the case at hand and has the potential to implicate Mr. Nicholson's real murderer."

"Very well," the judge said with a shrug. "Considering the reputation of the witness, and with no objection from the prosecution, I will allow his testimony with the understanding that Mr. Penrose will have all the time he needs to prepare for cross, should he request it. Understood, Mr. Davis?"

"Yes, Your Honor," I responded with a slight smile.

"Very well, step back," he instructed.

"Sheriff Chaffy will be added to the defense's witness list and called tomorrow," the judge announced. "Until then, this court stands adjourned until nine o'clock tomorrow morning."

Chapter Fifty-Five

The next morning, as Sandi and I walked up the hill to the courthouse, there was a cool June breeze blowing. The dog days of summer were fast approaching, so we enjoyed one of Gold City's last gasps of spring.

At precisely nine o'clock, we all stood as the ever-consistent Judge John Campbell entered the courtroom, called the court to order and asked the bailiff to bring in the jury.

Once the jury was seated, Judge Campbell looked at me and said, "Mr. Davis, you may call your next witness."

As planned, I called retired Quartz County Sheriff Samuel Chaffy, who was called into court from the outside hallway by the court bailiff. He came through the double doors in a wheelchair being pushed by his wife, Kim.

Chaffy had retired from the sheriff's office in ninety-one due to health problems. He had severe emphysema at the time of his retirement, due mostly from decades of heavy smoking. Attached to the wheelchair was an oxygen tank, and his mouth was covered by a breathing mask to ensure a constant flow of life's necessity.

Lately, arthritis had restricted his ambulatory abilities, and much of his movement outside the home was now with wheelchair assistance from his devoted wife of thirty-seven years.

He was not able to step up into the witness stand, so his wheelchair was placed in front of it, and he was sworn in. Kim removed the oxygen mask so her husband's answers to the court and the jury could be heard with clarity. Then the judge made it clear that if at any time the retired lawman needed oxygen, he would be given an opportunity to hook the system back up for a few minutes.

Once Chaffy was comfortable and ready to testify, I rose from my chair and walked over to be next to him.

"Thank you, Sheriff Chaffy, for appearing here today. We know it's very inconvenient for you to do so, but it is much appreciated."

"Happy to oblige," he said in an unsteady voice, trying his best to smile.

"Sir, you were sheriff of Quartz County from nineteen seventy-seven through September ninety-one, correct?"

"Correct."

"And you left early in your fourth term as sheriff because of health issues, is that right?"

"Yes, it is."

"During your term as sheriff you had a narcotics division, and two of your main investigative detectives were Tom Sadler and Mark Evans. Is that correct?"

"Yes, that's right."

"Now, Mr. Chaffy, you contacted me about five days ago, correct? I did not contact you?"

"Yes, that's correct," the former sheriff answered.

"Will you tell the court why you contacted me after this trial was already underway?"

The sheriff moved slightly in his wheelchair, adjusting his position for comfort.

"I contacted you hoping to testify in your murder trial because I had discovered something, I believed this jury and the court needed to hear. I did not have the information confirmed before the trial started, or I would have contacted you earlier."

"And, sir, please explain to the court and this jury what it is you discovered that you believe is of such importance to this trial," I asked, knowing that his testimony was about to shock the DA, the jury, Judge Campbell and the entire Gold City community.

It was time to pull that proverbial ace out of the deck and show our hand.

"In nineteen-ninety, about a year before I retired, Detective Sergeant Mark Evans was murdered; shot to death by two thirty-eight caliber bullets to the head. The murder was never solved, and no suspect was ever arrested. About a month ago, I reached out to our current sheriff, Milton West, and asked him if I could borrow one of the bullets from the Evans murder as well as have secure access to one of the bullets that killed Mr. Nicholson. Naturally, he wanted to know why, so I told him."

"And what did you tell Sheriff West?"

"I told him I had a hunch I wanted to pursue and that I would keep him informed of anything I found that would be of help and, of course, anything that was new."

"That was a pretty unusual request, wasn't it?" I asked.

"Yes," the former sheriff grinned, "but Milton—or Bud, as we all know him—and I have always enjoyed a great deal of mutual trust. And as some people might recall, he was my undersheriff the final few years I was in office."

"What happened after you contacted Sheriff West?"

"He agreed to accommodate my request and assigned an officer to assist me."

"And who was that officer?"

"Sergeant Dennis Miller, our ballistics expert. And once I got access to the bullets, Sergeant Miller and I took them to the state ballistic lab in Sacramento for testing. Naturally, Sheriff West wanted an ironclad record of the chain of custody for the bullets, so we made sure that such evidence protection was in place before they were taken to the state lab."

"What was the purpose of the test?"

"It was for comparison," he answered. "We already knew that the bullet that killed Mr. Nicholson came from your gun, but I wanted to know about the bullet that killed Detective Evans. I wanted to know if that bullet also came from your gun."

"And what, if anything, did you discover from the recent ballistic tests, Sheriff Chaffy?"

"The comparison testing was conclusive. There was no doubt about it—both bullets came from your gun."

"You are testifying that the bullets that killed both Detective Evans and Gary Nicholson came from my gun? The same gun the prosecution says I used to murder Mr. Nicholson?"

"That is correct," Chaffy said as he looked directly at the twelve jurors.

The courtroom erupted in loud chatter while jury members looked at each other in confusion. The prosecution team began shuffling papers as they whispered to each other.

"Quiet! Quiet in this courtroom," Judge Campbell shouted while slamming his gavel in an attempt to restore a sense of order.

"Well, sir, that's quite a revelation," I said as calmly as I could. "Sheriff Chaffy, do you happen to know where I was in nineteen ninety when Detective Evans was murdered?"

"Yes, I do," he answered. "Sergeant Miller and I verified during our investigation that when Evans was killed, you were in Phoenix, Arizona, attending classes at Arizona State University Law School."

"So, even though you have proven that my gun was the murder weapon in the killing of Detective Evans, would it be safe to say that I could not have killed him in nineteen ninety because, as you say, I was in Phoenix?"

"Yes, I believe it's safe to say you did not kill Detective Evans, because it was impossible for you to have been in Phoenix and Gold City simultaneously."

"Sheriff Chaffy, let's go one step further. You were sheriff in eighty-seven when I was arrested for drug distribution and possession. Correct?"

"Yes, I was."

"And you were involved in sending detectives Sadler and Evans to my home to search as ordered by the warrant?"

"Correct. I directed them to do so."

"And you directed the search because my home was outside of Gold City and was in your county jurisdiction, not Chief Kane's. Correct?"

"Yes, correct."

"You were also aware that three days after the nineteen eighty-seven search, my home was burglarized and in that burglary, my gun, this snub-nose thirty-eight that I am holding in my hand as a prosecution exhibit—the same gun that killed Gary Nicholson and Detective Mark Evans—was stolen in that burglary. Are you aware of that?"

"Yes, one of my deputies took the report and investigated your complaint."

"And are you also aware that I have always contended that whoever burglarized my home had to have known where that gun was kept? And only three people knew for sure: Lieutenant Sadler, Sergeant Evans and me?"

"I have heard about your theory, Mr. Davis, but I have no direct evidence as to its validity."

"Understood, sir, but they knew because I showed them where it was during the search of my home when they served the warrant. Lieutenant Sadler has earlier testified in this court that he did, in fact, know where the gun was kept. And I have always believed that one or both were involved in the burglary, so can you shed any light on my speculation?"

"Objection, Your Honor. As counsel just admitted, his question is based on speculation, is argumentative, and has no foundation," Penrose said.

"Overruled. I want to hear what the sheriff has to say," Campbell replied.

"No, I don't have any direct knowledge, but prior to Evans

being murdered I had undertaken multiple investigations of both Sadler and Evans for numerous complaints and credible rumors that had come back to me, or to the department, about them."

"Credible rumors and complaints about what, Mr. Chaffy?"

"We had complaints that Sadler and Evans were shaking down drug dealers for cash and drugs. And we heard rumors from reliable sources that seemed to validate the complaints."

"Did you ever find proof that they were doing these things?"

"No, not definitive proof; nothing that led us to an arrest or grounds for dismissal based on those rumors. However, there were other problems, especially with Evans."

"Yes, we will get to that in a minute," I said.

"Did you ever hear rumors or have actual knowledge of them having an inside source, a snitch, within the Quartz County drug world?" I asked. "Someone who was informing on other drug dealers to Sadler or Evans, so they could bust them?"

"Yes, we knew they had a snitch who was tipping them off to help our detectives bust other drug dealers in the county. That's why Sadler and Evans had the highest rate of drug-related arrests within their division."

"Do you have any idea who that informant was?"

"Yes, but I can't prove it, so I'm reluctant to speculate as to their identity."

"Fair enough," I said, "but getting back to Evans, and before his murder, did you have any disciplinary problems with him?"

"Yes," he answered. "In fact, he was on suspension at the time of his death. He was relieved of duty and ordered to drug rehab. By his own admission, he was addicted to cocaine and abusing the drug daily while on duty. His partner, Lieutenant Sadler, was the one who turned him in and requested that he be put in rehab. Evans was out of control, and we had no choice. Then, shortly after his suspension, he was killed."

"Sheriff, do you know who killed Detective Sergeant Mark

Evans?"

"I think I know, but I can't prove it. We never had a suspect, but I think it was someone who knew him well. I know you didn't kill him; that's for sure."

"Thank you, Sheriff Chaffy, nothing further," I said as I returned to the defense table after looking at the jury, absorbing their facial expressions and body language.

"That went well," Sandi whispered. "Good job."

"Do you have any questions for our former sheriff, Mr. Penrose?" the judge asked.

"Just a couple, Your Honor." Walking over to where Chaffy sat in his wheelchair, Penrose asked, "How did you confirm that Mr. Davis was actually in Arizona at the time of Sergeant Evans' death?"

"Sergeant Miller and I checked with the college administration office to see if he had any classes on the day of the murder. They informed us that Davis was registered for two classes on that day."

"But could they confirm that he actually attended those classes?"

"They could not positively confirm that he attended classes that day," Chaffy conceded, "but they were sure he did because his name was not listed on either classroom roster as having been absent. One professor might forget to list an absent student on any given day, we were told, but not two professors on the same day for the same student."

Penrose looked at Chaffy and realized what a blunder he had just made. He had violated the maxim that an attorney should never ask a question for which he didn't already know the answer. All the DA had done was confirm that I was in Arizona on the day Evans was killed.

Thank you, Thomas J. Penrose.

"The testimony you provided this court today is quite a

bombshell," Penrose said. "But why didn't you come to my office with this information rather than taking it to the defense?"

"Because this information would most certainly help the defense more than the prosecution, and I wanted to be sure the defense got it directly from me. Simple as that. Nothing personal, Tom, just a judgment call on my part."

Again, knowing that you never ask a question of a witness for which you don't know already the answer, Penrose said he had one last question for Chaffy.

"What caused you to undertake or question the comparison of bullets that killed both Evans and Nicholson?" he asked. "In other words, why did you suspect that both may have come from the defendant's gun?"

Penrose apparently hoped that the sheriff's answer would provide a hint of collusion between Chaffy and me. He was looking for an answer that would poke holes in Chaffey's testimony, but he fell well short of that goal.

Chaffy paused and looked directly at Penrose. "I took off my law enforcement hat and put on my thinking cap," he answered. "Can't say that I was totally convinced it might be the same gun, but when you sit in a wheelchair all day sucking on oxygen, you have lots of time to think. This case has been non-stop local news since Day One, and it's been on my mind a lot as well—especially since I know Davis didn't get a fair shake back in eighty-seven when he was arrested for dealing drugs. So, because the Evans murder had never been solved and both he and Nicholson were killed with a thirty-eight, I thought 'what the hell, let's see if the shoe fits.' And it fit perfectly."

"So, it seems Mr. Chaffy." Penrose paused then asked, "Final, final question, sir. Didn't you consider that this was quite a coincidence? That just maybe there was more to be considered, more questions to be asked and answered, more investigating to be done before bringing this damning information to open court?"

"Yes, as a thirty-year law enforcement officer, I considered many of those things, and rejected them. As Yogi Berra used to say, 'It was too coincidental to be a coincidence,'" the retired sheriff replied staring back at the DA.

There was silence in the courtroom, and Penrose stood near the jury staring at Chaffy. Finally, he said, "Nothing further, Your Honor."

"You are excused, Mr. Chaffy," the judge said, adding, "Let's take a short break and reconvene in twenty minutes."

As Chaffy was wheeled past our table by Kim, he looked my way and nodded, then winked. I smiled and nodded back because the former sheriff of Quartz County had just done us a huge favor.

Chapter Fifty-Six

When the court reconvened, Judge Campbell asked me to call my next witness. As I stood, I turned and scanned the crowded courtroom and realized that this trial had become the biggest show in town. The place was packed. Standing-room-only crowd.

That's not what Sandi and I had in mind when we developed our defense strategy, but I couldn't help but notice at lunch each day, and at dinner when Sandi and I ate out, that more and more people were smiling at me and fewer were glaring.

We needed the support of the jury, not the court of public opinion, but encouragement from friends and former customers certainly helped lift our spirits.

"I call Detective Lieutenant Sadler back to the stand, Your Honor."

As the lieutenant walked to the witness stand in his oversized suit, I addressed the court.

"Your Honor, given Mr. Chaffy's testimony, I would like to treat Lieutenant Sadler as a hostile witness. And I would like to ask the court to direct him to remove his firearm from his belt."

"Let's take your requests one at a time, OK?" the judge suggested.

"Your Honor, I think it was clear from Mr. Chaffy's testimony that Lieutenant Sadler has been implicated as a possible person of interest in these proceedings. And I intend to ask some direct questions of this witness that he may not want to answer. By having him declared as hostile, I will have greater leeway with regard to my questions."

And fewer objections from the district attorney.

"And as to the removal of his weapon?" Judge Campbell asked.

"Your Honor, I believe the wearing of his weapon—exposed as it is on his belt in open court—is threatening and prejudicial. He has already walked by the jury box with his jacket open and his weapon in plain sight. That might intimidate one or more jurors, Your Honor. Also, I intend to ask the witness some sensitive questions that may cause a reaction, not to his liking, and I would feel more comfortable if he did not have ready access to his firearm."

Judge Campbell paused before responding, clearly thinking about my arguments, then said, "You're certainly in no danger in this courtroom, Mr. Davis," he said, pointing toward the armed bailiff barely ten feet from the witness stand, "but you make a good point, and your requests are granted."

He then turned to Sadler and said, "Please remove your firearm, lieutenant, and hand it to the bailiff. You can retrieve it following your testimony."

The bailiff took custody of Sadler's handgun, and the judge announced, "You may begin, Mr. Davis."

"Lieutenant, you heard former Sheriff Chaffy's testimony, a few minutes ago, correct?" I asked.

"Yes," he said, as he hunched his shoulders, visibly uncomfortable at being asked to testify again.

"Do you remember, during your previous testimony, that we talked about me showing you where I kept my handgun in my house during your search in nineteen eighty-seven because you hadn't found it on your own?"

"Yes," he reluctantly agreed.

"Again, you couldn't find it because...?"

"Because it was well hidden in the bed, I guess." Again, it was a reluctant answer, but at least he was telling the truth.

"Yet, three days later, someone broke into my home, went directly to my bed and removed the gun from its hiding place, just as though they knew exactly where it was. You and Evans were the only people, other than myself, who knew where I kept my gun. Lieutenant Sadler, did you or Sergeant Evans steal my gun from my home three days after your search?"

My question was accusatory, but I felt there was a strong basis for the tone.

"Absolutely not," he excitedly answered. "That's ridiculous."

I moved closer to the witness stand after requesting to do so from Judge Campbell.

"The former sheriff also indicated that you and Evans were involved in some illicit activities while heading up the county's drug enforcement division. You heard him say that he had numerous complaints and heard credible rumors about you two ripping off—or shaking down—drug dealers for drugs or cash. Any truth to these allegations, lieutenant? And remember, sir, you are under oath."

"No, no truth to any of it. Zero truth." This time his voice was slightly louder.

I checked my notes at the table and briefly conferred with Sandi.

"Lieutenant how long were you and Sergeant Evans partners before his murder?"

"Just over ten years," he answered more calmly.

"And at the time he was murdered, he was a junkie—strung out on cocaine. Correct."

"Well...yeah, it seemed that he had a problem."

"Lieutenant, who do you think killed your partner?"

"I haven't a clue."

It was a caustic, short answer, but his tone and manner suggested to me that he might actually be telling the truth. But how could that be possible?

I had started out cordially, but I wasn't planning to continue in the same vein. I had one goal, and the jury's verdict was depending on my success. I had to push this witness to the limit. My job was to make him take the Fifth in open court and in front of the jury. There could be no stronger reasonable doubt than have an accuser, or hostile witness—especially one in law enforcement—take the Fifth and refuse to answer questions on grounds it may incriminate him. How could a jury vote guilty beyond a reasonably double after such action by a witness? We already had Nash and Parks take the Fifth. To ensure a not guilty verdict, Sandi and I believed you couldn't have too many witnesses take the Fifth or get caught in a lie.

"Why haven't you a clue?" I asked. "Didn't you investigate it along with the sheriff's homicide division?"

"Yes, I did, but so far we have been unable to settle on a suspect or a motive."

"Did you hear Mr. Chaffy testify that my gun, the same gun stolen from my house in eighty-seven, killed both your partner and Mr. Nicholson?"

"Yes, I heard him."

"How do you suppose that was possible? Three years after it was stolen, it was used to shoot your partner. Four years later it was used again, this time to kill Gary Nicholson. Who had access to that gun in both these instances?"

"I have no idea, Mr. Davis, the police, and the DA, think you did." He calmly answered, unfazed by my question.

"Well," I countered, pointing directly at Sadler, "I say it was you, lieutenant. I say you had access to that gun at the time both of these murders were committed."

"You're wrong, and you can't prove anything you're saying," Sadler angrily responded.

I walked toward the witness and asked in a loud voice, "Did you kill your partner and also kill Gary Nicholson?"

"Your Honor..." Judge Campbell sustained the objection before Penrose could complete it.

"Withdrawn," I said, stepping back from Sadler.

"Lieutenant," I continued, "let's talk about a motive for a moment. Your partner was strung out on cocaine and not thinking and acting rationally before his murder. Is that a fair characterization?"

"Yeah, that's fair," Sadler responded, looking at the jury.

"The more irrational and fog-headed thinking he projected, the more you worried about him doing something irrational and blowing your illicit activities. Isn't that correct?"

"No," he sharply responded. "There were no illicit activities."

"You say no, but I say yes. You even had him committed to a drug rehab clinic, not once, but twice, and both times he came out and went right back to coke as his crutch. Correct?"

"Yes," he answered. "He needed intervention, but rehab didn't seem to help. You can't fix *stupid*."

"Lieutenant, did you take my gun—the gun stolen from my home—and kill your partner? Did you shoot him twice in the head in order to prevent him from doing something *stupid* that would jeopardize your position with the sheriff's office and reveal your illicit activities through the years?"

Sadler turned to the judge and declared in a loud voice, "I don't have to answer these questions. I'm an officer of the law and should not be subjected to this line of questioning from a murder suspect."

"Actually, Lieutenant Sadler, you do have to answer these questions, unless I say you don't. And right now, I say you do, unless the answers to Mr. Davis's questions are self-incriminating. And if that's the case, I recommend you invoke the privilege you're entitled to under the Fifth Amendment and refuse to answer," the judge replied.

"In that case, Your Honor, I have no choice but to exercise my Fifth Amendment rights to self-incrimination," Sadler replied.

At that point, Sadler stood and began to walk away from the witness stand.

"Sit down, Lieutenant!" Judge Campbell ordered with a resounding voice of authority.

Sadler sat back down in a huff and, after a few moments of unrest and discussions within the court, order was restored. Judge Campbell then addressed a question to Lieutenant Sadler.

"Lieutenant, do I understand you correctly that you are refusing to answer counsel's questions because you wish to exercise your right under the Fifth Amendment of the Constitution of the United

States?"

"Yes, Your Honor, I'm declaring privilege. I won't sit here and be accused of murder with the threat of perjury hanging over my head should I answer one of his trick questions improperly. One inadvertent, mistaken word from me and I could find myself in jeopardy, so I choose to not answer any more of his questions."

The judge looked over at me and said, "Mr. Davis, you may continue, or not, knowing that the witness will no longer answer your questions."

"Thank you, Your Honor," I said. "I do have a few more questions for the witness if the court will indulge me."

"Proceed," the judge said.

"We understand from Mr. Chaffy that you and Evans had an inside informant. Is that correct?"

"As I said, I'm taking the Fifth," Sadler answered, crossing his arms.

I knew he wouldn't answer, but I wanted the jury to hear the questions.

"Do you want to tell the court who this informant is, or was?"

Sadler looked straight ahead and did not respond.

"What I don't understand is why you killed Gary Nicholson with my gun? Was it for revenge? A drug deal gone bad. He owed too much money, and you were collecting? Please, Lieutenant Sadler, tell us the truth."

Sadler again said nothing, staring straight ahead.

"Lieutenant, how involved are you in the Quartz County drug trade—the drug community if you will? How deep are you? Are you in so deep that killing another person became necessary to keep your head above water?"

Sadler sat rigid in the witness chair, looking out at the wall clock at the far end of the courtroom.

"Mr. Davis," Judge Campbell said, "it's obvious to this court that your witness is not going to respond, especially to your questions that could potentially be self-incriminating."

"I agree, Your Honor, so I have no further questions for this witness. But I think it's clear to the court that the witness is involved in this mess up to his eyes."

"Your Honor, I strenuously object," Penrose said as he rose from the prosecution table. "Nothing is clear to me except the fact that Mr. Davis killed Mr. Nicholson and is now trying to act like Perry Mason—exhausting one remote theory after another. Mr. Davis is on trial, Your Honor, not Detective Sadler."

"Enough from both of you," Campbell demanded above the din, then said, "Bailiff, please escort the jury from the courtroom."

When the jury was no longer present, Judge Campbell turned to Lieutenant Sadler and said, "Lieutenant, I am having you held for further questioning by homicide detectives in regard to both your partner's murder and Mr. Nicholson's. Bailiff, please take the lieutenant into custody."

As the bailiff approached the witness stand, the judge ordered both the prosecution and defense to meet with him in chambers.

By now I was getting to know the furnishings, wallpaper and wall hangings in Judge Campbell's chambers more intimately than I cared to. As we entered, Campbell removed his robe and motioned for counsel to take the chairs in front of his desk. Sandi and Penrose did so; I remained standing. He took his chair, leaned back looking at the ceiling, and exhaled loudly. As he leaned forward with a concerned look on his face, his eyes settled on me, then he said, "Please tell me, Mr. Davis, that it was not your plan all along to have Detective Sadler take the Fifth in front of my jury."

"Judge," I said, "I had no idea he was going to take the Fifth. I was pushing him, yes, because I wanted the answers to my questions, but I couldn't predict his reaction to those questions."

Penrose was shaking his head.

"You have something to add, Mr. Penrose?"

"Your Honor, I think opposing counsels have treated the court and the justice system with nothing but contempt from the start of this trial. He didn't even answer your question directed at him just now. Davis didn't say it wasn't his plan all along; he just said he had no idea. It just underlines the fact that defense counsel is sneaky and has tried to sabotage this trial from the start. He has now succeeded. Sadler was obviously a potential Fifth witness—a straw man he could set up in front of the jury, then badger into taking the Fifth. That was their plan all along, Your Honor, and if that's not a subverting of the adversarial system, then I don't know what is."

Sandi turned in her chair and glanced back at me to respond.

"Judge," I said calmly, "I can say only one thing to Mr. Penrose: Prove it. If he's so sure this was some kind of a master plan, then he needs to prove it. The truth is, my co-counsel and I only recently connected the dots to include Sadler in all this after we were contacted by Sheriff Chaffy. The police and the prosecution had ample opportunity of their own to connect the same dots, but either chose to ignore it or came up short of the mark. I think counsel's frustration with me largely stems from that, rather than the tactics I applied in the courtroom."

Judge Campbell, who was once again leaning back and looking at the ceiling, made a waving gesture with his hand. I wasn't sure what it meant.

"Judge," I asked, "what do you propose we do?"

Campbell swung the chair around and leaned forward, addressing the three of us.

"Mr. Penrose, I am informing you that when we go back out in that courtroom, I will give the jury a directed verdict of not guilty and excuse them. And when that formality is over, this trial will be over as well. Do you understand?"

"Your Honor, I respectfully disagree with that decision."

"Disagree, if you wish," the judge told him. "Hell, Tom, you can appeal my ruling if you think I've erred judicially, but that's what I'm going to do."

A directed verdict is a verdict ordered by the presiding judge preventing the matter from being considered any further by the jury. It is then determined by the judge by law, rather than by the facts. And Sandi and I knew the law was on our side. Facts were also on our side, of course, but it wasn't going to be necessary to prove any of them going forward.

"Your Honor," Penrose said, trying one more time to convince Judge Campbell that he was making a judicial mistake, "with all due respect, sir, you can't just stop this trial. Based on what? Surely the testimony of the last two witnesses couldn't have convinced you that the defendant had nothing to do with the murder of Mr. Nicholson. Mr. Davis may be a clever attorney; I'll give him that, but he has not proven reasonable doubt, Your Honor."

"Oh, but he has, Mr. Penrose, and only someone with blinders on could not see that Mr. Davis had nothing to do with this murder, never mind the murder of Sergeant Evans. This investigation needs to take another direction, and the truth needs to be uncovered, but not with this defendant on trial for a crime he didn't commit."

Penrose slumped, finally accepting reality.

"And it's time we take a fresh look at both Nicholson's and Evans murder, maybe it would be best to start with Lieutenant Sadler. He's now being held for that purpose, and he needs to answer some hard questions—Fifth Amendment be damned."

Judge Campbell looked at me for a moment, then at Sandi, and said, "Mr. Davis, you are free to go, with prejudice." Meaning, the dismissed charges could never be refiled against me in the future.

We had to restrain our smiles of relief knowing that this horrible nightmare had been settled and put to bed—forever.

"Thank you, Your Honor," Sandi and I said in unison.

We then shook Penrose's hand and exited the judge's chamber through the side door into the corridor—not the door that led back to the courtroom where, for nearly three weeks, Sandi and I had battled the DA while bonding with each other both professionally and personally.

As Judge Campbell had said—it was over. Now I knew who the informant was, but I didn't know the how or why behind all the carnage.

Next stop, the house on Veterans Avenue.

Chapter Fifty-Seven

Later that afternoon, shortly after four o'clock, Sandi and I, along with a patrol car from the Gold City P.D. and one from the Quartz County sheriff's office, pulled in front of a home on Veterans Avenue, across from the city park and not far from downtown.

Sandi and I walked up to the front door and knocked. A moment or two later the door opened, and Musette Parks greeted us. She saw four patrolmen standing behind us, then smiled as she opened the door and motioned for us to come in.

We went inside accompanied by two of the officers—sergeants from both the city police and sheriff's office. Musette was wearing jeans and a sweater with tennis shoes, her dark hair up in a bun. She looked refreshed and relaxed, as though she had been expecting friendly company. The house was clean and neat and looked pretty much like it had several years earlier when I used to come over to play cocaine cards.

She smiled and said, "Well, I guess congratulations are in order, eh?"

"Thanks, but I can't say you made it any easier." I lamented.

The Butterfly looked puzzled as to why we were there.

"This isn't a social call," Sandi told her.

"Really? Why, I thought you guys brought these cops along for a game of cards, like the old days Adrian, when you were a frequent guest of mine."

"No, not today," I replied. "We brought them with us to arrest you."

"You're shittin' me, right? Arrest me? For *what*? For not being the kind of witness, you hoped I'd be. That's not a crime, Adrian."

"You almost got away with it, but almost doesn't count when it comes to the law; almost isn't good enough." I looked at Sandi and winked. "Gary was your recent main supply source for your product, and you owed him thousands of dollars. You knew he usually kept a lot of cash in the house and a sizable stash of coke."

I paused to see how Musette would react. She looked me in the eyes for a couple of seconds then lowered her gaze, staring at the floor.

"So, you think you know the whole story, do you?" she said, turning and walking toward her living room sofa. "Well, you don't know shit, you asshole."

"Then why don't you fill in the blanks for us?" I asked.

She flopped on the sofa while Sandi and I sat in chairs across from her. The two officers stood behind us.

"Sadler hasn't admitted it—at least not yet—but he and Evans broke in my house and stole my gun, the jar of change, and my camera, didn't they?" I said it more as a statement of fact than a question, and we both knew the answer.

Madame Butterfly lit a cigarette, took a long drag then said, "Yes, Adrian, they stole that stuff from your house." She knew Sadler was, or would be soon, singing a tune to save himself.

"How did you end up with it?"

She again drew on her cigarette, then blew the smoke slowly back toward me and calmly said, "Yes, I ended up with your stuff."

"What happened?" I asked.

"Evans owed me quite a bit of money and gave me your things to help pay down his IOU for the coke he was pounding up his nose. I didn't know it was your gun or that the money was yours. Really, I didn't know it at the time, or I wouldn't have taken it from him. But there he was, handing me what seemed to be hundreds of dollars in coin."

"Didn't that seem strange?" I asked.

"Sure, but money's money, honey—right? And nothin' is strange in the coke business."

"And the gun?" I asked.

"I knew the gun had some cash value, so I took it and figured down the road I'd sell it to some paranoid doper. It had to be worth a couple hundred, maybe more. Same for the camera."

"When did you learn that the money and gun were mine?"

She inhaled another drag as her hands began shaking. "Oh, Adrian, it was years later; Sadler told me."

"When did you become their informant?"

Musette laughed nervously, but surprisingly at ease while she told a story that might implicate her in two murders.

"The snitch thing happened a long time ago. Sadler and Evans busted me in the early eighties with a small amount of coke and Evans approached me about keeping them informed about other dealers and drug deals I heard about. It was stupid, I know, but I was cocky and thought it would be smart to have two narcs in my pocket. And eventually, I was partying with both of 'em."

Her hands continued to shake as she lit another cigarette.

"I hung with Evans more than Sadler, because Sadler was married. Then I started fucking Evans to control him. He had a big dick, and he liked to use it at every opportunity. If he had just stuck to fucking and kept away from the coke, none of this would have happened."

"None of *what*?" I asked.

"Come on, Adrian, you're a smart attorney; haven't you figured it out yet?" The Butterfly asked as her upper lip began to quiver.

"I think so, but why did Sadler kill his partner? I'm assuming it was Sadler who shot Evans."

"Yeah, sure, it was Sadler. Evans was out of control; his coke habit was consuming him. He was fucked up all the time, making threats toward both Sadler and me. I couldn't control him any longer, and he was taking unnecessary risks on the job, jeopardizing Sadler's career. Sadler told me he was going to off him, but he needed a gun not tied to either of us."

"And you just happened to have what he needed?"

"Yes, I did," she said. "I told Sadler I still had a gun Evans had given me as payment for drugs, and that's when Sadler told me where it came from. You were in Arizona, enjoying a new life, and I didn't see the harm. I didn't think you'd ever show your face again in Gold City. And look at you now, eh?"

"So, what happened at Gary's the night he was killed? I assume it had to do with the money you owed him?"

"Yeah, it was about money...and something personal."

"Why did you come over after I left, and how did my gun and coat get in the mix?" I asked quietly, in an undemanding tone, hoping she would be honest. We had two witnesses to the conversation standing there in the room, so I was looking for answers that would take us to the actual murderer.

At that point, the sheriff's office sergeant informed Parks that she didn't need to answer any more of my questions without the Miranda warning and/or her attorney being present.

Musette said, "Fuck Miranda, I have two attorneys' sitting right in front of me. If they could get Adrian out of his mess, maybe they can help me as well. This fuckin' mess needs some fresh air." Musette continued, "After you left Gary's, he called me about two in the morning, yellin' and threatin' me. Sadler was here with me."

"Buying or selling?" I asked.

"Neither," she smiled. "He was here to get fucked—physically, not figuratively."

"Sadler?" Sandi said.

"Yeah, I started bangin' him after Evans went totally bonkers on coke. I wanted to keep Sadler close by for protection and fucking him regularly seemed to work. Gary was threatening me, Adrian; he wanted the money I owed him and said if I didn't pay him soon, he was going to the cartel to have them collect it from me."

She paused for a moment, looked at the two officers standing behind Sandi and me, and began to connect the final dots.

"Sadler and I knew it was time for Gary to go away. Permanently. There was more than one reason he needed to die, so I dug your gun up from the garden, and we went over to Gary's together. We sat in his front room listening to his bullshit while he screamed at me, demanding money. He told Sadler he was going to go to the sheriff and tell him all about his drug-dealing connections, and about the drugs and cash he was shaking down the dealers for, instead of bustin' 'em."

She then confirmed what we had suspected.

"We shot him to shut him up," she calmly said. "We didn't have any choice, and by killing him, we could take the money and the drugs he had in the house. I knew he kept it in the boat."

"So how did my jacket get into this?"

"It was laying on the sofa, we knew you just left, and when Gary was shot, blood sprayed all over the room, and some of it came down on your jacket, so when we were cleaning up to cover our tracks, I took it."

"You wanted to frame me? Why?"

"It was Sadler who suggested we frame you; it wasn't my idea. We had your jacket with Gary's blood on it, and we had your gun as the murder weapon. We knew you had been there earlier; it all just fit. It was easy for Sadler to get into your house and hide them."

"You didn't give a damn about framing me, did you?" I asked in a faint voice, shaking my head.

"Frankly, no," she said as I looked at her for some expression of remorse. "I'll have to admit; I didn't care *at all*. I just wanted to cover my ass. I had to choose between me going to prison or you going to prison, and that was a no-brainer."

"So, Sadler shot Gary, because killing people came easily to him. But it doesn't matter to the law, Musette. You were both there, so you are both equally guilty of first-degree murder because you took the gun there and planned to rob and kill him."

She smiled, then burst into laughter.

"Oh, Adrian, you fool, you are so wrong," she said between laughs.

Then, as suddenly as the laughter had started, it abruptly ended. She glared at me and said, "*I* shot the son of a bitch, not Sadler. And I'd shoot him again if I could. I hated him for what he did to my daughter."

"What did he do to your daughter?" Sandi asked.

"He killed my baby girl, that's what he did. He gave her AIDS and killed her." Musette Parks lowered her head and sobbed.

"What do you mean, he gave her AIDS?" I asked.

She looked up and shouted, "He was fucking her, for Christ sake! Don't you get the picture? He was coking her up, and fuckin' my daughter—and he gave her AIDS, that piece of shit."

Tears were running down her cheeks. I was shocked; truly shocked. I remembered the night at The Lumberjack Steakhouse when The Butterfly told me about her daughter's long, painful death. But AIDS? From my friend, Gary Nicholson?

"I'm so sorry, Musette, I really am. She was a beautiful girl."

Sitting in Musette's house, learning how her daughter had contracted AIDS and thinking about the past, I found myself reflecting on all the terrible things that had happened during those crazy, hedonistic years all of us had wasted. So much sadness for so many people.

"What a damn shame, Musette." I said sadly. "None of this had to happen—none of it. If only we had made better choices."

"Don't go gettin' sentimental on me, Davis; it's a wasted emotion with no cash value," she said with some sarcasm. "Now you're going to have these cops arrest me and take me to jail, aren't you?" she asked, wiping the tears from her cheeks with that hard look in her eyes staring directly at me.

I nodded.

"Well then it looks like I'll need a good lawyer, or two," she said, looking at both of us. "I'm glad it's over; will you two help me?" Parks asked, looking at Sandi and me. "I can pay you. I have money and the house."

We looked at each other and nodded in unison toward Musette.

Musette was placed under arrest, cuffed and advised of her rights by the city cop, then she looked back at me and asked, "What gave me away, Adrian? How did you finally figure it all out?"

I pointed at her neck.

"It was that beautiful gold nugget necklace you were wearing in court the other day; that's when it hit me," I told her. "At first, when I saw you wearing it at The Lumberjack that evening, I introduced you to Sandi, it didn't register with me. But when I called you to the witness stand in court the other day, and that big nugget was so radiant against the black sweater you were wearing, it all came back to me."

Musette knew what I meant; I could see it in her eyes.

"The night of Gary's murder, when I was at the house, he told me about the amount of money you owed him. He then showed me that necklace and said he was keeping it as collateral for your IOUs. The only way you could have had that necklace around your neck in the courtroom was if you had been at Gary's *after* I left that night. That's when I knew you were involved in Gary's murder."

"Well, bravo for you, Sherlock Holmes," the Butterfly said with some sarcasm as the officers began to walk her out of the house.

"But I never imagined that you were the one who pulled the trigger," I told her. "I thought for sure Sadler had done it, not you. But now, knowing the truth of why you pulled the trigger, I can understand your rage, so Sandi and I will help with your defense."

She didn't bother turning around to respond.

"Your place or mine?" Sandi asked as we stood on Musette's front porch watching her being gently placed in the rear seat of a patrol car. "All I know is that I'm starving, so do I cook, or do you cook?"

"Your place sounds like home to me," I told her.

"Maybe someday, but let's not get too far ahead of ourselves, OK?" she smiled.

The hug and kiss served as an hors d'oeuvre.

And I couldn't wait for dessert. Not the dessert of old, but a new dessert to be shared with Sandi for years to come.

Chapter Fifty-Eight

As I type these final thoughts, it is now August 31, 2012, my sixty-fifth birthday—a little more than five years since I began to record memories of a life split between utter self-destruction and blissful freedom. And it is Sandi—my beautiful wife, the love of my life—who has brought me the blissful part.

We began dating shortly after the trial and married Christmas Day nineteen ninety-five. I insisted on Christmas Day because I believed she was a gift from God—my own angel sent from Heaven above. Michael was born in November of ninety-six and is the great pride of my uneven life. Now fifteen, he's evolving from a boy to a man—and a wonderful young man, at that.

Looking back at this memoir, or whatever the hell it is, I guess I've painted a pretty candid picture regarding my sex life and its connected drug use. Some might call it great; some might say it was over the top. In hindsight, I realize how lucky I was. I never contracted an STD, or anything worse. I was a lucky guy.

When Sandi entered my life, I witnessed mental and physical pleasures not before seen—and all without the help of stimulants like drugs or alcohol. Oh, sure, we still enjoy a good bottle of wine occasionally, but that's as far as any outside stimulants have gone these past several years.

With Sandi, at times, I have reached beyond the plateaus of normal life. Each encounter has been unique, rising to a place where sensation is so intense that the rest of the universe doesn't matter to me. Living life with Sandi at my side is a pure thrill. Life is once again back in the ninetieth percentile. Remember, nothing is ever a hundred percent.

I began this manuscript of sorts in two thousand-seven when I celebrated my sixtieth birthday. It was absolute drudgery to start on this project, and it never got easier, but I was determined to do it—a chapter here, a chapter there. I wasn't sure how many years I had in front of me, and I wanted to record my memories while I was able.

This, then, represents the unabashed confessions of a former druggie who managed to pull himself out of the gutter just in time. Another couple of years of heavy coke use in those days, and I doubt I would be sitting here today, a successful attorney with a wonderful wife and teenage son.

Michael is still too young to understand what I did—nor do I want him to know just yet—but in time he will likely learn from others that a part of my young adult life was a cesspool filled with too much coke and not enough common sense. Maybe then—maybe—I will share this with him. Maybe I'll even share it with Sandi. I'm not sure.

Call it a catharsis, call it a confession. I don't exactly know what this exercise has produced, but in many ways, it represents what T. S. Eliot called, "These fragments I have shored against my ruin." And as scattered as these fragments of my life might appear, I have stayed a course faithful to the truth.

I still find life to be a never-ending surprise. We never know what will happen next, what we will see or hear, what important person will come into or leave our life. Life is a constant change. As I said before, nothing stays the same, and unless we are lucky enough to find comedy in it, change is usually a drama, if not a tragedy.

Along with the 'ten-percent factor' I mentioned earlier—I have another prescription for a long happy life—that is to believe that if we are lucky enough to be alive, we must give thanks for the miracle of life, and every moment of every day, no matter how flawed. And we must have faith in God, and a better tomorrow, even if that faith is not always deserved.

Thankfully, I'm now at a point in my life where I'm enjoying the present with Sandi, and looking forward to a long, long future with her. But I do think of my friends, and not so friendly, from years past. I think of them often.

Poppy, for instance, was a dear friend, and as far as I know, she's still with Google. She helped them when they were just an idea waiting to become a reality, and I couldn't be happier for her.

Shelly, unfortunately, went in a very different direction. She was a gorgeous young woman who became a haggard young woman before my eyes. Too much coke, too little sleep. She eventually moved away—to where I have no idea.

Asa was one of the few from those days of excessive sex and drugs who escaped Gold City. He met a guy from San Francisco, and they moved to Cape Ann, Massachusetts, in 2001.

London and Paris Maxx eventually divorced, and Paris sunk to depths I hate to be reminded of. She coked and drank herself to an early death. In the end, she was so bad she was vomiting blood into the washing machine in order to conceal her condition from her drug-dealing boyfriend. London followed suit a decade later when his own alcohol-ravaged body finally quit functioning. Damn, I loved that gal, and London was one of my best friends to the end.

Sergeant Ralph L. Pittman never made lieutenant, much less chief. He became a spiritual man. Much of what I have written about in these pages came from information Ralph shared with me a few years after the murder trial. After his divorce, he left the Gold City PD and went to Yemen with the United Nations Security Forces to make more money to pay alimony and child support. Didn't work out so well over there. He was shot and killed by the occupant of a house he was burglarizing. Karma?

Chief Abel Kane, by the way, sort of fell off the map. He retired shortly after the ninety-five trial and was never been heard from again. Then some years later we heard he was shot and killed by a bank robber as he was in the bank at the wrong time during a robbery. Seems he was trying to capture, or subdue the suspect, and was shot for his efforts. Can't say I was too bothered by the news.

District Attorney Thomas J. Penrose retired around 2003, and I see him occasionally at the grocery store. He doesn't seem to be doing much with himself, and he looks old and tired. I went on to keep beating his ass in court after my ninety-five victory. If my clients were guilty, I pled them out. If not, I took them to court and beat the DA consistently, because I was a better lawyer and had a reputation for winning. Revenge is sweet!

Former City Councilman Vance Egan somehow avoided jail for perpetrating his scams at Grizzly Bear Lodge, although it didn't end so well for him. The board threw him out of the lodge, he lost his next election, and his wife finally divorced him. And during the Wild West Days celebration, he was kicked in the head and killed by his horse. Seems he wasn't very kind to the horse, either––and horses have long memories.

Mayor and Councilman Arthur Fenwick worked until he was seventy, also retired from public life, and planned to travel and have fun. But on his first retirement trip—headed to Ireland to kiss the Blarney Stone and hoist a few pints—a terrorist bomb exploded, and his plane went down over the Atlantic. So much for a joyful retirement. Like Kane's demise, I shed no tears.

My doorman Wally retired from his truck driving job a couple of years ago. A great guy and the best bouncer any bar owner could ask for. He and his wife retired to Reno, Nevada, where he spends his days fishing in the Little Truckee River and hanging out at the Eldorado Race & Sports Book. We email each other every so often, but we haven't had a beer together in a couple of years. We need to do that, and soon.

Roxanne "Roxie" Meyers died of AIDS-related pneumonia in

2000. She was very sick at the end. Seems her being close to Nicholson and caring very much for him wasn't reciprocal, as she didn't learn that Nicholson had the HIV virus until it came out in court testimony. By then it was too late. Hopefully, not too late for her cousin.

Walter Nash, now in his eighties, is a broken man but continues to practice law. Following his testimony at my murder trial, Judge Campbell referred him to the state bar, and they suspended his license for a year. Now he's doing mostly probate, wills, trusts, and the like. Once a brilliant legal mind in tatters.

Musette "Madame Butterfly" Parks eventually cooperated with authorities in the murder of Sergeant Evans—which led to a Murder One conviction for Lieutenant Sadler—and a Murder Two/Grand Theft conviction for Gary Nicholson. Sadler planned the murder of his partner—Evans—planned the robbery of Nicholson the night of his murder, and he was present when Parks shot Gary. Sandi and I then pled Parks out to Man One/Grand Theft in the killing and robbery of Gary Nicholson. The DA gave her a break considering the AIDS death of her daughter as a partial motive for her killing Nicholson and her cooperation as a witness against Sadler. She served twelve years and was released. I have no idea where she is now.

As for Don—my brother took total control of Bogart's and made it a tremendous success. We were nearly in the dumpster when I left town for Arizona, but he rolled up his sleeves and made the joint what we had envisioned it to be when we took over our grandparents' one-room saloon and turned it into the biggest and busiest nightclub in the Sierra foothills.

Speaking of Arizona, my Playboy bunny pal graduated from Arizona State with a Master's in Education—summa cum laude, no less. Last, I heard, Kathy was happily married with a couple of kids, teaching English Lit at ASU. Good for her.

Dad died from prostate cancer in 2001. He was seventy-seven

and full of spunk right up to the end. He spent his last decade on earth traveling the country with Mom, gardening, fly fishing in all three forks of the Yuba River, and handling maintenance at Bogart's. Dad made sure the family trust included a clause that fully bequeathed the bar and building to Don, and that's the way it should have been.

As for Mom, she is still with us, but at eighty-five we have to accept the fact that she won't be with us much longer. She is feeling her age and misses Dad terribly. Since his death, she has taken care of the family home and spoils Don's kids at every opportunity.

God bless my parents.

My dog, Tonto, died a couple of years after I left Gold City for law school and it broke my heart.

EPILOGUE

It was nearly midnight in Washington, D. C., but not yet nine in Gold City when Michael Davis closed his father's memoirs and relaxed on his couch with one more glass of wine. He stared at the completed manuscript, contemplating and digesting what he had learned about his father's deepest, darkest secrets. Then he called his mother.

"Just finished Dad's manuscript," he said.

There was a long pause, then Sandi asked, "And...?"

"And, I had no idea what he had gone through in his life. I thought I knew, but I was wrong. And I'm really proud of how Dad turned his life around."

"He was a good man, Son, but it took him a long time to understand how good he was."

"You read all of it, right?" Michael asked.

"Yes, I did. I found it in your dad's office desk and spent a long night and early morning reading every page. I started reading it with a glass of your dad's favorite Cab in my hand and finished it with a pot of coffee sitting next to me."

"Did you understand it all?"

"Not sure what you mean by *understand*, Michael, but...yeah, I think so. Your dad sometimes wrote in a stream of consciousness style, so I guess some things were a little hazy, even to me. But how about you?" she asked. "Anything you didn't understand?"

"Well, for one thing, Benny Nicholson really didn't fit into the story much, and I don't understand what Benny's vendetta or motive was for killing Dad?"

"Well, besides Benny being mad that he didn't get off after his last drug arrest, he felt your father didn't do right by Gary—either in your dad's legal representation or the money issue—and he wanted revenge. And remember, your father was accused of killing Gary."

Sandi paused then said, "Michael, what few people know, and your dad didn't mention, is that Musette Parks is Benny's mother."

Michael was silent, trying to understand what his mom was telling him.

"Seems Gary and Musette knew each other as teens in Southern California and began dating," Sandi told her Son. "When she got pregnant in the mid-seventies, Gary dumped her and moved to Gold City. Then, a few years later, with a daughter from another relationship, she moved to Gold City and left Benny in Southern California with her sister to raise. When Benny was a teen, he ran away and came to Gold City to find his dad."

"You're kidding?"

"No, Son, that's what happened. Benny found Gary—who hadn't had anything to do with him as he grew up—and, once here, Gary let him move into his house. And for the next several years, Benny deliberately kept his distance from Musette because he was harboring a lot of hate."

"Why? Musette was his mother."

"Yes, but Benny was resentful that when she moved to Gold City to find Gary, she effectively abandoned him in Southern California. So, although Benny and his mom were living in the same small town, they were as estranged as any mother and child could have been. He wanted nothing to do with her. And very few people knew the true story about the mother-father-son relationship."

"So, Musette...or Madame Butterfly, or whatever the hell she called herself in those days, murdered Gary, the father of her son. And Gary killed Musette's daughter, Stacy, by giving her AIDS. Then, several years later, Musette and Gary's son, Benny, killed my father in the act of *revenge* for Gary's death, based on his perception that somehow Dad was at fault for that and more. Do I have all of that right, Mom?"

"That seems to be what happened, Son. It was a case of senseless tragedies being compounded by even more senseless tragedies."

Michael paused, trying to fully comprehend what he had learned from his dad's memoirs and the conversation with his mother, then said, "This is just one long, sad story, without a happy ending."

"Yes, many parts of your father's story are sad. A piece of me died with your father last week. But every time I think about him putting his forehead on mine and looking into my eyes, that is what love feels like, and I'll never forget that feeling. I'm so thankful I had twenty-five happy years with him away from all that drama. Often, he would ask me, 'What are you doing?' and I would answer, 'Making your life better.' Our years together were good years, they really were, and we had you to show for it. He adored you, Michael, and was so proud; never forget that."

"You know, Mom, it seems Dad's life was truly a miracle. He always said he was lucky, and God watched over him, and now I understand why he used to say that."

"Amen, Michael," his mother said with a crack in her voice.

Sandi Stassi Davis was alone in Gold City—without a husband next to her in bed and her son at law school, three time zones away.

"Amen!" she said again—this time louder, perhaps hoping Adrian would hear her.

"Goodnight, Mom," Michael said. "I love you."

"Goodnight, Son, and I love you too."

Sandi wiped away her tears and turned off the bedside light.

In the darkness, she instinctively reached over and felt Adrian's vacant pillow, then pulled it to her breasts and hugged it tightly— just as she had hugged Adrian for all those years and made his life better.

"Goodnight, my prince, at last, you are at peace."

—The End—

ACKNOWLEDGMENTS

Ultimately, every word in this book is my responsibility, but there are six people I would especially like to acknowledge:

Writer/historian Steve Cottrell provided some important conceptual input and historical insight.

Joy Porter, the owner of Winding Road Imagery, provided the professional photography for the front and back covers.

Attorney Allan Haley for his professional critique and advice on the law and court procedures.

Jack Campbell and Cyma Rubin read the manuscript as it evolved, and their early critique and advice helped shape the story's ebb and flow.

Most of all, however, I want to thank my wife, Robin Galvan-Davies, for her insistence that I finally write the story, and for her editorial and structural wisdom that made this a better book than it otherwise would have been.

Ernest Hemingway was right: "There is nothing to writing. All you do is sit down at a typewriter and bleed."

Amen to that.